AVON
PUBLISHERS OF BARD, CAMELOT, DISCUS AND FLARE BOOKS

SHADOWS OF SPLENDOR is an original publication of Avon Books. This work has never before appeared in book form. This work is a novel. Any similarity to actual persons or events is purely coincidental.

AVON BOOKS
A division of
The Hearst Corporation
1790 Broadway
New York, New York 10019

Copyright © 1987 by Jillian Hunter
Published by arrangement with the author
Library of Congress Catalog Card Number: 86-91027
ISBN: 0-380-75170-4

All rights reserved, which includes the right to reproduce this book or portions thereof in any form whatsoever except as provided by the U.S. Copyright Law. For information address Avon Books.

First Avon Printing: May 1987

AVON TRADEMARK REG. U.S. PAT. OFF. AND IN OTHER COUNTRIES, MARCA REGISTRADA, HECHO EN U.S.A.

Printed in the U.S.A.

K-R 10 9 8 7 6 5 4 3 2 1

THE AVON ROMANCE

Four years old and better than ever!

We're celebrating our fourth anniversary...and thanks to you, our loyal readers, "The Avon Romance" is stronger and more exciting than ever! You've been telling us what you're looking for in top-quality historical romance—and we've been delivering it, month after wonderful month.

Since 1982, Avon has been launching new writers of exceptional promise—writers to follow in the matchless tradition of such Avon superstars as Kathleen E. Woodiwiss, Johanna Lindsey, Shirlee Busbee and Laurie McBain. Distinguished by a ribbon motif on the front cover, these books were quickly discovered by romance readers everywhere and dubbed "the ribbon books."

Every month "The Avon Romance" has continued to deliver the best in historical romance. Sensual, fast-paced stories by new writers (and some favorite repeats like Linda Ladd!) guarantee reading *without* the predictable characters and plots of formula romances.

"The Avon Romance"—our promise of superior, unforgettable historical romance. Thanks for making us such a dazzling success!

Other Books in
THE AVON ROMANCE Series

ALYSSA *by Linda Lang Bartell*
BLAZING EMBERS *by Deborah Camp*
BY LOVE ALONE *by Judith E. French*
PASSION'S HONOR *by Diane Wicker Davis*
SILVERSWEPT *by Linda Ladd*
TEMPEST OF THE HEART *by Nancy Moulton*
UNCERTAIN MAGIC *by Laura Kinsale*

Coming Soon

MIDNIGHT DECEPTION *by Lindsey Hanks*
WINDSTORM *by Katherine Sutcliffe*

Avon Books are available at special quantity discounts for bulk purchases for sales promotions, premiums, fund raising or educational use. Special books, or book excerpts, can also be created to fit specific needs.

For details write or telephone the office of the Director of Special Markets, Avon Books, Dept. FP, 1790 Broadway, New York, New York 10019, 212-399-1357.

For my grandmother, with love

Chapter 1

**Boston Harbor
Summer, 1744**

Brant Layton's harshly formed features reflected cynical astonishment as he strode toward the gilt-haired young woman standing alone in the middle of the Long Wharf. With her delicate nose uptilted, she was pretending not to notice the group of sailors and porters staring at her, some flashing wistful glances, others openly lewd and insulting. Fresh from a boarding school on the outskirts of London, she was obviously unaccustomed to the attention her appearance drew from the average male.

Hellfire, there must be a mistake, Brant thought, his vibrant hazel eyes scanning the girl from her lopsided velvet hat with its sadly drooping ostrich plumage to her small, brocade-slippered feet. She couldn't be his uncle's betrothed. Against the background of rough harbor men and local prostitutes, she looked like a rose trying to bloom in a garden of weeds. She didn't fit Hugh's requirements for a wife at all. She looked too sweet, too unsophisticated, too . . . *vulnerable*.

He approached her uncertainly, circling her twice before finally stopping behind her. He didn't relish the prospect of bringing her back to the house. Maybe she wasn't as innocent as she looked. For her sake, he hoped so. "Lady Rosanne Mallory?"

Rosanne turned at the rich baritone voice, her midnight blue eyes assessing the athletically muscular man who had spoken her name. For a moment she forgot that she'd been made to stand there for the past three hours, enduring the humiliation of taunts and stares. She forgot her qualms about this strange country. She forgot her simmering anger at a man callously insensitive to her welfare. He would have a perfectly good excuse, of course, and she would be gracious enough to forgive him without a fuss. Relief eased the tension knotting her nerves. He wasn't what she'd expected. Nothing about him fit the image her father had painted of his old drinking friend, a man who'd struggled from poverty in London to a position of wealth and prominence in the New World. Nothing about him fit the frightful image she had begun to form of the man she was to marry. *Thank God.*

"Mr. Layton?"

"Yes," he responded without thinking. "Well, yes, but actually, I'm—" He broke off suddenly, frowning at the two black teenage boys perched on opposite ends of Rosanne's leather trunks, gawking at the ships entering the harbor.

"Luke! Ezekiel! Take Lady Rosanne's trunks to the cart, and tell the sedan-chair bearer he needn't wait for me. We're going back to the house."

Rosanne used the short lapse in their conversation to scrutinize the man more thoroughly. She guessed he was about twenty-five, so much younger than her father had led her to believe, and he was attractive, handsome in a pleasant but roughly imperfect way. He had a lean, sun-coppered face and heavily lashed hazel eyes that glinted with intelligence and roguish humor. The rather large nose was balanced by a firm, expressive mouth and decisively chiseled jawline. He looked in need of a shave, as though he'd left home in a hurry. But his hair was clean and softly curling, shining mahogany with warm reddish highlights and gathered at the back of his neck, into a queue with a ribbon. He wore a double-breasted royal blue velvet coat and matching knee breeches with a cream satin waistcoat and ruffled white silk shirt. The costume only slightly deemphasized the width of his shoulders and his powerful six feet two frame.

Rosanne noticed suddenly that his cambric stock was crooked, and for the first time in two months, she felt unafraid of the future.

He turned back to her then, his face relaxing. "I realize you disembarked some time ago. I trust your wait was uneventful."

Rosanne's soft red mouth tensed. Perhaps she ought to revise her opinion of him: attractive but inconsiderate. Charming but witless. Was that the best he could manage? No apologies? No excuses for this tardiness?

"Mr. Layton, during the three hours I've been standing here, I have had five invitations to dinner at the Bunch of Grapes, two at the Queen's Arms, and several others of an unrepeatable nature. A peddler tried to sell me a bottle of beaver oil to cure the warts I thankfully do not suffer from. A pair of poodles dancing the minuet escaped from their exhibit to christen my trunks. One of your two slaves tripped over his feet and knocked me to the ground. The second stomped on my hat while helping me up. Other than that, my wait has been quite uneventful."

A slow grin lit up Brant's face. Her forthright outburst took him completely off guard. He'd been anticipating tears or a tantrum, a spoiled young miss who would stamp her feet and pout.

"I *am* sorry, Lady Rosanne. You see, your ship came in earlier than expected, and my uncle was rushing out to a business appointment when he got news of your arrival. He sent the boys here to watch over you, but I guess they forgot to explain the delay. I came reluctantly, as a favor to my uncle and well, frankly, out of curiosity to meet the newest addition to the Layton family." He shook his head, struck anew by her appealing vulnerability. "Perhaps I should amend that to the Layton family's newest victim. Honestly, I'm not sure whether I should offer you my condolences or congratulations."

Rosanne stared at him, unable to make a grain of sense

out of anything he'd said. "Are you trying to tell me that if I didn't meet with your approval you'd send me back to England—or—or throw me over the wharf? And I don't understand what your uncle has to do with this. Why should it be his responsibility to meet me?"

"Because my uncle is the man you're engaged to marry, Lady Rosanne," he replied slowly, the amusement fading from his face. "My name is *Brant* Layton. I apologize for the misunderstanding."

"Well, I . . . Oh, damnation!" She glanced away, warm color staining her cheeks. Maybe she should throw herself off the wharf. She must have sounded like an utter numskull. God be thanked she'd discovered her error before she started chattering on about how many offspring they would produce! She should have known a man like Brant Layton wouldn't need to seek a bride beyond his own doorstep. Her dark eyebrows gathered into an unconscious frown. The situation really was his uncle's fault. Hugh Layton would have to make a flawless impression now to atone for what she'd endured this afternoon.

She subsided into the mood of grim resignation that had clouded her life since the day her father had informed her of the engagement. "I would have thought he'd at least make the effort to greet me," she said quietly, more upset than she cared to admit to herself.

Brant inhaled with slow deliberation, wanting to cast off the inappropriate sense of protectiveness that Rosanne stirred inside him. For a fanciful moment he entertained the possibility of marrying her himself—only to save her from Hugh, of course. Then, just as swiftly, he discarded the notion as ludicrous fantasy. He wasn't in the habit of rescuing damsels in distress; he had neither the time nor the interest for it. Anyway, she wasn't even his type.

She wasn't what he would call beautiful either . . . or was she? The color of her hair—bright, burnished gold—reminded him of sunshine on an October afternoon. He imagined pulling it out of that unflattering knot and watching it stream loose over her shoulders like satin wildfire. The spirit in her eyes belied the fragility of her finely boned features. Even in that simple brown muslin gown, there was something unmistakably, disturbingly, sensual about her. She was the kind of woman you would look at once and never forget, and that haunting quality went far beyond physical beauty.

No. He preferred soft-spoken, gentle-eyed girls like his own betrothed, Martha van Hoorn. A man would be begging for trouble if he became embroiled with this enticing minx. And the last thing he wanted was deeper involvement in Hugh's life.

He took her arm, guiding her past the numerous shops, warehouses, and counting houses that edged the north side of the pier.

"My uncle is a politician and a man of business above all else, Lady Rosanne. If you bear that in mind, you might find it easier to understand him. And if it's any consolation, I do know he has planned to take supper with you this evening."

"The honor overwhelms me."

Brant paused in midstride to stare down at her. "In future, my dear, I'd suggest you consider your thoughts more carefully before voicing them—if you want to please my uncle."

She looked up at him, her large blue eyes, edged in curling, gold-tipped lashes, steadily meeting his. "Are you insinuating that Hugh won't approve of me as I am?"

"Not at all. It simply occurred to me that you're not exactly what he's expecting."

A compliment or an insult? Rosanne couldn't decide. Fatigue and confusion had blunted her judgment. The sea voyage from London had been a nightmare. She would crystallize her own opinions about Hugh when she met him.

A small coach with four sturdy Narragansett pacers awaited them at the end of the wharf outside the Bunch of Grapes Tavern at the corner of Mackerel Lane.

"That's Daniel's coach," Brant commented in surprise. "I guess his wife decided to send it down for us. You'll be staying with them until Hugh finishes his business in

Boston and returns to his own home in New York. We won't have to ride in the cart after all."

Brant retained firm hold of Rosanne's arm as he pushed a path through the crowd of sailors, merchants, fishmongers, and local idlers congregating outside the popular tavern. It was approaching two o'clock, and men had gathered from their businesses around the wharf to await the dinner bell.

"Who is Daniel?" Rosanne asked loudly, to distract his attention from the embarrassing grumbling noises her stomach was making as the luscious aroma of roast suckling pig wafted to her from the tavern.

"Hugh's son."

They stopped again and stared at each other as the coachman recognized Brant and shouted an order over his shoulder to the footman. Brant shook his head in disbelief at the stunned expression settling over Rosanne's face.

"Good Lord, Lady Rosanne, don't tell me you weren't aware Hugh had a son."

"Yes, I knew," she said slowly. "But I thought—well, I assumed he was a child."

"Hell, no—he only acts like one."

Brant looked away and frowned, struck by the unpleasant realization that Daniel was even older than Rosanne, that this unaffected young woman was about to wed a politically ruthless and morally corrupt man who could pass as her father. Of course, he was judging his uncle on the basis of his own decaying relationship with him. Maybe Hugh would take into account Rosanne's inexperience and treat her with the tender consideration she deserved. But Brant wouldn't wager on it. Hugh viewed women as objects.

The footman moved between them to open the coach door and lower the steps, leaving Rosanne with no choice but to climb inside before Brant. For a second she faltered, glancing back at the full-masted ship that had carried her across the Atlantic, the *Broken Heart*, then at the huge brigantines which reminded her that she'd arrived in Boston the same week that war had been declared. In Europe it was called the War of the Austrian Succession, in the colonies, King George's War. It was yet another in the series of conflicts that had raged for over half a century between France and England for domination of North America. Would it be waged at sea? Would it be fought on the frontiers? Would it penetrate into the colonies? No one knew.

She climbed into the coach. What did she have to lose by marrying Hugh? She had nothing to return to in England. She'd left no one behind who would miss her, worry about her, write to her. Her mother had been dead for years. Her father hadn't even bothered to see her off. Her beloved nursemaid Gwennie had died on the voyage over, and her older sister Claire lived in the City of New York. Her paternal grandfather, the influential duke of Rydenham, was Rosanne's next closest known relative. But he had disowned her father, before she was even born, for marrying a common French actress, and he undoubtedly despised Rosanne as much as she did him.

"Welcome to America, Lady Rosanne. Welcome to your new home, my dear, dear girl. I can't tell you how I've looked forward to this day."

Rosanne froze and stared into the interior of the plushly upholstered coach at the owner of the suave male voice, an impeccably dressed man in his early forties who leaned forward to clasp her hands and draw her inside. Dazedly she studied him, her mind recording an absurd combination of details: his dark, fashionable Ramillies wig, his protruding ears, his hard amber eyes, his large yellow teeth and meticulously trimmed mustache, the ruby-studded lion's-head pin fastened on his stock.

She withdrew her hands from his clammy grasp, disliking him instantly.

"Well, for heaven's sake, Hugh, introduce yourself," scolded a sharp female voice from the opposite corner of the coach, and Rosanne's gaze swung briefly to a thin woman whose dark auburn hair formed a widow's peak on her unusually broad forehead.

"*You're* Hugh Layton?" Rosanne asked in an embarrassingly dismal tone, her gaze returning to the older man.

"I thought—well, your nephew said you were unable to meet me."

The bleak disappointment in her voice was too blatant for Hugh to miss. Insolent chit, he thought furiously. Typically arrogant little aristocratic bitch. He could tell she thought herself too good for him. Well, lady or not, she wasn't exactly what he had hoped for either. Not with that brilliant hair and those bold blue eyes, eyes that should be lowered before him in modest deference instead of expressing her distaste. Her deportment, or lack of it, was more indicative of an earthy peasant wench than the daughter of an earl he had expected. He was glad he'd taken the precaution of bringing her here to Boston before introducing her to New York society. He could see that his daughter-in-law would have her hands full before his betrothed satisfied his standards.

He forced a cordial smile, pretending not to have noticed her negative reaction. "Sit down, dear. I'm sure you're eager to be away from the wharf. My daughter-in-law and I were unavoidably detained. But I'll make up for my poor conduct later, I promise. After supper, we'll have time to become properly acquainted."

The subtle implication behind his words turned Rosanne's heart to lead. The mere suggestion of becoming intimate with him sickened her. *Father, how could you have done this to me?* She didn't care how wealthy he was. She didn't want to be his wife, for despite the elegantly tailored clothes, the smooth speech and practiced smile, she caught a hint of something coarse and repugnant about Hugh Layton, his manner striking false with the cold calculation in his eyes as he continued to stare at her.

She looked away indignantly. The way he was examining every facet of her appearance made her feel like a flawed diamond under a jeweler's microscope.

Sensing Brant behind her, Rosanne quickly seated herself next to the other woman, whose opaque green eyes regarded her with equally critical interest. Rosanne turned her head and watched Brant settle his tall frame beside his uncle. *Why couldn't it have been someone like him instead?*

Hugh reached for the silver-knobbed cane resting between his knees and rapped it against the roof of the coach. The vehicle rolled forward to turn left onto King Street. Folding his arms across his chest, he leaned backward against the cushioned seat.

"I understood that your old nursemaid was to accompany you on your voyage, Lady Rosanne. Did you send her to the house in the cart?"

"She died two weeks ago," Rosanne replied tightly. "And she was more a member of the family than a servant."

Hugh smiled to himself. The ancient crone had hated him, and he was delighted to hear of her long-overdue death. "She was an old woman, my dear. Anyway, I'm sorry, truly sorry, that you lost her. We'll see about finding you a proper maid in New York. My housekeeper will serve your needs until then."

Rosanne stared blindly out the window, aware but not caring that Hugh continued to talk to her. She was too miserable to mind if he thought her moody and ill-mannered. Forgotten was everything she'd learned at school about courtesy and correct behavior. She'd been taught how to read and write and cipher, but she had no idea how to conceal her emotions. She'd been prepared to accept an imperfect husband but could not imagine life with a man whose mere glance aroused revulsion within her.

". . . my daughter-in-law, Olivia," she heard Hugh saying, and she forced herself to feign interest as he finished introducing her to the woman on her right.

Olivia pounced on her with a fawning smile. "I'm the envy of all my friends, Lady Rosanne. Every woman I know has begged an invitation to tea so that she can brag she met you."

"You can't be serious."

"Oh, yes. Everyone has heard of the duke of Rydenham."

"Whatever your friends have heard about my grandfather has nothing to do with me." Rosanne's voice rose with resentment as she recalled the elderly nobleman she'd been schooled to hate since childhood. "The duke cut off my father's allowance upon his wedding day. As a result, we couldn't afford decent lodging or even a doctor when my mother took ill. I blame him indirectly for her death. He and I have nothing to do with each other. Nothing."

Bitter memories pricked Rosanne's mind, numbing her to the alarmed glances Hugh and Olivia exchanged across the coach. From a child's viewpoint, she hadn't considered that it might have been her father's own fault that his drinking and profligate ways had reduced him to a pauper, unable to provide for his own family. She hadn't considered that there could have been another side to the history of the estrangement between the duke and her father. She had been brought up to blame her grandfather for every misfortune that befell their household, and blame him she did.

Hugh's glance brushed across her with disapproval. "Your father assured me that he and your grandfather had overcome the enmity between them. Your mother was the only obstacle to their relationship."

"Then my father deceived you," Rosanne said stiffly. "He'd never forgive the duke. It was obviously a ploy to extract an offer for my hand, Mr. Layton, although I can't imagine why you'd want to form a friendship with a man like my grandfather."

Brant spoke for the first time since they had boarded the carriage, glancing at Rosanne with a wry smile. "Remember what I told you outside, Lady Rosanne."

Rosanne's thoughts somersaulted. Surely Hugh didn't hope that by marrying her he'd gain her grandfather's political patronage? The duke was a powerful man in England, with connections at the court of George II and in Parliament, it was true. But sweet heaven, if that was Hugh's intention, he'd have done better to wed a stranger unrelated to the duke than to marry her!

Hugh turned to glare at his nephew. "What the devil are you trying to do now, Brant? Have you been filling this poor girl's head with your usual nonsense? I suppose you made up some outrageous stories about me back there on the wharf to amuse yourself?"

"Now what could I tell her except the truth about you,

Hugh? She'll find out soon enough what an honest, scrupulous politician you are, how as a merchant you've won the respect of every man who's ever dealt with you—"

"That's enough, Brant."

"Brant is a disgraceful tease," Olivia said quickly. "He's not to be taken seriously. I'm sure we'll spend at least a week trying to undo all the mischief he's caused with his wicked tongue."

Hugh nodded in agreement, the civilized veneer slipping back into place over his steaming fury. God damn Brant and his irreverent sense of humor. Why in hell did the boy have to show up now of all times anyway? Brant knew how much this marriage meant to him, how painstakingly Hugh had constructed his life toward establishing a solid political future. Well, he and his nephew would have to have a grave talk when they reached the house. Brant's warped sensibilities and poorly timed visit were only minor issues compared to a more serious matter between them.

Calmer now, Hugh refastened his attention on Rosanne, his eyes tracing the outline of her high, generously rounded breasts and the slender indentation of her waist above the panniered skirts. It would be a severe trial to restrain himself from sampling her charms before they were married. Of course, he didn't want anything to spoil this wedding, not when he had been bragging publicly about his engagement for over four months now. Serving on New York's provincial council was no guarantee of the governor's favoritism. But this marriage would link him to one of the most illustrious old families in England. This marriage would pave his entrée into Governor Clinton's exclusive social circle, the New York aristocracy, which though built on New World land and wealth and power rather than on Old World bloodlines, still doted on English titles of nobility.

"It's been a long time since we met, Lady Rosanne," Hugh said, elevating his gaze to her face. "Six years ago, I believe, at Christmas."

Rosanne's mind raced as she tried to recall him among

the various male visitors her mother had entertained in their shabby London lodgings. Her eyes darkened with sudden anguish. Oh, God, could he have been one of her mother's secret lovers, one of the low-voiced strangers who had tried to buy her silence with sweetmeats? If he was, she didn't want to know. The idea that she would be marrying one of those shadowy figures from the past was too horrible to contemplate.

"I don't remember you."

"Of course you do, my dear," Hugh said. "Try to think back. Don't you remember the doll I gave you?"

"No. I don't."

Brant turned away from the window, his face taut with disgust. He remembered that winter six years ago. His Aunt Judith had died of a lingering illness, and Hugh had been in London—on business, or so he claimed. He hadn't even bothered to return in time to attend the funeral of the woman who had died after quietly suffering year upon year of his abuse, ambition, and infidelities.

"Six years ago, Hugh? Why, it's no wonder the young lady doesn't remember you. She's just eighteen now, isn't she? She would have been a mere child then."

The pointed reference to the age difference between Hugh and Rosanne struck its target with calculated force. Sparks of rage shot from Hugh's eyes, threatening to ignite the volatile atmosphere in the coach.

"You know, lad," Hugh said in a voice rich with warning, "I think perhaps living with those peasants and redskins has made you forget how to conduct yourself in genteel company."

"Forgive me, Uncle. I know how important it is to maintain an appearance of respectability—even while one is ruining lives or defrauding men of their land."

Hugh clenched his cane and leaned forward. "Have a care, Brant. I will not have you frightening my betrothed with your wild exaggerations. She doesn't know you well enough yet not to believe you."

"I wouldn't blame her if she wanted to sail straight back to England," Olivia added, dividing her time between glowering at Brant and patting Rosanne's hand. "Lord knows what she must think of us."

Rosanne glanced up, her large eyes meeting Brant's empathetic regard. She didn't know whether she should pay any attention to him or whether some desire for personal revenge had motivated him to speak out against his uncle. But she did know that she would be condemning herself to a lifetime of unhappiness if she married Hugh Layton, and that if she could find a way, she would break their engagement. But how—oh, God, how? Simply explain outright that she considered him too offensive to wed? Behave so obnoxiously that he would call off the betrothal himself? She would need an excuse, a sound excuse that would withstand his objections. He didn't appear to be a man who'd be easily put off.

"It really is a shame your father won't be able to attend the wedding, Lady Rosanne," Olivia said in an attempt to revive the conversation. "Of course, it's understandable, what with him taking a new bride himself."

"New bride?" Rosanne repeated numbly. "You must be mistaken."

But she could see the truth written on Hugh's face, and she knew then that her father had betrayed her mother's memory, that he *had* crawled back to the duke and begged forgiveness. He sent me away because he desired no reminders of his past with Mama, she thought bitterly. He wants to pretend we never existed. He's making a new life for himself, and I have no place in it. Why did the betrayal hurt so deeply when it was no more than what she might expect of her father?

She looked suddenly at Hugh, her expression hovering on belligerence. "Very well. Perhaps my father has made his peace with the duke. Perhaps he's even calling himself the earl of Brookbury again. But *I'll* never forgive my grandfather. Never. And another thing—I detest being called Lady Rosanne. I detest anything associated with the nobility."

"You cannot deny your birthright," Hugh said calmly.

"But bear in mind that after we're married, you will be known as Mrs. Hugh Layton."

Veering southwest onto the Cornhill thoroughfare, the coach rattled through a densely populated district. At the corner of Milk Street, where Cornhill became Marlborough Street, they passed a church, and the South End scenery took on a pleasantly rural tone with spacious houses situated between open meadows and cattle pastures. The scent of freshly cut field grasses laced the air with pungent sweetness. Presently there were fewer and fewer houses, and those Rosanne saw boasted large private gardens and fruit orchards.

Olivia nudged Rosanne from her trance as they turned onto Summer Street. "We're home, dear. You'll be staying here in Boston until right before the wedding. We thought it the proper thing to do, and it will give us the chance to become close friends." She lowered her voice. "I shouldn't tell you this, but Hugh has authorized an unlimited budget for your new wardrobe. I've already alerted the finest dressmaker in town—"

Rosanne peered outside while Olivia prattled on about visits to the milliner, the cobbler, the glover, the perfumer. The coach had slowed before an iron gate that was opened by two black men who had materialized from the small stable at the side of the house. It was an attractive two-story, gambrel-roofed structure that had orginally been covered with pine clapboard. Situated well off the street, it was enclosed in front by an eleven-foot-high fence and ornamental shrubbery; in back, by honeysuckle-draped granite walls.

The coach had barely passed through the gateway when Brant opened the door and jumped down onto the drive. Hugh dropped close behind him, muttering apologies over his shoulder to the women for his abrupt exit and for his nephew's unpardonable rudeness.

"Ungrateful, that's what Brant is," Olivia said with raw contempt in her voice. "A disrespectful and ungrateful savage. After all that Hugh has done for him too. Paying for his passage over from England, educating him—

not to mention taking him on as a land agent, when Hugh knew of a dozen more qualified men. I can't wait to see him return to his farms."

"Olivia—"

Olivia paused halfway out of the coach, her expression patient and solicitous. "Yes, dear?"

Rosanne hesitated. Should she confide in this woman? Against her better judgment, she plunged on. "Olivia, what if I told you that I don't want to marry Hugh? Well—that I've changed my mind?"

Chapter 2

"Changed your mind?" Olivia swung round with an incredulous laugh. "It's a little late for that, isn't it?" Then, as if realizing how menacing she sounded, she gave Rosanne a reassuring smile and caught the girl's hand as she stepped down from the coach.

"I know what's bothering you—it's Brant. He just brings out the worst in everyone. I think he's jealous of his uncle. Hugh has achieved so much compared to Brant's father, and all on his wits, without benefit of inheritance."

And at what cost? Rosanne was tempted to ask. But she merely nodded and held her thoughts, realizing, as she followed Olivia into the house, that her attempt at making an ally had failed. She was exhausted, hungry, and desperate for a bath after the miserable voyage. Perhaps by the next morning she would have thought of a graceful way to extricate herself from the betrothal.

Olivia, asking Rosanne to excuse her for a moment, disappeared into the rear of the house. Meanwhile, male voices, muted but angry, sounded from behind the library door and drifted to Rosanne in the receiving vestibule where she awaited Olivia's return. Were Brant and Hugh arguing about her? she wondered. As interesting as she found the notion, she realized that the disharmony between them had to lay more deeply rooted. She hadn't had time to analyze Brant's cryptic comments about his uncle, but she understood that he had meant to warn her. Against what? Tempted to eavesdrop, she was edging toward the closed door when Olivia reappeared with an older woman in tow

"I wanted to make sure that the water for your bath was heating before you dressed, dear," Olivia explained, her eyes slipping nervously from the library door to Rosanne's face. Distractedly she turned to the small, dour-looking woman behind her. "This is Hugh's housekeeper, Moira O'Rourke. She and his valet travel with him everywhere. She'll attend to your comfort while I have a word with my father-in-law about supper." And with a tight smile, Olivia hurried into the library and shut the door behind her before the angry male voices could escape into the vestibule.

Her face grim and unwelcoming, Moira shuffled forward and dropped Rosanne a stiff curtsy. " 'Tis an honor, m'lady," she muttered in a soft Irish brogue that indicated it was anything but. "If ye'll follow me upstairs then, I'll help ye unpack and lay out a fresh change of clothes." Her brown eyes swept disdainfully over Rosanne's gown. "Mr. Layton will want ye to dress for supper."

Irritation flared inside Rosanne at the woman's scantily masked insult. Heaven help her—was she to be bullied and criticized by everyone in this household, from her betrothed to his servants? Tomorrow she would definitely have to assert herself. For the moment, she was too tired to bother. She sighed, practically sprinting to keep up with the peculiar little Irishwoman. Weren't housekeepers supposed to be warm and maternal? she mused, suffering a fierce stab of loneliness for her old Gwennie.

Suddenly, as she reached the middle of the steep, narrow staircase, the library door below banged open and Brant stormed into the hall, a thunderous look on his face that cleared at once as he glanced up and noticed Rosanne. She smiled hesitantly, unsure of what to say in such an awkward situation. If she were a properly bred young lady, she would have undoubtedly kept walking up the stairs as if there were nothing unusual in his disorderly emergence. The trouble was, her upbringing had been for so many years neglected that not even the stern school mistresses had been able to subdue a natural penchant for mischief. Then Brant returned her smile, his eyes bright with wry amusement, and she decided impulsively that she would much rather stand here staring at him than pretend to be politely disinterested.

"Charming family, aren't we, Rosanne?" he asked ironically. "And just wait until supper—that's when we'll meet Olivia's husband—unless, of course, he's spending the day on one of the islands with his mistress. Not that I blame him—"

"You're disgusting, Brant!" Olivia hissed as she exited the library and swept past him. "For two shillings, I would—"

"You would what, Olivia?" he demanded softly, catching hold of her wrist. "And before you answer, let me remind you that I know enough about your and Hugh's illicit business practices to create a scandal that would send tremors rippling from here to New York."

He dropped her hand as though it were a venomous snake, then raised his head to address Moira at the top of the staircase. "Take care of my uncle's betrothed, Moira. She has no idea what a nest of adders she's marrying into."

To satisfy her curiosity, Rosanne would have liked to insist he explain what he meant. But Olivia standing below prevented a private conversation, and above her Moira was sighing and fidgeting with unconcealed impatience. Anyway, perhaps the less she learned about Hugh the better.

Brant watched Rosanne turn and follow Moira up the stairs, bewilderment etched on the girl's sculptured features. Why hadn't he just kept his mouth closed? She probably hadn't been given a choice about marrying Hugh. Spewing out his anger in front of her served no logical purpose. But didn't she have a right to know what sort of man she was engaged to?

He pivoted and strode down the passageway to the small drawing room that Olivia reserved for private business conferences. Conferences! A clandestine meeting with a ship's captain to discuss smuggling goods to Barbados. A port official come to collect his bribe. Common enough practices he knew, but the Layton family's involvement in duplicity had long ago begun to extend well beyond the usual victimless crimes.

Over the years Hugh had begun to eliminate political rivals and to force competitors into bankruptcy with blackmail and extortion. He had lured men into indenture with false promises, had cheated Indians of their land—Indians upon whom frontiersmen like Brant depended for protection from the French and other, hostile Indian tribes.

And now, Brant suspected, Hugh had had a man murdered. Of course, Hugh was too clever to dirty his own hands. He had let Olivia assign the sordid details to their network of well-paid agents. *Including me*, Brant thought with self-contempt. Lord, had there really been a time when he'd respected and admired his uncle?

He tried to evoke an image of himself nine years ago, a headstrong, independent seventeen-year-old, chafing beneath the authority of his father, Robert Layton, financial advisor to the Bank of England, director of three mercantile companies, and owner of a porter brewery in Hampshire. Domineering though Robert was, Brant adored his father. But he didn't want to follow his father into business or serve as an apprentice in the Layton brewery. He'd ached for adventure in those days. And adventure had beckoned, in the form of an offer from his uncle in New York—a position as Hugh's land agent in the Mohawk Valley wilderness. His initial duties would include recruiting settlers, clearing the land, and establishing a tenant-supported store.

He'd leaped at the opportunity, his imagination stirred by Hugh's grandiose description of the farming hamlet he envisioned. Brant spent the next three years receiving an education in the New World wilderness. Then he returned to England where, eager to prove himself, he soon persuaded twelve peasant families to indenture themselves to his uncle in return for passage to America and two hundred acres each of fertile virgin soil. With deplorable naiveté, he repeated to the settlers Hugh's promise that they would be eligible to purchase their leased farms at the end of their servitude. Little did Brant dream that those peasants were merely exchanging one feudal agricultural system for another. Hugh never intended to sell his land, and if he had, not one of his tenants, most of them free men now, could afford his grossly inflated asking price.

Brant eased his long body down onto Olivia's stuffed damask sofa and closed his eyes. He wished to God he could just walk away from the past nine years and pretend they had never happened. Of course he couldn't. He felt a responsibility to the Hemlock Creek settlers, if only to help them to relocate or, if they chose, to return to England. But the prospect of revealing to them the full extent of Hugh's deception was an emotional drain. He couldn't wait to be done with it. He couldn't wait to purge himself of Hugh's malignant influence. Six more months. That was how long he needed to pay his debt to the past. Then he could sever all connections with Hugh, taking with him his bitterness, disillusionment, and the experience he had gained at so great a cost.

A door slammed upstairs, diverting his thoughts to the present. In six more months that girl's troubles would only be starting. Not that that should concern him. No—with his wedding to Martha in the offing and the plans for his own land patent to be carried out, he couldn't afford to waste his energy worrying about Rosanne Mallory. Just the same, for some unfathomable reason, he did.

Moira watched Rosanne covertly as the girl sat on the edge of the bed, her still damp hair drying in tendrils around her pensive oval face. She wasn't at all what the housekeeper had hoped for. She wasn't brittle or worldly enough to withstand the humiliation she would have to endure. Even if Lady Rosanne was an earl's daughter and had been instructed in the social graces so that she could perform the duties of a councilor's wife, Moira doubted that the girl would have the sense to submit without a struggle to Hugh Layton's coarse sexual demands or to turn a blind eye to his flagrant womanizing. But that's no business of mine, the housekeeper reminded herself. The girl will either survive in this family or she won't.

"Let me help you, m'lady." She knelt before the bed to help Rosanne on with a pair of buckled, violet-dyed pumps, her arthritic fingers working clumsily at the task.

"You don't have to do that" Rosanne said, bending forward. "I'm not accustomed to being waited on hand and foot."

Moira shrugged and straightened, grimacing with what could have been either pain or disapproval. "If ye've no further need of me, then I'll be helpin' Mrs. Layton with supper."

Rosanne stood up, her dark blue eyes brimming with uncertainty. Her creased traveling clothes had been replaced by a blue-violet damask gown with a voluminous overskirt and quilted, bell-shaped petticoats. The low, square neckline and snug black silk stomacher accentuated her hourglass figure and made her feel unusually self-conscious. Remembering Hugh's burning scrutiny, she couldn't help thinking that a less revealing gown would make supper with him easier to bear. But Moira hadn't unpacked the trunk that contained her handkerchiefs or her older gowns with the modesty pieces attached.

"Moira, how long have you worked for Mr. Layton?"

"Twenty-odd years, m'lady," the housekeeper replied from the doorway.

"A long time." Rosanne traced a finger over the rice powder that had spilled on the dressing table, forcing nonchalance into her voice. "I suppose you're aware of the discord between him and his nephew . . . what caused it . . . ?"

"Master Brant and my son Patrick started a farming community for Mr. Layton out in the New York wilderness," the housekeeper said hesitantly, reluctant to talk. "For a few years it went well enough. But now Mr. Layton and his nephew hold differing opinions on nearly everything under the sun."

"That tells me absolutely nothing, Moira."

"I don't waste me time wonderin' about things I can't change. They aren't together often. Master Brant will be travelin' back to the City of New York soon to wed his sweetheart, and from there he will no doubt return to his own home."

"His sweetheart," Rosanne murmured, and felt a hope die inside her that had been so quietly conceived she hadn't known until now it even existed.

"I suggest ye rest until supper is served, m'lady. Enjoy an hour or two of peace."

"I take it peace is rarely known in this family?"

With a caustic smile as her reply, Moira slipped out into the hall, closing the door quietly behind her. Rosanne returned to the fireplace, avoiding her reflection in the mirror as she imagined Hugh's eyes feasting on her exposed flesh. To think that he'd have the right to touch her whenever he pleased—

Had she, perhaps, judged Hugh prematurely? Was she allowing a poor first impression to sway her? Her father, Edward Mallory, had never pretended even the smallest affection for her, but surely he wouldn't have entrusted her to a man who would possibly mistreat her. After all, her father had known Hugh for a long time. She didn't want to believe her father capable of such callous disregard for her welfare. And she didn't want to believe that he had turned hypocrite and gone groveling back to the duke for forgiveness.

It had to be true. In her heart she had always known that her father regretted marrying her mother, that he blamed Lisette for the loss of his inheritance. Accustomed to spending lavishly on the duke's credit, Edward had begun to squander Lisette's meager earnings soon after their marriage, continuing to drink and gamble as though he were still the affluent young lord. And when the theater where Lisette performed let her go because the duke threatened to withdraw his patronage if she stayed on as a player, Edward had started to take out his resentment on his bewildered young wife in cruel verbal abuse and prolonged absences from home. He'd had even less patience for his two daughters.

You were a fool, Mother, Rosanne thought sorrowfully. Why didn't you accept the duke's bribe when he tried to talk you out of marrying his son?

And she was a fool herself, she decided later as a maidservant showed her the way to the dining room. A fool for not insisting she meet the man her father had arranged for her to marry. But no more. Tomorrow she would explain her feelings to Hugh, offer him a chance to back out of the betrothal first to spare him any embarrassment. She would stay with her sister Claire until she charted a course for her future. Marriage had always been her assumed fate, but that could wait now until she chose her own husband, a man she would love without reservations—

"Still with us, I see."

"Brant."

She looked up, startled. He was waiting in the hall that led to the dining room, staring at her so intently she was amazed she hadn't sensed his presence. Without looking away—she was suddenly unable to—she dismissed the maidservant with a distractedly murmured thanks. It struck her as both perplexing and amusing that only a few moments ago she had been so lost in her own musings that she hadn't even noticed Brant. Now, if there was a single particle of her being that wasn't aware of him, she could not find it for the life of her.

Brant's eyes broke contact with hers to drift appreciatively over her gowned figure, lingering at the deep cleft of her breasts before lifting back to her face. Seductive angel, he thought with begrudging admiration. A woman who could make a man's life heaven or hell. Pity the poor fellow who loses his heart to her.

"I have been instructed to apologize for my conduct," he said.

Why? Rosanne wondered. Why had one man's gaze the power to flood her with weakening warmth while another's chilled her to the soul?

"Hugh made you apologize?" she asked.

"No. Moira."

She smiled at the way he'd lowered his voice, as if he were a small boy forced to express remorse he didn't really feel. "I suppose I wouldn't want her angry at me either."

"No. You wouldn't."

He placed his hand at the small of her back, guiding her over to a Newcastle glass window that overlooked a rose arbor. She looked lovely tonight, he thought, amused that only a few hours earlier he had found fault with her appearance. As fresh and lovely as the pink and golden blossoms outside. Suddenly he removed his hand, irritated that he'd felt compelled to touch her in the first place. Not since adolescence had he felt so unable to control his own behavior. It was unlike him.

"I fear I made a bad impression this afternoon," he said with a penitent smile. "I hope you understand it had nothing to do with you."

Rosanne nibbled the inside of her lip, trying to ignore the quivering in the middle of her stomach. Why could she still feel the imprint of his hand after he'd drawn it away? He was the kind of man her schoolmistresses had warned their young pupils against: darkly handsome, controlled, and bold, the kind of man who provoked impossible fantasies and imprudent behavior in starry-eyed young girls. Then again, she couldn't help wondering if she was attracted to him only because she found Hugh so unappealing by comparison.

It didn't really matter. Brant had his own life, and she had to concentrate her attention on untangling hers. She smiled up at him. "Am I to assume you were exaggerating this afternoon, that your uncle isn't the monster you led me to believe?"

The humorous glint in his eyes dimmed. "I have reason to believe that Hugh had his former business partner murdered, my dear."

"Well, well, now, what do we have here? Are you two

admiring Olivia's roses?" It was Hugh, his voice booming in an artificial attempt at pleasantness. "Her damask roses are exquisite—sometimes I just sit in the arbor and stare at them, pretending I'm back in England."

Rosanne turned her head, conscious of the sudden tension in Brant as his uncle walked toward them, suspicion lurking behind his smile. Brant's last words echoed a horrifying refrain in her mind. *Murder*. Should she take him literally? Why should she trust him at all?

"Brant and I had a nice conversation a little while ago, Rosanne," Hugh remarked, his gaze, dark with an underlying threat, swerving to Brant. "I can't promise it, but I think I've talked some manners back into him. He hasn't been misbehaving again, has he?"

Rosanne shook her head. "Not at all. We were—"

"Good, good," Hugh cut in, his eyes sliding over her with pleasure. "My, don't you look delightful?" he breathed. "Like a genuine lady tonight." He squeezed her hand, his fingers cold and possessive. "Go in to supper, Brant. You're not needed here."

"Fine," Brant said, his mouth hardening with distaste at the sight of Hugh gripping Rosanne's hand. "And by the way, Hugh, that nice little conversation didn't cover the reason for my visit to Boston. But that's all right. I've saved my speech for supper."

Rosanne pried her hand loose as Brant disappeared into the dining room. The fury on Hugh's face unsettled her. "Hugh, I wonder if we might talk privately—tomorrow morning?" She didn't relish the thought of facing him alone, but it was necessary. And the longer she postponed it, the harder it would become.

He looked down at her and grinned, obviously pleased. "Why wait? We'll take sherry alone in the drawing room after supper." He hooked his arm around her waist, holding her tightly as he turned them both away from the window. His voice deepened to a husky pitch. "Just between you and me, Rosanne, I'm going to have the devil's time waiting until our wedding night."

Her body stiffened. His touch was more abhorrent than she'd imagined it would be. And he already acted as if he owned her.

"Hugh, you haven't actually made the formal arrangements for the ceremony yet, have you?"

His amber eyes narrowed. He was too shrewd not to have detected the hopeful catch in her voice. He didn't like it at all: he had expected her total acquiescence.

"Rosanne," he said, his tone as hard as granite. "We are going to be married in New York in six weeks' time. Governor Clinton himself has promised to attend."

"Don't we—isn't it necessary to cry the banns first?"

"Oh, no, my dear. In New York we consider that a most vulgar custom."

"Six weeks," she murmured. "So soon." She glanced away, fear twisting her insides. He had everything planned from the perfume she would wear to their wedding guests. Clearly he wouldn't receive her rejection with a gracious shrug of his shoulders.

I have reason to believe that Hugh had his former business partner murdered. . . . There had been no sarcasm in Brant's voice when he had shared that fear with her. There would be no peace for her now in Hugh's presence either, with those darkly spoken words lingering in the back of her mind.

"Hugh, about your relationship with your nephew—"

Hugh sucked in his breath, his jaw tightening. He should have guessed something was going on when he'd walked in and found her and Brant talking so quietly.

"I don't know what he's been telling you now, but I'm fed up with it. You're not to talk to him again, do you hear? Thank God he's leaving in a few days. Until then I forbid you to converse with him alone."

An uncontrollable surge of resentment swept through Rosanne. "I'm perfectly capable of forming my own opinions, and I do not appreciate being ordered about like a servant."

She tried to wrench away from him, but he clamped his

arm painfully around her waist, forcing her against him in unpleasantly intimate contact. "Not servant, Rosanne, but wife. A wife who obeys me in all matters."

"Have you forgotten about supper, Hugh?" a third voice asked.

Olivia suddenly appeared behind them, coyly pretending she was embarrassed to catch Rosanne in her father-in-law's arms. But she had noticed Rosanne's angrily flushed cheeks, the way the girl jerked away from Hugh. Something wasn't quite right here, she realized. The Lady Rosanne had too much spirit for her liking. Composing her features to mask her disquietude, Olivia decided that she and Hugh would have to make a concerted effort to crush that streak of defiance.

"I trust you're refreshed after your bath, Lady Rosanne. You'll feel even better after supper."

Hugh, half amused, half annoyed by the cold look Rosanne shot him, bowed and motioned her forward. "After you, m'lady."

Rosanne escaped into the dining room without further prompting. Before Hugh had the chance to follow her though, Olivia blocked his path, speaking in an angry whisper.

"Couldn't you control yourself for once, Hugh? I told you earlier, she's not entirely thrilled to be marrying you as it is."

Hugh barely glanced at his daughter-in-law, his interest riveted on the supple figure standing in the dining room.

"There's no help for that now, is there, Olivia? Her father doesn't want anything more to do with her, and the only other person she could go to in the colonies is in the grave."

"I still think we should tell her that her sister died. She's bound to ask about her sooner or later. She's not going to believe Claire suddenly left New York, and if she hears—"

"She'll find out after we're married," he said emphatically, "and not a minute before. I'm not giving her any excuses to call the ceremony off. If you want to be helpful, try to inspire her with some enthusiasm toward becoming a devoted wife.''

"It would be a lot easier if you got rid of that nephew of yours. He's the one who's put her off you. He knows too much, Hugh, and I don't like it one bit."

Supper proved an ordeal for Rosanne. She sensed that the smoldering tension building all afternoon between Hugh and Brant had reached a dangerous pitch. At any moment either man could explode, breaking the bonds of social restraint. She had no desire to be caught centered between them when it happened.

"Was everything cooked to your liking, dear?" Olivia asked her for at least the fifth time. "Did you like the peach-walnut dressing? Were the veal cutlets tender enough?"

"Everything was excellent, Olivia."

Olivia's gaze strayed to the long-case clock in the corner. "I wonder what's keeping my husband. He knew this was to be a special supper. Perhaps he's still at work. Daniel will have to assume more business responsibilities now that his father has political duties on the council to consider. Hugh won't be able to travel to Boston as often as he likes in future."

Prodding herself to appear impressed, Rosanne managed a wan smile. "I understand Hugh's to be sworn in when he returns to New York."

Hugh preened, looking like a dandified lion in his frizzed wig and gold taffeta suit. "It's the beginning of a new life for me, Rosanne. I wish I could express my profound happiness at the thought that you'll be sharing it with me."

A string of distasteful images suddenly flashed across Rosanne's mind. Reciting vows of love and obedience to Hugh. Their wedding night. His thick body covering hers, committing the act that had been whispered about in the boarding school with equal amounts of dread and fascination. Forcing herself not to cringe at his touch. Bearing his children. Sitting at the same table with him night after night.

Panic welled up inside her. *No.* She closed her eyes briefly as the shadows of the future swept down upon her, shrouding all her young girl's hopes and dreams in lonely despair. Riches and social prominence were not enough, despite what her father claimed.

"Marrying for love is a fool's notion, Rosanne," he had told her harshly. "If I hadn't married your mother, I'd still be living on a grand estate."

She forced her eyes open to discover Hugh looking at her, his deep frown indicating that he'd been speaking and was upset at her inattention. "As a councilor's wife, you will have to sit through many a boring dinner, Rosanne," he said in the patronizing tone he might affect with a child. "I do hope you'll manage to at least pretend interest while the governor is talking."

She raised her head. "So long as I'm not expected to entertain him at the end of a seven-week voyage, I don't suppose I'll shame myself too dreadfully."

"Of course you won't," Olivia said, chastising her father-in-law with a quick scowl. Hugh looked shocked that Rosanne had dared to speak back to him in front of his family, shocked and coldly furious. She turned to Rosanne. "Hugh didn't mean to sound so—"

"Pompous?" Brant supplied, breaking his period of self-imposed silence. "Tyrannical?"

Hugh disregarded his nephew, his anger at Rosanne now screened behind an apologetic smile. "Olivia is right. I'm afraid the excitement of meeting you, and my new appointment, and, well . . ." His gaze strayed to Brant. "Well, personal matters have put me on edge."

His smile deepened, pleading for her understanding. "I cannot tell you how much this seat on the council means to me, Rosanne. To us. Governor Clinton has only been in office since last September, and he's still basically a naval officer, not a politician. He needs strong allies and reliable advisors more than ever, with this war going on. I intend to place myself completely at his service."

"Noble to the soul," Brant drawled, his long, restless fingers curling around the stem of his goblet. "Speaking of the governor, Hugh, did I mention that I met with him a few months ago at the Albany Indian conference?"

"You? Now what would the governor want with you, Brant?"

"For one thing, he was soliciting opinions from Mohawk Valley inhabitants on how to persuade the Iroquois to break their policy of neutrality and take up the hatchet against the French. For another, he wanted to inform me that my warrant for the parcel of land I purchased had been processed with his approval."

"I didn't authorize you to take out any more patents in my name, Brant."

"It wasn't in your name," Brant retorted with the smooth self-composure of a man who knew exactly what reaction to expect. "It was in mine, mine and about twenty-five other partners who signed it back over to me after the grant was approved. Fifty thousand acres of rich black soil on the north bank of the Mohawk that begins at the mouth of Olehisk Creek and encompasses an abandoned Mohawk village. Much of the land is watered by streams and has already been cleared by the Indians."

Fresh anger darkened Hugh's face. "Who are you trying to fool? I know that patent, and I know from my own experience that those goddamn savages refuse to sell it. Every land merchant in New York covets that tract."

"Oh, they didn't sell it. It was a gift."

Olivia pushed a silver dessert tray of spiced almonds, lemon suckets, and sugared rose petals in front of Rosanne, hoping to distract her, but the girl was more interested in the conversation than food.

"You're trying to tell me they just handed you title to their land?" Hugh laughed heartily. "How stupid do you think I am?"

Brant smiled. "I will pay them, Hugh—a fair price too. I know it's incomprehensible to your criminal mind, but we had no need to cheat them or get them drunk like your Albany burgher friends do. No fraudulent deeds. No bribes to the surveyor-general. No false boundary markers moved around at midnight. You've forgotten that Moira's son lives with me, and that he's married to a Mohawk sachem's daughter. Patrick and I are going into partnership together."

"But you work for me, Brant! I need you on Hemlock Creek. And you know I had plans to move you out into Cherry Valley, give you and Martha a little tract of your own to—"

"I've got my own land now, Hugh."

Rosanne could feel the rage rising from Hugh like steam. Then suddenly he smiled, a slow, unpleasant smile that had her sliding to the edge of her seat in tense anticipation. "Even if Clinton was persuaded to approve your patent, it won't make it through the council. I'll see to that personally, Brant."

"Oh, I think it will. You see, Hugh, if it doesn't, I'm going to expose you for the wretch you really are. I'm going to expose you for smuggling goods to our enemies in New France from Albany and from Daniel's warehouses here in Boston. I'm going to expose you for tampering with elections when you were an alderman and for helping your friends in the Assembly embezzle public funds."

He paused, his eyes glittering ruthlessly. "Another thing, Hugh. Your former partner, Franklin Newhouse, was on his way to New York to see me. Something about some evidence he thought the governor would be interested in. No one has seen him for over a month. I think you had him killed."

"Jesus God," Hugh gasped. "Did you hear that, Olivia?"

"That's an unforgivable accusation!" Olivia cried. "If anyone harmed Franklin, blame it on the unsavory people he began associating with after he and Hugh went their separate ways."

Brant shrugged. "I have no proof. But one day his corpse will turn up."

"And whose corpse is the subject of our suppertime conversation tonight?" inquired a plumpish young man from the doorway behind Rosanne. "Let me on the secret, someone. This sounds like more fun than a cockfight."

"Sit down and wipe that moronic grin off your face, Daniel," Olivia snapped. "Brant has provided all the aggravation we can stand. And you might at least apologize for being late."

"Yes, beloved," her husband said, instantly cowed. "I didn't mean to miss supper. There was much activity at the wharves today. We're doing a brisk business outfitting privateers for cruising expeditions. Governor Shirley is rumored to be calling for volunteers—"

Olivia broke in impatiently to introduce him to Rosanne, blatantly ignoring him after he bowed and took his place at the table. He was not an unattractive man, but Rosanne found his hangdog demeanor painful to observe, a pathetic contrast to the domineering arrogance of his wife and his father.

"And how do you find Boston so far, Lady Rosanne?" he asked her, looking nervously at his wife for fear he'd say the wrong thing. "Is it at all as you imagined?"

"Oh, it's—"

"She's too fatigued to answer your asinine questions, Daniel," Olivia said. "It's thoughtless of us all to keep her up when she's so obviously anxious to retire."

What was obvious, Rosanne thought, was that Olivia wanted her gone, and she was only too grateful to oblige. "Actually, I am exhausted, and before I go to bed I have to write a letter to Gwennie's brother in Kent, informing him of her death."

Hugh glanced up, frowning. "Don't go upstairs yet. We're going to have sherry together in the drawing room. I need only a minute to clear up a few things with my nephew."

"Tomorrow, please, Hugh." Rosanne eased back her chair and stood up. "Gwennie died so horribly, I can't forget about it, and I gave her my word I would write—"

"The old woman's been dead for weeks, hasn't she?" Hugh interrupted her with curt impatience. "One or two more days won't matter to her brother."

Rosanne's heartbeat accelerated with anger. "It matters to me."

"Rosanne, I said . . ." Hugh wavered at the mutinous gleam in her eye and abruptly softened his tactic. "We'll send that letter tomorrow, I promise you, and please give Gwennie's brother my personal condolences. In fact, I'll contact my agent in Kent and have him inquire discreetly whether the family is in need of a little financial assistance."

"That's very kind of you, Hugh," she said slowly.

"Think nothing of it, my dear."

What was wrong with the man? she wondered in bafflement. How could his behavior swing from coldly insensitive to charmingly considerate in a span of moments?

Hugh gave her an engaging smile. "Then you'll wait for me in the drawing room."

"I—I suppose so."

"I'll show you the way," Olivia offered.

"No. I remember passing it earlier."

Although aware that Hugh had gotten his way, Rosanne had chosen to concede. She could delay a private meeting with him, but she preferred to brave a confrontation and be done with it. She edged away from the table, bidding everyone goodnight, and as her gaze moved to Brant, she caught him regarding her again with that strange mixture of empathy, warning, and something indefinable that rushed through her like a whirlpool of liquified fire.

Her cheeks warm from his stare, she reached the doorway and paused for a moment as Brant's voice penetrated the confusion of her thoughts.

"I'll give you six months to find another land agent, Hugh, and that long only because I care too much about your tenants to leave them unprepared for the winter. That should also give you enough time to halt your illegal activities, and if you don't, by God, I'll ruin your golden political future, councilor."

A cloud of premonition followed Rosanne as she forced herself to walk down the hallway and into the lavishly appointed drawing room. She had entered this household at the peak of a crisis. She hoped she could escape before she became involved in the crimes Brant had accused his uncle of committing. Hugh, she remembered with a shiver, hadn't even bothered to deny Brant's charges but had merely brushed them off like so many ants at a picnic.

She looked around the room. Twisted rugs lay on the wooden floor. To her right was a large sofa and a pair of tulipwood tilt-top tea tables; to her left, a black walnut escritoire on bracket feet and a Chinese marble-topped sideboard. Four red leather-covered chairs on cabriole legs faced the massive stone fireplace with its brass-edged mantelpiece. Painted paper decorated with peacocks and exotic foliage covered the original whitewashed walls.

She felt uncomfortable here. Costly spermaceti candles burning in silver sconces failed to brighten the shadowed ambiance of the room, and Rosanne instinctively crossed to the window and parted the heavy red curtains to permit moonlight to spill into the darkness.

Footsteps in the hall, hurried and purposeful, alerted her to Hugh's approach. She turned to face the door, apprehension forming knots in her stomach. She prayed that he would not make a scene when she confronted him with her feelings.

He smiled as he entered the room and strode toward her, his hands stretching out to claim her in that possessive grasp. "I didn't give you a proper welcome, did I? All my family hovering around, never giving us the chance to be alone . . ."

She shrank away from him, easing her hands free. "I really didn't mind, Hugh. I enjoy being around people."

"I minded," he said thickly, his eyes suddenly heavy-lidded. "All through supper I couldn't eat a damned thing. I kept staring at your mouth, imagining how sweet it would taste."

"Hugh, please don't say things like that."

"Why not?"

She turned her head reflexively, her gaze drawn to a flash of movement outside the window—to the tall figure of Brant Layton standing in the garden. She couldn't quite make out his face, but as he raised a cigar to his mouth to light it, the brief red glow illuminated his features, and his expression indicated he could see inside the room. She forced her attention back to Hugh, her heart pounding with anxiety.

Chapter 3

"Let's have that sherry now, Hugh."

"The sherry will keep."

Rosanne edged around him. "It's late. I've been up—"

"Come here," he said roughly.

"No, no, I don't want—"

His hands closed round her waist and crushed her to him. His mouth descended on hers, slack and avid, cruelly imprisoning hers in a wet, bruising kiss. The feel of his fleshy tongue invading her mouth, forcing her lips apart, filled her with sick abhorrence. Twisting frantically, she lifted her hand and pushed his face sideways to her cheek. She gasped for breath, then heard his coarse, excited laughter in her ear as he dragged his mouth down her neck, kissing, biting her lightly, tracing patterns with his tongue.

"Please, please, Hugh," she cried, trembling, frightened at his strength, his persistance. "Stop it! Let me go!"

"Why?" he whispered. He dropped his head between the valley of her breasts, his hands creeping up her rib cage. "We're going to be man and wife soon anyway. I have a right. You have such beautiful breasts, Rosanne. Let me suckle them just once . . ."

"Excuse me. Am I interrupting?"

Hugh's face shot upward in outraged surprise, his frizzled wig askew. Rosanne snatched the opportunity to pry his hands from her waist. Whipping her head around, she stared at Brant in the doorway, her gratitude for his intrusion rendering her incapable of speech. Not that the scene needed an explanation. He had probably seen everything from the garden, anyway, she thought, flushing from the shameful realization as she covertly readjusted her gown.

"Am I interrupting?" Brant asked again, walking toward them with an expression of such studied innocence that Rosanne had to turn her head to hide a reluctant smile.

Hugh's lips twisted into a sneer. "That's pretty obvious, isn't it?" He tugged a handkerchief from his pocket and wiped it across his forehead, hope suddenly kindling in his eyes.

"If you are here to apologize, then I'll forgive the interruption. I know you didn't mean those things you said earlier, Brant. Be a good lad and apologize in front of my betrothed. Apologize and everything will return to normal."

Brant withdrew his attention from Hugh and glanced at Rosanne, observing her pale, frightened face, the small hand still clutched protectively to her bodice. Had that been her first kiss? he wondered. Would she ever discover that lovemaking could be a pleasurable act? He had watched through the window until he couldn't stand it another second. His uncle was a pig, he thought viciously. It was obscene to think that this lovely young girl was destined to end up as his aunt had. It was strangely sad to think she would never experience the ecstasy of a love that merged heart, body, and soul.

He smiled inwardly, suddenly amused at his own romantic musings. He wasn't sure he believed that such all-consuming love even existed. And if it did, he had never known it and wasn't sure he wanted to. He and Martha had a strong friendship to base their marriage upon. He needed a hard-working wife and a good mother to his children; romance had no place in his wilderness-oriented practicality.

"I'm waiting, Brant," Hugh said in growing irritation.

"I believe I must have lost my pocket watch somewhere in the sofa," Brant remarked coolly. "I was in here earlier. You don't mind if I look?"

"Damn your eyes, Brant," Hugh said tersely.

Frustrated anger spread across Hugh's features, his eyes burning against the blotchy pallor of his complexion. Helplessly, he stood back and watched as his nephew made a leisurely pretense of searching the sofa, upturning cushions and feeling along the seams before finally he straightened up muttering, "The devil! Where could it have gotten to?"

He turned back to Hugh and Rosanne, shaking his head in staged chagrin. "Well, I know I had it here. I remember sitting down and pulling it out—"

He plunged his hand into his pocket in a reenactment of the scene, pretending astonishment as he extracted the ivory-inlaid timepiece. Silence mounted in the room.

"Well, now, isn't this embarrassing?" Brant said at last, forcing a sheepish smile. "It was right here in my pocket all along. Imagine me thinking I'd lost it."

"I am trying to, Brant, but without much success," Hugh said through his teeth. "I swear, if there wasn't a lady present, I'd thrash some respect into you."

Rosanne's gaze crept to Brant. Her pulse had slowed to a less frantic pace, enabling her to calm her emotions. The relationship between Hugh and his nephew still puzzled her, but a stranger could see that Brant wasn't fazed by his uncle's threats. Hugh was the one who seemed more unnerved. Yet he didn't strike her as the type of man who would allow anyone to intimidate him either. Unless he feared that Brant *had* unearthed condemning evidence against him.

"I think you ought to leave now, Brant," Hugh said, his struggle for control straining his voice. "If not for me, then out of consideration for Lady Rosanne."

"Oh, I am leaving, Uncle. Moira is upstairs right now packing my bag. I don't intend to remain in this house a minute longer than necessary. I've said what I came to say."

Shoving his watch back into his pocket, Brant began to walk toward the door, then rotated slowly to address Rosanne. "If I were you, m'lady, I'd arrange passage back to England first thing tomorrow morning. No matter what he promises you, it won't be worth the price you'll have to pay." He closed the door behind him on a room filled with grim silence, his final words and fading footfalls echoing in Rosanne's mind.

"Damn him," Hugh muttered to himself. "Just like his father. Arrogant and self-righteous. Spouting his impossible principles. Damn him!"

He pushed past Rosanne and strode to the sideboard where a servant had placed a lacquered tray holding a crystal decanter and a set of matching glasses. His jaw clenched, he poured out two liberal sherries. Could Olivia be right? Would Brant make good his threats? Would he destroy everything Hugh had worked for with his stupid idealism?"

"Your sherry, my dear."

Rosanne was startled again by the sudden reversal in Hugh's manner, the hostility of the minute before now replaced by polite decorum. In wordless confusion, she accepted the proffered glass, not out of deference to him but because she felt in need of the instant fortification the sherry would provide.

"Sit with me on the sofa, Rosanne."

"I prefer to stand."

He shrugged and seated himself, his eyes gleaming with speculation. "I won't insist—but only because it is our first night together, and I respect your maidenly shyness. Naturally, after the wedding, I'll tolerate no disobedience. I trust that's understood."

She swallowed her sherry over the anger tightening her throat. What she understood was that he was determined to bend her to his will. She would be a receptacle for his lust when the mood struck him, a puppet who would move only when and how he manipulated her. The one advantage of being a neglected child was that no one had really cared where she went or what she did. Even at the boarding school she'd enjoyed a small amount of freedom in choosing her friends. She would never belong to herself again if she married Hugh.

She set her glass down on the sideboard. "I don't want

to marry you, Hugh," she said in an unstoppable rush of emotion. "I shouldn't have agreed to in the first place. I won't make the kind of wife you want. I'm sorry if this upsets your plans."

"Don't be childish, Rosanne," he said calmly. "You don't have a choice. You wouldn't want me to have to write to your father about your conduct, would you? He would be deeply distressed."

"Why the devil should I care about his feelings?" she cried. "He doesn't give a damn about mine. He can't even be bothered to attend the bloody wedding!"

"Please don't swear, Rosanne. I dislike hearing a lady employ foul language." Hugh put his own glass down on one of the tea tables and rose from the sofa. "Speaking of your family reminds me that we have a letter to write tomorrow morning."

"Yes, Hugh," she said, puzzled. "We're sending a letter to Gwennie's brother."

"Not that." He began to circle her, his brow furrowed in meditation. "You are going to write to your grandfather to tell him how happy you are that he and your father have made amends. Tell him about our engagement—he knows about it already, but that doesn't matter." He stopped directly in front of her. "Let him know how sorry you are that he has been ill recently and can't attend the wedding."

"You're deluding yourself, Hugh. My grandfather wouldn't waste his time attending my wedding, or even my funeral, for that matter."

"You're wrong, Rosanne. He's quite concerned about you. Why, my agents have confirmed that he's already begun investigating my background and has hinted that he'll pay me a visit as soon as he's physically able."

"I don't believe it."

"What you believe doesn't matter," he said coldly. "I want you to write to him."

Rosanne's mouth tightened with indignation. "I've never written or spoken a word to that miserable old man in my life. I do not intend to start now, and you'll not bully me into it. He ruined my mother's life, in the theater and at home. He planted seeds of discontent in my father's mind against her. They might have been happy if he hadn't interfered—"

"Your mother was a costly piece of tail from the alleys of Paris. Your father never should have given her his name. Oh, I understand well enough why he did it. She was a bewitching woman, but marrying her was a mistake."

Insensate fury ignited inside Rosanne. "How dare you speak of my mother that way!"

Hugh pivoted, scowling to himself, too absorbed in mentally composing the letter to heed the wild loathing on her face. It really was a shame Rydenham would be unable to attend the wedding. His presence would have been the social coup of the year. On the other hand, Hugh didn't want to appear overeager to curry the old man's favor. The duke had been involved in politics long enough to be able to sniff out a toadeater. But Rosanne was Rydenham's blood, and men tended to draw toward their own as they grew older.

He glanced at her, taken aback by the withering look she gave him. "Let us not argue about Lisette's virtue, for God's sake. I was fond of her too, but that doesn't change—" He cut himself off, his voice impatient. "I shall compose that letter for you, Rosanne. You'll copy it in your own hand."

"I won't write that letter. I'll despise that man until the day I die."

His face hardened. "When it comes to trivial matters, such as what color gown to wear, or which portrait to hang in the hall, then I'll gladly bend to your wishes. But in matters of importance, you will obey me."

"Importance? Tell me, Hugh, why is this letter so important to you?"

"An appointment to the council can be either a position of fruitless self-sacrifice or a stepping stone to greater achievements, depending on who supports me. With your grandfather's help, Rosanne, I could become mayor or maybe even receive a commission as lieutenant governor. After that, who can say?"

"I don't care if you're demoted to city rat-catcher, Hugh. I am not writing that letter. Now we've had our sherry, I'd like to go to my room."

He stared at her, aching to slap the belligerence from her lovely face. He would have too, if they'd been married. Edward should have warned him: Rosanne had inherited her mother's independent temperament. Fortunately, she was also blessed with Lisette's provocative sensuality, though Rosanne's was still unplumbed, unawakened. What a pleasure it would be to exploit it at his leisure.

"Go to bed, my dear. I think you'll look at this differently in the morning."

She hurried from the room, afraid he'd suffer another mood change and summon her back. Flinging open the door, she was startled to discover herself facing Olivia. Had the woman been eavesdropping, or was she about to enter the room?

"Good night, Olivia," she said tightly, not lingering to find the answer.

"Well, good night, dear," Olivia said, her face showing concern as Rosanne rushed by her toward the staircase.

But Olivia's expression of concern rapidly evolved into one of anger as she entered the drawing room and approached her father-in-law.

"I told you to let me handle this, Hugh. I thought that was why you were leaving her in Boston with me."

He sank down into a chair, his legs inelegantly sprawled out before him, his lower lip pouting. "I need her to write that damn letter, Olivia."

"It can wait a few days."

"And what about her attitude? It will do me more harm than good if she starts cursing Rydenham's name in public. I'll look a blasted fool."

"You'll look an even bigger fool if she refuses to marry you. The situation with her grandfather is obviously more delicate than Edward let on. She must be persuaded to forgive the duke."

"Then you persuade her, Olivia. You know I can't be bothered with petty details."

For an instant, deep-seated contempt sharpened the angular edges of Olivia's face, but it was gone before Hugh could notice it. "I suppose you'd like me to take care of Brant too."

"Brant? You're not going to change him. He's just a hothead. I don't think he'd really hurt me. We're family."

"Can you afford to test his loyalty, Hugh?"

He squirmed under her unflinching regard. God, she thought, he's just like his son. Strong willed when it meant satisfying his desires, pathetically craven when the situation demanded decisive action. If she had been a man, if she'd had *half* the opportunities granted him and Daniel, she wouldn't have allowed anyone or anything to thwart her own overpowering ambitions.

"Damnation, Olivia," he said raggedly. "What are you suggesting we do?"

"The wilderness is fraught with dangers, Hugh. Lawless men abound. Murder is commonplace. So are accidents."

"But I need him, Olivia. There are rumors of tenant unrest spreading through the Hudson Valley. Brant keeps our farmers in line and always delivers our wheat on schedule."

"Conrad Sluyter in Albany will find you another land agent before winter."

"I'm beginning to suspect you harbor more than a passing fondness for Conrad, Olivia."

"We were discussing your nephew," she said stiffly. "Are you forgetting he intends to abandon you?"

"He'll change his mind in a few months, once he marries and settles down."

"I don't believe it. You're making excuses for him. He could ruin you, Hugh." She turned to leave, then looked back with a taunting smile. "And do try to contain your lust for that girl until after the wedding. She's obviously not eager to share your bed. I can't say I blame her."

He cursed her silently as she left the room, regretting that he had ever forced Daniel to marry her, an ill-tempered bitch from the start, whose sole attraction had been a sizable dowry. In those days, however, Hugh himself had been an unimpressive tradesman, perched on the middle rungs of the social ladder. The eminent families he had urged his son to marry into had snubbed him with open scorn.

Those same families didn't laugh at him now, not that many years later, Hugh thought with smug satisfaction.

Or did they? Did they mock him behind his back? Despite his wealth, despite his lifetime nomination to the council, despite the favors he handed out freely, the elite social leaders of New York had never truly accepted him into their aristocratic circle. He had tried so hard to please them, perhaps too hard. But nothing he did seemed to win their lasting approval. Nothing he'd done as a child had won his father's approval either. His older brother Robert had claimed that. And a sizable family inheritance.

He glanced around the room, his anger rekindling as he his attention fell upon the sofa. Damn Brant! So much like Robert. Olivia had a point. But to have his own nephew murdered . . . Franklin Newhouse had deserved to die, a treacherous insect who toward the end of their partnership was attempting to extort a fortune from Hugh.

What was he supposed to do? he wondered tiredly. He couldn't let Brant spoil everything. Maybe the boy would cool down now that he'd gotten his anger out in the open. Hugh hoped so. If not, he would seriously have to consider Olivia's suggestion.

He stood and stretched, shoving guilt and regret aside. His fleeting experience with Rosanne had left him aching with frustrated lust. He needed a woman. Grinning in anticipation, he moved across the room to the bellpull. His valet, Leander, detested procuring harlots for his master, but he did have excellent taste, and he'd never brought home a diseased whore yet.

Chapter 4

Rosanne had tugged off her gown and flung herself across the bed in her chemise and petticoats. Sleep had overwhelmed her, a heavy but restless sleep haunted by impressions accumulated over the past two months. Hugh forcing himself upon her, his arm a manacle around her waist. Brant warning her to leave. Her father fetching her from boarding school, cold and eager to send her away. Gwennie eating tainted fish aboard the *Broken Heart*, and later her stomach becoming grotesquely bloated as she lay dying in agony.

"Promise me, my pet, that ye'll not bring that doctor in here to poke an' prod me. He couldn't help me now anyway. Promise me that ye'll not let them throw me overboard to feed the sharks. I want to be buried proper in a churchyard. 'Tis the only thing I've ever asked of ye in all the years."

"I promise, Gwennie," she'd whispered, believing that the old woman would surely survive, not considering that they had over two weeks left at sea.

She was shocked when Gwennie died that same night. Grief-stricken but bound by her promise, Rosanne had wrapped the body in coarse white sheets and told the other passengers that the old servant's seasickness had confined her to their cabin. But inevitably the corpse began to decay, and late one night Rosanne had awakened to see two large rats burrowing under the shroud.

She had screamed in horror, the bloodcurdling sound alerting the ship's watch and eventually drawing the captain to her cabin. Her secret had been discovered, the corpse flung overboard.

"What's happened, my dear? Are you all right?"

The nightmarish images receded as she opened her eyes to the reality of Brant leaning over the bed. Foggily she noted that he had changed into his traveling clothes—a coarse muslin shirt, buckskin breeches, a matching fringed jacket, and heavy jackboots. He looked utterly out of place in the delicately furnished bedchamber. He looked rugged and dangerously attractive.

"The r-rat . . ."

"A rat?" He glanced around the room, unable to suppress his amusement. "In Olivia's house? It wouldn't stand a chance." He sat down, bracing himself on the edge of the bed. "I was leaving my room when you screamed out. I've heard Indian war whoops that were less terrifying."

She sat up slowly, too shaken to understand his gentle teasing. "It was a dream, but it really happened—"

"Dreams can seem very real."

"No. It *happened*." And then, all at once, she found herself pouring out the misery of the past two months, the sentences tumbling over one another in whispered fragments that she knew dimly were only partially coherent. She felt responsible for Gwennie's death; she could not rid herself of the ghastly memory of discovering the rodents gnawing at the body of her beloved servant. There had been no one else to talk to until Brant, and even though she realized he couldn't possibly care what her life had been like, it felt so blessedly good to unload the burden of guilt she'd been carrying.

"They threw Gwennie's body overboard in the m-middle of the night without even a p-prayer. The captain said it could bring disease."

"He was right," Brant said gently.

"But I p-promised her."

"You did your best. I think she'd understand."

Their gazes caught and connected, Rosanne's glittering with emotion, Brant's as cool and compelling as a woodland glade. He knew he should leave. He was too uncomfortably conscious of her vulnerability, of her scantily clad woman's figure, its voluptuous curves and alluring recesses. Her hair was loose, as beautiful as he'd imagined it, reflecting the fading firelight. His eyes scorched a heated path down the honey cream flesh of her throat to the swell of her breasts above the chemise, where their light rose crests were provocatively visible through the edging of fine eggshell lace. He swallowed hard. He tried to conjure up Martha's face. The image blurred. He tried to rise from the bed. His body ignored the command.

"Rosanne, I should—"

"No, don't go yet."

She laid her hand on his thigh, not dreaming that his nerve endings leaped wildly at the unintentional intimacy of her touch. She only knew that when he left she would be alone in this house without an ally. She only knew that in Brant's presence she felt achingly aware of her femininity, her senses burgeoning in anticipation of an enigmatic destiny.

She heard him inhale forcefully. She felt his eyes gliding over her with restrained longing. Slowly, as if he were waging an inner battle of conscience against desire, he raised his hand to touch her cheek, his fingers deliberately brushing across her breast, in a movement as light and as tentative as a butterfly's flight. Her nipple hardened instantly into a taut, tingling bud, his caress sending pleasure streaming through her. She sensed that he would kiss her if she granted him the slightest encouragement, and suddenly she yearned for that kiss, yearned to feel his firm, sensitive mouth pressed to hers. In trustful expectation, she turned her face up to his, her eyes luminous blue sparks between their silken-lashed borders.

"Kiss me, Brant." Her voice was a dulcet-toned whisper, bold and irresistible in its innocence.

His hand dropped to her shoulder, his fingers curling as

he struggled to resist. "Oh, dear heaven," he groaned. "Why did you have to say that?"

"I thought you wanted to," she whispered.

"My sweet, innocent temptress, I should like to do so much more than just kiss you."

Caution slipped from Brant in insidious layers. It had been a month since he'd relieved his physical needs with Rachel Blakemoor, a young Mohawk Valley widow. It might be another fortnight before he could bed his betrothed. Rosanne tempted him dangerously, inflamed his parched senses. How easy it would be to forget time and place and propriety with her.

Besides, what harm could a single kiss hold?

He reclined over her, his strong arms cradling her as she melted back against the pillows with a shiver. Suddenly afraid of what she had touched off, ashamed of her own wantoness, she placed her palms against his chest to hold him back, all the while feeling the excited tempo of his heartbeat through his shirt, through warm flesh and hard pectoral muscle.

"Brant, maybe—"

"Too late," he whispered with a rueful smile that deepened the creases in his cheeks. His head dipped lower, his hazel eyes burning with hypnotic desire. "I suppose you don't know your own power yet, and I am sadly unaware of my weaknesses."

She gasped in surprise, the sound smothered by the meltingly exquisite warmth of his mouth possessing hers. His tongue outlined the lush contours of her mouth, sampling its innocent sweetness, coaxing her lips apart as the sun's rays coaxed the petals of a blossom to unfold. Instinct tutored her to follow his example as she moved her tongue against his.

"Rosanne— Oh, Lord," he murmured, his arms tightening around her. "What are you doing to me?"

Amazed to discover her inexperienced response challenging his control, Brant lengthened the kiss, refining his technique with practiced expertise. Suddenly, incredibly, he realized that her pleasure had become his pleasure . . .

that the need for satisfaction and the desire to satisfy had ignited into one consuming flame.

Wavelet upon wavelet of sensation engulfed Rosanne, leaving her weak even as they rushed through her body in delicious eddies that washed away all fear and resistance. So *this* was what it felt like to be kissed, she thought hazily, forgetting that less than an hour earlier Hugh's lips had ravaged hers in rapacious lust, forgetting that she was engaged to the uncle of the man devastating her with a tender seduction that she had invited. This was how it was supposed to be between a man and a woman, her heart told her. And she ached for completion, ached to delve deeper into the sensual secrets his kiss hinted at. Daringly she twined her arms around Brant's neck and shifted her small frame so that their bodies melded together in passion-heated contact.

Brant moaned in torment, conscious of the almost painful pressure building in his loins; conscious, oh Lord, all too conscious, of her soft, full-breasted figure beneath his. Tearing his mouth from hers, he wrenched her arms from his neck and straightened. His hands were actually *shaking*. He wasn't sure whether he could even stand. Another five minutes and God only knew what might have happened. He cringed at the possibilities. Tears. A humiliating scene. He might have ruined her life and his future with Martha; he might have made himself look like a total hypocrite in front of Hugh. He never lost control. What was wrong with him?

Rosanne dropped back against the pillows and stared at him, disoriented, as her spiraling senses slowly floated down to earth. Why had he stopped? Hugh? His betrothed? If they'd been alone in the house, would he have continued? Would she have let him? What would that heady kiss have led to? I'll never know, she thought heavily, and perhaps I should be grateful. I'm only a momentary diversion in his life. He'll have forgotten about me by tomorrow.

"I have to go," he said quietly. "I'm traveling for New York in the morning. I meant what I said about Hugh—"

A voice from the doorway interrupted him. "I've packed

yer belongings, Mr. Brant. Is there anythin' else ye'd like me to do before ye leave?"

He stood up quickly, annoyed at himself because he felt compelled to explain his presence in the room. "Lady Rosanne had a nightmare, Moira. I came in to investigate."

Rosanne sat up, her eyes seeking Brant's with wounded hesitation. He couldn't possibly have experienced the same soaring elation as she had and still stand there maintaining that cool self-possession. Was something wrong with her that she could be so easily devastated by a man's kiss? And yet Hugh's brutal caresses had disgusted her. They were incomparable, the feelings each man aroused inside her—a universe apart.

"It's true, Moira," she said. "I had a nightmare."

" 'Tain't none of my business, I'm sure," Moira said crisply. "I'm only a servant. If I worried about the strange goings on in this family, I'd have left years ago."

"Which is what I am about to do," Brant said, moving toward the door. His gaze drifted to Rosanne, lingering on her somber face. "Which is what you should do," he added softly.

And then he was following Moira into the hall, fighting an illogical reluctance to leave Rosanne, fighting the feverish spell that had threatened to drive reason from his mind.

Rosanne turned her face away from the door as it closed. What a senseless thing to have encouraged! She wished desperately that she had never learned how bittersweet a kiss could be. What had it done but fill her with restless discontent? What had it accomplished but to set a standard that would haunt her forever?

She settled back against the pillows and listened to the voices in the hallway. Brant was going. She could barely make out the deep tones of his voice as he descended the staircase.

"Kent and Mary Lawrence still own the Hunter and Hounds on Crabb Lane, don't they, Moira? It's more to my taste than the usual waterfront tavern."

"Aye, Mr. Brant."

The voices faded. On impulse Rosanne leaped out of

bed and ran to the window, wrenching it open in the hope it overlooked the stable yard. To her disappointment, she found herself staring down at a large fruit orchard interspersed with imported nut and shade trees. Then hoofbeats sounded. The entrance gate creaked open and shut.

He was gone, she thought, releasing her breath in a sigh. She returned to the bed, mechanically undressing and changing into the lawn nightdress Moira had laid out earlier, although she doubted she could sleep now.

A quarter of an hour dragged by. A man's laugh, low and muted, drifted to her from one of the bedchambers down the hall. She slid off the bed and walked to the door, listening intently, listening for that velvet voice. Had Brant returned? Had he changed his mind about leaving? Or had he merely forgotten something?

She opened the door and proceeded slowly along the dark passageway, drawn by emotions she couldn't name, emotions so young and fragile she was barely aware of their emergence. If she encountered Brant again, what would it change? They were each betrothed to others, pledged before they had even met. She could hear a woman's voice now too, rough and guttural, coming from the last chamber down the hall. Maybe he and Moira were arguing.

She pressed her hand against the door, hesitating, realizing she couldn't knock without a plausible excuse. She wanted to see him again—oh, she did—but what on earth would she say to him? Perhaps she could ask him to give her sister a message. Heavens, she thought suddenly, what if this were Olivia and Daniel's room?

She vacillated. She stepped backward, deciding she really ought to return to her own room. But the pressure of her knuckles had swung the door open. She stared into the chamber. The undulating flame of a single taper gilded the two naked figures locked in a carnal position upon the bed. Hugh—and beneath him a thin young woman, pressed stomach down across the bed. Her face was buried into a pillow while he thrust into her with tense concentration.

He had removed his wig, and candlelight glinted on his shoulders and closely shaven head.

"Oh, my God," Rosanne whispered.

She stood transfixed in the doorway, her oval face convulsed with disgust. She turned to flee, but it was too late. Hugh had heard her.

"Rosanne, oh, Sweet Jesus! I thought you were asleep."

Horrified and incredulous, Rosanne watched him shove the woman to the floor and knot a sheet around his thick waist as he jumped off the bed. "Put your clothes on, you dumb whore, and get the hell out of here!" he hissed at the prone figure sprawled at his feet.

"My goddamn pleasure!" the woman cried, rubbing her bruised hip as she scrambled for her dress. "You ain't normal anyway! I heard about men like you, but this was the first—"

"Shut up!" Hugh snarled. "Shut up, d'you hear me?" He began to approach Rosanne, his face beseeching and afraid. "My angel, you have to understand. You got me so excited tonight that I—"

He broke off as he noticed her gaze drop from his face to his lower torso. Glancing down, he realized that he was naked, that the sheet had fallen at the foot of the bed. He had never felt so foolish in his entire life.

"Why are you staring at me like that, Rosanne?" he asked defensively, stumbling backward to retrieve his clothes. "Didn't they teach you any manners at all in school?"

Rosanne shook her head in contempt. "Debauchery wasn't part of the curriculum, Hugh." Part of her wanted to laugh at the absurdity of the situation. Another part wanted to weep because her fate lay in the hands of this abhorrent man.

Behind Hugh, the whore laughed grimly and struggled to hook up her gown. "She's probably never seen anything as pathetic before, have you, sweetheart?"

Hugh, halfway into his breeches, staggered around with his right hand balling into a fist. "I told you to shut your mouth! My betrothed is a *lady*."

"Your betrothed, is she?" The woman hiked up her bodice and faced Rosanne. "Take my advice and find yourself another man, dearie. This one's a pervert if ever I've met one. You should hear the things he wanted to—"

Hugh lunged for her then, slamming her up against the wall. The woman's eyes widened in fear. Suddenly Hugh's fist smashed against her temple. Then again and again.

Outrage galvanized Rosanne. She darted forward. The woman had crumpled to the floor, whimpering softly, and Hugh was leaning over her with his arm drawn back.

"Stop it, Hugh!" she cried. She caught his arm in the upswing, pushing against his forearm with all her strength. "Stop it! You're going to kill her!"

"Don't interfere, Rosanne!"

Rosanne felt the tendons in his arm trembling as he turned his head to stare at her, his eyes bulging. "I believe every word she said about you, Hugh. And I am going to heed her advice. After what I've seen tonight, I couldn't possibly marry you!"

She released his arm and spun away from him, shaking violently but at the same time relieved. It was over. She would be free. She had found her excuse. He had humiliated himself; he had humiliated them both. He had no choice now but to let her go.

"Do you think you're too good for me, Rosanne?"

From the corner of her eye, Rosanne perceived a dark flash descending as Hugh brought his hand down in a vicious backhanded blow across her cheek. Flaming agony spread across the side of her face. He struck her again. Her eye burned and watered. Stunned, she reeled back into the cherrywood clothespress, regained her balance, and turned blindly. Hugh caught her before she could reach the door.

"Don't you . . . touch me!" she panted, her face numb with pain. "Don't touch me again!"

She fought to break his hold, disbelief and hatred throbbing in her veins. Even her father in his drunken tempers had never hit her or her mother. She could barely open her eyelid. She could taste blood on her rapidly swelling lip.

Her heart seethed with the desire for retaliation while her mind more wisely counseled her to escape.

She twisted back only to feel Hugh's blunt fingers jabbing into the tender flesh of her shoulders. He pressed his face close to hers. "Listen to me well, *milady*. Your father's blue blood may run in your veins, but so does your mother's. And your mother was a whore—"

"You're a liar!" she cried. "A madman—"

"A whore, Rosanne," he continued ruthlessly. "Just like that whimpering piece of trash on the floor there, and I should know. Why, your mother even lured me to her bed, inviting me with her lush whore's body as you were doing earlier."

"Inviting you?" she echoed incredulously. "Hugh, I was doing everything in my power to evade you!"

He smirked. "Is that so? Then why were you wearing a dress obviously fashioned to stir a man's senses?" He dragged one hand roughly along the slope of her shoulder to the silk ribbons at her throat, his voice taking on a husky timber. She had interrupted him before he'd found satisfaction with the prostitute, but it was Rosanne he really wanted.

"Why did you come to my bedchamber tonight, Rosanne? Are you ashamed to admit you want me? Your mother was like that too, playing her little love games. Oh, she swore she wasn't after me, pretended to fight me off, but I knew better . . ."

Rosanne wrenched his hand from her throat, her eyes blazing wildly. "My mother was a lonely woman, and maybe she did have lovers, but I don't believe she'd let anyone like you touch her!"

The memory of Lisette struggling beneath him jumped across Hugh's mind. Yes, she had put on quite an act, but he hadn't been fooled. She'd been flirting with him all evening, teasing him right under her husband's nose. And when Edward, as usual, had sunk into an alcoholic stupor at the table, Hugh had followed Lisette upstairs to her chamber and forced his way inside.

"You're repulsive to me, Hugh," he remembered her sobbing afterward. *"Repulsive . . ."*

With a start, Hugh snapped out of the past to realize Rosanne had just echoed her mother's exact words. Dazedly he looked down at her face, suddenly noticing the puffy eyelid and hideously swollen lip. Lord almighty! Had he done that? He hadn't meant to hurt her, he really hadn't, but there were times when he seemed to lose all control . . .

"Rosanne—" He reached for her, flinching as she turned instantly in a panic to escape.

"Good heavens! What's going on in here?"

Hugh and Rosanne looked around simultaneously as Olivia entered the room, her sharp green eyes missing nothing—from the prostitute cowering in the corner to Rosanne's face and disheveled state. Her lips tightened at the corners, the only indication of the fury raging through her. She felt she could strangle Hugh for jeopardizing their plans for a single night of pleasure.

"Olivia," Hugh began, holding out his hands to her in supplication. "It isn't as bad as it appears."

"Nothing is ever as bad as it appears, Hugh," she said, her words hanging like icicles in the chilled atmosphere. "I'm sure Rosanne will realize that in the morning, just as I'm sure you will promise her that nothing of this nature will ever happen again."

"Oh, it won't—it won't," he said hastily. "I made a terrible mistake tonight, and I lost my temper—"

"And I won't be here to let it happen again," Rosanne interjected furiously. "No one—no one has ever treated me like this before. I didn't want to marry you in the first place, Hugh. Now nothing on earth could force me."

"You're upset, my dear, and understandably so," Olivia said. "But Hugh has been under a tremendous strain lately—"

"I won't forgive him this, Olivia!" Rosanne cried. "Do you see my face? Do you know what he did to that wretched woman over there?" She tensed at the expression of patronizing sympathy Olivia had assumed. Olivia didn't believe her. She actually thought this incident would be forgotten overnight!

"I can't believe you would condone his behavior, Olivia."

The older woman gave her a tolerant smile. "I'm not condoning it at all, dear, but I am a little curious about what you were doing in his room. I thought you had gone to bed."

"I was looking for—" Instinct warned her not to mention Brant's name. "I was looking for you. I wanted a cup of tea to help me sleep."

Olivia sighed. "Go back to your room. I'll send Moira up with a pot of bee-balm tea and a vinegar compress for your cheek."

Rosanne walked rapidly to the door, her face expressionless. But then outside in the hallway her composure crumbled, and she had to lean against the wall to steady her nerves. Hugh wasn't mentally stable, and she realized now he wouldn't release her from the engagement without a fight. Her only course for a peaceful settlement was to appeal once again, privately, to Olivia.

The snatches of conversation that reached her ears from Hugh's bedchamber strangled that hope in its infancy.

"How could you, Hugh?" Olivia was demanding in a savage undertone. "Why couldn't you have gone to Mount Whoredom with that moron son of yours?"

Hugh hung his head, though he was sorely tempted to shout back that Daniel might not chase women if his wife weren't such an emasculating bitch. But he needed Olivia. Unfortunately, he was bound to her by an unholy alliance.

"A man of my position cannot be seen in public with a harlot, Olivia. And how was I supposed to know she'd wake up and wander into my room?"

"Couldn't you have thought to lock the door? And her face, Hugh!"

"I didn't mean to hurt her, Olivia. Oh, Christ, what am I going to do now? what if her grandfather finds out about tonight?"

Rosanne's stomach knotted in disgust. Hugh had turned from an enraged beast into a whimpering milksop within minutes. She leaned forward suddenly, shocked at Olivia's response.

"She's going to cause trouble for us now, Hugh. I can sense it. We'll have to watch her night and day until the wedding. And I don't care if I have to lock her in the wine cellar like a disobedient slave and then break her aristocratic fingers—she's going to write that letter to her grandfather!"

"Hellfire, Olivia, wouldn't it be easier to forge the letter ourselves?"

"You'll only encounter her defiance time and time again unless you assert yourself from the start. She has to understand her place."

"But you can't lock a young girl in a cellar, Olivia. It's—it's cruel."

"It's highly effective, take my word. My mother did it often enough to me. Now, tomorrow morning you give her that emerald necklace you were saving for her wedding gift. Promise to buy her whatever it takes to make her forget tonight. And get that harlot out of my house. . . ."

Rosanne fled down the hallway to her room, bolting the door behind her just as she heard Olivia emerging from Hugh's bedchamber. Surely they didn't really intend to make a prisoner of her until the wedding? Surely the fools didn't think they could buy her submission with jewels? The bitter irony of it all was that they hoped to use her to gain the support of a man who probably hated her as he'd hated her mother.

Belligerent anger bubbled inside her. She wouldn't remain in this house another hour. She'd go to her sister, offer herself as a nursemaid in exchange for a home. She pulled off her nightdress, wincing in pain as she yanked her chemise over her bruised cheekbone. Oh, the monster! she thought, and grabbed her damask gown off the peg rail in the hanger press. In an unthinking frenzy, she stuffed a few treasured belongings back into her portmanteau: an ivory comb, two rosemary washballs, her sister's last letter, a vellum-bound book of fairy tales, the leather pouch containing Gwennie's savings, which she vowed to repay the old woman's relatives as soon as she could. Gwennie would have understood. Gwennie would have *murdered* Hugh if she were alive!

A hasty check along the bottom of the portmanteau revealed that her mother's diamond ring was still sewn safely in the lining, exactly where Gwennie had hidden it.

A loud knock rattled the door. " 'Tis me, Moira. Mrs. Layton says ye fell out of bed and hurt yerself. I've tea and a compress for ye."

Fell out of bed! "I'm better now, Moira," she said, gritting her teeth. "I just want to sleep."

"Suit yerself."

She pulled a rich plum-colored velvet capuchin cloak from her trunk, throwing the silk-lined garment over her shoulders and raising the monk's hood. Carrying the bulging portmanteau, she tiptoed to the door and quietly unbolted it.

The hallway was deserted. She ventured out, but a noise stopped her cold at the top of the staircase. A husky manservant was stretched out on the tiny landing below. Her guard, no doubt.

She retreated from the staircase and back into her room, panic blanketing her mind. Almost a month of captivity in this house. Did Olivia really lock her slaves in the cellar as punishment? Did she starve them, deprive them of water and light? Rosanne shuddered convulsively. She wasn't a coward, but she was no martyr either. Who could help her? Perhaps Brant. But he'd left, swearing never to return.

She turned suddenly to the window and gazed down into the garden. Was it higher than the dormitory window at boarding school? Directly below grew a sturdy black walnut tree with thick, leafy limbs that beckoned like outstretched arms. She'd have to hang from the windowsill by her heels to touch its crown—a sobering thought. But she could attempt to drop onto one of the higher branches and swing to the ground. If she misjudged the distance and missed, she might break her legs. And Hugh would find her.

Chapter 5

A door opened from the servants' quarters below. Someone was leaving. Minutes whirled by. She gathered courage. Then, with her portmanteau tucked under her arm and her cloak wrapped tightly around her, she hoisted herself up and jumped.

Horror paralyzed her brain as she realized a split second too late that she was going to overshoot the tree by inches. She strained backward, contorting her spine in midair. Then spears of pain jolted up her legs, and snarled foliage slapped her arms as she landed in a teetering crouch across two intertwining limbs via a tangle of inhospitable branches.

The portmanteau thudded to the ground. She held her breath. The deep brown limbs beneath her sagged ominously. Crablike, she inched toward the furrowed trunk. Her cloak caught around her ankle: impatiently, she tugged it loose. The movement unbalanced her. Gasping, her arms flailing in circles like the wings of a fledgling ousted from its nest, she pitched forward to land on her folded knees with an excruciating thump.

In agony she crawled to the trunk of the tree and curled up in its protective darkness. Had anyone heard her? She listened intently, massaging her knee, positive she'd crippled herself. All was quiet. She stood up gingerly, picked up her portmanteau, and hobbled a few steps. Tears of pain burned her eyelids, but nothing seemed to be broken.

Clinging to the shrubbery, she limped toward the stables. She needed a horse. A cluster of clouds drifted past the half-moon, brightening her path. She froze.

Less than a yard ahead, a woman stood slumped against the garden gate. Too late Rosanne turned. The woman's head lifted, her black curls bobbing around her pretty, ashen face with its dark, lively eyes. Rosanne's heart careened with relief. The prostitute.

"What are you doing here?" two astonished female voices whispered in unison.

The woman pressed backward in alarm, her thin fingers fumbling to unlatch the gate. "I wasn't doin' nothing wrong, m'lady. Just waitin' for my head to stop spinnin'."

"You should see a doctor. Mr. Layton might have given you a concussion."

"A con— Oh, no. He looked clean enough, m'lady. Besides, I take mercury tablets imported from France to prevent the pox."

"No, no. Your *head*. I meant he might have hurt your head."

"Oh, that. Dizzy as the devil, but that's not unusual. Anyway you don't look that well yourself. Ladies have more delicate skin than whores, I guess." The woman's eyes lowered to the portmanteau. "You are takin' my advice."

Rosanne spoke hurriedly, reawakening to the danger of remaining on the grounds. "Are you familiar with the Hunter and Hounds on Crabb Lane?"

"The barkeep there don't encourage my type of business, but I know where it is." She squinted suspiciously. "Why?"

Rosanne sighed, bothered by the woman's curiosity, bothered even more by the sudden flutter her heart gave at the thought of seeing Brant again. "I have a friend there."

"Oh. I see."

"No, you don't. Please, Mrs.—"

"Barbara, m'lady," the prostitute supplied, opening the gate for Rosanne with an exaggerated curtsy. "I'll take you to your friend." And in silence they moved along the side of the house and made their way to the stables.

Their escape was accomplished so easily that suspicion began to mount inside Rosanne within seconds after riding from the house. Any common horse thief could have entered the stable and stolen this fine roan gelding, she thought. Why hadn't they encountered a single groom or stableboy? Why had the entrance gate been so carelessly left unlocked and unguarded? She urged the horse into a smart trot, glancing backward at the darkened house. Was that a woman's face in the hallway window? Or was it only a shadow?

Behind her Barbara squirmed in discomfort, the portmanteau wedged between them. "Can't you make this beast ride any smoother? I got thrown out of bed on my butt."

"I'm doing the best I can without a saddle," Rosanne retorted. "Don't wriggle about so, or we'll both fall."

They had ridden for only two minutes with Trinity Church looming ahead, and were turning right into Bishop's Alley when suddenly Barbara exclaimed softly and dug her knuckles between Rosanne's shoulder blades.

"Not down the middle of the street! That's the watch on the corner. Blast it, too late! They've seen us. You let me do the talkin', m'lady. My father always said I had a honeyed tongue, and he bein' a minister was pretty glib himself."

But Rosanne had no intention of testing Barbara's powers of persuasion on the two stout-figured officers advancing on them with raised, brass-tipped staves. Her mouth taut, she wrapped the reins around her wrists, lowered her head, and dug her heels into the gelding. The horse pricked his ears and lunged forward.

"Judas Iscariot!" Barbara gasped, flinging her arms around Rosanne's waist as the gelding veered off the street and bolted across an open pasture.

Reckless exhilaration coursed through Rosanne. "Can we reach Crabb Lane from here?" she shouted back to Barbara.

Barbara pried open one tightly closed eyelid to peer at

her surroundings. "If we don't break our necks first, m'lady!"

A stray cat stalking a field mouse arched its back in alarm and streaked across their path. Clumps of sod flew into the night. A window opened in a nearby house. Someone shouted curses. The stars in the clear summer sky blurred in their vision like madly dancing comets.

"I've got this horse under perfect control!" Rosanne boasted over the whistling air.

Then suddenly her bravado exploded into horror as she spotted a high stone wall in the distance. In their path. "Stop!" She yanked back on the reins to no avail. "Hell's bells, horse, *stop!*"

The horse continued on its galloping course; accustomed to plodding the crowded Boston streets, it was reveling in the freedom of the pasture. Panic-stricken, Rosanne dropped the reins and grabbed two fistfuls of mane. Instinctively she clamped her legs down tighter around the horse's sides, urging Barbara to do the same. Yet somewhere in the back of her mind, she heard her father instructing her mother that a horse's sides were extremely sensitive to pressure, that the harder you squeezed the faster the animal would go.

But if I loosen my grasp, I'll go flying through the air like a cannonball!

"We're going to be killed," Barbara sobbed. "Christ, I'm going to die in a stinking pile of cow dung—"

All of a sudden the horse dropped its head, turned sharply, and stopped—five feet from the wall, at the edge of a watering pond. Before she could lift her face, Rosanne felt herself plunging down the gelding's neck, skirts and petticoats smothering her terrified cry as Barbara somersaulted over her head and tumbled into the shallow, muddy water. Relieved of one unwanted burden, the horse backed up and tossed its head to deposit Rosanne at the pond's damp edge.

She lumbered to her feet, wincing, to help pull Barbara from the pond. She was astonished she could still stand;

her legs wobbled like hasty pudding. "Oh, heavens, are you all right, Barbara?"

"Do I look all right?" the woman snapped furiously, shaking out her skirts. Water streamed down her face and hair; thin rivulets of mud were turning the gold of her gown to brown. "If I had a pistol, I'd shoot that lousy horse. Where is it?"

The horse was standing several feet behind them, innocently munching on tender florets of vetch and milkweed. Rosanne approached him uneasily, persuading herself she had to remount. But Barbara, having located the portmanteau, insisted on walking; so, in apprehensive silence, the two women, one on horseback, the other on foot, continued cautiously along the edge of the pasture, staring into the fenced gardens of private homes before they discovered a pathway into Milk Street. From there they traveled a short distance east toward the waterfront until Barbara motioned Rosanne to swing north into Crabb Lane.

"There it is, m'lady." She pointed to a squat wooden inn, candlelight winking through the diamond-paned windows. "I'll see that this beast is stabled, and then you're on your own."

Rosanne slid from the horse's back to the street. "Sorry about the spill, Barbara. Thanks for your help."

"I'm only returning the favor you done me tonight by stopping old bugger-bones from beating me to a pulp," Barbara said. She tugged at the horse's reins, hopping back nervously as he surged toward her. "Don't return to that house, m'lady. Gentleman or not, he has a twisted soul, and that woman who was with him is even worse. An odd pair."

"Wait, Barbara. How shall I find—"

But Barbara had already vanished from view, and Rosanne didn't wish to linger outside. Squaring her shoulders, she trudged toward the inn's main entrance and pushed open the massive door. It was late, but the taproom was fairly crowded, most of the customers lonely travelers craving company and conversation.

Rosanne stared at the staircase rising from a dimly lit

corridor at the end of the taproom. What if Brant wasn't here? She couldn't very well present herself at every door. Perhaps a serving wench could direct her. She drew her hood down to hide her face. What if he wanted nothing to do with her and insisted on returning her to Olivia's house? What if she had imagined that gentleness beneath his rough surface?

"Damn my soul! Where did you come from, sweetheart?"

A portly, bearded man in a brass-buttoned coat reached out from a bench to grab her. Nimbly, she dodged the sinewy arm, spearing him with a disdainful look that would have wilted a sober man.

"I'm sailing for the Indies tomorrow, pretty pigeon. If you pleased me, I'd reward you with a bolt of silk the color of your hair, rubies to match your eyes—"

"Rubies to match my eyes? You're drunk, sir, and making quite a fool of yourself, I might add."

She whirled away from him in indignation, her gaze sweeping the length of the room. And then her heart stopped, knocking painfully against her breast. Brant. At a corner table, engrossed in an animated discussion with the attractive brunette sitting opposite him.

Irrational anger spurted through her. She was shocked to find him with another woman—shocked and, unreasonably, hurt. She wondered cynically whether all men were enslaved by their desires. Didn't it matter to him that he was engaged? Then, in a painful revelation of honesty, she admitted to herself that she didn't give a fig for his betrothed's feelings. She was reacting as though she were the one he'd betrayed, and yet she knew her reaction was inappropriate. In fact, she had no right to even bother him with her troubles. Her imagination had played her for a fool.

The kiss that had devastated her with its aching sweetness had meant nothing to him, she thought miserably, her heart shriveling at the realization. He had only been trifling with her after all. Perhaps . . . perhaps he'd been toying with her as a private insult to Hugh. She turned away. If she hurried, she might still be able to catch Barbara. Maybe the woman could find her a place for the night and help her locate a reliable guide to escort her to New York.

"Lady Rosanne?"

Brant stood swiftly and stepped around the table, overturning a stool in his haste. "God in heaven, Rosanne, is that you?"

She froze in consternation, tempted to pretend she hadn't heard him call her name. Then, slowly, she turned around. "Please, don't let me disturb your conversation—"

The woman behind them rose, smiling at Brant with politely contained curiosity. "Kent will be sorry he missed you, Brant. Give my love to Martha. Bring her with you next time you're in Boston."

"Yes. Good night, Mary," he murmured as she walked away. But his eyes never moved from Rosanne's face, half concealed by the folds of her hood.

Whatever had possessed her to track him down this late at night? How on earth had she made it here by herself? He'd been unable to stop thinking about her all evening, remembering her enchanting innocence and the sweet temptation of her body, of their kiss. Did the memory haunt her too? Had the dangerous spark that had flared between them lured her to him? It couldn't be. As enticing as the idea was, he sensed a stronger motive. Something in her voice had betrayed her. Desperation had driven her here.

"Rosanne?" His tone deepened with sudden understanding. "Rosanne, has something happened between you and my uncle?"

She nodded, her eyes flickering to his face. Standing this near him made her feel as though she were a candle melting beneath a flame, and it was a disconcertingly pleasant sensation. She looked away, willing herself to harness her wildly swaying emotions. Would he laugh at her when she told him what had happened?

"I'd rather not discuss it here, Brant. Could we—would you mind if I explained in your room? I'm afraid—"

His thoughts tumbled. Rosanne—alone with him in his room? Dear God, the delicious fantasies the simple suggestion spawned! He was about as far removed from sainthood as a man could possibly be, and this girl was tempting him unmercifully. But she obviously needed help. He couldn't turn her away.

"Are you afraid that Hugh might have followed you here?"

"Yes." She inhaled a ragged breath. "Actually, I doubt he's even discovered I'm gone yet, but—"

He took her arm, a tight smile lifting the corners of his mouth. "We won't take the chance."

They didn't speak again until they were inside Brant's chamber. Standing in front of the door, Rosanne watched him fumble with the tinderbox on the table, and seconds later soft, golden candlelight filled the room. For the first time in hours she relaxed, feeling protected in the haven his presence afforded. It was ridiculous, really, that a man she hardly knew should inspire her with such blind trust. But who else could she turn to? Indeed, she ought to bear in mind that he hadn't even agreed to help her yet.

"Sit down at the table across from me, Rosanne." As she obeyed, he removed his buckskin jacket and slung it over the back of his chair. "Now tell me, my dear, what can I do for you?"

She lowered her gaze from his bronzed face, down his throat, to the crisp, dark hair visible at the vee of his shirt. His hands were clasped before him on the table, his brown spatulate fingers callused and crisscrossed with several small white scars. Those hands bore the evidence of a wilderness existence, and yet they had touched her with exquisite gentleness. Those hands had touched her face, her breast, with the promise of a sweet fulfillment to which, given another chance, she would abandon herself without shame or hesitation.

She blinked guiltily. The tip of her tongue glided around the edges of her mouth and reached her swollen underlip. "I—I need you to take me to the City of New York with you. I'll pay for your services as a guide. My sister will help me after that."

He flexed his supple fingers, frowning as he considered her proposal. "Your sister?"

"Mrs. Lowell Winston. Her husband is an attorney. Your uncle is supposed to be helping him establish his reputation."

"Lord, that's laughable," Brant said with unthinking bitterness. "But Winston . . . I'm sure I've heard that name mentioned recently, though I can't recall in what context."

"Claire and I were very close. When she learns of what Hugh did to me tonight, she will insist her husband end their relationship."

Brant lifted his head slowly. "Exactly what did my uncle do, Rosanne?" His voice was deceptively soft, but there was an undertone of pure steel running through it.

She acted as if she hadn't heard him, busying herself with removing her sister's last letter from her portmanteau. She would just as soon forget that humiliating scene with Hugh. "I—I have her address here somewhere."

His hand shot across the table and captured her wrist, his fingers locking around the delicate bones. "Why did you run away from Hugh?"

"I—I just don't want to marry him."

An ugly suspicion festered in Brant's mind. He withdrew his hand, unable to suppress the shattering memories of coming home to find his aunt hiding from his uncle, sobbing, and showing the marks of a beating. Not once had she accused Hugh of striking her. Not once had Brant actually caught his uncle at it. And every time Brant had tried to confront Hugh, Judith had rushed to her husband's defense.

" 'Tis close in here, Rosanne. Take off your cloak."

"Not yet. I—"

He had risen and moved around the table before she could protest; his hand reached down and gently pushed the hood to her shoulders.

"Oh, my God."

His horrified stare encompassed the bruise emerging on her cheek, the deep purplish tinge around her partially closed eyelid, the split lower lip.

"Did Hugh do this to you?" He sounded as if the words

were strangling his vocal chords. He clutched her by the shoulders and hauled her from the chair so that she could not avoid his scrutiny. "Answer me, Rosanne!"

"He— I—I found him in his room . . ."

Word by word the story stumbled out, Rosanne shaking all the while with pent-up fright, dimly wondering whether she made any sense at all. She wanted to tell Brant that he was hurting her, that his fingers were pressing into the bruises that Hugh had given her little more than an hour before. But that would only fuel his fury against his uncle. And suddenly she was afraid for Brant, afraid that the pinpoints of flame in his eyes portended danger for them both.

"Please, Brant! As it is, he doesn't know where I am, and I don't want to involve you any more deeply in this wretched affair than I have to. What happened to me should not upset your life."

Gradually Brant eased his hold as her plea penetrated the red fog that clouded his mind. She was right. He shouldn't react this way. That was the sensible course, he knew. Still, the thought of Hugh hurting her, of Hugh befouling her with his depravity, consumed him with savage rage. My uncle doesn't deserve her, he thought. His aunt Judith had forbidden Brant to interfere in *her* marriage, forcing him to witness her slow disintegration in helpless anger. He would not allow that to happen again. Damn, but he wouldn't.

"Sit down at the table again, Rosanne. I'll go downstairs to ask Mary for something to bathe your face with."

She trailed him to the door, clenching her hands, her eyes dark with anxiety. "She won't let Hugh know I'm here?"

"He won't find you, Rosanne, if you're sure that's what you want."

"Of course it's what I want!" she cried hotly. "What kind of woman do you think I am?"

He shook his head. "I don't know. Wealth is a powerful intoxicant. Women have sacrificed more to possess it. Hugh lives in a magnificent mansion with over a dozen servants. His rooms are filled with costly furnishings. The entrance lobby is inlaid with black and white marble tiles imported from Italy."

"I don't care! I wouldn't care if the hall was inlaid with diamonds."

He returned fifteen minutes later, carrying a tray that contained a cotton cloth, two fragrantly steaming mugs, and an earthenware bowl of a pungent, pulpy, greenish liquid. He had also brought her writing materials for the letter to Gwennie's brother that weighed so heavily on her conscience.

Rosanne stared in revulsion as he soaked the cloth in the murky substance. "You don't mean to put *that* on me! What is it?"

"An Iroquois remedy: boiled garlic, wintergreen, and witch-hazel leaves."

"It stinks to heaven."

He pulled up a chair beside hers, squeezing out the cloth with a grim smile. "Drink the hot flip first, and maybe you won't mind the stink."

She was glad afterward that he'd made her drink the strong rum and beer beverage, sweetened with sugar and thickened with beaten eggs, for the aromatic infusion stung her skin, and even the gentle pressure he applied brought tears to her eyes.

"I apologize if I am hurting you, Rosanne."

" 'Tis all right." She couldn't help staring at him as he leaned over her, his eyes hooded as if to hide the intensity of his unspoken thoughts. "What are you thinking about, Brant? You look positively ominous."

A slight smile eased his expression. "I was imagining skewering Hugh to the wall with my sword. I was imagining watching him writhe."

Rosanne's thoughts raced in sudden wild confusion. His admission should have repulsed her, but it hadn't. Frightened her, yes, for she had no doubt that he was angry enough to kill Hugh. Yet even stronger than her fear was the bewilderingly fierce longing that blossomed from the core of her being. The spot on her shoulder where his free hand rested radiated rippling warmth that melted her inhibitions. A languid ache spread through her loins. Her lips parted in unconsious invitation.

Brant removed the cloth from her face, the shift in her mood hitting him with the impact of an unexpected physical blow. His eyes explored the depths of hers and summoned her into his soul. He wanted to kiss her again, if only to prove to himself that the first time could not possibly have been as exciting as he remembered it. She wanted it too. He could sense the sudden quickening of her breathing, the subtle surrender in her posture. It took every atom of his will not to succumb. God help me, he thought. This must stop. I am an idiot to have gotten involved with her. The reckless passion she kindled in him could only amount to disaster for them both. He should never have kissed her. If only he could obliterate the sensual remembrance of the silken fullness of her breasts pressed to his chest. If only she wouldn't stare at him with those spellbinding velvet eyes.

As if she felt his inner withdrawal, Rosanne broke their gaze and gingerly touched her fingertips to her face. "I look awful, don't I?"

Brant's throat contracted with an unsettling blend of desire and compassion. "Bruises notwithstanding, you look more beautiful than any woman has a right to do," he said in a rough voice, and looked down at his hands.

"More beautiful than your betrothed?"

He stiffened, sobered by the reminder of Martha. "That's a rude question, and I don't think I should answer it."

An awkward silence lengthened, Brant wishing he could retract the compliment he had given so impulsively. Why had he told her he found her beautiful? *Because it's the truth, you simpleton.* And, he admitted to himself reluctantly, it was also true that in a few tension-fraught hours she had half bewitched him with her fragile sensuality and unspoiled nature. Of course, he wasn't about to reveal that to her—no doubt it was only a temporary infatuation on his part that would wear off in another day or so. After all, he would be with Martha soon, a sensible and beautiful young woman in her own fashion; the woman who had been his first adult sweetheart, to whom he'd offered wedlock and fidelity. He and Martha had outlined their future together in meticulous detail. It was unthinkable that this little minx with her tumbled yellow hair and artless allure could disrupt his plans.

He sighed, perturbed to notice Rosanne watching him with devilish lights dancing in her eyes. "You have a peculiar effect on me, Rosanne. I can't say I like it."

What was he talking about? Rosanne wondered. Had he suffered the same horrible emotional tumult that had swept through her a few moments ago? If so, he'd obviously fought against it and won. For an instant she'd believed he would kiss her again. But it would have been wanton and unladylike to encourage him a second time, even if their current circumstances did not call for the usual rules of conduct.

"How long has it been since you've seen this Martha, anyway?"

Annoyance tempered with amusement flitted across his face. "Almost a year, I guess."

"A year, Brant? That's a long time. Aren't you afraid she'll have changed? What would she think if she knew you had another woman in your room right now?" She nearly asked him what he would do if Martha had fallen in love with another man, but the possibility seemed sadly too farfetched to consider.

"You have an impertinent tongue, Lady Rosanne."

"What would she think if she knew I was going to spend the night here?" she persisted.

A tidal wave of arousal flushed through Brant's body. He shook his head as if to clear it of the tantalizing vision of taking her, right there on the bed behind them. He was embarrassed to look down at his breeches, and he prayed she wouldn't notice either. Damnation! Didn't she know better than to taunt a man with those innocently provocative innuendoes? She had no idea what she was doing to him. Heaven knew he'd been guilty of a few sexual indiscretions over the past year. But this was different.

This involved more than carnal need. He could not seduce Rosanne Mallory and hope to stroll casually away afterward. She was the sort of girl over whom men made great fools of themselves. That she was unaware of her own attractiveness lent her added appeal.

"I think the less I tell Martha about you, the better."

Rosanne suddenly felt ashamed of herself. It wasn't nice of her to goad him when he was putting himself out to help her. She didn't know why it should bother her that he belonged to someone else. After all, she would probably never see him again after their journey together ended.

"I wish I needn't have involved you in this," she said, her manner subdued. "I don't want to cause trouble between you and Martha. I—I simply knew of no one else to ask for help."

Brant threw down the cloth and stood up. The only trouble he could envision at the moment was what would happen if he stayed alone with her much longer. "Go to sleep," he said gruffly. "You can write your letter first thing tomorrow. We're leaving shortly after dawn. Mary's letting me have another room."

She sprang to her feet. "Must you leave me here alone? What if Hugh finds me in the middle of the night?"

"Hell, I can't sleep in here with you, Rosanne." He reached down for his jacket, glanced back at her with a resigned sigh, and then slowly lowered himself back into the chair.

"I'll sit here until you fall asleep. If Hugh hasn't found you by now, I think we can assume you're safe for the night. I'm going to face the wall so that you can undress."

"Thank you." She went to the bed and sat down, kicking off her muddy shoes and raising her skirts to remove her stockings. "Will you remember to lock the door from the outside?"

"Yes."

Oh, God! He gnashed his teeth together and swung his head toward the wall, squeezing his eyes shut to blot out the sidelong glimpse he'd caught of her white, exquisitely shaped legs. Heat rushed to his face, to his groin in throbbing waves. He thrust the horrendous yet perversely pleasing thought of rape from his mind. *Think of something else. Make conversation.*

"How—how the blazes did you find your way here anyway, Rosanne?"

"The prostitute. We stole one of Hugh's horses and rode here. The big brute almost killed us."

Brant grinned. "A roan gelding?"

"Yes."

"That's Rupert, one of my uncle's favorite horses."

"I'm not surprised," Rosanne said ill-humoredly. "Neither of them seems to like women very much."

She slid under the cool, lavender-scented sheets in her chemise and stared at the back of his head, at the gleaming brown hair lying on his tanned neck. She recalled how crisp it had felt beneath her fingers earlier; she recalled the gentle strength of his arms as he'd held her . . . as he'd held himself in check. What a shame that Martha had met him first, she mused, and then she turned onto her stomach with a deep, rueful sigh, admonishing herself for even contemplating the unlikely notion of a match between herself and Brant. How could she forget that he was Hugh's nephew? Hugh. The name alone filled her with disgusted anger. He and Brant were total opposites, she decided. And then, as she closed her eyes, her thoughts subsiding in a wave of tiredness, she remembered Brant telling her she was beautiful.

Brant sat in rigid discomfort, wishing he hadn't heard her petticoats slip to the floor. Was she lying naked under the covers? Would she resist if he got into bed beside her and spent the night worshipping and awakening her delicious young body?

Nine days of her unaffected charm. Nine nights of maddening temptation. And he had only himself to blame. He was the one who had encouraged her to escape from Hugh. If he hadn't interfered, she might have accepted her forthcoming marriage as a cross to be borne, like so many other unhappily wed women before her. But now he'd assumed the responsibility of taking her to New York, and he would have to protect her until he delivered her into her sister's care. He couldn't even entrust her to an experienced guide. Not as long as there was a chance that Hugh would come after her, would force her to return to him. Brant couldn't let that happen.

Chapter 6

Rosanne tugged open the warped casement window and inhaled the perfume of Boston. From the waterfront drifted the pungent smell of codfish and whale curing on the wharves, of tar and seasoned lumber in the shipyards. Mingling unpleasantly with the maritime fragrance was an acrid odor made up of the smell of sewage, vats of boiling soap, breweries, bakeries, and dye pits.

Pearly streaks of dawn tinged the horizon. Ribbons of moisture glinted off the rooftops, steeples, and hundreds of chimneys that crowded the skyline. The cobbled streets below echoed with the clattering of oxen-drawn carts and wagons en route to Boston's three market squares. In half an hour, the town clerk would ring his bell to announce that marketing could begin.

She backed away from the window in restless agitation. Where was Brant? She didn't want to remain in Boston a minute more than necessary. Had he changed his mind? She'd sensed a reluctance in him last night—a reluctance, no doubt, to become embroiled in the miserable mess of her life.

She dropped down onto the bed beside her neatly packed portmanteau. If he failed to appear within ten minutes, she would assume he had rethought his decision to help her.

A knock at the door abruptly ended her worried reverie, and then Brant's voice reached her, deep but subdued, as if he wasn't alone.

She rose and slowly crossed the floor to the door, dark suspicion stealing through her. What if he'd summoned his uncle? What if his kindness last night had been a ploy to placate her until he contacted Hugh?

The key turned in the lock. She opened the door.

Brant stared at her for a moment, taken aback once again by her loveliness, his brow furrowing in displeasure at the bruise she had tried to conceal with rice powder. "Good morning," he managed to say finally, moving into the chamber. "The cook's sending up some cold pie from last night's supper so we won't waste time over breakfast. You may leave your letter on the table. Mary has promised to send it out on the next packet."

She stood back, her relieved gaze veering from his face to the slatternly girl who had squeezed into the room behind him. "Who is this?" she asked suspiciously.

"Her name is Polly Andrews. She's a maidservant just arrived in town seeking work. I hired her to accompany you to New York. She understands you're not obligated to keep her on after that."

Rosanne felt the girl studying her with barely bridled insolence. "I don't need a servant. I'll pay her a day's wages now and she can leave." She hurried to the bed and unstrapped her portmanteau. "What's a fair price?"

"Put the purse away, Rosanne," he said, distinctly annoyed.

"I've plenty of money. I don't expect you to pay my traveling expenses. Besides, I really don't need a servant."

"Put the purse away. She's coming with us."

She turned toward him. "Why?"

"Because—" He glanced back at Polly and motioned her out into the hall. "Go downstairs and remind Mrs. Lawrence we'll need to hire a horse as well as a saddle for the lady's mount."

The girl obeyed, casting a covetous look at Rosanne's portmanteau as she slipped past him.

"Why, Brant?" Rosanne repeated.

He moved to the table, avoiding her gaze. It was a liberal age, and chaperonage in the colonies was not rigidly enforced. A young gentlewoman traveling alone with a guide might raise a few eyebrows, but it was not unheard of. Oh, hell, he thought. Whom was he hoping to deceive? He'd hired the wench on impulse so that she could serve as a barrier between himself and Rosanne, an obstacle to keep temptation at bay. If, for some unanticipated reason, Rosanne did decide to forgive his uncle, Brant could release her to him pure and untouched. If Martha interrogated him about his fidelity, he could look her in the eye with passable conviction, discounting the few necessary but casual encounters he'd engaged in since their separation.

"Because I said so."

"Because you . . . Well, one can hardly argue with such profound reasoning. And I am in no position to argue." She seated herself at the table, drumming her fingers against the edge. "All I want to do is leave Boston before Hugh discovers I'm gone."

"Even if he finds you, you need not return to him. The choice is yours."

Her jaw firmed. "Why do I get the impression you expect me to change my mind? Why would I want to marry a man like him?"

"I told you. Wealth, security, social prominence." He shrugged. "Not everyone marries for love."

"And you?"

"That sounds like old Ned leaving our tray at the door," he said, pointedly evading her question. "I wonder why that damn girl isn't back. And don't throw your money around in front of strangers." He went to the door, glancing back at her as he opened it, his expression softening. "By the way, you've got a black eye, but the swelling has come down considerably. Goddamn my uncle," he added feelingly.

"A black eye?" She lifted her hand to her face. "I didn't have a decent mirror. I shall have to wear my hood up again, or everyone will stare."

"You'll attract more notice covered up like a monk in this heat than with your face bruised. Besides, Hugh won't realize you're gone until we're miles away."

Rosanne prayed fervently that he was right. The cold pigeon pie and ale she took for breakfast congealed along with her fear to form a sodden lump in her stomach as they left the inn. With luck, Hugh wouldn't discover her gone for another hour. And when he did, she doubted he'd think of Brant as her accomplice. Moira might, however— although it seemed unlikely she would talk, especially if, as Rosanne suspected, it had been the dour housekeeper who had enabled her to escape so easily.

The streets were already clogged and bustling with activity, though dawn had just fully broken. Here and there sleepy apprentice boys in leather aprons scrubbed the doorsteps of their masters' shops. Merchants straightened hastily donned periwigs as they rode in one-horse chaises on their way to counting houses along the wharves. Farmers and coachmen argued in narrow lanes over who had the right of way.

To avoid the congestion, they bypassed the main thoroughfares and rode a northwesterly route of small lanes and tiny, dark alleyways. Presently the sounds of the awakening town faded behind them into a dull cacophony: the tinkling of doorbells as shopkeepers opened for business; the hammering of cobblers, joiners, carpenters, and blacksmiths; the musical shouting of slaves in the market squares bargaining off their owners' produce; the livestock in their stake pens providing a raucous chorus.

Rosanne allowed herself to relax only after they reached the sparsely settled town outskirts and had ridden unmolested through the guarded gate. But as they passed the gallows outside, her heartbeat quickened with anxiety. What if Hugh caught up with her and had her arrested for horse theft? Would he dare? Not if he wanted her grandfather's patronage, she decided. Not if he believed she could help him obtain it. Yet last night he'd behaved with such irrational anger that she wasn't sure he could control his own actions. She had no intention of becoming better acquainted with him to satisfy her curiosity.

Other than by boat, the only route out of Boston was over the Roxbury Neck, a narrow stretch of partially paved road surrounded by sandy marshlands that flooded at high tide. Cutthroats and hunters haunted this lonely area. At night travelers losing their way often wandered off into the marshes, never to be seen again.

Rosanne stared up and down the low, desolate track, apprehension creeping back to undermine her newfound complacency. Red-winged blackbirds trilled and foraged for insects in the bordering trees, cattails, and tall marsh grasses. The road was deserted and, except for the occasional traveler, would probably remain so until the market closed at one o'clock when farmers began returning home to neighboring valleys.

"Is it safe to ride this way, Brant?"

"That depends." He looked back at her with a wry smile. "Hugh wouldn't expect you to find your own way here, if that's what's worrying you."

She expelled a sigh. The farther they rode from the town, the easier she seemed to breathe.

Birdsong echoing through the marsh and the rhythmic clopping of hooves had just begun to lull her into a tranquil mood when suddenly she felt something hard jab at the small of her back.

"What the—"

"Don't make a fuss now, mistress," Polly whispered from behind her, her horse's shoulder rubbing the rump of Rosanne's gelding.

Rosanne jerked her head around indignantly, gasping in disbelief as she discovered the girl holding a flintlock hunting pistol. "Why, you sneaky little bitch! What do you think you're doing? Brant, she's got a pistol!"

She twisted around toward him, her mind gratefully registering the fact that he had automatically raised his rifle. Why hadn't he listened to her about the girl? "Brant, *do* something." She stared at him in confusion, wondering why he didn't order Polly to drop her weapon, why he was lowering his rifle. Then she saw his gaze was focused over her shoulder.

Dear Lord, she thought, her breath catching. His expression could mean only one thing: Hugh had found her. Her eyes dark with dread, she forced herself to turn around again in time to see two horsemen emerge from behind a clump of maples. One had a bloated white face half covered by a shaggy golden beard. The other had coarse features and, she noted with alarm, the cropped ears of an ex-felon. Each carried a musket. Were these Hugh's henchmen? Did he have such close connections with the criminal element that he could procure two ruffians overnight to find her?

"I'm not going back with you," she told them, her voice quaking with both fear and determination. "I'll fight and scream every step of the way. You'll never—"

"Shut your mouth!" the coarse-featured man snapped, and she did. His musket raised, he nudged his horse toward Brant. "Drop the rifle." Brant hesitated, his eyes fastened on the gold-bearded man, who had moved next to Rosanne. "Drop it, or Jack'll blow her pretty head off. I'll have your purse too."

Brant let his tall Pennsylvania rifle fall to the ground and carefully removed a heavy pouch of coins from his coat, taut lines of tension forming around his mouth as the second man grinningly lifted his musket barrel level with Rosanne's temple. She looked more furious than afraid, and he prayed she would do exactly as they asked. Polly had dismounted and unstrapped Rosanne's portmanteau, lifting it down and rifling through it on her knees until the pouch spilled out onto her lap.

"Found it," she sang out jubilantly.

Rosanne clenched her fists in impotent fury. Gwennie's savings—the money she needed to pay her way to New York! How dare that slattern paw through her personal belongings and steal what the old woman had taken a lifetime to save! This revolting threesome clearly hadn't been hired by Hugh but the realization did nothing to console her. She knew she couldn't reason with them. Their kind held sentiment in contempt.

Polly stood up, greasy hair escaping her mobcap, and strode over to Rosanne's gelding. "Get off. I've a fancy to ride on a velvet sidesaddle myself."

Rosanne glared down in defiance, conscious of the musket aimed at her head, terrified it would go off the moment she dismounted. Were they really despicable enough to commit murder over a purse of coins? If she galloped off, would they shoot her? She hazarded a look at Jack and shivered at the bloodlust in his eyes. She shifted her attention to Brant, wishing she could read his thoughts behind his stony features. Was he counting on another traveler happening by to rescue them? His expression seemed to be cautioning her, but against what?

"Polly told you to get down!" Suddenly Jack leaned over and shoved her viciously, forcing her to slide off Rupert with her foot still caught painfully in the stirrup. As she worked herself loose and finally got to her feet, she heard Polly cry out a warning.

Rosanne's eyes widened in panic. Brant had jumped off his horse and dragged Jack to the ground, pummeling his bearded face with a series of swift powerful punches. The musket landed three feet behind them. Could she reach it? Would they guess she didn't know how to use it if she did? She started forward and then froze. The other man had clubbed Brant across the back of the head with the butt of his own musket and was hauling him off Jack. For a horrifying moment she thought Brant had been killed, and she couldn't breathe for the suffocating fear that swelled her chest. Then she heard him moan.

Brant straightened up, pain pounding through his skull in sickening waves. Good God! he thought, still dazed, that had to rank as one of the stupidest things he'd ever done in his life. He couldn't believe the strength of his own reaction to the sight of that bloated pig assaulting Rosanne; it had driven every rational thought from his mind. As much as he'd enjoyed smashing that fat face, he doubted that his life was worth the spurt of savage satisfaction he'd felt. He had a knife strapped inside his boot; he would have slit the bastard's gullet if he hadn't feared they would take immediate revenge on Rosanne.

Jack staggered to his feet, blood streaming down his swollen nose onto his beard. "Polly, hand me my musket.

You take care of the girl. The marsh reeds will cover their bodies."

Rosanne's heart lodged in her throat. They coldbloodedly intended to kill them! Polly darted forward. Without considering the consequences, Rosanne swung her foot out and tripped the girl; then she threw herself onto Polly's back and clung like a limpet, tumbling her to the ground. Polly grunted and bucked, trying to dislodge her, but Rosanne held fast until suddenly Jack shouted behind them. She looked up, past Polly's sweating face. Brant had almost reached the rifle.

"Riders coming down the road!" Jack shouted, and scrambled back onto his horse.

His companion wheeled his horse around without a second's hesitation. "Move on, Polly! We got what we wanted!"

Polly finally shook herself free of Rosanne and ran over to the gelding, swearing in frustration as he shied away and refused to let her mount him. "Goddamn this horse!" she cried. "Jack, blast your ass, help me!"

"No time, Poll. Take the tavern nag instead!"

Releasing a stream of vile curses, Polly obeyed. As the three riders thundered away, Rosanne retrieved the musket and thrust it at Brant. "Shoot them! Stop them! You can't let them take our money."

"Dammit! Don't you know better than to handle a loaded firearm as if it were a child's toy? They're well out of range by now." He picked up his rifle and stalked toward the edge of the road where his horse had wandered. His head felt like a boiled pumpkin, and all she could talk about was her damned money. The girl had impudence.

She stared after him, guilt and concern flooding her as she noticed droplets of rich red blood on his queue and jacket collar. He had been hurt far more seriously than she'd realized, and he had received his injuries defending her. Ashamed of her selfish preoccupation with her purse, she hurried after him.

"Brant, let me look at your wound."

Hoofbeats behind them distracted him before he could

respond. He and Rosanne turned at the same time to watch two elderly gentlemen reining in alongside them. One had drawn his sword, noticing the contents of Rosanne's portmanteau strewn across the road.

"Anything wrong here?"

Rosanne opened her mouth to answer, but Brant spoke first. "Just a bad spill. Thanks for your concern."

"This is a nasty road for cutthroats," the man remarked, sheathing his sword. "Glad to hear there's been no trouble."

Her face dropping in dismay, Rosanne stood back as the two men rode on. "Why didn't you tell them what happened?" she demanded, turning to Brant. "They might have helped us. I intend to get my money back and see those three clapped in gaol."

"Is it important enough to return to town and wait to give a report to the constable?"

"Oh. I hadn't considered that." She raised her eyes to his face, her teeth tugging at the inside of her lip. "Perhaps we should return anyway and have a doctor look at your head."

"If there's anything wrong with my head, I can't blame it on a musket blow." He gave her a humorless smile and dragged the reins over his mare's neck to lead her back onto the road. 'Gather up your things."

More badly shaken from the robbery than she had realized, Rosanne felt her temper rising at the edge in his voice, which implied that somehow she was at fault for his injury. "I didn't hire that slatternly little bitch, Brant. You did. And I didn't ask you to charge that bearded ox as though you were some medieval knight either." She swooped down and began snatching up her belongings, cramming them back willy-nilly into the portmanteau. "I don't know what came over you anyway, to take such a stupid risk."

He was massaging the back of his throbbing neck and watching her, his own irritation mounting, though he wasn't sure whether it was directed at her or himself. "Maybe it was because I reckoned you were about to do something even stupider, like ride off and get yourself shot."

She straightened slowly. "Was it that obvious?"

He didn't answer but wrested the portmanteau from her hands and restrapped it to her saddle. "Just consider yourself fortunate to have escaped with your life."

"Fortunate? That was all the money I had, and it wasn't even rightfully mine. How am I supposed to pay for my food and lodgings now?"

"I suppose I'll have to pay for you, won't I?" he said as he came close, positioning himself to help boost her onto Rupert's back.

Rosanne placed her hands on his shoulders, acutely conscious of the powerfully toned muscles tensing beneath her fingertips, muscles that had become hard as steel from swinging an ax and clearing forest into field. Her blood burned with sweet fire as he held her close for an instant, his eyes locking with hers. Was he as keenly aware of her as she was of him? she wondered. Did even this casual contact sear his senses and fill him with bewildering longing? Was it her imagination, or had his hazel eyes kindled in response to the forbidden attraction she felt for him?

Cold reality intruded on her wistful musings as he hoisted her roughly onto the saddle. Her face clouded. "I can't let you pay for me, Brant. Anyway, you've forgotten—your money was stolen too. How will we manage now?"

He stepped back quickly, averting his gaze so that he wouldn't be tortured again by another glimpse of her legs. It was all he could do not to touch that delicately sculpted ankle, not to slide his hand up that gracefully shaped calf. Had she noticed that he'd held her far longer than was necessary? Did she have any idea that she had stirred up a maelstrom of sensations inside him? Trouble, he thought ruefully. The girl spelled trouble all the way up to her bright golden tresses.

"My money wasn't stolen," he said. "I always carry a second purse of counterfeit coins. Jack and Polly may yet be arrested.

"Brant, I—I promise I'll repay you."

"Good."

She stiffened, piqued by his cool nod. "You're sorry you agreed to help me, aren't you?"

"Maybe."

"Well, maybe I'm sorry I asked you!"

Smiling tightly, he finished checking her mount's girth and then backed away from the horse. "I believe that makes us a damned sorry pair, doesn't it?"

Amusement flickered in his eyes at her soft, disconcerted gasp. He swung on his heel to return to his mare, his thoughts in a tangle. He would not let her make him feel guilty. He wouldn't. The situation couldn't possibly be more uncomfortable for her than it was for him, could it? He felt as though he were being dipped in a pool of flames every time he touched her. The odd thing was that he couldn't remember ever suffering like that around Martha. He supposed he should be grateful that his betrothed didn't upset his inner equilibrium. Rosanne always seemed to keep him slightly off balance, unsure of what she would do or say next. Of course, it was pointless to compare them. The two young women were as dissimilar as fire and rain.

As she watched him remount, Rosanne pressed her lips together to subdue an urge to laugh. Counterfeit coins indeed. No wonder he'd taken such an off handed attitude about the robbery. *He* hadn't lost anything. But he might have, she realized, sobering as she felt a stab of conscience. He could make all the biting comments he liked. That didn't alter the fact that he was putting himself to considerable inconvenience to befriend her, or that he'd risked his life to protect her. That one act in itself belied a thousand cynical remarks.

"What the deuce are you waiting for now, Rosanne? Another robbery?"

She stirred, setting her heel to the gelding's side. Bright tatters of sunlight had begun to penetrate the morning haze. At any moment now, Hugh would discover her absence.

Chapter 7

How could she have spent five whole days with Brant and yet know nothing more about him than when they'd left Boston, except that he disliked peas? Was she overly sensitive, or did he sincerely regret agreeing to help her? Sometimes he seemed to stare right past her as if she were invisible, and then, at other times, when he thought she wasn't watching, his gaze practically scorched her skin.

Their first day together they followed the Post Road to Dedham, past hamlets and farmhouses and gentleman's seats, and through a swamp to a village, where they stayed the night in a rambling, century-old inn. In separate rooms.

For Rosanne the next three days passed in a blur of fording rivers and crossing ferries and climbing hills with low-branched trees that scratched her dusty face and barberry bushes that snagged her skirts. At night she tumbled into bed and sank into immediate blissful sleep, her muscles twitching with exhaustion, her mind so weary she could hardly remember exactly why she was running at all.

Brant's behavior throughout their journey both annoyed and puzzled her. Although he hadn't actually shared any private thoughts with her—God, what an understatement!—she suspected his conscience was bothering him, possibly in regard to Martha. But what could he have done to feel guilty about? she mused in exasperation. He could not have gone to greater lengths to avoid physical contact with her if they'd lived on separate continents. In fact, it was downright insulting, the way his jaw clamped shut and his whole body recoiled whenever she asked him to help her mount Rupert.

What had she done wrong? She realized she wasn't exactly as fresh as a spring violet; her waist-length hair would be snarled after five minutes of riding, and her skirts always seemed to be spattered with mud. But he hadn't bathed or shaved either.

Now she stared at him as he slowed his horse before a weatherworn wooden bridge that spanned a swiftly flowing river. The relentless pace he'd kept up since they'd left Boston made her wonder whether he was secretly hoping to lose her along the way, or whether he was so eager to reach New York that he didn't feel the physical strain. It was just dusk, but she had been ready to stop hours ago.

"Brant?"

He looked back at her briefly, guiding his mare sideways along the shore. "Yes?"

"I need a bath."

"You need a—"

"I—we both should bathe."

His eyes widened, flickering at her with sparks of amusement. "Right now?"

"No, of course not." She shifted her weight, her spine throbbing from the unaccustomed hours in the saddle. "Why did we leave the main road? There's not a place to stop in sight."

"Just a precaution."

Fear surged through her, displacing fatigue. A precaution against Hugh. She had almost managed to banish him completely from her thoughts. "Do you think he's following us?"

"I doubt it. Come here, Rosanne. I'm going to guide your horse across the ford."

"What's wrong with the bridge?"

"The postrider said it was unsafe. Probably rotted from floods."

"It looks fine to me. Anyway, this horse makes me nervous whenever he's near water."

He rode up alongside her, stretching over the pommel to seize her hand. The electricity generated by the contact startled them both into silence. Yet neither made to move away. At length, Brant spoke. "Don't expect me to dive in after you if you fall. I agreed to serve as guide, not as nursemaid."

"I won't fall."

She tugged her hand free, her fingers tingling from the pressure he had exerted, and coaxed the gelding onto the creaking walkway. The bridge trembled, and as Rosanne gazed down at the dark, rushing current, she almost turned around. She didn't dare glance back at Brant, but she knew he was watching with disapproval, anticipating her fall. Then, midway across the bridge, the horse stumbled over a loose, warped plank. Rosanne held her breath. Visions of herself plunging downstream into deep, stone-pitted waters crowded her mind. A moment later, to her relief, the horse regained his footing and clumped to the tree-fringed shore.

Beneath a spreading veil of dogwood branches, she lifted her hand to Brant in a smug little wave.

He smiled, slowly spurring his horse onto the bridge. Suddenly he was tired of trying to ignore her, of pretending to disapprove of everything she did or said. She was a delightful traveling companion, energetic and uncomplaining and full of high spirits, even if she provoked him relentlessly. Since when had he become so stolid that he could resist a lovely young girl's challenge?

He proceeded with reckless confidence, at a faster gait than Rosanne had dared, slowing only when the bridge began to shudder under his weight. Sudden unease filled Rosanne as she watched him approach the halfway point.

"Brant, be careful."

He didn't hear her. Her voice was lost in the mare's alarmed whickering as two rotted planks splintered and gave way. Her right foreleg treading air, the horse panicked and surged forward.

"Back up, Gemma," he ordered, struggling to keep his seat.

The mare tried to obey, throwing her weight frantically onto her hind legs. But in her fall, she'd caught her hoof between the dangling planks. In desperation she worked herself free, tearing out two more planks and hurling Brant against the rickety railing in the process. A second later she lunged straight ahead, over the gaping hole in the bridge, to the shore. The horse reached safety. Her rider hadn't.

Rosanne dismounted hurriedly. "Brant, are you all right?"

"No! I've bruised every inch of my a—"

A sudden ominous crack interrupted him as the railing collapsed, followed by a loud splash and a simultaneous explosion of the most graphic curses Rosanne had ever heard. Then nerve-stretching silence. Her heart thumping with alarm, she hitched up her skirts and scrambled down the muddy embankment. Had he knocked his head against the railing? Would he be swept unconscious downstream before she could reach him?

She froze in relief, chiding herself for letting her fears run rampant, as she saw him rising to stand knee-high in the shallow water. Her conscience stung her at the expression of disgusted embarrassment on his face. "I thought it was deeper," she said lamely, trying not to laugh. "Did you hurt yourself?"

He slogged across the gravelly bottom, water sloshing over the folded tops of his boots, one dripping hand outstretched. "Do you still want that bath?"

She danced back gingerly. "Brant, please. You frightened me. It wasn't my fault."

"Perhaps not," he said in crisp irritation as he climbed toward her. "But there is something about you that attracts troub—" He broke off, raising a hand to his forehead in disbelief. "My God, I'm bleeding. At this rate I won't have a brain left in my head before we reach New York."

"Let me see."

"No. Don't touch me. It hurts. I think I might even faint."

"Don't be such a baby. Kneel down while I rinse your

handkerchief in the river to wash the blood away. It looks like a tiny scratch."

"I'd rather you gathered squaw wood for a fire. There's nothing worse than wet buckskins."

"After I tend your head."

He winced and complained under his breath at the slightest pressure she applied, but Rosanne appreciated the opportunity to repay the concern he had shown her the night she escaped from Hugh. The tactile memory of his firm, yet tender, fingers on her cheek still had the power to inundate her senses with unbearable yearning. A yearning she would never satisfy. With a softly drawn sigh, she reminded herself that he belonged to another woman and that she should respect him for his fidelity.

But Rosanne's ministrations had pressed Brant's self-control to an aching limit. Truthfully, he found resisting the temptation to touch her more painful than the cut on his forehead, his body responding to her nearness with alarming excitement. What was it about her that made him suspect he was missing something in his relationship with Martha? Did he desire Rosanne only because she was forbidden to him? In a different situation, would her sweet, easy laughter haunt him like a siren's song? If he felt free to make her his, would the tender torment inside him abate? He doubted it. He doubted there was a man alive who could resist her enchanting allure of spirit, gentleness, and delicate sensuality. It was a damned good thing for them both that their journey was almost over.

Scowling at his own thoughts, he drew away from her abruptly. "That's good enough."

She stared at him with guileless eyes, offended by his unnecessarily brsuque tone. "Why have you come to dislike me so intensely, Brant?"

The accusation was so at odds with the truth that he nearly laughed. "Dislike you?"

"Yes. You make it insultingly clear in your every word and gesture. Perhaps it would be better for us if I hired a real guide at the next town."

He said nothing. Rosanne didn't know herself how she'd

expected him to react, but of all the possibilities, his silence seemed the most disheartening. In it she read that she had guessed correctly, that he wished he had never agreed to bring her with him.

She wasn't quite sure how it happened. One moment she was rising swiftly to her feet to remount the gelding, and the following she found herself entangled in Brant's arms, her lower body pinned to his lap by the firm-muscled leg he'd thrown over her knees.

He kissed her then, without explanation or apology, and her own utter lack of resistance shocked her to the soul. Need for him flamed in every particle of her body, burning her hurt anger into ashes. Even more astonishing was her awareness, for the first time, of the deep desire he harbored for her and had so desperately tried to smother beneath his ill-humored detachment. She felt his desire in the impatience of his large hands cupping her head as it lolled back in languid surrender, in the way his tongue penetrated and sought sweet possession of her mouth. She felt his desire in the trembling of his fingers as he brushed past the barrier of skirts and petticoats to glide in gossamer-light circles along the inside of her thigh, to her softly curved hip, across her belly. And lower.

"So now you know how foolish your question was, Rosanne," he whispered in a voice ragged with finally acknowledged passion and self-disappointment.

The truth flooded her in waves of inner warmth. She gazed up at him, her eyelids half closed under the weight of her lashes as she examined the harsh planes and contours of his face. The fluttering sensations flowing through her had devastated her self-possession. She felt weightless, her mind enshrouded in mist, her bones dissolving into steam. Around them the delicate fragrance of the lady's slipper orchids that flourished on the embankment spiced the air. She noticed that he hadn't shaved again that morning; a sensual urge to stroke his shadowed jaw rose inside her and begged to be fulfilled.

"I had no idea," she breathed. "It never occurred to me that you—"

"That I wanted you? That I shake and flush like a man with ague whenever we touch? That I close my eyes at night, trying to recall Martha's face, only to realize I can't force you from my mind long enough to picture her?"

His admission lifted Rosanne onto a golden cloud, affirming her secret hope for what could develop between them. Until then she hadn't dared confront the extent of her feelings for him. She hadn't dared give herself permission to dream.

Brant pressed his face against her throat, moaning as his lips rubbed the silken spill of her breasts above the bodice he had begun to unlace. His hand curled around her hip and flattened across her belly, the warmth and creamy texture of her skin heating his palm and assailing him with fierce need. Quivering flames raced through his tall frame. She was so sweet and vulnerable, from the small-boned fingers resting trustingly on his shoulder to the temptingly curved mouth parted in expectation of another kiss. It would be so easy to take her, so good to lose himself inside her snug, heated depths.

He bowed his head again, his mouth enveloping hers in a long-drawn kiss that lingered and provoked, that satisfied as it aroused. His hand wandered lower still, seeking her velvet-soft flesh. She squeezed her thighs together in an instinctively protective movement, closing them around his hand but not discouraging his quest.

"I would not hurt you, angel," he whispered. "Are you afraid of me?"

"Oh, no, Brant," she said softly, moving against his hand. "Not of you, but maybe of *this*. I've never been with a man before."

She felt him tense. She felt him slowly draw his hand away to tighten into a fist at his hip. What had she said wrong?

"Damn!" The tersely uttered expletive struck a discordant note in their tranquil twilight surroundings. It was not for him to take her innocence. Why had he hoped he could forget that? "I'm sorry, Rosanne. You arouse feelings in me I never knew I could experience, feelings that would probably be better left unexplored."

The shimmering heat building in Rosanne's belly evaporated. The triumph she had savored minutes before faded as she realized the conflict in his heart had only been momentarily stilled and not resolved. He could not offer her love. Nothing would prevent him from marrying Martha, and that was as it should be. The realization hollowed out the joy that had welled up inside her and left in its place a cold, miserable void.

He watched her face, relieved to discern no evidence of tears. "I can't become involved with you and then put you out of my mind once we reach New York," he said gently. "The attraction between us is like a spark under a haystack. Smother it immediately, and you'll only burn your fingers. Fan it just a little, and it rages out of control." He paused, realizing she had turned to stone in his arms. "You don't understand, do you?"

"No." Hurt, confused, and humiliated by his rejection, she attempted to struggle away from him, but he did not release her.

"Hold still," he ordered softly. "A sweet young woman like you doesn't want to give herself to some tough-skinned farmer like me. What do I have to offer? A few hours of pleasure that we would both regret later. I'll be investing the next twenty years of my future in establishing a wilderness town. Martha is committed to helping me. It's already all planned."

She swung her head to the side, finally succeeding in unmeshing herself from his arms. She was unable to imagine what the next twenty minutes would hold, let alone two long decades. Her father had always manipulated her life, as had her schoolmistresses after him. But no one had prepared her for the wrenching disappointment she felt at this moment. Was it possible to plan one's life to avoid this kind of pain? She stood up, wheeled stiffly, and bent to dip the handkerchief in the river, splashing water over her stinging cheeks.

"I think I will hire a guide after all, Brant." She turned,

emitting a cry as she felt him haul her against his body. "Oh, don't!"

An emotion she was unable to decipher darkened his countenance. "You can't hire a guide. You have no money. And even if you did, I would not entrust your safety to a stranger."

"Why not?"

He let her go, his voice deepening, hesitant. "I suppose I can't help regretting that I won't be the first man in your life, little one. I suppose I can't help wondering what you and I might share if Hugh and Martha didn't exist."

More confused than enlightened by his reluctant confession, she heard him whistle softly for his mount and watched as he crouched in the lengthening shadows to examine the mare's leg. Without being reminded, she began to gather wood for a fire. They didn't speak: they didn't know what to say. The course of their relationship had unexpectedly shifted direction. Neither of them could guess where it would lead next. Neither dared speculate.

Rosanne awoke with a soundless cry, panicking at the feel of the callused hand closing over her mouth, the large male body looming beside the bed. Mindless fear shredded the cobwebs of a pleasant dream. Hugh! He'd finally found—

"Stop wriggling, for God's sake. It's only me."

Her frightened eyes focused. Her furiously pumping heart slowed. Brant. "I'm going to take my hand away. Do not raise your voice. Olivia's warehouse manager is in the room across the hall, and one of her porters is waiting below in the taproom. Hugh must have sent them out to scout for you. We're going to leave before they can recognize you or Rupert."

She nodded, her heart resuming its frantic pounding as he peeled back the calico coverlet. "What were you doing downstairs? I thought you'd gone to bed."

"I had." He smiled ruefully, his teeth gleaming white in his swarthy face. "Sleeplessness seems to be a recent affliction for me. You'll have to dress without a candle."

She was too distressed to care about modesty or to blush with maidenly embarrassment when he tossed her her crumpled petticoats and helped lace her stays. She was glad they had both bathed and eaten earlier, but Lord, she was exhausted. "Are you sure they haven't already seen us?"

"I don't think so. They're not asking questions or putting up placards seeking information about your whereabouts. Hugh is keeping the matter quiet." He draped her cloak around her shoulders. "Let's go. We can catch up on our sleep tomorrow."

They reached the stables without incident and rode through the night, hazarding rock-strewn roads and black, hilly passages. A little after dawn they passed a postrider and halted at a tiny inn tucked away off the main road. Brant paid a shilling for two breakfasts of tough beefsteak, tasteless boiled mutton, Indian bread, and beans washed down with an inferior red wine. They ate in Rosanne's room.

"I don't feel well at all," she said suddenly, rising from the table.

He looked down at her empty plate. "I shouldn't wonder. You stuffed yourself like an animal preparing to winter. Lie down and sleep off your gluttony."

She stretched out across the bed. "I'm too tired to even take off my shoes. Too tired . . ." Her voice trailed off in a yawn.

He finished his wine, watching her with subdued desire. Then slowly he got up and walked to the side of the bed. She was already fast asleep, her long golden hair spilling across her face. Frowning, he knelt and removed her shoes, noticing that the soles were nearly as worn through as was their owner. Unthinkingly he brushed her hair from her face, his fingers lingering on the discoloration that remained above her cheekbone. Anger slammed through him, anger mingled with the hot, stabbing hunger that he was trying so unsuccessfully to quell. He pulled his hand back, his eyes falling to her throat, to the deep indentation between her milky white breasts. He turned his head, turned it so sharply that his neck muscles ached. God, he wanted her. It was insanity . . . and once again he felt an almost wild relief that their journey was almost at its end. Neither he nor Rosanne could resist this tension much longer. And yet it seemed harder for him, harder because he was fighting something within himself, while Rosanne seemed more in touch with her emotions.

"You are trouble, girl," he whispered, and swiftly stood up and left the chamber before he could capitulate to the madness inside him tempting him to stay.

Chapter 8

They rode into the City of New York ten days after leaving Boston. Sapped of energy by the heat, wrapped in separate worlds of secret thought, they spoke infrequently. Earlier, at breakfast, the strain between them had suddenly become too unbearable to ignore, and they had lapsed into forced, trivial chatter, expressing their relief that their destination was at hand. Still, a pale shadow of unacknowledged regret at their imminent separation had already begun to darken that relief.

I should be delighted to be rid of the chit, Brant thought tiredly. What a blessing it would be to sleep peacefully at night instead of lying awake fantasizing about her like a virgin schoolboy. It might seem rude, but he planned on depositing her right on her sister's doorstep before any of Martha's acquaintances had a chance to spot him. He couldn't imagine explaining his involvement with Rosanne to anyone else when he was unable to do so to himself. Actually, he wasn't sure he wanted to examine the feelings she stirred inside him, for every time he attempted it, he sensed chaotic emotions clamoring beyond his control, emotions that would challenge the intended course of his life.

For Rosanne's part, she could not decide which had suffered more over the past two weeks: her self-confidence or her stiff, bruised body. If I had it to do over again, she reflected, I would most assuredly hire a guide. A guide would not have been so cursedly moody—or if he had, she wouldn't have been personally offended by his behavior. A guide would not have awakened this achingly sweet awareness within her. But that would fade away in a week or so, she consoled herself. It had to, didn't it? She could not envision living with so much unexpressed emotion trapped inside her.

She looked up, studying her surroundings with reluctant interest. The streets were generally laid with cobblestone, although some were still of dirt and littered with refuse that provided fodder for the pigs that roamed in droves. In pleasant contrast were the principal thoroughfares, several shaded with elm, lime, shade-giving water beech, and locust trees, the latter clustered with pendulous white blossoms that exuded a delightful fragrance.

The majority of the city's houses were constructed of brick, the older dwellings with tiny dormer windows and gable ends facing the street. Homes several stories high were common; their roofs were covered either with white-pine shingles, so dangerous in a fire, or with red and black tiles, testimony to the Dutch influence, when New York had been Nieuw Amsterdam.

Although it was still early, the thriving seaport city pulsed with life beneath is deceptively pious skyline of numerous church spires. It was a Friday, the day designated by ordinance for any muck accumulated in front of residences to be swept up and disposed of. Rosanne noticed far more slaves about than she had in Boston, some riding their masters' horses to be watered, others carrying buckets to fill with tea water at the wells.

Claire and Lowell lived on Pearl Street, and Brant found his way easily to the attractive, two-story brick house with its garden reaching down to the East River. He slowed his horse the moment the residence came into view. He knew Rosanne would invite him inside to meet her relatives. He also knew he was treading dangerous ground by remaining in her company: Martha's father associated with several merchants in this neighborhood.

"So," he said, tilting his head to look at her, a frown

furrowing his brow. "I've delivered you safely, as promised." His gaze swept up her travel-wrinkled gown to her serious face with its appealingly sunburned little nose. "A trifle rumpled, but in one piece." *A most delicious piece, at that,* he thought, and looked away.

A trifle rumpled but minus my heart, she corrected him silently. At any other time she would have smiled and tossed him a teasing remark. But it was impossible to feign a sunny smile while she had to concentrate all her efforts on suppressing a horrible inclination to cry.

"You will come into the house so that Lowell may repay you, won't you?" she asked softly, a note of entreaty slipping unbidden into her voice.

He slapped the reins across his knee, debating whether it would help or harm her case against Hugh if he explained the situation in person. He disliked the thought of bringing her all this way only to have her brother-in-law refuse to offer her refuge. After all, the fellow enjoyed a relationship with his uncle and perhaps would side with Hugh in this mess. And yet what could he, Brant, accomplish by meeting Lowell Winston? This was a matter to be handled with discretion. His presence might eventually turn into an embarrassment for both himself and Rosanne.

"No," he said at length. "I think we'd be wiser to part in private."

She could feel an artificial smile forming on her lips as numbing pain seeped through her. He was going to ride away, out of her life, leaving her in emotional turmoil, and she could do nothing to stop him. She hadn't realized until now how much she had dreaded this day, how deeply she'd come to care for him, to enjoy his company, his wry humor and gentle strength. "You—you won't even let us offer you some refreshment?"

He shook his head. "No."

"But I must repay you."

"I'll accept no money from you, Rosanne," he said quickly. "The journey was . . . well, it was an experience. I don't believe I'll ever forget it. Perhaps I'll come to visit you later at your sister's."

She felt dangerously lightheaded, swinging on a wild pendulum that hovered between joy and anxiety. Was he teasing her, tactfully putting her off? Did he mean he wanted to see her again? "Please, Brant. You must at least meet Claire."

"No. I have business to attend—"

"Martha," she said without thinking, the pendulum knocking her to earth on its downswing. "You're eager to see your betrothed, of course, and it's inconsiderate of me to hold you back. I wasn't thinking—it must be the heat. I'm not used to it, and I am sweltering in these stupid stays. . . ."

He stared at her as she rambled on about how her stupid stays must have obstructed the flow of blood to her brain. He'd come to appreciate her candor, he realized in surprise. He'd come to relish not knowing what would befall them next, to relish the delicious—albeit maddening—friction between them. He would miss the excitement of her presence—he would miss this straightforward little minx—and he would have a hellish time readjusting to the rules of polite behavior, which they had temporarily dispensed with. Life would lose a certain luster without Rosanne. And Martha was the furthest thing from his mind . . .

He looked up abruptly, his thoughts scattering as he heard her whispered good-bye. She was guiding her horse past his, riding out from the concealing shade of a water beech tree and into the sunshine. A sedan chair briefly blocked her progress. He glanced over toward the Winston house, frowning, intending to wait until she was safely inside—

"Rosanne! Turn around—*now!*"

She could scarcely hear him call through her haze of misery. Hesitantly, she glanced back at him. The sedan chair had moved out of her path. What else could they say to each other? Why prolong the pain? Then all at once Brant was riding the narrow distance separating them, his eyes catching hers in a glance that communicated danger. She wheeled her horse around.

"Good girl," he said, grateful that she had the presence of mind to react without questioning him. "Just keep riding beside me to the end of the street. No, don't turn around. One of Olivia's men has just led his horse into your sister's stable. A servant showed him right into the house when he knocked. Hugh must have guessed you'd come here."

"Oh, God," she whispered. "Why would Claire allow them into her home? Something must be wrong, Brant. She would never let them set foot inside her door if she knew what had happened."

"If she knew. Would you expect Hugh to admit why you ran away from him?" He shortened his reins to turn the mare. "There's a water cart on the corner. Stay behind it until I return."

He shared her feeling that something was wrong in her sister's house, but he didn't learn what it was until almost twenty minutes later, when he intercepted a young maidservant leaving the grounds on an errand.

"I am looking for the residence of a Mrs. Walton from England, girl," he called down to her from his horse. "I believe she lives hereabouts."

The girl's brow puckered in thought beneath her frilled calico cap. "Mrs. Walton? No, sir. A Mrs. *Winston* was my mistress, and from England too, but she died in childbirth two months ago." The girl bit her lip, belatedly remembering Mr. Winston's strict orders against divulging news of his wife's death to strangers. But it was really Mrs. Winston's sister he wished to keep the news from, wasn't it? So that the poor young lady's wedding wouldn't be ruined. Not, she thought privately, that one could hide such a tragedy . . . "She's buried in Trinity churchyard. Could she be the same, sir?"

He drew in a sharp breath, forcing himself to display no other reaction. Suddenly he remembered why the name Winston had struck a familiar note in his memory. He had overheard Hugh and Olivia discussing Claire's death, but at the time the young woman's name had meant nothing to him. How would he break this terrible news to Rosanne? What would become of her now?

"Thank you anyway, girl," he said slowly and dropped a coin into her empty basket. "But the woman I seek is an elderly widow. She could not possibly have been your mistress."

Chapter 9

Rosanne numbly accepted the glass of mulled wine that Brant pressed into her hand. She didn't want to believe him. It had to be a mistake. Tears gathered on her lower lashes and flowed in furrows down her face. She had always taken Gwennie and her sister for granted. Now they were both dead, taken away suddenly, and she was truly alone, alone in a hostile world.

She drank the wine without tasting a drop. Brant had brought her to a pleasant tavern on Maiden Lane and had paid for a chamber just so that she might have the privacy to grieve. She had cried for three solid hours, and she realized dimly that she must look like a vision from a nightmare, with her streaming red eyes and uncombed hair.

"I—I won't be able to repay you now, Brant," she said brokenly. "Not until I find work or s-sell my mother's ring." Her voice rose and quavered, plunging to a whisper. "I do not want to go to my brother-in-law. I always thought he sounded like a pompous p-pig."

He scowled, the desperation on her face wrenching his heart. "You won't have to. And you don't owe me anything. I've told you that. Here."

She blew her nose on the handkerchief he handed her. "Lord, you must be fed up with me by now."

"Did I imply that? Look, I know nothing I say will comfort you, Rosanne, but I am sorry about your sister.

Hugh should have told you. I would like to think he withheld the truth for your own good, but unfortunately I don't believe it. In any account, you couldn't have saved her."

"But I—I wish I could have at least seen her one last time," she whispered, fresh tears surging. "Poor, poor Claire." She gave a heartrending sob and buried her face in the crook of her arm, her hair hanging down over the edge of the table. "I hope she didn't suffer, like Gwennie . . ."

"Hush now. I'm sure she had a doctor with her." He watched her for several minutes more, feeling helpless, uncomfortable and unsure of how to console her. His own sister had died when she was only two and he, four, so the memory was blurred, the pain indistinct. It upset him deeply to see Rosanne in this state after she had held herself together without any show of weakness throughout their difficult journey. And emotionally charged situations always distressed him. He had been brought up in the belief that one should keep one's feelings tightly lidded. Then gradually her sobbing abated, and he released a quiet sigh of relief.

"I am so dreadfully tired," she murmured. "My head aches."

"And no wonder. You've been through more in the past ten days than most women could stand. You'll feel better if you sleep. The wine should help."

Suddenly he stood up, lifted her into his arms, and carried her across the room to the large mahogany bedstead. "But I can't sleep," she protested. "It's the middle of the day, and I have to decide where to go—"

"We shall decide that after you rest. Sleep, while I attend to my business about the city."

"But Martha—"

"Martha will wait until evening," he said, spilling her down gently on the bed. "She doesn't even know I've left the frontier. My return should come as a complete surprise."

Rosanne awakened at dusk, feeling completely drained.

Listlessly she rummaged through her portmanteau for a comb, hairpins, and rosemary soap. The uncomplicated ritual of pinning her hair back into a knot with a few natural curls falling around her face soothed her shattered spirits. She could not allow Brant to pity her: the thought was abhorrent. She would pull herself together and find a way to relieve him of the burden she had imposed on him.

She repacked her belongings and sat down at the table to await his return. She would go far away from the city, sell her mother's ring, and travel somewhere Hugh wouldn't think to find her. She could boast of no outstanding skills to any prospective employer. She could sew and cook well enough, but at school she had shown a natural aptitude for mathematics, an aptitude her schoolmistresses had counseled her to keep hidden, as it was deemed a most inappropriate and worthless talent for a young lady to possess.

"I knocked, but I imagine you didn't hear me. Are you feeling better?"

She turned her head, so immersed in her thoughts that she hadn't heard Brant's entry. She could hardly see him behind the towering pile of boxes in his arms. She got up to close the door after him. But he failed to notice her approach and they collided, scattering the parcels.

She knelt hastily to collect the boxes. "I hope I haven't broken—" She halted in midthought as she glimpsed the sheen of a dove gray taffeta gown beneath layers of tissue. He had been buying presents for his betrothed. In her clumsiness, she had spilled Martha's gifts all over the rough pine floor. Hurt and furious at herself because she had no right to feel hurt, she gathered the boxes into a tottering stack. "Nothing appears damaged." She sat back on her heels, her heart leaden with unhappiness. "Martha should be delighted."

He gave her a peculiar smile. "I don't think so." He leaned down to lift the boxes and toss them behind him onto the bed. "They're for you."

She glanced up at him in disbelief, all at once noticing that he had visited a barber and that his comfortable traveling clothes had been replaced by a black brocade buckram-lined coat that fell to his knees, a silver-figured silk waistcoat, and close-fitting black brocade breeches. The silver buckles on his new shoes shone in the fading twilight. He had a black hat too, three-cornered and trimmed with silver braid. Rosanne decided that she liked him far better in his old buckskins, with his lean copper face unshaven. He looked suddenly like a stranger to her, a stranger who belonged to another woman.

"I don't believe you." She got up awkwardly. "You just decided to give these to me because you're sorry about my sister."

"When I originally ordered the clothes, they *were* meant for Martha—that's true." He threw his hat down on the bed beside the boxes. "But I changed my mind."

"Because you feel sorry for me."

"I don't know why." He lifted a chemise from one of the boxes, caressing its smooth texture with his thumb, picturing it against Rosanne's fine-grained skin, soft white silk upon even paler, even softer flesh. "I've ordered an early supper for us to share before I leave. Try the clothes on while we wait for our food."

She could not find it in herself to deny him; his kindness pierced her fragile defenses. Behind the dressing screen, stripping off her soiled clothes, she tried to decide exactly when she had surrendered her pride. And for what. For love, a resigned voice answered softly inside her. Yes, she loved Brant. The thought she might never see him again stabbed at her heart like a fiery thorn. She would have chanced shame and scandal to remain with him. She would have defied Hugh, her father, and even Governor Clinton to stay at his side. If he had wanted her. But of course he didn't. He'd made that clear.

She had no mirror, but she could tell that the heavily embroidered skirts were too long, the pointed bodice a little tight. A white lace fichu saved the deeply scalloped neckline from indecency. She hadn't found any stockings among the boxes, so she stepped out barelegged for Brant's inspection.

"What do you think?"

His eyes swept over her, flaming with the fierce desire his mind struggled to deny. His heart thudded painfully against the broad confines of his chest. Tantalizing thoughts and possibilities ran through his brain. He could postpone his marriage. He could make Rosanne his mistress. Set her up in Albany and visit her twice a month. On, dear Christ, what was happening to him? How could he offer one woman a lifetime of marriage while scheming to seduce another?

"I'll put on my shoes and stockings." She turned away, unnerved by his silence, uncertain what it meant.

"There's a new pair of stockings on the bed," he said hoarsely. "And a riding habit. I did not have time for shoes. I'm sorry. I know you need them."

She sat down at the table, her heart missing a beat as he knelt at her side with a small, rectangular box. "Why are you doing this?" she whispered.

He shook his head, his eyes searching her face as if it might hold the answer. "I'm not sure. I want—I want to put the stockings on you, Rosanne," he finished, his voice strangely harsh. "I want to touch you. Please."

Scarlet heat blossomed inside her belly and spread through her insides in a rush of pleasurable sensation as she considered his request. It was the last thing either of them had expected him to say. But this she had to deny him, deny them both. He would hate her if she came between him and Martha. She could not bear that. "Is that wise, Brant? Is it right?"

"Wise, no. Right . . . ? I honestly cannot say." He glanced down at the stockings he had unwrapped. "All right. Put the damned things on quickly. I find my self-control is dangerously frayed."

A half hour later they sat down again together at that same table to a meal of plump boiled shrimp, hot rabbit pie, salad, and a flagon of dry white wine. Neither of them ate much, though they were both hungry. A frail thread of temptation hung between them, a dangling, tenuous fiber that neither dared touch.

"I'll probably have supper again tonight with Martha

anyway," Brant said moodily. "Her mother and her rich Dutch cooking . . ." He pushed his plate away. "Tomorrow we'll decide what to do about you. I suppose you would prefer to return to your relatives in England. I'll send you back if—"

"I have no one there. No one."

He nodded, fleetingly recalling her hostility toward her father and grandfather. "Then perhaps I shall try to enlist Martha's help. Women are better at figuring out these problems than men are. You can't stay here in the city."

"No." She toyed with a shrimp on her plate and shoved it to one side, staring at it until its tiny veins blurred before her eyes. I'd die before I would accept Martha's help, she thought. I shall be gone the moment he tells me he is bringing her to meet me. I couldn't bear to see them together. It would be too much . . . too cruel.

Brant stood up, and she lifted her gaze unwillingly to watch him slip a small jeweler's box into his pocket. Her heart sank heavily in her breast, aching with anticipated loss. The box contained Martha's ring; she knew because she'd peeked at it when he had answered the door.

"Well, wish me luck, Rosanne."

She got up and walked toward the bed, fighting back the impulse to beg him to stay. Did he have any notion that her heart would break when he walked out that door? Undoubtedly not. He was too full of his plans to notice all the telltale signs of her silly lovesickness. She supposed she ought to be thankful she hadn't made a fool of herself by admitting how she felt toward him.

"You've forgotten your hat, Brant."

"Oh, yes." He took it from her and hovered at the door, not knowing how to leave—not, in fact, wanting to.

"Your damn stock isn't folded properly again," she said, lifting her hands to his throat and feeling her own tighten with emotion. "I'll fix it for you."

He inhaled sharply, bracing himself for the devastating gentleness of her touch, for the sensual urges it inevitably stimulated. From between half-closed eyelids he studied her face, compassion and regret mingling inside him. For the first time in his life, he wished he were a man given to reckless impulse. He could not help wondering what would have happened had he followed his feelings for her. Ridiculous, he chided himself. And even more ridiculous was that he felt, suddenly, a horrible reluctance to proceed with his marriage to Martha, a painful tugging between what his heart desired and what his mind coldly decreed he should have. *Sheer folly.* It was not even his decision to make! This wayward little enchantress would set her life straight and have no further use for him. His infatuation for her would quietly die. He and Martha would make a comfortable, if not love-filled, life for themselves . . .

"There's some money on the table in case you want something else to eat while I'm gone," he said, exhaling as she lowered her hands. "I don't know what time I'll be back. The van Hoorn house is on Stone Street—"

"Good luck, Brant," she interjected softly. "Don't spoil your evening with Martha by worrying about me."

Brant stood alone in the long, candlelit hallway, staring morosely at the wainscotted walls that boasted a beaten-gold mirror and gilt-framed portraits, several of past van Hoorns, one a Rembrandt. Wrought silver candlesticks graced delicately carved tables. Silk-upholstered Windsor chairs hugged corner recesses. The house and its furnishings exuded an atmosphere of Old World wealth and unpretentious elegance.

The van Hoorns were entertaining. From the small ballroom came the rustle of lace and lutestring as the musicians broke into a spirited gavotte. Cornelius van Hoorn would be very displeased if Brant appeared after a year's absence only to announce that he could not marry his beloved daughter after all. . . .

Brant eyed the front door with ferocious yearning. He looked forward to facing Martha with about as much enthusiasm as he'd felt that afternoon years ago when his friend and partner, Patrick, had yanked out his hindmost molars. How should he go about this? He had no desire to hurt Martha. He did not want to lose his friendship with her brother Hans or to give up the financial backing of the van Hoorn family. He told himself that his aversion to going through with the wedding was perfectly normal, a simple case of a bachelor balking at the impending loss of his freedom. He told himself that he needed a wife; a lonely man on the frontier craved female companionship. He told himself that a bewitching waif named Rosanne Mallory had nothing, nothing whatsoever to do with his unwillingness to wed his betrothed. But he wasn't sure. Perhaps, if he had another month to reconsider, he would come to his senses and realize— Realize what? Would Martha understand? Would she forgive him for calling off their engagement?

And as it happened, he never had the chance to test her temper. He never had, in fact, the chance or the need even to voice his own recent and violent opposition to marrying her, for he found he had arrived, unexpected and unannounced, at the van Hoorn home just in time to interrupt Martha's engagement party to Wouter Jansen, a wealthy, middle-aged ship builder. Brant's appearance caused an uncomfortable but temporary hiatus in the festivities until Martha spirited him away to the parlor to explain the situation. In all fairness, Brant could not blame her. After all, he had never made much of an effort to keep their relationship alive. He heard out her awkward apology with stoic acceptance, resenting only the way she had broken their engagement. Not a letter. Not a word of warning. But then perhaps he had secretly hoped for this all along.

If Martha had harbored any doubts about ending their prolonged engagement, Brant's calm resignation dispersed them. And in the end, there was really nothing left for him to do but drink a toast to the happiness of the betrothed couple and then quietly make his way back to the woman who had bedeviled his thoughts and his life for the past ten days.

Chapter 10

An hour dragged by with unbearable slowness. Rosanne brooded by the unlit hearth, awash in self-pity, feeling like Perrault's Cinderella left alone on the night of the ball. Was Brant holding Martha in his arms at this very moment? Was he whispering tender love words in her ear, telling her how much he had missed her? He'll resent me for having to return to the tavern afterward, she thought dismally. But then perhaps he wouldn't return at all. Perhaps he would spend the night with Martha . . .

And it was a night made for love. Glittering stars adorned the sky like a far-flung necklace of diamonds, and the evening air wafting in through the opened window enveloped her in its sultry summer warmth. It was a night made for lovers to stroll down leafy lanes and to share kisses in the starlight.

She sighed and walked to the window, picking up Brant's old jacket and hugging it to her, inhaling the faint, musky fragrance of his skin and the stronger aroma of the awful cigars he smoked which clung to it. She stared outside. Attached to the back of the two-story stone building was a bowling green and a large, lantern-illuminated garden set out with tables and benches. The meeting of a weekly social club had just broken up in the garden, and its affluent young members were spilling outside to plot their evening's entertainment.

She squeezed her eyes shut to force back a fresh deluge

of tears, and when she opened them again, she saw a table of five roguish young men looking up at her and raising their tankards to her in a toast.

"What's your name, sweeting? Mine is Leonard!"

"Cinderella," she answered, smiling, in spite of herself, at their uninhibited exuberance.

"C'mon belowstairs and talk to us, darling!" another shouted, his four rakish companions nodding and clapping in agreement.

She shook her head and drew back from the window, sighing tearfully. She envied them their spirits, even if they had been loosened by strong rum punch. If she hadn't had a deep abhorrence for alcohol taken to excess, she might have gotten stinking drunk herself.

"I believe the maiden's frightened of us, lads," a third youth cried, and at that a chorus of slurred male voices began pleading with her to reappear.

Eventually she did, half reclining across the windowsill with a glass of wine in her hand, listening amusedly as they introduced themselves and tried to entice her into joining them for a late supper. Their attention was flattering and frivolous, but she felt relieved when they finally abandoned their attempts to lure her downstairs and turned their questionable charms on the untidy serving wench who arrived to take their orders.

The serving wench. Rosanne leaned farther out the window as the girl sashayed away from the table with her striped muslin petticoats flouncing. She couldn't see the wench's face clearly, but she recognized her haughty demeanor. It was Polly, the vile slattern who had robbed her on the Neck.

Rosanne bolted from the room on stockinged feet and flew down the dark wooden stairs. Eyes widened as she darted through the taproom, but she moved too fast for anyone to detain her. Bursting into the garden, she caught sight of the girl returning from the kitchens with two earthenware platters of fried scallops and pickled mussels.

"Someone stop her!" Rosanne shouted to her table of

startled admirers. "She's a thief—oh, I'll wager she bought those petticoats with *my* money!"

The young rake who had introduced himself as Leonard rose to her assistance. Unsheathing his sword, he scrambled over the table, upsetting his companions' tankards, and jumped behind the bewildered serving girl. "Take off your petticoats, wench, and surrender them to their rightful owner!"

The girl gave a terrified shriek, dropped both seafood platters, and whirled to flee. Leonard and his four companions chased after her with jeering taunts, knocking over tables, chairs, and patrons in their frenzy. The girl had little chance of escaping, and within two minutes Leonard had cornered her in the kitchen garden.

"Got her!" He glanced back across the garden at Rosanne, waving her toward him. "What should we do with her?"

Rosanne squeezed through the small crowd that had converged. "Nothing. Ask her where my—Oh, *no!* It can't be . . ."

The girl was not Polly. She was the innkeeper's daughter, the favorite child of the florid-faced man who came charging out of the taproom with a musket and his two husky sons.

" 'Tis all that woman's f-fault, Papa! She told those m-men to chase me. She accused me of stealing her p-petticoats—"

"She did what?" roared the innkeeper, turning on Rosanne. "Explain yourself, mistress."

She melted back in mortification. "She—she looked like the girl who stole my purse. Truly. I am sorry if I frightened her, but thank God there was no damage done."

"Wasn't there now?" the innkeeper's wife demanded, joining them in the kitchen garden after a hasty inspection of the premises. "And who's to pay for the damage caused? Who's to pay for the broken bottles of wine, the wasted food, the cracked earthenware, and Lord knows what else?"

"I didn't cause all that damage," Rosanne said indignantly. "These gentlemen here—" She turned, but they had vanished, vanished in the confusion and left her to accept the blame.

The money Brant had left her was not nearly enough to cover the alleged damages, and within half an hour she found herself locked out of their chamber and shown to the street, Rupert being held as collateral until Brant returned to pay the staggering bill. She had no choice but to wait for him. She hadn't the money to hire a sedan chair, and where could she go? Certainly not to the van Hoorn house, she thought, giggling nervously at the image of presenting herself at Martha's door. She looked around in dejection. This was hardly the way she wanted to end her relationship with Brant, to repay his kindness. But then, if it were up to her, their relationship wouldn't end at all.

A bright yellow carriage suddenly pulled up alongside her, the rakehell named Leonard hanging out the door. "Are you in need of assistance, Cinderella? Some lively company, perhaps? We've a rousing evening planned—wrenching off door knockers and breaking streetlamps. Would you care to come along for the ride?"

"Oh, go to the devil, you overgrown juvenile!" she said angrily. "I've had all the assistance from you I can afford."

The carriage clattered away. Then, moments later, a chorus of loud clinking thuds drew her attention farther down the street. She blinked, disbelieving. Leonard and his cohorts were taking turns hurling stones at a streetlamp in a contest to see who could break it first. The metallic pinging of coins pitched against the second-story windows of a darkened house followed. Then the lamp shattered to a rousing cheer. Two windows cracked. Applause broke out.

Mohocks, she thought disgustedly. Gangs of bored young gentlemen who amused themselves by raising mayhem in the streets. Every law-abiding Londoner feared them, but she hadn't realized they also existed in the colonies. She edged back into the shadows. It would be just her luck if the watch arrived and she got herself arrested along with these drunken vandals. It would be just her luck if Brant had to abandon his betrothed to bail her out of gaol.

Chapter 11

Brant seemed only mildly surprised to find Rosanne waiting for him on the corner of the street. Or was he drunk? she wondered disdainfully, catching a whiff of alcoholic fumes as he leaned down from Gemma to talk to her.

"I suppose there is a good reason why you are prowling about like a streetwalker and not waiting for me in your chamber?" he asked in an indolent voice.

"It was not my fault," she began, her nose crinkling in disapproval at the scent of rum that laced his breath. "I didn't realize—"

He held out a hand to interrupt her. "Don't tell me. Let it be a surprise. This seems to be my night for them."

She peered up at him, an unbearably delicious suspicion slipping into her mind. "How did your reunion go with Mistress van Hoorn?"

"Oh, well enough. I arrived in the middle of her engagement party, had a few drinks with her newly betrothed, and nibbled some sugar cookies on which their initials had been imprinted. All in all, it was a jovial affair—very civilized, actually."

"Oh, Brant," she said softly. "How dreadful . . ." *How wonderful!* "I am sorry—well, I truly am."

"Hmm. Come closer." She did, and for a moment he seemed to be regarding her as though she were about as pleasant as a pebble in his shoe. "You weren't thrown out of the inn, by any chance, were you, Rosanne?" At her tiny embarrassed nod, he sighed and reached down to lift her up onto the horse.

"Am I going to be arrested if we try to return, Rosanne?"

"No . . . but it might cost you a little more than the price of the chamber alone."

His arm closed around her waist as the mare moved forward, her hooves clopping on the cobbles. "What am I going to do with you, little nuisance?" he asked with another sigh.

Little nuisance, she thought, stung by the unflattering term. Was that all he considered her? Was he going to take out his private misery over losing Martha on her now?

"I am neither your responsibility nor your possession," she said with injured hauteur. "I'm grateful for your help so far, but believe me, I do not enjoy having to depend on you any more than you do. In fact, if you'd set me back down on the ground, I shall—"

"You will what? It's almost midnight. You have no friends, no money. Where would you go?"

"To my brother-in-law, if I must."

"That pompous pig? He'll send you right back to Hugh."

"Perhaps not." She pushed down against his arm, anger and resentment flaring like fireworks inside her. It was not fair of him to take out his disappointment on her, to try to frighten and intimidate her, even if she knew he was right and didn't want to admit it. "Set me down, Brant!"

His arm tightened around her midriff, drawing her deeper into the immovable barricade of his chest. His breath ruffled her hair as he spoke. "Convince me that you've changed your mind about Hugh, and I'll take you straight to his house, where you'll be cared for until he can come for you."

"I'm under no obligation to convince you of anything," she said breathlessly, twisting to break his hold. "You brought me safely to New York, but you needn't put yourself to any more bother. Can we not leave it at that?"

She had succeeded in wriggling around so that although she was not an inch closer to escape, she *was* in a position that any passerby would assume was a passionate embrace. Brant looked down into her angry, uptilted face, aware only of the sweet turmoil she never failed to arouse inside him. "No. We cannot leave it at that."

"Why the devil not?" she cried. "You can't deny I'm a burden to you—a nuisance. Why would you not be delighted to be relieved of me?"

"Because I—I—" He shook his head, floundering for the logical explanation that eluded him. "Must we argue about this in the middle of the street? And stop squirming, would you. I'd hate to end the evening landing in gaol for abduction. You are staying with me, and that's all there is to it."

It wasn't the gruffness in his voice but rather the emotional entreaty beneath it that pierced her defensive shield of hurt indignation. Did he want her with him only to ease the pain of Martha's rejection, or was there more? Was it possible that this day would finish sweetly after all?

They had almost reached the inn when unexpectedly a bright yellow carriage rounded the corner and rattled toward them at a breakneck pace. Cursing, Brant urged his mare to the side of the street. Rosanne leaned into him, willing herself invisible. The carriage slowed. *Please, Leonard, you idiot, don't spoil this for me . . .*

"If it isn't Cinderella again!" a drunkenly familiar voice shouted from the window. "Did you find your prinsh?"

The carriage lurched forward and sped away, leaving Brant staring after it in bemusement. "What the hell was that all about?" he demanded, angling his head to look down at Rosanne.

"I've no idea," she lied unconvincingly. "You know how drunkards rave."

His mouth slanted into a rueful smile. He did not believe her for a moment, but he decided that for the sake of his own peace of mind he'd be wiser to accept her bald lie. Peace of mind—as if that were possible with her sweet female form clasped so tightly in his arms, her presence teasing him deliciously and chasing his thoughts around in disturbingly erotic circles. Dear God, how could he even entertain such notions when he'd just lost the woman he intended to marry? Shouldn't he force himself to pass at least one night of brooding regret?

He appeased the innkeeper with a promise to pay for the damages in the morning. Inside the chamber he lit three tallow candles and opened a bottle of wine while Rosanne stepped out her slippers and pulled the pins from her hair. He debated asking her to join him in a drink, but he knew damn well what that might lead to, and it seemed wrong to take advantage of her at a time when her emotions were vulnerable. He could stay with her another ten minutes at most. He needed to think. Could he still depend on Martha's brother to invest in his sawmill? He would have to meet with Hans tomorrow. And it was necessary to decide where he could take Rosanne next to keep her out of his uncle's reach. God, was nothing in his life destined to run smoothly?

A gentle voice intruded on his thoughts, and he looked up in surprise to discover Rosanne standing before him. "I think she was a fool, Brant, if my opinion matters." Her gaze dropped to the bottle balanced loosely between his knees. "And I think you'll feel far worse in the morning if you don't stop drinking."

He smiled to himself. She thought he was drinking to ease the hurt of losing Martha. Maybe he should tell her he had planned to break the betrothal himself. Actually, it had worked out better this way. The van Hoorn family still liked him. He and Hans would remain friends. Would Rosanne understand why he had suddenly realized he couldn't wed Martha? Might she possess some special insight to enlighten him?

"You should take a syllabub of cream and crushed snail shells before you go to bed," she continued. " 'Twill prevent a pounding head in the morning."

He chuckled quietly. "How would you know? I find it hard to believe you've ever once sought comfort in a bottle. Anyway, I'm celebrating."

"My father often 'celebrated' too, always to the misery of those around him." She leaned over him to take the bottle and place it on the table. Her unbound hair brushed his face, and she drew back as she noticed him stiffen in reaction. "I suppose there are better ways to seek comfort. Or to celebrate," she finished softly.

He frowned, forcing his eyes to the door. "I should go. We'll decide what to do with you in the morning."

"You—you could take me with you to your home," she blurted out. She stepped back slowly, aghast at her own audacity. "Well, why not? I'd as soon work for you as for a stranger."

He smiled. What a preposterous thought. "It's out of the question."

"I don't see why. I have to work for someone. At least you wouldn't beat me or force me to—to—"

"Damn, Rosanne!" he exclaimed quietly, gripping the edge of the table. "Have you ever looked a rattlesnake in the eye? Have you ever awakened in the dead of night to hear a panther scream? Have you any idea what it is to live in constant fear of an Indian attack?"

"No—no to all those things! But if Martha was willing to take the risk, why do you think I would not?"

His face hardened. "Martha grew up on a farm with her aunt in Albany. She hasn't led a sheltered life. And, anyway, as it turned out, she was not willing to take the risk." He leaned forward, preparing to rise. "It's late. I've asked for another room for the night."

"Why?"

"Why? Rosanne, please—"

"I—I want you to stay with me, Brant. I don't want to be alone tonight. I don't want to start thinking about Claire again."

Heat tinged Rosanne's cheeks as he raised his head to stare at her. Although she meant every word she had said, she was only vaguely aware of the invitation implicit in her plea. He might simply rebuff her, unwilling to become entangled with her, she realized, her heart thudding hurtfully against her breast.

"We're both vulnerable right now, Rosanne," he said in a low, strained voice. "I do not think you fully realize what might happen if I stayed alone with you tonight."

"I think I do." She drew an uneven breath, twisting her fingers together behind her back. "Perhaps it's shameful to admit that to a man. But I can't help it. It's the truth. Does that mean there's something wrong with me?"

"No. Oh, God, no—"

He reached out suddenly and pulled her down onto his lap, his answer a tortured whisper that sent sweet shivers of longing through her. "You are a warm and passionate woman, angel. There isn't a damned thing wrong with you."

He braced one hand across her hip to support her weight. The other he slipped up along her back to the nape of her neck, exerting gentle pressure to bring her face to his. She closed her eyes, yielding with a ragged whimper that hovered between relief and trepidation. His mouth brushed across the lushness of hers, persuading, instructing, arousing until she parted her lips in eager response and welcomed the exploration of his tongue. Lightheaded, she clasped his shoulders and swayed against the granite support of his chest, her hair swinging down to cover their faces like a curtain.

White-hot lightning flashed through Brant's body, searing reason, scorching senses. Tomorrow, he knew, he would regret this. But tomorrow was a lifetime away. The promise of pleasure the evening offered tempted him too strongly to haggle over its price.

His mouth broke contact with hers, his warm, wine-scented breath blending with her softly uttered murmur of protest that he had ended the kiss. He rested his cheek against her temple, inhaling the sweet herbal fragrance of rosemary soap that lingered on her skin as he waited for the roaring in his ears to subside. Carefully he stood up, lifting her with ease, one arm behind her back, the other hooked under her knees. He hoped he would be able to reach the bed without falling to the floor to ravish her. He had denied his desire for her for so long it was suddenly unleashing itself in torrents of scalding need.

Rosanne laid her head against his chest and heard the

chaotic tempo of his heartbeat playing in concert with the wild rhythm of her own. She had hoped for this, had willed this moment into existence. Still, she trembled at its arrival, her senses rising in a whirlwind of heady anticipation. Gazing up at the man who held her, she felt her heart tighten at the realization that soon she would belong to him.

He kissed her again as they reached the featherbed, collapsing beside her as he lowered her onto the swanskin coverlet. Each time their lips met, each time his tongue swirled around hers in playfully sensual circles, Rosanne felt herself sinking deeper into a quicksand of pleasurable acquiescence, her whole being submerged in torpid warmth. He unlaced her corset, his mouth bent into a faint anticipatory smile, and slowly pulled the drawstring of her chemise. He untied the sleeves of her gown, muttering, "Why didn't I have the foresight to buy you a sacque instead?" as his deft fingers worked and finally pushed the loosened cloth from her shoulders so that her rounded ivory breasts were bared to his gaze. A groan of sublime appreciation for her loveliness broke low in his throat, and the hot, lustful look in his eyes as they lifted back to her face brought a blush of belated modesty to her cheeks. It was as if he had the uncanny power to sear through her skin to her soul—yes, the wildest, darkest, deepest part of herself was surging up through all her inhibitions to welcome, to invite him. It was as if she had been fragmented until they had met. And now they would be as one again, as perhaps in another time and place they had begun.

"You're shaking, Rosanne," he said hoarsely, his breath a sweetly scented caress upon her cheek. "Are you afraid of me?"

"A l-little. Oh, yes . . ."

"There is no need, angel," he said soothingly. "No need to fear me at all."

Would it ease her mind, he wondered, if he were to admit he was more than a little frightened himself of her effect on him, both physically and emotionally? Every nerve ending in his body trembled in heightened expectation of what was to come. He prayed for the willpower and patience to keep the promise he had made her.

"Relax, Rosanne. It'll be so good. I'll make it good for you . . ." His mouth dropped to hers, caught her lips in a hard, hungry kiss. "For us," he murmured roughly.

He branded her face, her throat, her collarbone, with quick burning kisses, and she fisted her hands and curved her back in passionate enjoyment as his mouth descended and her nipples peaked and tautened beneath his flickering tongue. She was quivering uncontrollably by the time he drew back on his knees to remove her petticoats, her garters, her stockings, containing his passion so that he could pause to kiss the tension from her sweetly molded mouth and to admire the lovely body that he ached to possess. And when finally he flung the last confining garment to the floor, he had become so highly aroused that for a moment he was forced to stop himself, deriving the most unexpectedly intense pleasure from simply holding her and trying to accept the fact that she was actually giving herself to *him*. Oh, Lord, how her nakedness excited him. She was exquisitely formed, her legs long and curvaceous, her hips sensuously rounded, her breasts ripe and heavy. He longed to sink into the hidden velvet of her, but she was no whore to be ravaged in mindless lust and cast away afterward. The precious offering of her innocence could not be accepted lightly. Her initiation could not be rushed. Gently he released her and leaned back to strip off his own clothing. He couldn't wait to feel her flesh against his, to press his body to the cream-satin softness of her curves, to press himself inside her.

Rosanne's eyes widened as she watched him, her pulse throbbing in wonderful torment. Aside from her unsavory experience with Hugh, she had never seen a naked man before, and Brant was magnificent—sleek, well-toned, long, his sun-burnished torso and chest corded with muscle, ridged with suppressed strength. Her gaze lowered slowly to the shadowed junction between his thighs, to the thick, jutting staff, and a small inaudible gasp escaped her. Would he hurt her? she wondered, glancing away in a sudden surge of panic. Were those boarding-school whispers true?

"I'll try not to cause you pain, little one."

She looked up into his face, embarrassed that her anxiety was that transparent, and the desire emblazoned on his dark features swiftly swept that fear aside and ignited wanton wildfire in her blood. Intuitively she understood that if he brought her great pain, he would also give her an equal amount of pleasure. She gazed steadily into his eyes, her expression open and trusting.

He smiled tenderly and brushed the curve of her cheek with his knuckles, then stretched out alongside her for a timeless moment, his fingers stroking the surface of her belly, the outline of her ribcage, leaving behind a trail of quivering warmth. Rosanne sighed and curled up against him, feeling the crisp black matting of his chest tickle the sensitive tips of her breasts. Gradually his hand dipped between her modestly clenched thighs, his fingers sliding between the damp, silken folds and probing carefully inside her, preparing his entry. Heat rushed into her loins, building, building, building, threatening to consume her in its uncontrollable conflagration. What did it matter that she had known him less than a fortnight? Her heart had acknowledged him as her destiny from that very first day, and she would give herself to him without shame. God forgive her, she felt no shame.

"Love," he whispered, his voice rough edged with restraint. "Put your hands on my shoulders."

With gentle force he pressed her back down beside him, one knee clefting her thighs, his other leg locking possessively around her hips so that she lay cradled against him. He arranged his arms around her waist and kissed her, murmuring reassuringly against her lips, his mouth absorbing her little sighs of contentment. The thought streaked through his mind that but for a quirk of fate, another woman would be lying in his bed tonight. But suddenly there was no other woman in his past, perhaps even in his future, except Rosanne. Yet he was fiercely glad to be the first man who would know her. This moment had been inevitable from the start. And, he remembered vaguely, he had suspected from the start that it would lead to danger. But, God help him, he didn't care.

Mesmerized by his eyes, by the embers of passion smoldering in their depths, Rosanne reached up and tugged the ribbon from his queue so that his hair tumbled around his bronze neck in soft, dark waves. Aflame with need, she stared up at him and smiled, her heart whispering, *I love you, Brant. I love you so.* He rose above her then, towering, his shoulders so broad they blocked the candlelight so that for an instant, as he poised unmoving, they were both plunged into warm and pagan shadows.

There was a sudden shock of burning pain. Another kiss, and then they melted together in a fusion of liquid flame. Caught in a wildly racing current of heated sensations, Rosanne clung to his shoulders and surrendered herself to his mastery, allowing him to sweep them both toward the shores of a faraway rapture. Her blood surged in molten arousal. She arched into him, moaning, her head thrashing on the pillow. Her heart pounded, harder and harder, until at last, when she thought she might shatter from the exquisite pressure of the pleasure mounting inside her, her senses burst in sweet rebellion, a myriad of sparks shooting through her belly. From far above her then, she heard Brant growl, a primitive sound of possession and relief that reverberated through her quaking body and struck to her very soul. His large frame shuddered. He gripped her to him almost violently. She closed her eyes tightly, overcome with the force of her own emotions, and now that it was over and she lay enmeshed in his embrace, she felt above all else a fervent gladness flooding her being.

For an eternity they remained enveloped in a warm cocoon of intimate silence. Neither heard the pup whining below, the door creaking open as a kindhearted servant sneaked the creature into the kitchen for the night. If another world existed beyond their bedchamber, they wanted no part of it. The experience had lifted them into a higher dimension, had changed the pattern of their lives forever, intertwined them for all time.

Rosanne, who could summon nothing from her past to

compare it to, lay quietly basking in the radiant satisfaction of the moment. She had known so little happiness in her life that she felt an almost superstitious fear of questioning it when it fell her way. Perhaps, if she analyzed it too deeply, that happiness would be snatched away from her. So, with fragile faith, she accepted what she and Brant had shared and contented herself with the present. What the future held, she dared not guess. Earlier that evening, she had resigned herself to losing him forever. And if—as a coldly demoralizing little voice whispered inside her—if he had only taken her in a storm of passion and would abandon her with the dawn, she would still not regret this night. For the first time in her life she had tasted the heady sweetness of wanting and being wanted in return. She could spend a lifetime with Hugh and never dream that such meltingly tender passion could exist between a man and a woman. But she and Brant had shared that precious knowledge tonight. No one could take that away from her now. The memory was indelibly branded upon her heart and soul.

But Brant, who had known many women, who did have a wealth of past experience to compare their lovemaking to, lay beside her overwhelmed by a deluge of feelings that were so intense, so foreign to his character, that he instinctively shied away from scrutinizing them. Above all, he felt an uncomfortable longing to comfort Rosanne, to woo her with promises that he doubted he could keep. They were so clearly unsuited to each other—he, a middling-class adventurer-farmer; she, a runaway aristocrat who would be flagrantly out of her element in the land he loved. For no matter how she resented it, Rosanne had been born a lady. Would she be able to adjust to the harshness of the life he led? She had surprised him so far with her endurance and her inner strength, and tonight— Lord, tonight—with her passionate response. But she had been thrown into her relationship with him out of necessity, and he had witnessed countless times that the wilderness tended to bring out either the best or the worst in a man. How would it affect a tenderly bred girl like Rosanne?

Damn, maybe he didn't understand women as well as he liked to think he did. He had expected Martha to wait for him forever. Plainly he had overestimated his importance in her world. And he had definitely underestimated the power of the gilt-haired nymph in his arms.

He turned to her, smiling inwardly at what a fool he'd been to hope that once he had possessed her, the fever in his blood would cool. Instead, he found that he ached to make love to her again and again, to spill out his soul to her, to share his secret thoughts as easily as he had shared his body's demands. Oh, sweet Jesus! Hadn't he feared this would happen? Hadn't he feared that once he succumbed to their mutual attraction he would be unable to stop himself?

"I'm sorry, Rosanne," he said, the words forced huskily past the tightness of his throat. He hesitated, struck afresh by the vulnerability revealed on her lovely oval face, a vulnerability he had used to selfish, carnal advantage. "I am truly sorry."

She leaned her head back and gazed evenly into his eyes. "And I am not," she said, her voice steady with acceptance. And when, a minute later, he mounted her again, filling her with hard satin heat, she reveled in the sensations he sparked inside her and in the sweet anticipation of knowing she would awaken beside him with the sun.

Chapter 12

Brant woke in reluctant stages with a pounding head and a racing heart, hoping to find that the events of the previous evening belonged to an erotic dream. Presently he became conscious of the lush feminine curves fitted up against his back. Oh, Lord, what had he done? Robbed a young girl of her maidenhead. No, it was worse. Rosanne wasn't just any young girl. She was an earl's daughter, his uncle's betrothed, for God's sake! Surely he could have exercised a little more self-discipline. Surely he could have forced himself to walk out of this room when his mind had alerted him. He groaned faintly as fragments of memory drifted through his awareness. He could not use drunkeness as an excuse. He would probably seduce her again if placed in the same situation. His body wanted to seduce her now. God, he disgusted himself.

He sat up abruptly, clapping a hand over his eyes to shut out the insolent sunshine pouring through the partially shuttered window. "Lord," he muttered, sinking back down onto the bed.

"I think," Rosanne said quietly, "that you had best stay here while I dress and have breakfast sent up. You'll feel better after you eat."

He turned toward her, a stricken look on his face. "Oh, God, Rosanne, I am so sorry—"

"And I told you that I am not. Lift your arm, would

you. You're pulling my hair. Please, Brant, move off. My stomach is so empty it hurts."

He almost laughed. She was as charming as a child in many respects, so plainspoken and unversed in deception. But last night she had been all woman. Last night . . .

"Did I hurt you?"

She nodded, twisting away from him to sit up in a sudden burst of shyness, and as she did, the swanskin coverlet slipped from her shoulders to reveal her nakedness. Her lustrous hair veiled her breasts—though the pink-tinted peaks showed prominently through the gilded strands—and tumbled in disarray past her small waist and softly padded buttocks. Brant groaned again and swung his legs over the side of the bed, his elbows braced on his knees, his hammering head cradled in his hands.

"Get dressed, Rosanne," he said unsteadily. "It is effort enough for me to gather my wits this morning without fighting the temptation of your charms. I—I find it impossible to think and look at you at the same time."

She moistened her lips, noticing that they still felt tender from the fervent kisses he had given her throughout the night. "What do you have to think about that cannot wait until after breakfast?"

"You. Me. Hugh. *Us*. Last night. How in God's name can you act as if nothing happened?" He stood up and walked to the table, lifting the flagon of wine to his parched mouth. Deliberately he faced the wall, afraid to turn around until he heard her leave the bed. All it would take was one look at her again, and they would be back in that bed for the rest of the day.

Rosanne slipped past him and collected her clothes from the floor, darting behind the screen to dress. She fought back a wave of anxiety. What was he going to do? Why did he have to decide their entire futures before breakfast? Why couldn't he simply accept what had happened between them? Her spirits sagged as she recalled the expression of shocked remorse she had glimpsed on his face when he awoke to find her beside him. It could not have been further from the dawning look of love she'd hoped for. He couldn't have remained unaffected by last night, could he? Could it be that he hadn't shared in the soaring magic, the sublime spell that had linked body to soul? She knew that she loved Brant, more than ever now, but it was beyond her limited experience to interpret his feelings for her.

She stepped clumsily into her shoes, so distracted by her thoughts that she bumped backward into the screen and sent it crashing to the floor. Brant merely shook his head in mute chagrin, sitting on the bed dressed in shirt and breeches. He had shuttered the window, and although she could perceive only the outline of his darkly shaded face, it was enough to make her feel a sick twist of foreboding in the pit of her abdomen.

He's going to send me away, she thought wildly. First he'll lecture me like a spinsterly aunt about my shameless behavior last night, then he'll express his own remorse, perhaps offer to recompense me for the loss of my virginity. Pain, humiliation, and uncertainty cascaded over her in rampant waves. What was the going price these days for deflowering an earl's daughter?

"I have reached a decision."

The rough resonance of his voice reached into every corner of the darkened chamber, into every corner, it seemed, of her consciousness. He paused, and the thought ran through her mind that he was pontificating as if he were a judge about to announce a fearfully awaited verdict. She wanted to swear at him for his unwarranted solemnity, for dragging out her agony. But she couldn't. She was too intent on maintaining her composure.

"Last night wasn't planned, Rosanne," he said with a deep frown. "I hope you believe that."

Her throat swelled. Here it comes, she thought miserably, bracing herself for the inevitable rejection. Well, damn him! I'll not salve his stupid conscience by accepting his apology. Nor shall I apologize for my part in what happened. Let him suffer his guilt alone.

"Faith," she drawled, bending to raise the screen, " 'tis amazing to me you haven't filed a lawsuit against France and England for beginning a war you hadn't planned."

He lifted his head and his eyes narrowed at her acid-tinged tones. So, she, too, had begun to regret last night, had she? Or was she possibly afraid that he'd abandon her now, send her back to Hugh with a courteous note of apology for the taking of her innocence? That option was, of course, completely out of the question, considering his uncle's depravity and the sweet, troublesome secret that now bound him and Rosanne together. Another fork in the road, he thought ruefully, and he found himself at a loss to choose the right path. How had he come this far in his life with so little self-awareness? It seemed that everything, everyone, he had believed in had been an illusion. His uncle. Martha. Especially himself. And what was this blue-eyed brat? An angel of salvation or a demoness tempting him to damnation?

"I have reached a decision," he repeated cautiously. "We'll be married in Albany. I must stop there anyway for supplies."

Rosanne could only stare at him in mute disconcertment as a host of conflicting emotions gathered like a gale inside her. He wasn't going to send her away. She would not have to return to Hugh or, God forbid, to England to beg assistance of her grandfather. She could live with Brant as his wife, could lie beside him on sultry summer nights, cuddle with him on freezing winter mornings. But—and it was this thought that dominated, that rose above the clamor of the others—he had asked her to marry him in the same tone of voice he might have used to admit he was suffering from an incurable illness. He was an honorable man seeking to redress a wrong. He didn't love her at all. He desired her. She understood the difference.

She drew in a sharp breath. "I will not marry you."

His heavy brows steepled in surprise. "Why not?"

"Why should I?"

A gauntlet tossed. She waited in agonized silence for him to pick it up, aching to hear that he wanted her for any reason at all so long as it wasn't rational. Pulsing tension closed around them. She studied his face for a hint of his mood, her gaze hovering just below his.

He groped for answers, too unsure of his feelings to share them. Yet, in the nebulous depths of his uncertainty, an emotion stirred, unidentifiable, intense, and unquestionably perilous. He pushed it back firmly before it could surface.

"I can see no other way to solve your—our—dilemma," he said at last. "It's only a matter of time before Hugh traces you to me. You'll have my name and my protection. He'll be forced to leave you alone."

Glacial disappointment crept through her. What had she expected? Would she have wanted him to lie? "What about Martha, Brant?" she forced herself to ask. "She might still change her mind. If you pursued her, tried to persuade her that she was making a mistake—"

"She's doing the right thing," he said quietly. "And she has nothing to do with us." He glanced away, wondering irrelevantly how Rosanne would fare after a few months on the frontier, whether the first wolf or naked Indian she encountered would send her sailing back to London. He himself had longed for the secure confines of the city more than once during his first year in the Mohawk Valley.

"What about your plans?" she asked archly. "Your hopes for your own wilderness community?"

He shrugged, slowly buttoning his shirt. "My plans haven't changed. I had intended to bring home a wife. It is true that life might be difficult for you at first, but you indicated last night that you would be willing to try. And considering your alternative— Well, I don't think either of us could stomach that now, do you?"

Hugh, she thought, her gaze drifting downward to her bare toes. And that was what *she* felt like—a female version of Hugh—as if she were forcing Brant into a marriage he was obviously unhappy about. She couldn't marry him under those conditions. She knew too well the malignant resentment that could grow between a husband and wife when their affections for each other were unequal. She'd seen it in her parents. The man she married would need her, adore her, cherish her—as she would him. And yet, she could not let Brant go. She had given him her heart as foolishly and as irrevocably as she had her body.

A compromise, perhaps . . . A reckless gamble taken on the chance that one day he might return her love, ask her to be his wife for that reason alone. And he was right. What alternative did she have?

"I shall go with you, Brant, but not as your wife. I'll wash, cook, sew, scrub floors if I must, but I insist on earning my keep."

"Don't be absurd."

"You need help, don't you?"

"Of course. Always. But I have a housekeeper. And, damnation, Rosanne, like it or not, you are a *lady*."

"If I were your wife, I'd keep your house, wouldn't I? You'd not expect me to lounge about all day gorging on sweetmeats."

He came to his feet, muttering, "God in heaven, girl! Do you have any idea what kind of arrangement you are proposing? It leaves too much room for complications." He stopped. All at once, without understanding how it had happened, he realized that their positions had been reversed, that it was he who was left without a satisfactory alternative. She wouldn't marry him. Should he react with relief or disappointment? Was it possible to feel both? He couldn't really imagine a spirited young beauty like her sharing the hardships of his life, could he? Why was he surprised that she was adamantly refusing to marry him? Why should he even care?

And yet he wanted her with him. It made no sense, he knew. It defied logic, reached beyond the passion he had experienced with her last night. He didn't understand any of it. He didn't especially want to.

He put on his shoes and stockings, his manner suddenly decisive. "You will stay here while I return to the van Hoorn home. It might be a good idea if Hans took Rupert in exchange for another horse for you."

"You're taking me with you?"

"Yes."

"Are you going to see her again?"

"That isn't my intention. Her brother has expressed an

interest in building a sawmill on my land for a share of the profits. We couldn't talk business last night, but I suspect that even old Wouter is interested in the proposition. Would you like anything besides food before I leave?"

"I'd like to place some flowers on Claire's grave."

"I'll see to it later. 'Twouldn't be wise for you to visit the churchyard. It's an obvious place to catch you." He picked up his hat and walked to the door. "In fact, Rosanne, I think you'd better not leave this room at all. Hugh pays me well, but I can't afford another bill like the one you incurred last night."

"Oh!" she cried, her composure cracking. "I told you it wasn't—"

The door closed, and for a terrible moment she stood paralyzed, certain he intended to desert her. Martha had had an entire night to rethink her decision. She might be waiting for Brant, hoping he'd return. But I trust him, Rosanne thought in defiance of her fears. I trusted him from the day I met him, and I trust him now. He doesn't have to take me with him. It isn't impossible that he might come to care for me one day.

And then, as she turned woodenly from the door, a small object lying on the table caught her attention. The ring. He'd left the ring. He wasn't going to offer it to Martha again. For now that was enough evidence to disperse the doubts overshadowing her heart.

They sailed up the Hudson River with the horses to Albany, arriving three days later to breakfast in an old Dutch farmhouse that had been converted into an inn several years before when immigrants had begun a westward surge. Rosanne accompanied Brant while he visited the few local merchants he trusted and hired two packhorses to carry the supplies he purchased back to Hemlock Creek.

They ate a heavy meal of fried slices of scrapple—a mixture of pork and cornmeal mush—and olykoeks—sweet, doughy cakes studded with fruit and raisins. As they were finishing their hard cider, Rosanne noticed a thin, sallow-complexioned man enter the dining room, or rather he noticed Brant and then her, his sunken eyes raking her with crude appraisal.

Brant, observing her sudden expression of distaste, glanced back at the man with a scowl. "Turn your face away," he said quickly. "And for God's sake, don't reveal who you are if he asks for an introduction. His name is Conrad Sluyter, and his father is one of Hugh's closest business associates. He wanted my job as land agent, and he wanted my patent even more. He's an unscrupulous little bas—"

"Back already, Layton?" Conrad drawled, his voice loud enough to interrupt conversation at nearby tables. "Don't tell me Miss van Hoorn has changed her mind. I understood there was to be a wedding."

"And so there shall be." Brant leaned back, eyeing Sluyter disdainfully over the rim of his leather mug. "Martha is marrying Wouter Jansen, the shipbuilder. But I've a feeling you already knew that, didn't you, Sluyter?"

Conrad's lips stretched into a gloating grin. "Well, I did introduce Wouter to Mynheer van Hoorn while I was in the city last winter."

"If that's all you wished to say, Sluyter, I suggest you leave." His face deceptively complacent, Brant put down his mug and sat forward. "We were enjoying our food until you appeared."

The pretense of pleasantness fled Conrad's face, leaving a sneer to tighten his gauntly drawn cheeks. "Between you and me, Layton, Miss van Hoorn always seemed rather insipid. Not at all the type for the hotblooded buck you fancy yourself to be." He reached out a long, bony forefinger and plucked at a lock of Rosanne's hair. "Now this pretty little piece looks like she'd set a man's bed afire—"

Brant shot up from the table, punched Conrad in the abdomen and again in the jaw before the Dutchman could raise an arm in his own defense. Staggering back, Sluyter collapsed across a chair with blood dribbling from the side of his mouth. With a glaring gaze fixed on Brant, he yanked out a handkerchief and spat a rotted tooth into it.

"My tooth!" he said in shrill disbelief. "You barbarian,

you knocked my tooth out!" He uncurled his body and suddenly charged at Brant with an outraged snarl, swinging his long arms like windmill blades.

"Wait for me outside," Brant ordered Rosanne tersely, swiftly stepping in front of her with his knees bent and his weight evenly balanced. He grabbed her arm and pulled her around the table. "*Now!*"

Chapter 13

Conrad attacked Brant with several inexpertly thrown punches before Brant had time to push Rosanne to the door. The tables around them emptied instantly, men grabbing their trenchers and retreating to the taproom where they could watch the fight in safety.

Brant feinted and ducked, circling the Dutchman slowly, goading him with his eyes, allowing Conrad to exhaust himself. Soon Sluyter's swinging arms slowed, and his chest rose and fell as he panted with exertion, his breath becoming fast and labored. And it was then that Brant began jabbing with his left, almost playfully at first, knocking his knuckles under the other man's chin, a little harder each time.

"I think you ought to apologize for what you said about the young lady, don't you, Sluyter?"

Conrad's head jerked upward, and he smiled with taunting defiance, blood tinting his teeth as he answered. "I'll not apologize for anything. Especially not for what I said about your whore."

Brant swung fiercely with his right. Screaming as the powerful fist connected with his jaw, Conrad zigzagged backward into Rosanne. Senseless from the blow, he swayed straight toward her cringing figure and crumpled at her side. Horrified, she wrenched her skirts back to avoid contact with him and inched away from his prone figure. She glanced up at Brant, reassuring herself that he had only received an abrasion on his cheek and, undoubtedly, badly bruised knuckles. Why had he allowed Sluyter to provoke him? She tried to motion Brant quietly to the door, hoping they could escape before Conrad roused to resume the fight, but Brant was watching two men shouldering a path through the spectators in the taproom. One was a younger, huskier version of Conrad, the other a grim-faced merchant in his fifties.

The younger arrival rushed to Conrad's assistance, helping him into a chair. The older man had focused his interest on Brant, controlled rage molding his blunt features. "What have you done to my son this time, Layton?"

"Simply reminded him to watch his manners."

Rosanne noticed that Brant's rifle had come to rest at his side. She also noticed the furious disapproval in his eyes as his gaze flickered over her and he realized she had disobeyed his order to go outside.

"Shall we fetch the sheriff, Jacobus?"

Jacobus Sluyter glanced down at his eldest son, who was slumped over in the chair, and slowly shook his head. Favors asked of the sheriff had to be saved for important matters. He and his friends could handle this independent English upstart on the quiet. Though few in number, Brant Layton and his brash breed were the thorn in the side of every Albany fur merchant, attracting traders and Indians alike with their fair dealings and low prices. Their competitive spirit threatened to break the lucrative Albany monopoly. They had to be stopped before they established a dangerous precedent. But they had to be stopped with caution.

"You could learn from your uncle, Layton," Jacobus said heavily.

"I have." Brant grabbed his hat, his mouth hardening as he turned to regard Rosanne. He motioned to the door impatiently. "Let's go."

Just then, Huybert, the youngest Sluyter, straightened up swinging a stool above his head, and launched himself at Brant. Out of sheer instinct Rosanne flung her portmanteau at Huybert's chest, the momentum of the wallop she dealt him sending her stumbling back against a table. Nimble for his bulk, Huybert jumped over the portmanteau as it fell to his feet, but her tactic had succeeded in deflecting his aim, so that the flying stool glanced off Brant's swiftly upraised rifle and not off his head, as intended.

By the time Rosanne recovered her portmanteau and Brant had hauled her behind him, Jacobus had calmed Huybert and Conrad had managed to stand up. Fingering his jawbone, he watched Brant steer Rosanne to the door, his eyes following them with burning hatred.

"I won't forget this, Layton," he said, angrily brushing away the hand his father laid on his arm. "Your land grant still hasn't cleared the council. You may not live long enough to learn whether it ever does."

"Watch what you say, Conrad," Jacobus warned in an undertone, lifting his head to indicate the silent audience behind them.

Rosanne paled at Conrad's threat as Brant opened the door and unceremoniously shoved her out onto the *stoep*, glancing back at Conrad with his own calmly uttered warning: "Insult a woman of my acquaintance again, Sluyter, and you'll lose more than a tooth."

Huybert swore and started back toward Brant, but Jacobus caught the boy's arm and twisted it upward in a paralyzing hold.

"Good day," Brant said pleasantly, inclining his head in a mockingly courteous farewell.

Rosanne expressed a loud sigh of relief when at last she saw Brant coming through the door, half expecting he'd emerge bloody and beaten. She had been trying to decide what had sparked his anger. Was it Conrad's remarks about Martha or those about herself? Martha still touches off a sensitive nerve in him, she realized dejectedly. How long would it take him to forget her? Or would he ever? He didn't behave like heartbroken suitor; indeed, his spirits had lifted noticeably since Martha had terminated their engagement. But then it might be an act, a masquerade contrived to conceal his true feelings until his masculine pride mended. She did not know him well enough yet to analyze his actions for ulterior motives. She took him at his word. She accepted him for whatever he might be, for in their emotionally charged fortnight together, he had treated her with more tenderness than she'd ever known before. And even now, as he confronted her with his exploding anger, grabbing her arm and roughly marching her toward the stables, she loved him.

"That man actually threatened your life, Brant," she said breathlessly, casting a furtive backward glance across the stable yard.

"I thought it was understood you would obey me," Brant said through his teeth, so furious he was unable to look at her. Ordering the stableboy to leave them alone, he dragged her through the stables and shoved her into Gemma's stall.

She retreated to an opposite corner, hot indignation flowing through her. "I was afraid something would happen to you, but if I'd known you'd react like this I'd have let the lump-headed hulk brain you!"

"And if I'd known you would make such a disobedient servant, I'd never have agreed to employ you."

"Servant? I'm not a—"

"No," he interjected forcefully, moving out of the stall to test that the wooden harnesses were secured comfortably on the two packhorses. "You are not a servant. And I doubt you know a kettle from a frying pan."

She whirled to face the door, angry that he'd bent her own words to prove his point. Was that his intention—to goad her into admitting she didn't fit into his life? Why did he assume she'd been raised like a princess of the blood? Or was his ill temper merely a screen? Was he lashing out at her because Conrad had flung Martha's rejection in his face? The thought came to her suddenly that he might not understand his own motivations any better than she did.

Brant looked up, observing Rosanne's haughtily indignant profile, and it was all he could do to keep a straight face. And then he remembered her throwing her portmanteau at Huybert, uncaring that the oaf was thrice her size and could snap her spine like a twig. His heart had stopped in sickening anxiety as he'd watched her place herself in Huybert's path. What had gotten into her? All at once, he found himself recalling the incident on the Neck not that long ago, when he had risked his life just as unthinkingly. He would have done it again today, he admitted to himself in bewilderment. Huybert had no idea how fortunate he was he hadn't laid a hand on Rosanne.

Brant moved away from the horses. Why was it that he and Rosanne together sparked such irrational behavior? He was not in the habit of brawling in taverns, and he doubted she was either.

He came up behind her, his anger draining away. He ached to touch her but didn't dare it, searingly aware of what that contact would erupt into. They hadn't made love since that one voluptuous night; they hadn't had the privacy. But he feared that the moment an opportunity presented itself again, the temptation would have to be met and conquered. They would soon reach Hemlock Creek, he thought worriedly. Would a raw setting heighten or equalize the differences in their backgrounds?

"I'm sorry I lost my temper."

She turned stiffly, her eyes probing his for a trace of mockery. Finding none, she began to feel her own annoyance abate. "You shouldn't have hit that odious man, Brant. It wasn't worth it."

The image of Conrad's skeletal finger toying with her hair leapt into his mind. His jaw clenched. "You're right," he said roughly. "I should have killed him instead. Stay here with the horses."

"Brant, *no*—"

He turned, backing away slowly, his hazel eyes bright with wicked amusement. "Come on, little bruiser. I'll finish Conrad, and you handle Huybert. Whoever gets done first takes on the father."

She picked up a handful of oats from a feedbag to hurl at him, but before she could unclench her fist, the stable door swung open. She and Brant wheeled around at the same time, both expecting the Sluyter family to come bursting into the stables. They saw instead the large-framed woman who'd served them. Fortyish and attractive in her starched lace cap, velvet bodice, and short skirts, she called out to them timidly:

"You dropped your hat, Mr. Layton."

"I also forgot to settle the bill." He tucked the hat under his arm, withdrew his purse, and pressed several coins into her palm. "Apologize to your mistress for what happened."

"The sniveling little swine had it coming," the woman said feelingly. "He and his father act as if they own the very air that surrounds Albany. Oh, and that brings to mind a sad business—I am sorry about your friend, Mr. Layton. I've had nightmares about his murder."

Brant frowned. "Are you talking about Franklin Newhouse?"

"Yes, sir. A shepherd found the body in the foothills a sennight ago. He'd been killed with a tomahawk. The sheriff claimed it was the work of an Indian or a runaway slave, but that's what he always says. Strange little man, your friend. He stayed here overnight before he was murdered. He seemed so uneasy, Mr. Layton, as though he feared he was being followed."

"Which he probably was," Brant said with a grim sigh. "Thank you for letting me know this, Katrina. And thank you for my hat."

Rosanne could feel the suspicion building inside Brant as they walked Katrina to the stable yard. "You don't really believe Hugh is involved in the man's murder, do you, Brant?" she asked in a nervous whisper, although there wasn't a soul except a stableboy within earshot.

"Franklin was a dead man from the minute he threatened to expose Olivia and my uncle. Conrad probably arranged the murder. Unfortunately, no one will ever prove anything, despite my warning to Hugh in Boston."

As she listened to him, her own thoughts took an alarming turn. For the first time, she wondered if she might be jeopardizing Brant's life by involving him in her escape from his uncle. Would Hugh retaliate when he finally realized who had helped her? If he found her, he would make her life hell for defying him, for humiliating him. Would his rage extend to seeking a dangerous revenge against Brant?

"Brant, if Hugh becomes truly desperate, do you think he'll try to hurt you?"

He shook his head. "As corrupt as he is, I don't think he'd go that far. He's counting on my family loyalty to keep me silent. Until the actual time comes, I am not sure myself what I'll do. I can't turn a blind eye on murder. And I cannot forget the men whose lives he's ruined while they're my neighbors."

"I believe you're still very fond of him," Rosanne said quietly.

"Mostly I hate him, not only for what he's done, but also because it was unnecessary. A man of his intelligence should be helping people instead of hurting them."

Conversation ceased between them as they approached the stableboy who held their horses. Brant asked him to fetch the pack animals and then helped Rosanne mount the mild-tempered bay Hans had sold him. His hands lingered above her waist, aching to haul her down and hold her close against him. He wanted to carry her across the yard to the meadow behind the inn, to remove the royal blue velvet riding habit he'd bought her, and to love her in a private haven of waist-high grasses and fragrant clover. He wanted to bury his face between her breasts and crush their fullness against his naked chest. Their gazes joined, Rosanne's clouded with concern and unashamed longing, his troubled and flaming with flagrant passion. He yanked his hands down abruptly and turned to his own horse before he could become entangled in the sensual web closing around them.

He had offered her marriage. Neither gracefully nor willingly, he had to confess. But the offer had been made, and she had refused him. Sooner or later she would weary of staying with him anyway, of the relentless sunrise-to-sunset farm household routine. Maybe Hugh would even appeal to her after a few shivering mornings washing laundry at the creek, or a week of tedious candle dipping in the kitchen. Had she ever done anything more strenuous in her life than lift a teacup to those kissable scarlet lips?

It would not do for him to become too attached to her.

He mounted his horse, a sigh escaping him. If they were to part, he hoped it would happen soon. Every moment he spent with her left him a little more captivated by her sweet disposition, a little more uncertain of his own intentions.

"Are you ready, Rosanne?" he asked, resurfacing briefly from his deep reverie as the stableboy reappeared.

"Yes."

He clucked his tongue. The mare surged forward, trailed by Rosanne's bay and the two heavily laden packhorses. God, what a situation to carry home with him. He had always managed to master his emotions in the past where women were concerned. It annoyed him unbearably that the only female his uncle coveted should prove to be the exception.

But she was.

And the intensity of his feelings for her, the rampant pattern of their growth, shook him to the core. Perhaps, he thought hopefully, perhaps he was trying to transfer the affection he once felt for Martha to Rosanne so as not to upset the even keel of his life. Perhaps he was only trying to protect her from Hugh because he'd failed to protect his aunt. Perhaps he unconsciously wanted to get back at Hugh by taking Rosanne with him.

No.

The truth was that everything he felt for her came from the shadows of his own soul.

Chapter 14

Rosanne watched Brant in moody contemplation as they rode away from Albany and its stone fort, her emotions uncoiling painfully inside her heart. She had witnessed the battle of desire against reason in his eyes when he'd held her a few minutes ago. What did it mean? Would their relationship perish before it took root? She wondered whether it had been a mistake to give herself to him so freely that night. She thought of her mother, of Hugh's horrid accusations, and worried that she had inherited Lisette's wantonness.

Should she have accepted Brant's offer of marriage? He might well never broach the subject again. Would marrying him now have made everything all right?

No.

She yearned for him to reciprocate her love, but it had to happen naturally. The notion of forcing herself on him—of him marrying her out of pity, guilt, or obligation—twisted inside her like a serrated dagger. He must come to love her of his own volition. What did she have to lose by waiting? What could he take from her that she hadn't already given willingly?

For the next twenty miles they traveled across a stretch of sandy pine plains broken only by an occasional isolated cabin. Against her protests, Brant had smeared a tarry salve across her face.

"You're too damned adorable to let the bugs feast on you, angel," he said, grinning at her messy little face.

She rubbed her nose furiously. "How do I know you're not just trying to make me look stupid?"

"Wipe it off and find out. But don't cry to me about it later."

"Why aren't you wearing any?"

His grin widened. "I guess my hide is too tough for the bugs to bite."

They continued in comfortable silence. All Brant's senses were attuned to his environment, alert for timber rattlesnakes, for hostile Indians, for the lawless trappers who lived in makeshift huts in the hills during the summer trading season. His rifle rested with reassuring weight across the crook of his arm. Drop by drop he felt the tension of the past few weeks draining from his body. The hazards the wilderness posed suddenly seemed tame compared with those he was encountering as he explored the unfamiliar terrain of his own heart.

Rosanne absorbed the alien atmosphere in wide-eyed wonder as the horses trod along a path padded with lichen and pine needles, their tails swishing to flick away a host of bothersome black flies. The curiosity and excitement that consumed her left no room for fear to flourish: there were too many new sights to marvel over.

The strident trumpeting of a blue jay drifted down from the towering pitch pines interspersed with smaller oaks that rose around the trail. Delighted, she spotted a white-tailed deer hidden in a shady hollow above a brackish stream that was clogged with decomposing leaves. Bracken fern and bladderwort covered its shallow banks. Mosquitoes bred on its sluggish surface. A red squirrel scuttered up an oak, pausing briefly on a leafy bough to scold. Amid the mossy roots below, a woodcock chiseled with its long beak for a beetle.

The landscape altered again by the time they reached the Dutch town of Schenectady, a modest replica of Albany that the Iroquois called The Place Beyond the Pine Plains. They stopped only long enough for a dinner of hodgepodge soup and dumplings, then rode to the common wharf to board a flat-bottomed bateau. Rosanne's ears burned from the lusty, uninhibited language employed by the boatmen as they wielded their poles up the Mohawk River. But, delicate sensibilities aside, she was privately grateful for the respite from riding a horse. The muscles of her inner thighs were quivering from the exertion of days in the saddle. Her spine felt brittle, the vertebrae disconnected.

They disembarked and resumed their trip on horseback, along a trail that cut through a cluster of low-lying hills that were settling down for the night beneath a slowly descending cloak of twilight. Brant glanced back frequently, amused at Rosanne wobbling in the saddle, valiantly fighting to keep her seat. To her credit, she hadn't complained once. Not a murmur. Determined little chit. He admired her for that.

"It won't be long now," he reassured her. "We'll be spending the night with friends."

Her eyes stabbed the shadows. She slapped away a mosquito hovering near her wrist. She shuddered as a vixen sprang out from a thicket and pounced on a juicy frog resting by a stream. Suddenly the trail led them into a clearing. A crudely constructed cabin chinked with moss and clay loomed against a backdrop of timbered hills and stump-studded fields. Feeble candlelight glowed behind the oiled-paper windows. Rosanne slumped forward against the saddle pommel. She would not have cared if she slept in a cave that night.

"That you, Layton?

A short, muscular man stepped out from the woodshed attached to the cabin. His dark eyes glinted in welcoming recognition. He swung down his axe. "Ye've brought yer bride. She looks to be a fine lass. Bring her inside."

"She's not my bride, Lorne," Brant said uncomfortably as he dismounted. "She's my—my—"

"Servant," Rosanne said.

Lorne MacGavin's eyebrows lifted and dropped. "Alison! Fenella!" he bellowed, striding forward to take Rosanne's horse. "We've visitors!"

A pair of russet-haired teenage girls with dark, laughing eyes tumbled out of the cabin, five skinny hounds tangling around their ragged homespun skirts and barking excitedly.

"Who is it, Da?"

"Oooh, it's Mr. Layton!"

The girls flew at Brant in a rapture of giggles, flinging suspicious but not unfriendly looks at Rosanne, who hung back shyly near the woodshed.

"She doesn't look like a maidservant," Fenella, the elder of the two, observed. "Are ye sure she isn't your—"

A stern glance from her father shamed her into silence. Lorne MacGavin was one of the feisty Scotch-Irish New World settlers whose ancestors had spilled over the Scottish borders and crossed the Irish Sea to put down roots in Ulster over a century before. Proud, poor, unlettered, and recently widowed, he supported his family by hunting, and he kept the girls in line with infrequent Biblical sermons and a leather strap.

They ate a solemn supper of squirrel stew with rye bread and a wilted salad of watercress, wild garlic, bitter grapevine shoots, and dandelion greens. Fenella served a runny strawberry fool for dessert. Talk turned to weather and then the war, Lorne's voice dropping as he repeated to Brant his plan to conceal the girls in the root cellar in the event of an attack by the French and their allied Indians. Rosanne, dozing off on the puncheon bench, snapped to attention.

Frowning, Brant got up to light his cigar at the fire where Fenella was heating a kettle of water for washing. "Governor Clinton is talking about imposing a levy for a militia."

"I wish him luck," Lorne said dourly.

"You and the girls could move into my land, Lorne," Brant went on. "You've nothing invested here but the cabin."

"I'm a free man now. I hunt for what we eat. The girls manage. I'll not indenture myself again."

"I didn't mean that. You were a carpenter in Ulster. I'd like to hire you, in return for a small tract."

"Aye. Well, I'll consider it."

Brant returned to his seat and glanced across the table at

Rosanne; he'd noticed her reaction at the mention of an Indian attack. Hadn't she listened to his warnings? The last thing he needed was a hysterical female clinging to his shirtsleeves every time an Indian came to trade. He exhaled a cloud of smoke, watching her through the blue-gray billows. That was unfair. She was a brave little brat, too damned brave. Lovely too, he mused, with her blue eyes reflecting the firelight like sunshine on a lake. Thank God he was too exhausted tonight to lie awake craving the softness of her body beneath his, craving the heaven he had experienced with her that unforgettable night. Oh, damn, if only he could put that memory from his mind! If only it hadn't been so perfect, so right, so natural . . .

"It's late," he said suddenly, rising. "I'm for bed."

Fenella turned to Rosanne, her eyes narrowing in her small, monkey face. "Ye'll need a blanket. It's damp in the barn."

"The barn—"

Lorne leaned across the table and cuffed his elder daughter on the ear. "Ye're not to give yerself airs, miss. She'll sleep in the loft with you and yer sister."

"But, Da, she's a servant!"

"Aye, and so were yer parents."

Several minutes later, as she settled under a deerskin blanket on a corn-husk mattress, Rosanne wondered if she would indeed not have been more comfortable in the barn. It was stuffy in the windowless loft, and Fenella didn't bother to hide her hostility at having to share her sleeping quarters with a stranger. Rosanne closed her eyes. She was so exhausted she didn't even protest when the young girl's elbow persistently prodded her in the small of the back.

"She's lovely, Fenella, don't ye think?" Alison whispered, lying on the other side of Rosanne.

"If ye like bright hair and funny little noses," Fenella said with a disdainful sniff. "I know one thing—she's no servant. She's his lover woman!"

Rosanne flushed hot red from her chest to her hair follicles. Was it that obvious? How could Fenella tell? She, Rosanne, and Brant hadn't exchanged more than four sentences all evening, let alone touched each another!

"Stop your blethering, Fenella!" Lorne shouted, and the loft shook as he banged the ladder against the ceiling below.

Presently, Rosanne felt herself drifting off to sleep. Alison was already snoring. Fenella was scratching and muttering to herself. Did the girl have fleas? Suddenly Rosanne felt a large furry object at her feet, burrowing beneath the blanket, squeezing into the warm tunnel between herself and Alison. A cold nose bumped her shoulder. A slobbery tongue scraped against her cheek. She cracked open an eyelid, slowly turning her head. It was one of the underfed Irish wolfhounds, commonly called a wolfdog, the smallest of the litter. Sensing a soft heart, he crawled up on her shoulder and stretched out across her chest, his tail thumping Alison's face.

"Oh, no, Fenella," Alison said groggily, pushing the dog's vibrating rump from her face. "Ye know Da'll flay your hide if he catches this whelp up here."

Fenella sat up and yanked the dog from Rosanne's chest, hugging him so fiercely that he gave a small protesting yelp. "Da's going to shoot him tomorrow anyway. I'm going to love him all night long so he'll have happy memories to take to heaven."

"Dogs don't go to heaven, ninny," Alison said, snuggling back down under the blanket.

"Oh, yes, they do!" Fenella cried. "They do!" She turned drowning eyes on Rosanne. "Tell her."

"Well, why wouldn't they?" Rosanne hoisted herself up on her elbow, reaching out her other hand to pet the wolfhound. "You weren't serious, were you? About your father shooting the dog?"

"Aye, I was. He's a mean old man. He hates my wee Tynan 'cause he eats a lot and chases the hens. Da says we canna afford to feed him."

"If I hear one more peep from up there, ye'll all sleep in the barn!" Lorne roared from below.

At the sound of the loud, ugly voice, Tynan wriggled from Fenella's arms and retreated to the end of the loft, curling up into a ball with a soulful sigh. Rosanne turned onto her side, a lump of emotion rising in her throat. There had been so many times during her childhood when she'd felt unwanted herself, a worthless burden to her parents, a resented demand on their time and money. To be sure, her mother had played with her and petted her when the mood struck, or when Lisette didn't have friends to entertain. But her father had never spared a loving word or gesture for her or Claire. Oh, God. Even Brant thought she was a nuisance. Silent tears seeped from between her closed lids. Had anyone ever truly cared for her except Gwennie and Claire? Would anyone ever care for her again? Would she ever have a home of her own, a husband to spoil, babies upon whom she could lavish all the love she had craved as a child and had never known?

She peeled off the blanket and crawled across the loft to Tynan, wrapping her arms around his thin neck and burying her damp face in his rough grayish coat. "It's all right, boy," she whispered. "I'll not let him hurt you. It's all right."

Every muscle in Rosanne's body pleaded for at least another day of rest. Her eyes kept drifting shut as she laced her bodice and leaned backward so that Alison could comb out her hair. It was not yet dawn. But she could hear Brant and Lorne stirring below, conversing in low tones about fishing, the fur trade, the price of pelts on the European market.

As she climbed down the ladder, she noticed Fenella already at the table, ladling bean porridge into pine-knot bowls. She glanced about the dimly lit room, her gaze frantically hunting for Tynan's long wiry body beneath the trestle table. Had Fenella hidden the dog from her father? Had the awful deed been accomplished yet? She was afraid to ask, in case Lorne had forgotten what he'd threatened to do.

"Is there anything I can do to help, Fenella?" she asked.

"After we eat," the girl replied ungraciously, banging Rosanne's bowl down on the table.

Rosanne sat down and dipped a wooden spoon into the lumpy porridge. Her eyes met Brant's across the table. He's waiting for me to complain about the food, she thought, to demand Congo tea and kidney pie for breakfast.

"Lovely porridge, Fenella," she said, almost choking on both the porridge and the lie.

Fenella's upper lip curled in derision. "Do I look bloody simple? The porridge tastes like cow—" She broke off at a scowl from her father. "Speaking of cows, ye'll not mind helping me freshen the hay in their stalls, will ye?"

Rosanne slipped a hopeful glance at Brant, but his eyes remained downcast, dark with private mirth. He did not mean to come to her rescue, damn him. He thought it was amusing.

"No. I don't mind."

As soon as Fenella cleared the table, Rosanne got up and walked to the door, practically stepping over Alison, who was already hard at work beside the hearth, scrubbing out the kettle with a corn husk and sand. Fenella handed Rosanne a smoking betty lamp and then lifted the latch.

"Alison, remember you're milking after ye wash the dishes." She gave Rosanne an intolerant look. "Come on, you. And don't be starting a fire with that lamp or lettin' it go out on the way. 'Tis dark at the back of the barn."

It was also barbarically dark outside, Rosanne thought, tramping after Fenella along the sloping, weed-edged path. The barn was twice as large as the cabin and enveloped them in a dusky atmosphere that was pungent with the ripe fragrance of hay, leather, and fresh manure. Rosanne hung the lamp safely on a nail above the haymow door.

"Shall we muck out the horses' stalls first?"

"We have no horses. Clean up after yer own." Fenella handed Rosanne a wooden shovel, smiling slyly. "We're not fancy like yer man. We live simple."

Rosanne shook her head, refusing to let the sour remarks upset her. What young girl wouldn't become embittered living this way?

Fenella moved toward the mow to remove a pitchfork hanging on the wall, and Rosanne bent at the waist to roll up her skirts and petticoats, thinking that Brant had better not make any rude remarks about how she smelled afterward. As she straightened, she thought she detected a shadow falling across the corncrib. She tilted her head and stared, tiny spears of unease pricking her skin. The shadow vanished.

"Fenella—"

The girl interrupted her with a shrill cry. "Oooh, naughty Tynan—pissing on Nella's egg basket!" Then, "Damn it to hell! Look at all these feathers! A fox must've got to one of my hens again. I've told that nitwit Alison to keep the doors closed."

Well, at least the dog is safe for now, Rosanne thought wryly, turning away with a sigh. Then suddenly a soft whoosh rippled the air behind her. The light from the lamp dimmed and died. Tynan growled. Something dropped to the hay with a muffled thud.

Rosanne revolved, one apprehensive inch at a time. Tynan's growls rose over the ominous sound of something heavy—Fenella hauling a sack of grain?—being dragged across the floor. Then another thud. Her gaze jerked over the corncrib to the hay wagon. Fenella's legs, encased in threadbare worsted stockings, dangled over the side. A silverish blade sliced upward into the shadows above the girl.

A tomahawk!

"Oh, God, no!" Rosanne cried involuntarily, her fingers tightening around the shovel. In horror she perceived the bulky outline of a man springing to his feet in the wagon bed, a man dressed in dirty buckskins with a tomahawk poised in the hand of his uplifted arm.

A scream clawed its way up through her chest and tore from her throat as a broken croak. "No—no, don't!" Too late she regretted calling attention to herself as the man's head snapped around in her direction, his long black hair swinging over shoulders as massive as twin hillocks. A scrawny chicken, its neck wrung, dangled from a brass game ring on the scalp belt at his hip.

Rosanne froze in shocked fascination, unable to tear her eyes from his face—a hideous vermilion-painted oval with a central blob of scar tissue where a nose belonged. The beads on his leggings clacked as he jumped from the wagon and advanced on her in a slow, stalking crouch.

Her mind raced, and yet she could not move. Had he murdered Fenella? Had she interrupted him in time to save the other girl's life? The clacking grew louder. The revolting stench of rum, sweat, and rancid animal blood, all now absorbed by the leather of his buckskins, clogged her nostrils. Still she couldn't move. She felt as though her feet were chained by invisible manacles to the floor.

Then she saw him raise the tomahawk again, and primitive instinct lent life to her paralyzed limbs, carrying her backward, crashing through the door of an empty stall. She called out shrilly for help, knowing hopelessly that no one in the house could possibly hear her. Unexpectedly, Tynan responded, springing out from beneath the wagon to launch his wiry weight at the menacing figure. The man grunted angrily and kicked at the dog, but Tynan had gotten hold of his ankle and clung to it fiercely with his fangs. Rosanne watched in dread as the tomahawk flashed downward.

"Oh, no," she whispered. "T-Tynan, look out!"

To her limitless relief the dog retreated just as the tomahawk descended to chop air. Suddenly the rear door that gave into the cow pen banged open. Pinkish streaks of dawn penetrated the gloom. Rosanne spun around, her anxiety increasing a hundredfold as she realized it wasn't Lorne or Brant or even Alison standing before her, but another dangerous intruder, tall and raw-boned, with a fur cap pulled down low to obscure his features. She felt his gaze swing to her, though she could not see his face. Without realizing it, she had raised the shovel to defend herself. Tynan stood before her, his spindly legs planted apart in a defensive stance.

The newcomer closed the door behind him, his flintlock

coldly leveled at Rosanne. In a harsh guttural tongue she didn't recognize, he called his companion to his side. They exchanged a few words. Then the man with the hideous face ran outside. Rosanne's stomach lurched when she noticed Fenella's shawl fluttering like a trophy from his belt. Intuitively she realized that he had been instructed to stand guard.

She looked up, her heart racing. The man at the door began moving toward her, his musket held steadily, his shaded eyes attacking her with the lawless lust of a man who needed a woman and didn't care how or where he had her.

"Stay away from me," she warned ineffectually. "If you—"

The shovel slipped from her hands. She started forward to flee.

He was on her faster than a red-tailed hawk on a hare, wrapping a sinewy arm around her throat, smothering her cries with a filthy, rough-textured palm. She struggled, desperate for breath. He slammed her up against the stall door, grunting with exertion, for she was stronger than he expected. Her head hit the door. A trail of golden stars exploded between her temples. A hoe bounced off the wall and clattered beside them. Foggily she was aware of Tynan leaping at her assailant in a relentless frenzy, snarling as he tore into the man's leggings with tooth and claw.

The man would soon smother her, she realized in dim panic as her lungs expanded until she felt they would burst, and he was whispering something again and again, a girl's name, or so it sounded. Darkness swirled around her, and her last lucid thought was that he had managed to kick Tynan out of the stall and slammed the door on the wolfdog's snapping jaws.

Unexpectedly sunrise flooded the barn. Her eyelids flickered apart as the suffocating band around her throat loosened. Disoriented, her chest heaving, she could not bring herself to look into the man's face, though she sensed his alarm as he threw a backward glance at Alison standing horrified in the doorway. For a moment he seemed to hesitate, leaving both girls suspended in terror. Then, cursing in that alien tongue, he reached down for the musket propped against the wall and flung Rosanne to the hay. Belatedly, his companion burst into the rear of the barn, gesturing him frantically to leave.

Rosanne fell to her knees, her body rigid in grim anticipation. Would he shoot her in the head? Would it hurt very much to die?

"Oh my God," Alison whimpered, her milk buckets knocking together as she whirled and fled in shrieking panic, Tynan racing beside her. "Da! Mr. Layton! Help! Oh, Da—"

Chapter 15

The fatalistically anticipated shot never came. When Rosanne finally forced her eyes open, her assailant was gone, and the door to the outside cow pen was reverberating slightly. She braced her hands against the rough wall and hauled herself upright, shivers convulsing her frame. She felt furious at herself for not fighting him harder, and yet a dim part of her mind reassured her that she had done the right thing. At least she was alive. But Fenella . . .

Brant ran into the barn and gently drew her out of the stall, stroking the hair from her fear-bleached face, patiently trying to coax sense out of her when, to her frustration, she could hear herself gibbering incoherently.

"The t-tomahawk, Brant. Fenella's legs . . . Oh, the wagon. He had a tomahawk, and the chicken's neck was wrung."

"Did he hurt *you*, Rosanne? Are you injured anywhere or just badly shaken?" He held her away from him and subjected her to a quick, searching study, a shaft of fury stabbing him at the red fingerprints embossed upon her colorless cheeks. "Please, Rosanne," he said urgently. "Tell me if you are hurt."

"No, no." Her blue eyes slowly lost their wildness, and she felt ashamed that he had witnessed her temporary lack of control, though God knew it would have been a harrowing experience for anyone. "I'm fine," she said hoarsely, "but Fenella—"

"God Almighty, there's blood on your skirts, Rosanne!" He knelt swiftly, concern twisting his features into a horrified mask.

She giggled, needing to release some of her tension. "No, Brant. Not my blood. The dog bit him. Oh, Fenella, we must help her. . . ."

He stood up hurriedly. "Stay here. Alison is tending to her sister."

"Don't go after them, Brant! They're dangerous!"

"I'll be all right."

He disengaged himself from her icy hands and ran outside to the cow pen, rage burning through his veins like vitriol. Scanning the perimeters of the clearing, he vaulted the low chestnut fence and took an instinctive route toward the hills. His eyes combed the ground for tracks while his long legs carried him with tireless strides. On occasion he would race for sport in contests against Mohawk braves in the valley. But these bastards had gotten a lead on him that he had lengthened while he reassured himself that Rosanne was unharmed.

At the peak of the hill he paused, his gaze following the trail of footprints to a steep-banked stream. Moccasin tracks, not surprisingly. One pair belonged to a tall, lightly built man who appeared to favor his right leg; the other indicated an owner abnormally large but fast for his size. Both sets of heelprints were sunk deeply into the ground, revealing that the men had been carrying something heavy over their shoulders.

Thank God it wasn't Rosanne. He still felt sick inside with the panic that had gripped him when Alison ran into the cabin screaming that a man was attacking Rosanne in the barn.

He listened. Soft birdsong floated from across the stream, which meant that no threatening humans were lurking below in the thickets. Beyond the banks he spotted canoe tracks leading to the water. Whoever they were they had probably spent the night in the MacGavins' barn and had now fled downstream. Indians? Not unless they were drunk on rum. They were trappers, most likely, a class of men often wilder than the animals they hunted.

The sound of rocks skittering down the hillside disrupted his thoughts. He grabbed his rifle and bolted behind a bush; then he grinned as he saw the wolfdog scrambling toward him. The hound explored his ankles; then he sniffed the ground and trotted in overlapping circles until he reached the tracks. He was young, but he showed a keen nose for scent. Brant wondered idly whether he was worth training.

"Another time, boy," he said softly. "We've lost them for now."

Lorne appeared next, lumbering up on bare feet whose soles were hardened to the consistency of bark. "Goddamn savages! Made off with me sow and a calf!"

"Never mind the livestock, man," Brant said impatiently. "Is Fenella all right?"

"Fenella?" Lorne possessed the grace to look bleakly shamefaced for checking his animals' welfare before even considering his own daughter's safety. "Aye, she must be, or we'd have heard Alison shrieking her lungs out by now." He wheeled and spat, muttering to himself as he started down the hill. "Filthy, stealin' heathens! What are ye sniffin' at, ye worthless bag of bones? Who let ye out of the woodshed anyway?"

Inside the barn they found all three girls safe but understandably frightened. Fenella was the center of attention, insisting everyone feel the bump on her noggin, big as a goose egg, or so she claimed. Rosanne listened to Fenella's recitation with grudging amusement, wishing she'd been the one to lie blissfully unconscious throughout the ghastly ordeal.

"And then I looked down and saw this man asleep in the straw with the strangled hen. I didn't have a chance to scream. He popped up all of a sudden—" And at this point Fenella paused dramatically, waiting for Brant and her father to enter the barn.

"The little twit is too stupid to realize she almost ended up like her hen," Brant whispered into Rosanne's ear as he came up behind her. "Did you get a close look at them, sweet?"

She turned, leaning into him with a sigh. "Not really. The man with the tomahawk had his face painted, but it was scarred horribly, as if he'd been mutilated. It was dark, and I—"

"Indians," Fenella said, eavesdropping.

Alison shook her head in disagreement. "The man holding the musket had queer light eyes. Of course, I couldn't be *positive*."

Brant guided Rosanne toward the door, his arm resting lightly around her waist before he lifted it away. "Are you ready to go home?"

"Oh, yes."

It was already warm outside; the sunlight gilding the clearing held the promise of another hot day, but Rosanne could not suppress the tiny chills that coursed through her as she realized how close to death she had come.

Home, he had said. How safe and inviting that rough velvet voice made it sound. How it filled her heart with tremulous hope. She didn't care if he lived in a two-room cabin like the MacGavins'. The smaller the better; the more chance she would have of encountering him at unexpected moments, of gaining a foothold in his affections.

Home. She suspected she had imbued that word with more meaning than he'd intended. But she couldn't help herself. And for the present, she had no reason to try.

Rosanne soon recovered from her experience in the barn with her usual resilience, but the incident had left Brant unnerved and on edge, reminding him to be on constant guard against the amoral element that abounded in the woods and posed a greater danger than marauding Indians and wild animals combined. Every mile they traveled carried them deeper into a wilderness where the laws of nature and survival regularly overrode those society had contrived. Every mile they rode made them more dependent on and conscious of each other.

Brant decided he would have to teach Rosanne the

rudiments of shooting. He'd already begun training Tynan to protect her, and he smiled at the sight of the wolfdog trotting alongside his new mistress with his aristocratic muzzle held high. How could anyone conceive of destroying such a dignified creature? How could he refuse Rosanne's plea to take the dog home with them?

Aside from the fact that Tynan's impulsive forays into the foothills tended to lengthen their journey, the dog showed intelligence and an unbounded capacity for devotion. But then Tynan claimed descent from an ancient Celtic breed whose courage and loyalty were legend. The wolfdog was the dog of the nobility, and that, Brant thought wryly, made Tynan a better-suited companion to Rosanne than himself, with his common background. But he and the hound shared an instinctive desire to guard her from harm.

They followed the Great Central Iroquois Trail, which served as the colonial highway. They passed a few scattered hamlets, a flourishing farmstead here and there, an occasional palisaded Indian village on a hilltop. At Rosanne's request they stopped to sample the wild strawberries that grew along the river lowlands, along the fertile banks of the river the Iroquois called Tenonanatche, The River Running Through the Mountains. Frequently the road meandered along an ancient hunting trail, narrow, twisting, plunging into the heart of primeval forest that yet remained untouched, untamed by the centuries and by so-called civilization.

At first the silence unsettled Rosanne as they rode through the living tunnel of lavender-green twilight, flanked on either side by massive-trunked elms, pines, and sugar maples. The cool, resinous fragrance of evergreen forest mingled with the earthy odor of leaf mold and the spicy scent of pine needles crushed beneath the horses' hooves to form a pungent potpourri whose aroma filled the air. Gradually she came to lose her fear of the shadows, sensing that the secrets they held would not hurt her.

"Brant," she said, conscious of the way her voice was

absorbed into the stillness. "It is not at all like England, is it?"

He glanced around thoughtfully. The Old World forests of his memory whispered of a fading magnificence, while the New World wilderness pulsed with the promise of an exciting destiny still unfolding.

"No," he said at length. "It's not. Do you miss it?"

"No." Her voice descended an octave. "Brant, is it my imagination, or is that a wolf's head carved into that tree?"

"That's an hereditary marking. The wolf is the symbol of one of three Mohawk clans."

This was the land of the legendary Hiawatha, sixteenth-century Mohawk sage, prophet, and reformer, whose dream of uniting his people in peace had resulted in the formation of a democratic league that supported its member nations' independence and right to self-rule. This was the land of the Iroquois, the powerful Six Nations who called themselves, *Ongwe-Honwe*, real men—men mightier than all others, who dwelled within a figurative long house that reached from the Hudson River to the shores of Lake Erie. The Mohawks, most feared, most respected nation of the league, protected the eastern door of the symbolic dwelling house; the Senecas, the western.

"The Mohawks—they are friendly toward the English, aren't they, Brant?"

"Yes, though heaven knows why or for how much longer, considering how often we've cheated and deceived them. The French, as it happens, have treated the Indians more humanely on the whole, viewing them not as savages to be eliminated but as souls to be redeemed."

"Fenella told me—she said the Indians were cannibals."

"Not any longer. But in fact, they do believe that torture is a way to honor their enemies."

"What would happen if the Mohawks decided to switch their allegiance to the French?"

"Our scalps would dangle from the belt of some Abnaki brave, I suppose. The Iroquois are our only barrier against attack here on the frontier. The Caughnawaga, cousins of our Mohawks, have already thrown their support to the French."

"You're trying to frighten me."

"Not at all," he said placidly. "But Hemlock Creek is well stockaded, an unlikely target in the event of a raid. Are you having second thoughts? I realize that wilderness living was hardly one of the options for a future which you and your delicately reared friends discussed at tea parties."

There it was again—another caustic reminder that he considered her birthright to be some kind of handicap, as if her entire existence had been devoted to luxurious pursuits! In his way he was as bad as Hugh, who believed that by marrying her he would miraculously assume an aristocratic bloodline.

"You would be surprised by what young ladies really discuss at tea parties, Brant."

"What sorts of things, then? The correct form of address for an earl's toenail, or the proper way to bite into a biscuit?"

She gritted her teeth. "No. Men."

Insulted to learn he still viewed her as something freakish, she kneed her mount and overtook Brant on the trail. Indignation stiffened her spine, indignation and habit ingrained by cruel months of wearing a backboard harness strapped inside her gown at boarding school. As she passed him, she heard him chuckling at her answer, which only heaped fuel on her anger. It was one thing for her to denounce her own lineage, quite another for someone she adored to attack her for it.

"I suppose," she called at him archly over her shoulder, "that your after-supper conversations cover such fascinating topics as the proper way to shovel up sheep dung, or the correct form of address for a broody hen."

"Sometimes they're even more exciting," he said, his eyes gleaming with enjoyment. "Sometimes we spend an entire evening discussing how to lay up a fence. But tell me—I was but a lad when I left England and you've piqued my interest—what sort of men do well-bred young English ladies discuss over their tea?"

"Oh, all sorts. Farmers and lords, rogues and bad-mannered colonials. Young ladies in London are especially fond of discussing colonials."

"In flattering terms, I trust."

"Oh, heavens, no. You see, colonial men are always making such great fools of themselves. Their misdeeds provide us with an endless source of amusement."

"And pleasure?"

"Wha—"

She broke off with an astonished gasp as he rode up beside her and boldly hauled her off her saddle and onto his horse, securing the reins of her mount around his pommel. She clung to him in genuine alarm. "What are you doing, Brant? I shall fall!"

"I won't let you."

He lifted her onto his muscular thighs and wrapped an arm around her waist, nuzzling the back of her neck with his jaw and scraping the silken lobe of her ear with his stubbled cheek. Perhaps it was the primitive isolation of their surroundings, perhaps it was the challenging provocation in her eyes or the saucy bouncing of her breasts as she'd ridden past him; whatever the cause, Brant found himself suddenly seized by an irresistible desire to kiss her pouting mouth, to lay her beneath him on a fragrant bed of pine needles.

His voice, rich and deep with desire, fell into the golden hair spilling loose from its knot. "Be still, my lady, and you'll have another colonial misdeed to relate to your wide-eyed and well-bred acquaintances when you return to London. Think how it would thrill their sheltered souls to hear how you were ravished on horseback—"

"I am not returning to London! Oh, Brant, behave yourself! Stop this . . ."

Her protests faded into a helpless cry as his hand crept up her waist, tauntingly circled her breasts, and gently but firmly closed around her jaw, effectively silencing any further objections. His lips grazed hers, at once rough and gentle, sampled their sweetness, teased and lingered like a hummingbird hovering above an exotic blossom. Staring up dizzily into his face, she caught the glitter of triumphant conquest in his heavy-lidded hazel eyes. Her lips parted. Her mind waged a futile protest against her body's mutinous response; its most alarming symptom was the telltale hammering of her heart, which surely he could hear, or feel, so tightly was he holding her to him. This isn't fair, she thought frantically. I mustn't let him know that he has only to touch me and I melt inside like a spring thaw.

"Brant, d-don't," she whispered, but her words were hollow and betrayed a humiliating lack of conviction. "I'm angry with you. I'm tired of you teasing me about my background."

Gentle humor vibrated in his baritone voice. "Are you tired of my kisses, my angry rose?" His tongue darted into her mouth, igniting a flame in her belly that Rosanne knew from her brief experience would soon blaze throughout her entire body unless she squelched it immediately.

"Brant, listen! The dog is barking! Perhaps we're being followed."

"The stupid creature is barking at me, Rosanne," he said amusedly. "But that was a pretty good ploy."

She forced her head back, feeling his arm tighten about her as if to remind her she couldn't escape without his consent. "He thinks you're hurting me."

Brant grinned down at the dog. "Be quiet, mongrel. You're not supposed to protect her from me. Can't you tell that we're playing?"

"Good boy, Tynan," Rosanne said. "Now put me back on my own horse, Brant. 'Tis uncomfortable riding this way."

"I find it extremely comfortable. In fact—"

Rosanne felt him reach around her for his rifle before she realized he had stopped talking. Craning her neck, she traced the direction of his gaze several yards down the trail toward a scraggly procession of traders and Indians laden with their burdens of blankets, kettles, hunting bundles, and wooden eating utensils.

"I want you to look carefully at those men as we ride

by, Rosanne," he said quietly. "Study each of their faces."

"Who are they?" she whispered.

"Traders on their way to Fort Hunter. Those traveling as far west as Oswego will probably stop to barter at our store."

Several of the trapper-traders recognized Brant and greeted him with gruff invitations to share a jug of diluted rum. Brant declined politely but engaged in deliberately lengthy conversation, admiring bundles of beaver pelts strapped across the underfed string of pack mules. Rosanne examined the copper-skinned faces of the Indians with their tumplines strapped across their foreheads, the traders with their gnarled beards and leathery cheeks.

"I didn't recognize any of them," she said quietly as they left the plodding entourage behind. "Neither did Tynan."

"That's too bad," Brant said. "I'm of a mind to finish what that dog started."

His arms settled around her waist again, not forceful now but protective. Lord, he thought, what a relief it would be to reach Hemlock Creek. There he would be too busy during the day to let her distract him, and if he worked even half as hard as he usually did, he would be too exhausted most nights to do anything more dangerous than dream. It was a hellish way for any healthy man to live, but he suspected she wouldn't last the summer; she would surely leave him before its end. Unless . . . unless he found a way to make her want to stay.

His pulse beating unevenly, he shifted her off his lap. "You had better get back onto your own horse," he said reluctantly. "I don't want to give that randy herd back there any ideas."

Two hours into the morning they rode past the palisaded Fort Hunter, where soldiers were unloading cannon and ammunition from ox-drawn carts. Nearby sprawled the bark long houses of Teantotologo, the Lower Mohawk Castle. Here Indian braves sat in the sunshine repairing fishing nets and elm-bark canoes for starlit journeys on the rivers of the Adirondacks. Squaws tended the ripening fields: hoeing, weeding, and smoking out ground squirrels; praying, while they labored, for the blessings of the Three Sisters: the Spirit of the Beans, the Spirit of Maize, and the Spirit of Squash.

Later that evening they crested a hill and paused to gaze down on the peaceful farming community of Hemlock Creek, which would have been classified as a fort had Hugh not shunned the martial title. Brant's gaze slowly moved past the organized complex of tenants' cabins, ripening fields, and the outbuildings beyond. Enclosed within a vertical-stake stockade were his home, a barn, a smithy, the store and trading post, and a smokehouse. Years of love for this land showed in every orderly acre, and soon he would leave it all behind to begin the same backbreaking process anew on his own tract of wilderness.

Slowly he turned his head and shifted his meditative gaze to Rosanne's face, bewitchingly outlined in silver filaments of moonlight. Despite his cynicism and his disillusionment over his uncle's deceptions, he felt proud of what he'd accomplished here, and unconsciously he had been anticipating her praise. He quelled an eager impulse to ask what her first impression might be. He wanted her reaction to be as spontaneous as always. Hemlock Creek was one of the finest communities in the valley—she could not help noticing that. In fact, if Hugh had kept only a fraction of his promises, Brant might have been tempted to remain on indefinitely.

Rosanne felt his gaze on her face, felt the emotion emanating from his dark eyes. She suddenly thought how painful this moment had to be for him. He had expected to bring home a bride. He had expected to share this view with Martha, perhaps discuss with her on this very spot how many children they intended to have and their plans for the patent on the north side of the river. Tears misted her eyes and temporarily blinded her. She was unable to observe and therefore appreciate the craftsmanship that had gone into the solid two-story oak-timbered house with its gabled roof and enormous stone chimney that released welcoming whorls of grayish smoke into the night. She was unable to see the expectancy in his look.

She ached to tell him how grateful she was that he had helped her, that he'd brought her here to this haven in the wilderness. Her gaze swept past the log stockade to the blockhouse that stood opposite them on a grassy knoll. Hemlock Creek was so much more than she'd dared hope for, but she couldn't admit that now, not when he was obviously struggling to subdue his own emotions. For once she would hold her tongue, respect his mood. She owed him at least that much.

She would be safe here . . . even if she wasn't the woman he wanted.

Brant watched her and waited. Finally he released his breath and glanced away, reluctantly accepting the fact that no praise would be forthcoming. Her uncharacteristic lack of enthusiasm wounded more than his pride. Suddenly he felt a fool. Why had he thought she would look on this place as anything more than a cluster of cabins and cornfields?

Why had he placed so much importance on her reaction? Had he been secretly, foolishly, hoping that she could come to share his dreams? Whatever it was that lovely young ladies from London dreamed about, he doubted bitterly that it included boiling their own soap and entertaining half-naked Indians by the fireside.

"Let us go to the house," he said curtly, kneeing his horse past her. "It's late. Everyone here rises at dawn."

The house, not home. They had an arrangement, not a relationship.

The disappointment in his voice substantiated her fears. He had been in a pleasant enough mood not half an hour earlier. She hadn't said anything since to cause the strange resentment she sensed radiating from him. She hadn't done anything wrong, had she? Unless, of course, he resented her simply because she wasn't Martha van Hoorn. Well, she couldn't help that. Nor would she apologize for it. But all at once, as she followed Brant past the creek from which the community derived its name, a feeling of cold desolation brushed her heart, and she wondered if the painful pattern of loneliness and rejection she had known all her life was about to be repeated.

Peter Ericsson was sick of living like a wild animal. He was tired of hiding out in the hills. He was tired of sleeping on hemlock boughs and stuffing his moccasins with moss to protect his feet.

He laid his head back against the rough bark of a white pine, his legs stretched out before him. His hair, pale as the midnight sun, dripped water onto his shoulders, cold water from the creek where he'd washed out the charcoal and bear grease he used to disguise his fair coloring. He had that sensitive Scandinavian skin that didn't weather the elements well, but his features were clean and chiseled. A shoulder of fresh pork sizzled on the pit in front of him and sent fragrant smoke through the evening woods. Saliva filled his mouth at the savory aroma.

"That pig should be done by now, Luther."

The buckskin-clad man turning the spit glanced over one big shoulder and grunted, the flames from the campfire throwing his ghastly features into relief.

Peter turned his head away in automatic revulsion, crying sharply, "Watch the fire, you idiot! You're burning that sow to cinders."

Mother of God, what a face, he thought, and time had only made it uglier. It was seven years since he and the escaped bond servant had been caught and tortured by Huron Indians during a trapping expedition in New France, seven years since Peter had run the gauntlet and jeering squaws and their children had hacked off Luther's nose and tongue with their blunt, rusty knives. How both men had survived and later managed to escape was a story Peter had tired of bragging about, but he was plainly the more fortunate of the two. The whips and birchbark torches that had descended on his back had left him a mass of scars from his buttocks to his shoulders. Yet the tavern whores he associated with still found him attractive, giving him an evening's pleasure for the same amount of wampum they charged other trappers for an hour.

"I need a woman, Luther," he said idly. "Maybe I should marry another Mohawk squaw, just for the summer." His gray eyes glinted. "God, even that skinny calf you stole is better than you with your slobbering grunts. Just looking at that face curdles my stomach."

He jumped up restlessly, massaging his left knee. He was only twenty-nine, whipcord-lean and agile, but like so many other trappers and *voyageurs*, he had already begun to suffer the first twinges of rheumatism. The incredible physical demands of canoeing, skating, and trapping game winter after winter took its toll on even the hardiest constitution, white and Indian alike.

"I need a woman," he muttered again. "Preferably with golden hair and sweet-smelling skin like the one I almost had in the barn."

Luther's shoulders shook with laughter, and Peter, in a sudden overwhelming rage, unsheathed his knife. He knew why Luther was so amused. He knew a woman like that would rather die than submit to a trapper like Peter Ericsson. He would need fine clothes and pretty manners, a wash with soap and a shave before she'd even grace him with a smile. He needed money, he thought angrily. And spring trapping had been only fair. He'd lost a valuable pack of beaver and lynx pelts negotiating the falls.

"We're going into Albany soon, Luther, to collect the money Conrad Sluyter owes us."

Luther grunted, then shot up from the log that had been his seat as Peter's knife landed with a quivering thud at his heel.

"Pay attention, Luther. That could have been a scalping knife lifting your lovely black locks."

He retrieved the knife, wiped it on his breeches, and edged closer to the fire, his eyes scanning the tree-lined darkness around them. The Mohawks who inhabited this valley were harmless enough for now, but he had vowed he would commit suicide before he would be taken captive again by another savage. God, he was sick of this life.

Money. He needed money again, money to take him back to Sweden. He had stolen a small fortune once, fifteen years before, from the silversmith he'd been indentured to in Philadelphia. His master and mistress had returned home early from church one Sunday and had caught him in the act. Peter had been forced to kill them before he could escape, and he had been murdering for money ever since.

He crouched down before the fire, his gaze leveled above the flames, and motioned to Luther to cut him a chunk of charred meat. He had no definite plans in mind as yet, but he knew he would not spend another winter in the wilderness. Maybe Conrad Sluyter would require his services again. Peter ate rapidly, methodically, his thoughts fading. He could not afford to let his guard down at night. Anyway, he felt confident that something would turn up for him. It always had.

Chapter 16

"It must be the dark. Ye look different than I remember ye, Martha. Of course, that was a few years back. But ye seem prettier, softer, somehow. Have ye put some meat on yer bones, girl? Well, don't be bashful. Give me a hug!"

"I'm not M— Ooof!" The breath whooshed out of Rosanne's lungs as she felt herself pulled from her horse and heartily crushed in the Irishman's embrace.

The Mohawks called Patrick O'Rourke Walking Oak, for he carried two hundred and twenty pounds on a six-feet-three frame, a frame with a torso as thick as a tree trunk and limbs knotted with muscle.

"Ye're not Martha!"

Red cheeked and speechless, Rosanne shook her head as the auburn-haired blacksmith quickly lowered her to the ground.

"Why didn't anyone tell me?"

"I believe she tried," Brant said dryly, swinging down from his own mount. There was an awkward pause, which Brant finally broke with a stilted introduction. If Patrick was embarrassed about his blunder, he was even more astounded that his friend hadn't brought home the bride everyone expected. "Is your wife still awake, Patrick?" Brant asked, moving around the dumbfounded Irishman to lead the two horses to the stables.

"I am here, my friend." A slender young Indian woman walked forward from the front of the house toward the small gathering. She wore a deerskin tunic decorated with dyed-porcupine quills and a necklace of fragrant swamp grasses and bear claws. Her hair fell to her hips, sleek and oiled, a swatch of black satin fastened in a clamshell disk. Her Iroquois name, Deosongwa, translated into English as Deep Spring, but her husband called her, simply and lovingly, Spring.

She smiled at Brant, her eyes warm with welcome. "Did Corlaer Clinton's council approve the gift my father made to you?"

"Not yet, but there's no doubt that it will pass." He turned to Rosanne, quelling the impulse to slip his arm around her waist. "Deep Spring, this is Rosanne Mallory. She'll be staying with us for a while, helping around the house. I would appreciate it if you'd take her inside and have Mrs. Dare give her something to eat."

Rosanne stared into the darkness of the surrounding hills, her throat aching with unshed tears. It was rude, she knew, but it required more effort than she could muster to return the woman's smile. *She'll be staying with us for awhile.* Not forever. For awhile. Until he tired of her or could work out how to send her away. She stepped back stonily as he retrieved her mount's reins and turned to walk the horses to the stable. Am I dismissed? she felt like shouting after him.

"Come," Deep Spring beckoned. "The venison stew is still warm."

What else could she do? Tearing her gaze from Brant, Rosanne called to Tynan and followed the graceful Indian woman into the house, Patrick lagging behind with a perplexed frown. Deep Spring led her into a large, candlelit parlor with a cavernous fieldstone fireplace. Behind it, a narrow wooden staircase climbed to the second floor. Before it, sprawled across the floor on a circular woolen carpet, were two Mohawk braves wearing breechcloths and beaded ankle moccasins. Both had shaven their heads on either side and left strips of bristled hair, scalp locks, as a deliberate challenge to any enemies to try to lift their scalps. Neither looked half as intimidating as the elderly gray-haired housekeeper who sat knitting on the worn Turkey-work upholstered settee, her lips pursed in silent speculation beneath a thin, pointed nose.

Deep Spring made the introductions. Her English was practically faultless; she had worked as a translator for the reverend of Queen Anne's chapel at Fort Hunter years ago. She had met Patrick there, during a smallpox epidemic that had raged through the valley.

Mrs. Dare, without dropping a stitch, gave Rosanne a hesitant smile and Tynan, a definite scowl. Three young people seated in tall, carved chairs at the rectangular pinewood table rose politely from their card game to acknowledge her. All three were Mrs. Dare's grandchildren, she told Rosanne, the offspring of the daughter and son-in-law she had lost to smallpox. Simon, at seventeen, was reed slim and soft-spoken, a passionate aspiring botanist, by the look of the plants and flowers spread across his place at the table in interesting little clumps. Sally and Priscilla were eighteen and nineteen, respectively, strong-looking freckled blondes, the pair of them, who performed the bulk of the household duties with good-natured efficiency. Their smiles of greeting, it seemed, were genuine but plainly curious.

Mrs. Dare snapped at Sally to fetch a bowl of stew, then at Priscilla to run upstairs and prepare a bed. With a shy glance at Rosanne, Simon gathered up his precious collection and excused himself for the night, which left Mrs. Dare on the settee and Deep Spring and Patrick on the floor, talking animatedly to the two braves in their guttural Mohawk tongue.

Rosanne stared down at the bowl of stew Sally placed before her. An hour before she could have devoured a potful. Now she felt too tired, too self-conscious, to force down even a bite. She fished several hunks of venison from the bowl and fed them to Tynan under the table. She felt like an intruder in this house, a beggar who had been let in on a compassionate impulse.

A large hand fell lightly on her shoulder, its strange yet familiar touch sending sparks through her sagging frame.

"Go to bed, Rosanne," Brant said, his own voice weary. "Priscilla is upstairs waiting."

She didn't argue with him. But as she stood up, swaying against the table, she realized that throughout their journey she had been forcing herself not to surrender to the bone-deep exhaustion that suddenly made its existence known, from the numbness of her neck down to the muscle spasms in her calves. She approached the staircase steadily. She couldn't allow herself to wilt now, not in front of all these people whose eyes seemed to be focused on her in judgment, brimming with questions about her relationship with Brant, her place in this house.

Climbing the staircase, she realized that she'd forgotten her portmanteau and that if she didn't braid or at least comb out her hair, it would be a tumble of snarls in the morning. She turned. And then Patrick's voice floated up around her like a thundercloud.

"That's no scullery maid! Who the hell is she?"

She didn't hear Brant's answer, but Patrick's subsequent growled response carried up the staircase with resounding clarity.

"An *aristocrat?* Ye're beggin' for trouble! Christ, I thought we'd agreed we wanted nothing more to do with your uncle. What have we been breakin' our backs for then? Oh, Brant—to bring that girl here. I'm sorry about you and Martha, lad, but ye could've found any other number of girls to console ye. Why her? Why ask for trouble?"

"What the devil was I supposed to do with her?" Brant retorted, his own rich voice raised in anger. "You don't know how miserable Hugh would have—"

"And what will he do to you? Ye shouldn't have gotten involved. It wasn't yer place."

Priscilla appeared at the top of the staircase then, her friendly flow of chatter preventing Rosanne from catching Brant's next response. "I've made your bed. There's an extra blanket in the chest, but I doubt you'll need it. I've put out a clean towel, fresh water in the washbasin, and a bowl for the dog too."

"Thank you, Priscilla," Rosanne said quietly and resumed her ascent, absorbed in her fretful thoughts. Then, on the last step, she heard Patrick's voice again, shaking with resentment, the resentment ingrained by generations of his peasant ancestors who had suffered oppression under the English nobility.

"Shall I melt down the silver candlesticks to make her a fancy chamberpot to piss in? Are we to mince and scrape every time she enters a room?"

Priscilla glanced back with a gasp, her eyes meeting Rosanne's before drifting away in embarrassment.

Rosanne hesitated, torn between pretending she hadn't overheard Patrick and running downstairs to defend herself. Before she could decide which course to take, she was astounded to hear Brant take up the challenge.

"Shut your big, blustering mouth, Patrick. She isn't like that!"

Rosanne could not bear to listen another moment. Lifting her head, she followed Priscilla down the hallway to her room, her portmanteau forgotten—everything, in fact, forgotten except the shock of hearing Brant leap to her defense against his best friend. It seemed there was no end to the trouble she caused him.

Priscilla led her into a simply furnished room that had been rented out to travelers during the early days of the community. Moonlight peeked through the bleached muslin curtains hanging at the small dormer window that looked out onto the wooded hills. A large, brass-hinged teakwood chest sat at the foot of the rope bed. In one corner there was a cherrywood washstand that held a Delft bowl, and a linen towel was draped over a peg beneath. Opposite the door stood a plain pine clothespress.

"The moon is so bright tonight, I forgot to leave you a candle," Priscilla said awkwardly, the lingering aftereffect of Patrick's outburst straining the atmosphere between them. "I'll fetch you one so you can see to put away your clothes."

"There's no need," Rosanne said. "I'm so tired, I shall probably fall asleep the moment you leave."

She was wrong. She was still awake when the moon's radiance faded from the hills and the sky began to lighten. She kept thinking about the hostility her presence had generated between Brant and Patrick, about how Brant had protected her during the past fortnight and of what price he might have to pay for his gallantry. And why—*why* had he brought her here?

Downstairs Brant escaped into the musty clutter of his office and quietly closed the door behind him, wishing it were possible to remain hidden away there until his life straightened itself out. He understood all too well, though, that most of his problems were inescapable and that the bottle of Priscilla's sour-watermelon wine he held in his hand would help but temporarily.

He sighed, moving toward the desk to light the lamp.

She isn't like that.

He uncorked the bottle and drank deeply, coughing at the vinegary fire that burned his esophagus. Why then had he taunted her about her high-born status? Why had he expected her to shed her beguiling sweetness and suddenly show herself to be a spoiled little brat? Had he read too much into her reaction, or absence of it, to his home tonight? It had been late when they arrived. She was exhausted and probably reluctant to comment for fear she might offend him.

He set the bottle down with a grimace. Patrick was right about one thing, he thought tiredly. Rosanne and he should never have crossed paths. He had probably done her more harm than good by bringing her here. If he had any sense at all, he would insist she return to London, even if he paid her passage himself and discreetly entreated his mother to help Rosanne when she arrived there.

"If I had any sense," he muttered.

"Ye'd be drinking my whiskey and getting pleasantly drunk by now."

Brant looked up at the broad figure leaning against the doorjamb. He realized that the offer was as close to an apology as he could expect from Patrick, and he accepted it. "I'll have a dram."

Patrick entered the room, placing a bottle and two small glasses on the desktop. They sipped in enjoyment for several moments, falling back into their usual comfortable camaraderie, and seeking safer ground for conversation.

Brant leaned back in his chair, his eyelids drooping. "Finish telling me what has happened while I was gone. Have you talked with William Johnson about the possibility of a French attack in the valley?"

William Johnson was another Irish landowner and trader who lived on the northern bank of the river, so respectful of and respected by the Mohawks that Governor Clinton continually sought his advice as an Indian authority.

"He thinks we're safe enough here," Patrick said, settling a heavy thigh against the desk. "In his opinion the most vulnerable to attack are those outposts farther northeast, around Saratoga. I agree."

Brant nodded, stroking his jaw. "God, I'm tired."

"Aye. Either so tired or so besotted with your little lady that ye haven't even bothered to ask how the clearing goes on the new tract. I took it upon myself to start." There was no trace of malice in Patrick's voice. "I've a feeling ye'll be moving there sooner than ye intended, unless Hugh calls yer bluff and convinces his cronies on the council not to approve yer grant."

"He won't."

"Aye, well, he'll not take kindly to yer hidin' his woman under yer bedclothes."

Brant lifted his head, his eyes revealing more than he realized. "She is not his woman. And that's not how it is between us."

"No?" Patrick fingered his reddish beard, exhaling a deep sigh. " 'Tis surely not my place to judge ye. Ye stood by me when I married Spring, when half the men in the valley thought me mad for marrying a Mohawk."

"As I recall, the other half thought her mad for marrying you."

Patrick shifted his weight to the floor. "Ye don't suppose the lass heard what I said about her? 'Twas my temper talking."

"Patrick, every living soul within the stockade heard you."

"Maybe I should apologize to her."

Maybe we both should, Brant thought uncomfortably but said instead, to distract himself, "Your mother helped her escape."

"No! How is the sour old hen anyway?"

"As sour as ever," Brant replied, affection in his voice. "And in an odd fashion, loyal to my uncle."

"He'll try to ruin ye when he finds out about the girl," Patrick said, on edge again. "If he doesn't decide ye deserve a fate like Franklin Newhouse. Aye, I heard last week, and wasn't surprised."

"The sheriff said he was murdered by Indians."

"Naturally. The coroner's report for yer death will probably claim the same."

"Come now. Hugh won't go that far. It's Rosanne I'm worried about. He'll want her back."

"And ye'll not give her up? Here, have a splash more whiskey. I think I know the answer."

The house was dark and creaking with the usual nighttime settlings as they mounted the stairs and parted in amiable silence. As Brant approached his room, he looked down the hallway to the closed door at the end; his thoughts centered on the woman asleep behind it. Sweet temptation tugged at him, a beckoning urge to crawl into that comfortable bed beside her, to sleep pressed against her soft curves. Regretfully he stifled the impulse. But she would still be here tomorrow and the next day. As long as he could keep her here at Hemlock Creek, he would remain content to let their relationship follow its natural course.

Chapter 17

Everyone here rises at dawn. . . .
Late morning sunshine poured into the room. Rosanne opened her eyes and remained motionless for countless moments until she remembered why it was so important that she not oversleep. Which she had. She rolled off the bed and flew to the washstand, then danced about pulling on her clothes, her uncombed hair whirling around her shoulders. She was furious at herself. She had still been awake at sunrise, lying in bed listening for someone else in the house to stir. She had wanted to prove herself a willing worker from the start.

Tynan trotting at her heels, she hurried downstairs to the kitchen. It was the largest room in the house, with a double-layered plank floor for insulation, a long trestle table, and a huge brick fireplace in which the embers were never allowed to die. Smoked hams, dried onions, ears of corn, and bunches of herbs hung from the low-raftered ceiling between rows of brightly dyed yarn. Polished pewterware ranged along the stout mantelpiece, and copper-banded barrels of wheaten flour and cornmeal lined an entire wall.

Mrs. Dare was struggling to lift a heavy, blackened kettle onto the fireplace crane. Rosanne bolted forward to help.

"No, don't, girl!" the woman cried. "You'll dirty your dress, and I can manage myself. Oh, you clumsy thing!

You've knocked the bowl of chopped herbs all over my swept floor."

Rosanne hadn't been anywhere near the table, but out of respect for the woman's advanced age, she clamped her mouth shut and stepped away from the fireplace. She winced as she watched the old housekeeper absentmindedly tossing gnarled handful after handful of salt into the beginnings of a soup.

"Shall I chop more herbs, Mrs. Dare?"

"No. I'll use the ones you dropped. Don't tell Deep Spring though. The girl insists any food that falls on the floor must be left for the spirits of the dead. There are corn cakes left over from breakfast if you're hungry. Tea's gone cold in the pot, but you wouldn't want me to go to all the trouble of heating fresh water, I'm sure. Mr. Layton said you were to rest. Damn my soul, did I just add salt or cornmeal to my soup?"

"Salt—quite a lot of it too."

Mrs. Dare looked up with an impatient sigh. "Go and eat, missy. You're addling my brains. And take that cur outside."

"Mrs. Dare, I'd like to help."

"Help me by leaving me in peace. You're only in the way here."

Rosanne surreptitiously prepared a bowl of cold venison stew for the dog and took a corn cake to appease her own hunger. Feeling ill at ease, she wandered through the house and eventually found her way into Brant's office. She knew it was his by the silver-braided hat hanging from the antlers of a stag's head mounted on one of the three walls paneled in bare white oak; bookshelves reached from floor to ceiling of the fourth. A large pine desk dominated the room, littered with ledgers, receipts, sketches of the future settlement, and two dirty glasses smelling faintly of whiskey. Her dusty portmanteau leaned against the desk, next to a big, squarish portrait draped in a linen sheet.

Curiosity overcame her. She raised an edge of the sheet, steeling herself to uncover what she was sure would be Martha's likeness. But it was only an old portrait of an attractive couple—Brant's parents, she imagined, judging by the woman's clear hazel eyes and the man's dark wavy hair, both traits Brant had inherited. The pair in the painting looked at peace with themselves and deeply enamored of each other. She envied them with all her aching heart. Had her parents felt like that once?

I'm prying, she thought, carefully redraping the portrait. She picked up her portmanteau and slipped out of the office, guilt, longing, and uncertainty following her. It wasn't Martha's memory that posed the greatest threat to her and Brant. Something intangible but far more difficult to breach stood between them. Their different backgrounds? Could it be that simple? Perhaps it was merely the unsavory chain of events that had drawn them into the awkward alliance they shared. Their relationship had been enshrouded in shadows from the start. Brant seemed unable to accept her for what she was—hardly surprising, since her own father had had the same difficulty. Was there something wrong with her, some horrible flaw of which she was unaware? Had she made her love for Brant so obvious that it repulsed him, frightened him? Take care, a distant voice from childhood warned her. Her father had abhorred her clinging attachment, her pathetic attempts to please.

Get away from me, you little grub. Your voice grates on my nerves. Lisette, send her outside. I have a headache.

She wiped at her eyes almost guiltily and found her way outside, out of the house where she wanted so desperately to belong and knew she did not. Whatever was wrong between her and Brant demanded greater wisdom to comprehend than she possessed.

She passed the kitchen garden, where Deep Spring, wearing an embroidered deerskin vest, white lace petticoats, and a calamanco skirt, was on her knees, busily weeding. She saw Sally and Priscilla up at the hillside creek; they were stretching freshly washed sheets over sun-warmed boulders and flirting with two traders who had come to do business at the store. Brant was nowhere in sight, and she wondered whether that was deliberate on his part, whether he'd taken to heart Patrick's advice.

"Simon is leaving for Schenectady, Spring!" she heard the Irishman shout from the smithy where he and another man were struggling to shoe an ox, which they had lifted into the air by means of a leather harness. "Do ye want him to pick ye some more black ferns if he finds 'em?"

Everyone here served a function, an essential purpose. Everyone helped hold the community together in his own way, like threads in a tapestry. Except her. She watched Simon amble toward the stable, loaded down with a shot pouch, powder horn, and musket that he didn't look aggressive enough to use. If she were to ride out and never return, no one would miss her. Brant, bad moods and enigmatic motives notwithstanding, was too kindhearted to actually force her to leave, but he would probably react with relief if she took it upon herself to do so.

So she did.

But first she returned to his office to write him a polite note explaining her departure, promising she would repay him one day for the money she already owed him and for the coins she found scattered on his desktop and took with her. She saddled the bay and called Tynan to follow her. The two sentries in the blockhouse, trained to watch only for those entering the stockade, assumed she was riding out after Simon; they noted her leave-taking and thought no more of it. She planned vaguely to go to Schenectady, sell her mother's ring, and seek employment as a chambermaid at an inn. She would still be close enough to Brant to keep hope for them alive in her heart. But she would not be a *nuisance*. If he cared to resume their relationship, he could; but, of course, he would be under no obligation even to contact her. She would not impose her presence on him any longer. It wasn't fair to either of them.

She could not have selected an easier person to follow. Simon proved himself a hopelessly inept woodsman, inattentive and unaware he was being trailed, his interest focused on the wildflowers and wayside plants he frequently dismounted to admire.

Three hours later he stopped at a stream to rest and eat. Rosanne, some distance back, dismounted and crouched behind a blackberry thicket, her insides churning as she watched him devour four chicken legs and half a dozen corn cakes. She considered announcing her presence and asking to ride with him. More important, he might ask her to share his meal.

"Get back here, dog!" she whispered as Tynan suddenly picked up an interesting scent and set off up a grassy slope at a sniffing run. When she turned her attention back to the stream, Simon had disappeared.

She remounted in annoyance and rode along the road, following it until it forked into two wilderness trails. Which way had he gone? Toward the river? Among the countless tracks left by summer traders, how could she distinguish those made by Simon's horse?

She guided her mount onto the path that looked most frequented, a pleasant hunting trail patterned with puddles of sunlight that splashed down through the intertwined branches of hemlock and pine. Riding slowly, she took careful note of a lightning-riven stump, a bear-scratched log, the remnants of a campfire—landmarks, in case she had to return.

By dusk she admitted to herself she was lost, lost in a warren of wildness. She dismounted and quickly began retracing her route, hoping to find her way back to the highway before darkness fell.

In the waning light nothing looked familiar—or reassuring. Oak trees became ogres with gigantic arms outstretched to ensnare her. The ferns brushing her skirts were the feathers of Indians lying in wait. In the murmuring of a brooklet, she heard them discussing how they planned to torture her. Danger lurked behind every rock, in every shadow.

"I will not panic. There is nothing to be afraid of," she said aloud to allay her mounting unease. She stopped and tethered her horse to a sugar-maple sapling so that she could shred the hem of her petticoats. Then she remounted and rode on, leaving a dainty trail of lace behind her.

After twenty minutes she stumbled down a stony hillock and found herself at a wide stream where salt licks had been laid to attract deer. She got down from her horse and stretched out on the bank. After Tynan had lapped his fill of the sweet water, she leaned back on her elbows and studied the stream's course, wondering where it led, whether there was a remote chance that it was the one in over a hundred that could guide her back to the settlement. She was not particularly frightened of spending the night alone in the woods . . . until she realized that she wasn't at all by herself. A feeling of being watched came slowly over her. She glanced across to the opposite bank and noticed a doe, motionless against a stand of elms, its soft large eyes studying her warily until it was startled by a crackling sound from the adjacent underbrush. All at once the creature bounded off into a cover of darkness. Barely a second later, the roar of a musket broke the silence.

Tynan flew to the water's edge, barking wildly at both doe and musket fire. Rosanne sprang to her feet, unable to perceive anything across the water but a fading puff of black smoke. Hunters? Trappers? Indians? Her frightening experience in the MacGavins' barn lay too near the surface of her memory for her to risk flirting with greater peril. She swung around and clambered up the embankment and on up the hillock that seemed ten times steeper now than on the descent. There was no time to rest, even at the crest. Terror spurred her on as she detected loud, splashing footfalls through the stream below.

She ran blindly, her long legs pumping to propel her against the weight of her skirts, her petticoats. Sharp three-cornered rocks pierced the soles of her worn shoes, tridents of agony that stabbed her feet. Her lungs bursting, she slapped away low-hanging hornbeam branches and plunged, to her regret, through a prickly bramble. Droplets of blood erupted over her face and forearms, over every exposed inch of her flesh, or so it felt, not already covered by the reddened bumps of mosquito bites. She stumbled over a sprawling network of roots, her skidding feet annihilating a microcosm of lichen and toadstools. Grabbing a dangling grapevine, she yanked herself upright and swung forward to embrace an elm, only to fly backward into the underbrush as a screech owl swooped down at her head, its golden eyes glowing.

I can't run anymore, she thought frantically, her hands pressed to the jabbing stitch in her side. But she could hear the footsteps gaining on her, could hear the frustrated panting of her pursuer as she continued to elude him. The possibility that he might not be an enemy, that he might even help her if she gave him the chance flitted across her mind. But she was unable to shake off the ugly memory of the doe leaping for its life, barely escaping death from the musket of her pursuer. He still had that firearm, and wilderness wisdom as well. She was alone—except for her hound—and she was acutely aware of her lack of defenses.

She burst into a moon-dappled glade, her bright hair, snarled and studded with twigs, swirling loose from its knot. "Tynan, hurry!" she whispered, unaware that the dog stood waiting patiently behind her. And then the hound growled, his alert ears perceiving the tread of a moccasin-clad foot. She turned again and ran.

Suddenly the ground swung out from under her feet. She felt herself falling, skirts and tattered petticoats billowing out so that she looked like a mushroom as she dropped into a man-made pocket of darkness. She landed with a crash on her rump, sobbing at the crippling pain that traveled up her spinal column. The log covering above her head snapped back into place, showering her upturned face with dirt, leaves, and brown pine needles. She was imprisoned in a dank, dark hole. Oh, God, God, trapped like an animal.

It was a wolf deadfall, a trap dug ten feet into the ground. The air was rank with the odor of fear and humus and wolf urine from a recent captive. She groped along the ground, recoiling as her fingers closed around the mossy skull of a small mammal, a skunk perhaps, that had served as bait. A fungus gnat danced across her cheek. She shuddered, swatting at the darkness, and hit her nose instead. She could not see her fingers in front of her face.

She took several deep breaths, trying to retrieve her wits. She dared not lean back against the walls of the pit for fear a snake would strike at her. Even a harmless black racer would unnerve her in the darkness. No doubt I deserve whatever happens, she thought dolefully. This is probably my punishment for slipping that eel under Mistress Marsh's skirts at school during chapel. She briefly considered digging footholds to climb to freedom but gave up the notion at the realization that she would be unable to push the trapdoor open even if she were to reach it.

Above her Tynan whined and pressed his nose between the logs, his paws scratching frantically in a futile effort to free her. "Fetch Brant!" she cried. "*Find Brant!*"

Moments later she felt the vibration of footfalls above the pit. Horrified, she remembered the man or men chasing her and realized she was utterly at their mercy. The covering was cautiously raised on the supple rawhide straps that were wound around a row of wooden stakes. A face stared down at her, a curious Indian face, the hawkish nose studded with a dangling string of purple beads. Fear jolted through her, rendering her momentarily speechless and immobile. The Indian squatted and leaned over the pit, shaking his head at her predicament, his tufted scalp lock reminding her of a rooster's comb—and she, a worm in the earth, exposed and helpless for the plucking.

He laid down his musket, bending lower to examine her, almost as if she were one of the wonders exhibited on the Boston wharves. No one could save her now, she thought. It was pointless to scream. She didn't even have a weapon to defend herself with.

She reached behind her. "Go away!" she shouted, and hurled the skull at the Indian, missing him by several inches. He jumped back in surprise. Then all at once a birchbark torch flared, and four more faces were gazing down at her, their dark liquid eyes glistening with varying degrees of amusement. They're laughing at me, she thought, fear giving way to indignant disbelief. They're laughing at the stupid white woman who got herself caught in a wolf trap. Then suddenly another face appeared, nearly as darkly hued as the others, certainly more forbidding and frightening in the intensity of the anger it reflected.

"Brant! Oh, thank heaven . . ."

He leaned down into the pit, a muscle twitching in agitation along the edge of his knotted jaw. "My dear Lady Trouble," he said softly, menacingly, "if I left you here alone all night, it would be no less than you deserved. Doubtless you believe me too tenderhearted to close the trapdoor on those big blue eyes." He rocked back onto his haunches, making as if to rise. "The temptation, you see, is not to punish you but to gain the peace of mind knowing that as long as you are down there, you can cause me no further worry. . . ."

Chapter 18

He did not trust himself to continue speaking. He felt utterly incapable of articulating either his relief at finding her unhurt or the anger that had swept over him at discovering she had left the stockade by herself. He was afraid of the tumult of his own thoughts, afraid that the emotions dammed up inside him would finally burst loose in an uncontrollable wave. And heaven help them then.

He hadn't realized until tonight what it would mean to lose her.

He hadn't realized before how much he had come to rely on Rosanne to counteract the cynicism that had begun to corrode his soul.

His deepest fear was manifesting itself: he was fighting to hold her to him when in his heart he knew it would lead to pain. He could not understand what had happened to him since he had met her. It was as though a hobgoblin had crept into his life, torn it into a thousand pieces, and left him struggling to fit them back together. But nothing matched up anymore.

"Damnation," he muttered. "Perhaps I should have jumped into that pitfall myself."

Rosanne, riding behind him, perked up at the sound of his voice. Was he swearing to himself again? How had her intention of making his life easier turned into this dreadful humiliation? He hadn't spoken a syllable to her since that awful moment when she feared he would carry through his threat of leaving her overnight in the pitfall. He had, in fact, lowered the trapdoor and left her alone for another twenty minutes, long enough for the black panic to begin welling up again.

His silence hurt her even as it reawakened an achingly poignant hope inside her. Had he begun to care about her? Was it possible he cared without even realizing it himself? She was exhausted, her imagination was overstimulated, but she felt certain she had seen a look of vulnerability in his eyes as he'd helped lift her from the pitfall.

But when he found her horse, he had roughly hoisted her over the saddle, his face showing no emotion as she winced at the pressure of sitting on her bruised rump. From what she gathered he had recruited a small hunting party of Mohawks to help search for her. Ironically, she now realized she had been running from a young brave who would have led her to safety. She sensed that her thwarted departure from Hemlock Creek had deeply touched Brant. She sensed his coldly controlled fury, his confusion, his reluctant caring. She only wished she knew which emotion would prevail.

Lord, how long had they been riding? Two—perhaps three—hours. His Indian friends had long since gone their separate ways, and she and Brant rode alone. At times she caught herself sliding out of the saddle, half asleep and drugged with fatigue. She had to break the tautening length of silence. She couldn't stand the suspense another moment.

"Are—are we very far from Hemlock Creek?"

At first she thought he hadn't heard her, he took so long to answer. But then she saw his shoulders stiffen beneath his rough linen shirt.

"Far enough."

"Oh. That far."

He glanced at her from the edge of his eye. It was a fairly easy ride back to Hemlock Creek, but she didn't look as though she would last another mile. Besides, he wasn't ready himself to return to Patrick's gloating face and smug "I-told-ye-so."

They made camp in a small clearing sheltered by a ring

of pines, on a slope with a southeastern exposure that would be warmed by the rising sun. Rosanne spread out the blankets Brant flung at her feet. Then she curled up and watched him feed twigs into the fire, until she could no longer keep her eyes open. She was safe. He wouldn't let anything harm her.

His voice lashed out unexpectedly and shook her out of her stupor. "I had no idea you were that desperate to leave me. You didn't have to run away from me. I'm not Hugh. I offered to send you back to London."

She sat up slowly and stared at him, her hair spilling around the edges of the woolen blanket she held clutched to her neck. "I wasn't running away from you, Brant. Not you."

He turned his head, his eyes dark with doubt. "Then what? Why?"

"I—I saw today that I'd become a burden to you. I saw that I don't belong at Hemlock Creek."

"I tried to tell you that before," he said harshly. "I warned you what my life was like. What did you expect, a palace in the wilderness, with crystal chandeliers instead of tallow candles?"

Tears burned behind her eyelids. "Don't," she whispered. "Don't put words in my mouth again. That wasn't what I meant. How could I stay there knowing I'd come not only between you and your uncle but also between you and Patrick?"

He inhaled the smoky night air, wanting to believe her. It was possible, he admitted silently. He might have been so involved in fighting down his own emotions that he'd given her the impression he didn't want her in his life. He teased her often enough about the trouble she caused him. But what did she want? Not to marry him, naturally. Perhaps she had no answers either.

"I can't deny that any affection I had for Hugh died the night I saw what he did to you, Rosanne. But the rift between him and me was already irreparable before you set foot in Boston. As for Patrick—well, I think you'll discover he isn't really such a fool if you give him another chance."

She bit her lip. "Mrs. Dare certainly didn't want me in her kitchen."

"That was my fault. I told her you needed to rest today."

The blanket slipped down to her shoulder, and Brant's eyes followed its descent, followed with concern the crisscross of scratches on her neck and chest. He forced his attention back to the fire, tension twisting the muscles of his neck into knots. He remembered the fear and helpless anger he'd felt when he found her note, and now he groped for the remnants of that anger to rescue him from the sudden flood of desire pounding through him as a drowning man would grope for a raft. Anger, at least, was an emotion he could understand and deal with, unlike the tenderness she summoned inside him. His throat worked as he held back the soft words he wanted to whisper to her. No. That wouldn't do. He wasn't good with words. He wasn't as clever as Hugh. He would sound like a fool, and she would laugh at him, this fairy princess, she would laugh at his clumsy woodsman's attempt to woo her. And that would be more than even he could endure.

"Do you mind telling me what you planned to do once you reached Schenectady?"

"Find a position as a chambermaid at an inn."

"How long do you suppose you'd have lasted, with men pawing and grabbing you every time you turned around?"

"Well, actually, I had—I'd planned to work in a decent place."

"A decent place."

He hurled a green stick into the fire and watched it smoke until his eyes watered. "This is the wilderness, Rosanne," he said fiercely. "A trapper who hasn't seen a woman in months has little interest in decency, for God's sake. Here men take what they want—when they want it and with no thought for the consequences."

"Even you, Brant?"

He got up at that and strode toward her, dropping

smoothly to his knees to grip her forearms and lift her against him roughly, hungrily. His face was savage in the firelight, his eyes burning with raw need above the harshly sculptured planes of his cheekbones. He frightened her then, at that moment; he seemed like a stranger and yet was so dear to her that she could only catch her breath and prepare herself to accept whatever he chose to mete out to her.

"Even me—at times. Oh, God, Rosanne, Rosanne . . ."

His voice was hoarse as he whispered her name repeatedly in a litany of longing, his big hands sliding up her back and plunging through her shimmering hair before he lowered his head to kiss her. He couldn't fight it again tonight. He made no pretense of trying to.

Soft whimpers broke in Rosanne's throat as she parted her lips to his. Her body curved upward into his embrace, opened, arched, clung like a blossoming summer rose to a trellis, clung to his long, muscular torso for support. His hand drifted slowly down her shoulder, down her side to her hips, to mold her to him. Anticipation coursed through her, mingling with the ebb and flow of her emotions, the love she bore him, the pain it caused her to hold that sentiment inside. His mouth moved against hers with tender urgency, every thrust of his tongue intensifying the joyous turmoil within her. His was a kiss that held a burning sweetness, lit beneath the surface by the fires of denial. She sensed the conflict in him again, his reluctance, his need for her, the battle against whatever it was he felt but seemed afraid to face. She was afraid of it too, afraid of this dark bewilderment inside him, a bewilderment that left her heart suspended between rapture and despair. And yet for her there was no choice.

They sank to the blanket, Brant drawing her onto his lap to deepen the kiss, holding her so tightly he knew she could feel his thick arousal, could hear his wildly thudding heartbeat. He was lost in a labyrinth of emotion and sensation and did not want to be found. It was too late now anyway, he thought distantly. Too late . . . It broke inside him like waves thundering on a shore, his hunger for her, this relentless aching to make them one. He felt her fingers slipping beneath his shirt and tracing a shy trail that made his muscles contract with delighted surprise, that sent the blood surging to his head in a heated roar. With a groan, he spilled her down beneath him and began to unlace her gown. Oh, God, what would he have done if something had happened to her tonight?

Rosanne watched his face as he undressed her, watched the play of pleasure in his eyes as his rough yet infinitely sensitive hands bared her flesh in unhurried enjoyment. She loved his hands—erotic, eloquent, as adept at giving pleasure as at honest toil. She felt beautiful beneath their sensual exploration, felt herself flowering beneath their skillful quest. Her gown fell loose. Her lips parted on a low, unbidden moan. She wanted to drag him down on top of her, to feel his body melded to hers again, to welcome the hard, forceful weight of him. Shivers rippled through her at the thought.

"Are you cold?" he asked hoarsely.

"I'm burning, Brant," she whispered. "Burning for you."

He squeezed his eyes shut as if to collect himself. "Oh, Lord, little one," he groaned. Only she could do this to him, he thought. Only she could devastate him with one candid utterance.

He swung away suddenly to tear off his shirt, stood fleetingly to remove his buckskin breeches, his eyes opening to capture hers with hypnotic concentration, not breaking their gaze even when he reached back to bring his rifle and hatchet beside him. He moved with agile animal grace, his superbly conditioned body with its muscular ridges and indentations framed in firelight. Rosanne raised her hands slowly to touch him, to press her palms to his burnished chest, to tease him with her fingertips. She heard him gasp at the unexpectedly intimate contact, as if she had scalded his senses, and then he lay stretched out next to her, his mouth at her throat, his arms closing around her to fit them together, pliant curves to angular frame, so different and yet so compatible. There was no hesitation in him now, she noticed. How could either of them have fought this?

Moonlight silvered their entwined limbs, glistening with ivory radiance in the cleft between Rosanne's breasts as Brant cradled their globular fullness in his palms. His thumbs circled upward, summoning sensation, scaling the stiff little peaks. She could still feel his eyes on her face, could sense him reveling in her response. Slowly his head lowered from her view, his lips tracing downward from her throat in hot, feathery strokes. She felt herself trembling, her heart accelerating in passionate excitement. His mouth fastened around her nipple, and she held her breath in sweet suspense, her eyelids fluttering at the tugging pleasure of it, at the white-hot pleasure that was his tongue streaking across her senses.

"You're so lovely—I still can't believe you're allowing me to touch you," he whispered, rubbing his cheek against the softly swelling underside of her breast. "I can't believe anything as sweet and unspoiled exists in this world . . . in my world."

"Oh, Brant," she cried softly, her fingers sinking, twining in his thick, dark hair. "Please don't be angry at me for what I did. The last thing I want is to cause you trouble. I—I need you—"

"Then let me love you, little temptress." His hands curled around her ribcage and slid sensuously down her spine to form a hammock beneath her buttocks. His mouth brushed hers, a kiss of flame. "Let me love you, Rosanne," he whispered again, and pressed himself inside her, his entry smooth and deep and tempered with rapidly eroding restraint.

"Oh, yes," she breathed. "Oh, yes, yes, please . . ." It did not occur to her to discourage him, to withhold this precious part of herself. Games and guiles did not come to her naturally. But loving this man, aching so desperately to belong to him did. Her doubts faded into delicious nothingness. Thought fled in a rush of wanton surrender. From the moment he began moving inside her, there was only the reality of him, the spark-centered awareness of arousal until her body caught the cadence of his movements, until, at last, her body caught fire.

It was more than an hour later when in the distant darkness a panther screamed, the high-pitched sound echoing across the foothills where the creature prowled. Brant had laid a hunter's hardwood fire, which would burn low but steadily through the night, its ring of golden luminance not quite reaching the two figures lying together on the blanket. Clouds passed across the moon, casting the floor of the timeless forest into shadow. Tynan slept contentedly behind them.

"Stay with me for the summer, Rosanne," Brant whispered. He leaned his head back and smoothed her hair away from her face, his fingers touching a scratch on her chin. "Please."

He sensed her surprise at his request, and he realized suddenly he wasn't sure himself why he wanted her to stay, or how a few months could change anything between them. Was he hesitant to let her go because he felt somehow responsible for what had befallen her, felt ashamed that he had taken advantage of her defenselessness? What difference would another month or so make when it was inevitable that he would lose her? By summer's end he expected his conflicts with Hugh to be resolved, and it would be safer for her to leave then. Or to stay, he thought, his heart tightening.

"Will you stay, Rosanne?"

A bittersweet pain pierced her heart. Only the summer. No mention of marriage this time. He had made the offer before, as she'd suspected, only to absolve the guilt he had suffered over the taking of her virginity. Would he ever feel anything for her deeper than desire? Would he fight against it if he did? She buried her face in the muscular curve of his shoulder, wondering again if it was only her hopeful imagination that made it seem he had become tense in anticipation of her answer, wondering whether her reply mattered more than he was able to admit.

"Yes, Brant," she whispered. "I'll stay."

Chapter 19

By midmorning they reached the small ravine that was Brant's two-mile landmark from Hemlock Creek. A silvery brook splashed down its eastern wall over a natural slate staircase and flowed through the chasm's floor, where it was diverted into a deep, boulder-edged pool. Hemlocks hovered along the edge of the water like a parade of shaggy, benign beasts. Sweet ferns flourished in their underlying shade, their delicate fronds dipping flirtatiously toward the pool's surface. Herbs and wildflowers carpeted the moist banks: swanweed, angel's hair, bright touch-me-nots, and tiny bluets with their starry petals and yellow centers uplifted to the butterflies dancing above them.

As she guided her bay along the path, Rosanne stared down at the water with longing. She had tried unsuccessfully to drag her comb through her hopelessly tangled hair, and she was hot, sweaty, scratched, bruised, and insect-bitten. In her deplorable state, she wished they could return to the house under the cover of nightfall instead of making their entrance at a time when everyone was bound to see them.

"Brant, do you think I—" She cut her sentence short and sighed. He was so uncommunicative and irritable that morning that she decided any tenderness he'd shown her last night was accidental. And so far he had given her no inkling of what he felt about last night. For all she knew he was trying to forget it. Her own feelings always bubbled to the surface, no matter how hard she struggled to suppress them. But Brant's emotions seemed to run as dark and mysterious as the spring that fed the pool below. Oh, that pool . . .

Brant glanced back at her and frowned. How could anyone look so damned appealing despite those big red blotches and scratches and wildly tumbling tresses? Oh, he knew exactly what she was hinting at. A bath. As if he were suppposed to let the settlement go to Hades while he played handmaiden to her Cleopatra.

"Rosanne—"

"Brant," she interrupted with a beguiling smile. "I'll wash your back."

He swore softly. The girl had more brass than a wagonload of gypsies at a fair. Not that he wouldn't enjoy a dip in that pool himself. The Indians believed those particular waters were healing—though not, he doubted wryly, for his particular malady. But they were too near home, and the risk of being seen was very real. He had, after all, a certain position of authority to maintain, even though Rosanne made him feel he lacked control of his own behavior, let alone the actions of an entire community.

"Hurry up," he growled. "I have work to get back to. And be careful going down those rocks. Hold on to the overhanging branches until you reach the bottom."

She slid down from her horse. "Aren't you coming too?"

He dismounted, tethered their horses to a sturdy young pine, and stretched out across the rocky ledge that overlooked the ravine. "I'll keep guard. It's safer."

Rosanne descended the moss-slick staircase to the ravine floor, holding her skirts in one hand and a branch in the other. Disrobing hurriedly, she shook the dust from her clothes and draped them over a boulder that partially sheltered her from Brant's sight. Wondering with a little smile why she bothered with modesty after the events of the previous night, she waited until he turned his head before she slipped into the pool.

It was paradise. The fresh water that lapped around her

shoulders was pure and tingling cold, stinging at first and then soothing to her welts and scratches. Clinging with her toes to the smooth-pebbled bottom and enjoying the feeling of the long water grasses swaying sensuously around her ankles, she closed her eyes, sighed luxuriously, and arched her neck backward to rinse her hair.

All at once a brown muscular arm slipped around her waist, while an agile-fingered hand broke the water's surface with a splash and cupped her breast. Startled, she gasped and twisted around, her eyes flying open.

"Did I frighten you?" Brant was grinning down at her, droplets of water clustering on his thick black lashes, his long hair slicked back seallike over his scalp.

"I thought you were a trout."

"With hands?" He leaned backward into the pool, dragging her between his powerful thighs. Rosanne could feel his manhood rising taut across her loins, a flaming sword pressed to her flesh. Her insides melted. The soles of her feet tingled. Was it her imagination, or was the water heating up around them too?

"Who's keeping guard?"

"Tynan."

She looked up at the dog sitting placidly on the ledge above them. Brant had left his clothing and rifle within arm's reach on a flat-topped boulder. "I thought you had work to do," she whispered impishly.

"Don't remind me of that."

He closed his eyes, concentrating on overcoming the treacherous urges of his body. Lord, she was sweet. She'd looked like a naughty woodland naiad gliding around the pool with her rose-centered breasts skimming the glassy surface. And he'd had to watch her only for several moments to be made achingly aware of his own mortal foibles.

"Brant—" She lowered her head to kiss him. At that first tender touching of their lips, she felt herself dissolving into limpid fire, into the water around them. "Brant," she repeated. "What if—what if I told you that I love you?"

A blush of embarrassment brought warmth to her face. Oh, sweet heaven above, it was out, and she regretted her words immediately! She should have kept her secret, saved it for a time when she was more sure of him. But she could not hold it in another second, the love for him that overflowed her heart. Would her declaration make a difference?

He opened his eyes and stared at her as if she'd shaken him awake from a dream; his body suddenly became rigid, the warm, relaxed muscles hardening into marble. Was she serious? Was she testing her power over him, that considerable power of her femininity?

"Have any other young men ever courted you, Rosanne?"

"No." She dropped her eyes, feeling unbearably vulnerable because of what she'd revealed. He was not pleased, she knew. Not pleased at all.

"Had you ever been kissed before that night in the drawing room with Hugh?"

"No." She shook her head, her chest hurting. She should not have told him. Oh, to be able to take back those words!

"Then how can you be certain that you're in love with me?" He hesitated as if waiting for her to convince him, and when she didn't even try, he continued in the same heavy tone. "I'm the first man you've ever shared intimacies with, little one. How could I help but compare favorably to Hugh? You've been forced to rely on me. It's not as if you had much choice in the matter. Isn't it possible you've mistaken gratitude for love?"

Tynan began to bark. They ignored him.

"It is possible," she said in a tremulous voice. He didn't want to believe her, she thought. He was offering her a way to save face. He really didn't want to be emotionally involved with her. "It is possible, but not—"

He shoved her away from him before she could finish, his head swerving toward the ledge where the dog had been. "Put your clothes on and get behind that boulder!"

"Why—?"

"Do as I tell you!"

She glanced up and noticed that Tynan had disappeared, though she saw no other evidence of anything amiss. Nonetheless, she started for the bank. Before she could reach the edge of the pool, Brant had scaled the ravine, his rifle and clothes in hand, and was running toward a dense tangle of underbrush. There was no room amidst the devastation of her emotions to feel threatened by whatever he'd gone chasing after. She suspected he would welcome even an Indian attack as an excuse to end their conversation. She wrung out her hair and let it hang over her shoulder like a coil of golden hemp. She wanted to sink to the bottom of the pool, melt into her misery, and never, never resurface. Why had he asked her to stay?

Brant's face reflected the grim twist his own thoughts had taken as he sprinted toward the pines. Damnation! All he needed was to be caught bare-assed like some Adamite by one of the tenant farmers' brats. He assumed—he hoped—that was all that had set off the territorial scolding of two blue jays in the grove and the wolfdog's alarmed barking.

He crouched before a blueberry thicket, scowling as he watched the hound whine and circle in agitation. As far as he knew, bears derived no gratification from peeping at naked humans. But someone had been watching them; he felt it in the marrow of his bones. And whoever it was had covered his tracks well. Too well for a child. He touched the ground. The animal tracks were a day old. He dressed quickly.

"Goddamn it," he muttered. He debated spending the rest of the morning combing the woods for at least one identifying clue, but he suddenly remembered he'd left Rosanne alone at the ravine. He straightened up. Then, as he was turning away from the thicket, he stopped dead and raised his face. A warm breeze rippled over him, bringing with it the lingering fumes of a bitter, medicinal scent. Where had he smelled that before? he wondered as he walked back through the pines.

He caught sight of Rosanne struggling to climb the slippery rock staircase, her skirts and petticoats drenched at the hem. Sighing at her stubborn refusal to stay hidden as he'd asked her to, he reached down and hauled her onto the ledge.

"I would have managed it myself," she said haughtily. "I told you to stay below."

She gained her footing, pulling away from him as though he'd touched her with poison ivy. He stared suspiciously at the wetness lingering on her cheeks.

"Are you all right?"

"Of course." She noted with relief that her voice did not betray the pain numbing her heart. At least she had a thread of pride left somewhere inside her.

Brant watched her walk to her horse, the breeze lifting the dampened hem of her gown. Sweet little innocent, he thought wistfully. Friendless in a foreign land, she had been forced to depend on him, and he had turned that trust into a torment for them both. If they'd met under different circumstances, would she have given him a second glance? It was difficult to imagine such an enchanting young woman selecting *him* over some witty young lord who could whisper poetic flatteries in her ear while dancing a faultless minuet. He followed her slowly. Could she love him? No, he dared not believe that. But he wanted to resume their conversation, wanted to hear her shyly whisper those sweet words again, whether untrue or not.

He grinned with rueful humor. She looked so upset with him right now that he decided she probably wished he would drop the subject. That was what he should do as a gentleman, of course, and he would. But only temporarily. The thought of Rosanne falling in love with a hard-bitten farmer like himself was too intriguing not to pursue. In fact, the more he considered it, the more the idea tantalized him.

"Smells like rain," he said conversationally, strolling forward to help her remount. "The Iroquois call July the Month of the Thundershowers. It doesn't help the haying."

He's patronizing me, she thought furiously. Acting as if I'd never mentioned how I felt. Maybe this is his way of telling me that love is out of the question. If that's the case, why will he not admit it outright? Oh, he was so infuriating!

"What were you chasing after?" She didn't care actually, but it provided an excuse to keep the conversation on even ground. She hoped she could stay angry with him for a long time, long enough to recover from the hurt and humiliation of offering her heart to him and having that tender gift thrown right back in her face.

He glanced up at her. "I don't know who it was. Probably one of the boys from Hemlock Creek running away from his father's strap. We desperately need that school Hugh promised to support. It's one of my priorities for the village—a school where white and Indian children can learn there is more to life than hunting or breaking your back at a plough."

Rosanne stared down at her lap. A school, she thought with grudging excitement. She was certainly qualified to teach, and she enjoyed children, but she was not about to offer her services merely to receive another rejection.

Brant's eyes narrowed in disappointment. She did not seem the least bit interested in what he'd said. But why should that surprise him? His life, his goals, were far from thrilling by a high-spirited young girl's standards. Still, he could not help thinking how enjoyable it would be if she could share his vision. Having her to come home to would most assuredly lighten his labors.

"Come. It's almost noon."

"I want no special treatment when we return to the house, Brant. I intend to do my share of work along with everyone else."

He climbed onto his mare. "I gave Mrs. Dare orders that you were to rest a day before you took on any duties. However, if you're that eager to work, I'll have her start you this afternoon."

"Fine."

A few droplets of rain splashed across his bronzed cheekbone, and he brushed them away distractedly, still looking at Rosanne. She had no idea what she was asking for. But one thing was certain: she would have no energy to run away from him again once she became involved in the grueling household routine. How long would she hold up? Damn. Judging by the brat's determination, by the wearing misery he suffered trying to restrain himself when he was around her, he had no doubt he'd be the one to collapse at the end of the summer.

Moments after they rode from the ravine, a light thunderstorm erupted, as if to accentuate the tension between them. But as they passed swiftly through the stockade gates, they were forced to set aside their personal problems. From sentry to bondservant, the entire community of Hemlock Creek was abuzz with fearful speculation. Men, women, and children—Mohawk and white settler alike—had clustered around the small, log-hewn store and trading post. No one seemed to notice the fat, warm raindrops pattering down.

A shriveled gnome of a man, a weather-wizened old trader with a flowing white beard, was holding court before an enthralled audience. He had just traveled down through the Adirondack Mountains and had sighted Abnaki scouts in the foothills above Saratoga.

He couldn't say where. He couldn't say when. But he promised there would be a French-Indian raid somewhere along the frontier before winter. Blood would be spilled, he predicted, and scalps would be taken.

"Does he truly know what he's talking about?" Rosanne whispered.

Brant's face looked distressingly grim. "I don't know. But I've heard that he's never wrong. Come along. We've got work to do."

Within the next week, sentries were doubled; cellars provisioned; extra bullets molded; and muskets cleaned, loaded, and primed. Farmers took turns guarding the fields where their neighbors labored. Children practiced sitting for hours without making a sound. Women threatened to leave their husbands and move to Albany. More than one family along the remote northernmost British outposts had already packed up its belongings and fled south for safety. Stories of past massacres, actual and fabricated, spread up and down the Mohawk Valley to fan the flames of hysteria.

Another fortnight passed. The air was sweetly redolent of freshly mown clover, for haying was well underway, and the farmlands echoed with the slashing of scythes and the pounding of hammers on anvils as farmers paused to beat dents out of their blades. Overactive imaginations still had Indians skulking behind the haycocks in shorn fields, but for the most part, fatalism and fatigue had replaced fear.

Chapter 20

Brant made good his promise to keep Rosanne occupied. She pressed cheese, churned butter, and sanded the pitch-pine floors. She baked. She quilted. She treated rattlesnake bites. She scoured kettles and bleached linen and mended shirts. She whitewashed walls. She carried corn cakes and pitchers of cool, sweet cider to Brant as he chopped wood or helped in the fields with the haying or the oat harvesting.

She grumbled and complained good-naturedly about her duties, along with Sally and Priscilla, and she loved every minute of it.

She felt appreciated for the first time in her memory. True, she was working harder than she ever had, but every task represented a labor of love and brought its quiet reward. She began to believe that she belonged after all. She was accepted. Outwardly, at least, life was simple.

To her chagrin, however, she hadn't been able to stay angry with Brant. How could she ignore him when he stole kisses from her in the woodshed, kisses that turned her bones to water? Oh, she tried; she tried to treat him with casual indifference, but it was difficult not to soften when he bragged to everyone who would listen that she made the most delicious peach dumplings he'd ever tasted. She told herself that since that morning at the ravine, they hadn't had a proper chance to talk again. But she wondered privately whether she was deceiving herself. Perhaps he was deliberately evading the issue. In any event, he'd never spoken at length with her since, and she had never repeated her admission of love.

And the summer was almost over.

She stretched out on the ropebed with a sigh, waves of weariness engulfing her. There was only a sliver of moon that night, and it was so hot that she'd left the window open, the coverlet drawn back. She turned onto her side and listened as Tynan jumped off the bed, his nails clicking against the bare wooden floor. She could hear wolves howling in the nearby hills, and she began to drift off with their lonely dirge lulling her to sleep.

Her eyes snapped open. Tynan had raced across the room and skidded to a halt beneath the window, deep, ominous growls rising from his chest, his legs planted squarely apart.

"Oh, not again tonight." She raised her head from the pillow. "Shut up, you great stupid thing. Those wolves are—"

Fright slammed through her and shocked her into silence. In the large leafy boughs of the oak that stood outside her window, she saw two pairs of dark, glistening eyes staring into the room, eyes embedded in masklike faces. Indian faces, she thought, covered with black war paint. Oh, dear Lord, how had they gotten into the stockade?

She had to warn the others, had to force herself to cross the floor to the door and give the alert. She slithered to the edge of the bed. She dropped silently over the side. Her heart was leaping in her chest like an apoplectic frog. And then, drawn despite her dread, she hazarded another look out the window. A third face moved into the moonlight. Her eyes widened.

Racoons.

The war party was, in actuality, a mother racoon and her two offspring out on a nocturnal jaunt. Rosanne walked to the door, collapsing weakly against it in silent, relieved laughter. She had almost raised an alarm against a family of racoons. She would never have lived it down.

* * *

Brant was unable to sleep. The August air wafting in through the window was unpleasantly heavy, stifling. He imagined it carried the bewitching scent of rosemary soap. Rosanne. He remembered her mouth, how sweet her scarlet lips had tasted. He remembered the satin lushness of her breasts and belly and thighs pressed against his. He remembered the wild ecstasy of sinking inside her to the hilt, of impaling her with his hot passion. She was gentle and caring and giving. She was everything a man could want in a woman, too precious for someone as tired and jaded as he to dream of possessing. But dream of her he did. Every damn night, and it was unbearable.

He heard the wolfdog growling and he grinned into the darkness. "Protect your princess, you noble hound," he whispered. "One of these nights my resolve will weaken and I'll charge into that chamber and really give you something to bark about."

He flopped onto his stomach, groaning at the constrictive heat in his loins. God! He couldn't live like this much longer. He and Rosanne had to come to some resolution of their relationship soon or he'd disintegrate from the strain. Thank the Lord he had plans to occupy his mind and his absorption in the problems of the day-to-day management of Hemlock Creek to beat down the desires of his body.

He'd selected the clearing for his cabin. Now he awaited only the approval of the governor's council, the test of the threat he had made against Hugh. In his mind he'd already girdled the trees, plowed a field, and planted his first crop of corn. Next he'd build his own trading post, and near it a sawmill. He would give first choice of his tracts to the Hemlock Creek farmers who were as disillusioned with Hugh as he was. So far he'd delayed telling them he was leaving, though most had already guessed. He'd lost several friends, made a few enemies. It couldn't be avoided.

Restless, he rose from the bed and pulled on his breeches. He'd do as well to spend his time reviewing the store ledgers as to toss in his bed all night. Patrick had botched the books during his absence, but then they hadn't been kept all that well to begin with. And no matter how much work it took, Brant refused to give Hugh the satisfaction of being able to claim he'd been cheated out of money by his own nephew.

On the other hand, Brant wouldn't bother to deny that he'd taken Rosanne into safekeeping, once Hugh finally realized where she had gone and who had helped her.

I won't let him take her back, he thought vehemently. Hugh would not lay his sordid hands on Rosanne again if he could prevent it.

He opened the door to the hallway, his head snapping around in stunned recognition of the feminine shape tiptoeing toward the stairs. "Rosanne—what the devil?"

"I'm going downstairs to make a cup of sassafras tea," she whispered, then began laughing softly. "I scared myself stupid. There were three racoons in the tree outside my window, and I thought—"

"—they were Indians." He smiled, and drew closer to her, his gaze flickering unwillingly downward to the enticing glimpses of pink and white skin beneath her nightdress, one of Priscilla's cast-offs. He could see her nipples thrusting through the threadbare gauze, like tiny puckered rosebuds. "It's nerves," he said roughly, dragging his eyes upward to a safe focus on the wall. "When Patrick first came here, he shot a coil of rope in the barn because he thought it was a rattlesnake. To this day, he still swears it moved."

"What's all the fuss?"

They both jumped as the subject of their discussion himself crept up beside them, unabashedly naked, a fierce-looking tomahawk in his hand. Deep Spring was standing in the bedchamber doorway behind him, draped in a blanket and armed with a knife and hunting musket.

Brant looked away, his eyes meeting Rosanne's in a shared look of amusement. "It's nothing, Patrick. Go back to sleep."

Rosanne smiled, trying to keep her gaze above Patrick's neck. "I thought I saw Indians in the tree—"

"What Indians? Where?"

"Racoons, Patrick," Brant explained with a smile. "They had climbed the tree outside her window."

There was a creak behind them then, and Mrs. Dare emerged from her room, a peculiar spectacle with her iron-gray hair streaming loose over her frail shoulders and her shrunken frame lost somewhere beneath the folds of her late husband's nightshirt. An ancient blunderbuss was tucked firmly under her arm.

"Is there trouble?" she asked, her eyes moving over Patrick in widening shock.

The Irishman drew back into his own doorway, hastily covering himself with the blanket his wife gave him. "It's all right, Beatrice. Go back to bed, and for God's sake, don't point that relic at anyone."

Mrs. Dare retreated, but not without a reproachful reminder for Rosanne. "We begin candlemaking tomorrow. I shall expect you to rise early to help."

"Yes, Mrs. Dare. I remember."

Several seconds later, Brant and Rosanne were alone again, both feeling self-conscious and embarrassed at having awakened the others. "Would you like a cup of tea?" Rosanne asked him quietly.

"No. But I wouldn't mind a nip of Mrs. Dare's raspberry brandy. Here. Take my arm going down the stairs. Can't afford to have a good servant laid up, can we?"

Inside the kitchen, they sat down opposite each other at the pine trestle table, Brant nearly falling off the bench when his foot brushed Rosanne's bare ankle. The sensation raced through every nerve in his leg and slammed into his groin like a lightning bolt. She looked so sweetly rumpled and defenseless in that old nightdress that he felt ashamed of himself for his predatory urges. Still, they didn't go away.

"You look tired, Brant," she remarked, wondering at his suddenly pained expression. "I'm sorry if I woke you."

"I was awake. We've all been on edge lately." He took a deep breath and tried to converse naturally, as if there were no ferocious battle raging inside him. He hurt with wanting her. "There's always the chance of a raid, even though we're better protected than most. As you go to and from the fields, or out fishing—it always happens the moment you let your guard down." He reached across the table and touched her elbow, his expression becoming serious. "I warned you it wouldn't be easy to adapt to my way of life. Especially for someone of your upbringing."

She stared at him, her jaw setting. She'd had all she could stand of such remarks about her background. She had worked bloody hard to prove herself to him the past month, and that he chose to overlook her efforts made her wonder if perhaps he was deliberately searching for reasons why they didn't belong together. Perhaps it was time to enlighten him. Perhaps it was time to dredge up all the memories of childhood that she'd locked away.

"Exactly what kind of upbringing do you imagine I've had?"

He seemed not to notice the chill edging her voice. "The daughter of an earl? Well, pampered, of course. Sheltered and secure—with servants, I suppose."

"Do you think I felt pampered when I had to mop up my father's drunken vomit because my mother was too disgusted to do it? There were no servants. We couldn't afford them."

"You had a nursemaid—"

"Who stayed with us out of loyalty and who almost went blind sewing to help support the family." Unshed tears thickened her voice as the hurt resentment that had gathered inside her all the years was finally released. "There was no love in our home. Only hatred."

He frowned, growing uneasy at the turn of the conversation. "I understood your father was a wealthy man, that he frequented the same clubs as Hugh . . ."

"When the winnings were good, we lived in a fine townhouse on St. James's Square, but when there were no winnings, as was more often the case, shelter was an ancient half-timbered hovel above a bawdyhouse in a London alley where the sun never shone and rats bred in the stinking laystalls below my window."

"I had no idea," he said slowly. "That first day, when we were riding in the coach to Olivia's house, you sounded bitter toward your father, but I thought it was because you resented having to marry Hugh. My mind was preoccupied with my own problems."

Her lower lip trembled as she went on: "Security was crawling out through broken windows to escape creditors banging at the door and threatening us with debtors' prison. Security was watching my mother sell herself—" She stood up, emotion constricting her chest, her throat. "Hugh said she was a whore. Well, perhaps I didn't want to face the truth. But if she accepted money for her body, she did it because she had to feed her family and couldn't find work—and because she was a passionate woman who craved attention. She felt guilty, I think, guilty that my sister and I had been deprived of our supposedly noble heritage. I know she died believing that she wasn't good enough for my father." She lowered her eyes to the table as she was drawn back into the hurtful memories. "He hated me, hated the sight of me. Claire was older and clever enough to stay out of his way. But I kept after him like a dumb puppy, begging him to love me—"

"You need tell me no more, Rosanne," he said in an anguished voice. "You don't have to give yourself pain in order to convince me of anything—it's unnecessary."

She continued tonelessly. "Your uncle told me I was just like my mother. He said that I had her blood—that I was a whore—"

"Stop it!"

She couldn't stop. The words were wrenched from her secret self, from the sad, lonely child who still dwelt in the shadows of the loving woman she had become.

"I know how my mother felt, Brant. I know now what it is for a woman to feel that she isn't enough, that no matter how hard she tries to prove her worth, she cannot change what she is. All right, I'm an aristocrat, and yes, if you must know, I've even been told I have royal blood somewhere in my background. Well, I won't be ashamed of it anymore. I am not ashamed of giving myself to you either, but I don't think I—I don't think I can bear—"

He swung off the bench and moved around the table to envelop her in his arms, holding her as the tears came, holding her until she had to accept the comfort he ached to offer. "I am the one who should feel ashamed," he whispered. "Please believe I have suffered my share of guilt over what I've done to you. I'm sorry, Rosanne, sorry for any pain I've unwittingly caused you. Forgive me, little one. Forgive me for adding to your hurt with my insensitivity. I can't change what your father did, but I promise that one day Hugh will regret what he said to you. It was a lie, a vicious lie."

The import of his words sank slowly into her consciousness, penetrated her heart with ice-cold comprehension. Was he admitting that he pitied her? Dearest God, did he pity her as if she were some unwanted animal like Tynan that he'd taken under his protection? Pity and desire. What an ugly combination! The humiliation of it almost knocked her to her knees. He was a compassionate man and yet he was being unknowingly cruel. Had she been deluding herself about his feelings after all?

She lifted her face from his chest, pushed his arms away as if they were shackles, and began to back away from him. "We'll both be dead tired in the morning."

"What's the matter?"

She turned her head. "Nothing."

"What did I say? Rosanne—"

He reached out for her again, caught her arm and held it fast. He could feel her withdrawing emotionally, withdrawing beyond his grasp, and it frightened him more than her running away had done. Suddenly she was a stranger, or perhaps he was looking past the lovely, lighthearted girl he thought he knew and seeing the true Rosanne Mallory for the first time, with all her private insecurities and endearing imperfections. And he had never felt closer to her.

"Tell me what's wrong," he said gently, his thumb massaging her arm, his forehead touching hers. "What is it?"

She shook her head as tears threatened to spill anew. "You . . . you feel *sorry* for me. You—you're keeping me here because you feel guilty about . . . about . . ."

"No. Oh, God, no, Rosanne. I wish it were that simple." He sighed, his eyes probing hers. "You're wrong. Whatever I feel for you has nothing to do with pity."

"But you—"

His voice was very low. "I've been thinking about that day in the ravine, when you told me you loved me. I was wondering whether you still felt that way."

Her eyes filled with confusion and uncertainty. Would she ever understand him? But she wouldn't lie. At this point, pride no longer mattered. "I love you, Brant," she said huskily. "I fear I always will."

"You're sure?"

"Oh, yes."

Relief washed over him, relief and a joy so piercingly sweet he trembled with it. It was true. This beautiful, complex creature of girlish naughtiness and womanly mystery loved him. He wouldn't lose her. At a loss for words, he realized he had to show her how he felt. He would give her the home she had never had. She would never feel unwanted again.

"I have to go into Albany tomorrow," he said quietly. "Would you like to come with me? I'll buy you a new gown."

She looked at him as though he were speaking a foreign language. A profound change had taken place inside him; she sensed it, but she was unsure of what it was, or what it meant, or how it would affect her.

"I can't go with you," she said after a long hesitation. "Mrs. Dare needs my help this week. You heard her."

"Next time then." He loosened his grip, his fingers tangling with hers as he drew his arm back to his side. "Go to bed, sweet. We'll talk when I return. You understand, don't you, that this situation is intolerable, that we can't continue this way?"

What did he mean? What in God's name was he trying to tell her? She turned in the doorway to look at him, and the unexpected tenderness on his face was a balm to the bewilderment inside her.

"Be careful while you're gone, Brant," she said impulsively.

"And you stay out of trouble," he returned with mock gruffness. "Don't go wandering off into the woods by yourself." Then, with a slow, intimate smile that made her heartbeat quicken, he added under his breath, "I'll miss you, imp. Wait for me."

Peter Ericsson sat naked in the ennervating humidity of the Indian steamhouse. His eyelids were closed; his thin face was impassive. A compress of tobacco leaves soaked in bear grease and bitternut-hickory oil was wrapped around his left knee. Behind him, dressed only in a deerskin skirt, a *ga-ka-ah*, a Mohawk maiden poured water onto heated stones so that hissing steam rose to the ceiling of the willow-withe hut.

At the moment he was not aware of either his rheumatism or the submissive squaw who would share his bearskin that night. He had just returned from Albany with his final payment from Conrad Sluyter for the tomahawking of Franklin Newhouse. And, also through Sluyter, he had received a request for another murder that would pay him more than he could earn in seven good trapping seasons. He didn't ask the name of his employer. He didn't care. He would have murdered Brant Layton for half the amount he'd been offered.

It would be a challenge. He rarely knew his victims. He rarely remained in the area where he had killed them longer than it took to collect his fee. It was a shame, really, that Layton wouldn't recognize him, would not realize that his murderer was the same man whose jaw he had broken six years ago over Peter's mistreatment of his young Mohawk wife.

Ericsson stirred angrily, his grey eyes darkening to pewter. He could still feel the stunning agony of that sledgehammer fist, as if it had been only days ago that Layton had caught him beating the girl outside the fort. She had refused to return with Peter to their hut after that, choosing to work instead on Layton's settlement, and Ericsson had divorced her shortly afterward. He knew she had later married an Irish blacksmith in a Christian ceremony, but she avoided him whenever he came to trade at the post.

He would have to study Layton's habits, watch him, find more excuses to frequent the settlement. In fact, he had already begun. With a tight smile, he recalled that summer morning a few weeks earlier when he had accidentally stumbled on Layton and his golden-haired companion in the pool. It had been her, the same girl he'd almost had in the barn. Was she Layton's wife, his mistress? Perhaps he'd take her away with him when he left America. He would have enough money for their passage. She looked so much like his sister, as he imagined his sister would have looked had she lived. One way or another, he would have to work her into his plans.

Chapter 21

For three days Rosanne had helped dip candles—hundreds, thousands, millions of them. Even in her sleep she was melting the smelly tallow, tediously threading hemp wicks, withdrawing the slender, cooled tapers from their tin molds. Her hands and the insides of her arms were scalded bright scarlet from being splattered with the hot animal fat.

Mrs. Dare didn't wish to bother with fancy bayberry or other scented candles, which meant that the house would stink of scalded deer suet all winter long.

"Gran is out of her mind," Priscilla had grumbled mutinously. "We're dipping weeks before anyone else in the settlement, and if the damned things melt in the heat, she'll make us do it all over again."

Sally lifted her skirts and dabbed at her perspiring forehead. "When I marry, I'll have a candlemaker come to my house to run beeswax candles into his own molds."

"Then you'd better marry a wealthier man than Garth Hitchcock," her grandmother retorted from behind her. "But in the meantime be grateful you're not hand-dipping, and stop spilling fat on the floor."

Soap making, today's task, had been another nightmare. But at least she'd been able to work outdoors, taking turns with Sally and Priscilla to stir the great black kettle's hideous concoction of grease and wood-ash lye until, with luck and constant attention, it cooked into a mushy soap.

We look, Rosanne decided wryly, like a triad of neophyte witches watching over some foul potion. Inspired by the thought, she grabbed the long wooden ladle just as the soap came to a rolling boil and began to dance around the kettle, cackling: "Double, double, toil and trouble. Fire burn and cauldron bubble."

"What's the matter with her?" Sally whispered to her sister.

"The heat, I think," Priscilla replied. "Rosanne, sit down in the shade."

Sally shook her head. "It looks like an Iroquois ceremonial dance. "Hey, Deep Spring! Come and look at this!"

Rosanne straightened her spine, the ladle swinging to her side. "Haven't either of you two dunderheads ever read *Macbeth*? I'm supposed to be one of the three witches in the cavern."

"I don't know how to read," Priscilla said.

"And if I could, I wouldn't care for a book about three witches chanting over a soap kettle," Sally added scornfully.

Woefully shaking her head at their ignorance, Rosanne left them giggling and wandered over to the orchard where she ate a few ripe peaches and played with Tynan until they were both panting and exhausted. I should have asked Brant to bring back some scented washballs for me so that I do not have to use that dreadful lye soap, she mused as she trudged toward the house.

Brant! Her hands flew to the lopsided knot of hair at the nape of her neck. He was due back from Albany that day, and she looked and smelled as if she belonged in a barnyard. She had to bathe and wash her hair. He was always complimenting her about how clean she smelled. He'd faint dead away if he got a whiff of her now.

Unfortunately, Priscilla had already appropriated the leaky copper-banded tub that had been dragged into the kitchen from the dairy, and Sally, who was being courted by Garth Hitchcock, Hemlock Creek's overseer, was next in line.

"Make them hurry, Mrs. Dare," Rosanne pleaded. "This is urgent."

The elderly woman snorted. "Love's always urgent.

Anyway, a rough cloth and vinegar serves as well as bath. Sponge off at the creek if you're that desperate."

"Honest to God, Grandmother," Sally said. "If she does as you say, she'll either smell like a sallet or have every farmer for miles peering through his cornstalks for a look at her."

Rosanne sighed. She had begged to be treated as an equal, and so she was. "I'll have to go to the pool at the ravine."

"Not alone, you won't, young lady," Mrs. Dare said. "You take Simon to stand guard. Wash that dog of yours while you're there."

Simon welcomed the opportunity to leave the gloomy interior of the trading post and walk with Rosanne through the woods. It was early September, and goldenrod blazed in burnished glory in the fields they left behind. Along the way they admired the shaggy purple asters that had just begun to appear by the wayside. At Simon's insistence, they also examined the mushrooms that had sprouted up in shady places since the last thundershower. There were golden-capped chanterelles nestled among sprawling oak roots. And when he spotted a colony of sticky fawn mushrooms crowded into a rotted tree stump, he took out his knife and began digging them up.

"I'll take these home for supper."

Rosanne watched over his shoulder. "They're not poisonous, are they?"

" 'Course they ain't." He got up, picking leaves from his homespun breeches, and bit a cap from its stem, chewing it with a beatific expression. "See?"

She gave him a skeptical frown. "If you take sick, I'll leave you for the wolves."

They fell into step together, enjoying the coolness of the tree-shaded trail. "Patrick says the wolves get bolder every year," Simon commented. "The settlers are driving them out of the hills."

"That's sad," Rosanne murmured.

Simon stopped and stared at her with renewed respect, his eyes widening. "I think so too, and everyone always makes fun of me when I defend them, but I reckon wolves have as much right to live as people. Anyway, they only worry you when you're wounded."

"So you keep telling me. I hope I never encounter any though, harmless or not."

As soon as they reached the ravine, Simon wandered off to explore the hemlock undergrowth, staying within shouting distance of Rosanne. She stripped down to her chemise and took Tynan into the pool with her, scrubbing them both with the last precious sliver of her rosemary soap. As she leaned backward into the water, her hair fanning about her like wet cornsilk, she daydreamed about Brant, about their reunion and their future, if one existed. Overhead, patches of fading turquoise sky showed through the raggedly connected canopy of pine and hemlock. She didn't care if he bought her a hundred gowns. All she wanted was to see that expression in his eyes again, the tender expression that told her his feelings for her had nothing to do with pity. They'd had over a week apart to mull over their relationship, and while her love for him remained unchanged, she had come to realize that she could not stay at Hemlock Creek, in his house, unless he wanted her enough to make her his wife. She needed that now. She had once thought that she would accept whatever terms he laid down. But she had changed.

And somehow, no matter what happened, she also knew she would survive. At least that was what her mind told her now. It might be another thing entirely to leave Brant, if it came to that. But she would know soon enough where she stood with him, she thought soberly. And in the meantime, her heart hung in the balance, hung and brimmed with a love she believed would follow her into eternity.

"Are you all right, Rosanne?" Simon shouted to her. "Sun's setting. We should start back soon."

"Just let me dry off," she called back.

She dressed and climbed onto the ravine ledge to comb the tangles from her hair. Disgusted with her attempts to groom him, Tynan had taken off after Simon.

She'd almost finished pulling on her white cotton stockings, silently lamenting that they were more holes than fabric, when she heard a commotion in the thicket behind her. She froze. A man's voice, low and taunting, drifted across the still conifer stand and was answered by a weak but angry growl.

She flattened herself against the ledge, squeezing into its large crevice like a salamander, and waited. Brant had warned her that from spring until autumn black bears liked to feast on the berry bushes that edged the forest groves. Although generally harmless to humans unless provoked, a bear was unpredictable.

Twigs popped. Branches splintered, and suddenly a large black bear stumbled into the clearing, panting heavily. A heartbeat later a hunter burst from the thicket, his white-blond hair plastered to his neck in sweat-clumped strands. His shirtfront was stained crimson, and Rosanne wondered how he had the strength to stand, let alone fight so energetically, after losing that much blood.

Unexpectedly the bear swiped a paw at the man's head, missed, and turned, rolling first to the left and circling next to the right in confusion. Dark clots of blood matted its massive, glossy-coated chest. The hunter pivoted gracefully on the balls of his moccasin-clad feet and danced into the animal's path, a hunting knife in one hand, a long, bloodied lance in the other. An expression of malevolent enjoyment gripped his handsome features. He prodded at the bear's belly with his knife and poked the lance through its ears as the beast roared in pain.

"Come on, you big stupid bastard," he taunted softly. "Try to hit me again."

Rosanne's stomach curdled at the hunter's senseless cruelty. Her first impression had been wrong. He hadn't received a scratch, though the bear was bleeding heavily. He was tormenting the animal, torturing it, prolonging its suffering for sport. She scrambled out of her hiding place in red-hot rage. She didn't pause to think. She reacted.

She scooped up a handful of loose rocks and hurled them at the hunter's head. He heard her, for all at once he swerved in her direction, reflexively flinging up a hand to protect his face from the shower of sharp missiles. His gray eyes widened in astonished recognition as they swept over her, and then again in pain as the bear swiped its paw across his shoulder, shredding linen and flesh into bloody strips.

"Jesus!" The hunter gazed down at his shoulder in white-faced shock, then swiftly recovered and drew his lance back for the kill.

But by then the bear had already wheeled and was galloping in Rosanne's direction on its columnar legs, its shaggy pelt rippling. Afraid to move, Rosanne stood helplessly as the beast rolled toward her in pain-induced panic. One razor-sharp swat could kill her instantly or send her crashing to her death on the boulders below. From the side of her eye she saw the hunter raise his lance and aim. Oh, God, don't let him hit me, she prayed. Don't let him miss!

Suddenly the bear swung behind her, as if using her as a shield, and plunged back into the thicket. The pale-haired man lowered his lance with a snarl of disgust, but when he turned his attention back to Rosanne, all traces of anger were wiped from his face. He sheathed his knife and smiled resignedly, touching a hand to his shoulder like a little boy showing a hurt to his mother.

"Why did you throw the rocks at me?" he asked her quietly.

She pressed her hands to her face, sick inside with guilt over what had happened to his shoulder, yet relieved that the bear had managed to escape. Still, because of her interference, this man had been injured, perhaps seriously.

"Let—let me look at your shoulder."

"Happily."

She hurried to his side, her eyes riveted on the blood oozing down his arm. As her fingers carefully peeled away the remnants of his shirt, Peter looked away, his thin lips curling sensuously at the unexpected assault of pleasure upon pain. He couldn't remember when anyone had touched him with so much gentleness. She appeared not to recognize him, but he had visited the trading post twice in the past few weeks hoping to see her, at a time when other traders were moving west. And he had been haunting the ravine like a crow seeking carrion since that day he had watched her in the pool with Layton.

"It looks bad," she said, her feathery brows gathering into a worried frown. "You must come back to the house and let me dress it properly."

He glanced at her, his eyes narrowing. "Won't your husband mind, gentle lady?"

"I'm not married." Now it was Rosanne who looked up, feeling an inexplicable prickle of disquietude as she studied the hunter's face. "Do I know you?"

"My name is Peter Ericsson," he said evenly. "If we'd met before, I would surely have remembered. I'm a trader and trapper by profession. Perhaps you've seen me in passing." He lifted the hand of his wounded arm and lightly touched her wrist. "I don't know what to call you."

"Rosanne M—" She recoiled, breaking their body contact and instinctively withholding her surname. "My name is Rosanne."

"A pretty name. *Ja*, it suits you well. But tell me, Rosanne, why did you interrupt my sport? Bear steaks make good eating."

Angry color blossomed in her cheekbones at the reminder of his cruelty. "It was unnecessary to torment the poor beast. Obviously it was in pain. Why didn't you use a musket and kill it quickly?"

"If an animal is terrified before its death, its meat is exceptionally tender."

She shuddered. "That's terrible. I'm glad the bear got away!"

"In Sweden my father hunted bears and killed them for the entertainment of royalty."

"How barbaric. Any sport that involves cruelty toward animals—bearbaiting, cockfighting—sickens me."

"My mother felt the same." His face hardened around the edges. "Unfortunately, her tenderheartedness did not extend to her own children. When my father fell ill, she ran away from home with my sister and me and indentured us all in exchange for passage to the New World. Then when we put in for water at Bermuda, she and a Spanish sailor jumped ship together. My sister died a week before we reached America. It was a blessing that she didn't have to live through the humiliation of becoming a bondslave." His eyes moved over Rosanne's face, feature by feature, with an intensity she found deeply unsettling. "You look like Kerstin, or as I imagine she might have looked today. She had the same golden hair."

"Hey! What's going on here?"

It was Simon. Suspicious when Rosanne hadn't answered his last call, he had climbed out of the ravine and was rushing toward them, holding his musket awkwardly in one hand and a growling Tynan by the scruff in the other. The dog was straining to get at Peter, his teeth bared ferociously.

"Is this man bothering you, Rosanne?"

She turned, her mouth drawing into a rueful smile. "I'm afraid it was the other way around. Tynan, mind your manners. What's come over you?"

"He smells the bear's blood," Peter said quickly, before Simon could venture an opinion. "He's a hunting dog, isn't he? It's in the breeding."

"Simon, take my badly bred dog home," Rosanne said. "We'll walk behind you."

Simon hesitated, his face dark with distrust. "I'm not leaving you here alone. Gran would have my head on a platter."

"Will you stand here arguing with me while this poor man bleeds to death?" Rosanne asked sharply.

Reluctantly Simon obeyed and started toward the trail, dragging the wolfdog beside him. Rosanne turned back to Peter with an apologetic smile.

"They are both very protective of you," Peter observed. "I can understand why."

She felt another stab of unease and chided herself for her suspicious nature. She was the one who had assaulted the man, who had virtually caused him to be mauled by the bear. He hadn't sought her out. She might not care for his kind of person, but what reason did she have for this feeling of apprehension he aroused inside her?

"We will walk slowly," she said. "It isn't far." They were almost home, she reasoned, and Simon was only a few steps away with his musket. What could possibly happen to her between here and the settlement?

Chapter 22

They proceeded across the clearing, but after only several steps Peter stumbled and clutched her arm, his face twisting in pain. He grunted and pulled back, shaking his head in self-disgust. "I'm sorry, mistress. I felt lightheaded for a moment."

She bit her lip, her gaze following the fresh rivulet of blood trickling down his arm. "Lean on me, Peter. I'm strong enough to support you."

"I couldn't. I might get blood on your gown."

"It's old anyway. I can wash it later." She moved behind him to his right side, the side at which hung his tomahawk and shot pouch, and hooked her arm around his waist. "Now put your arm around my shoulder. Didn't you have a musket with you?"

"I left it in the thicket, but it will be all right. My partner will find it."

He shifted the lance back to his bad arm to accommodate her. As they continued down the trail, he was careful not to burden her with his full weight. He gave no thought to his shoulder. Meeting the girl was worth the pain.

He could feel that she was tiring, that she was trying not to hurt him. He remembered musingly that he, too, had once been trusting, before his mother had sold him and Kerstin to that slobbering Philadelphian merchant and his shrewish wife. Innocence never lasted. Corruption was the way of the world.

"Are you all right, Mr. Ericsson? We've only a little farther to go."

"I'm fine. Tell me if I am too heavy for you."

He glanced back over his shoulder. He'd instructed Luther to stay clear of Hemlock Creek until their work was finished there. One look at that grotesque face would undoubtedly jog Rosanne's memory. He turned his head, his gaze amused. He could see Simon skulking through the trees ahead of them, all big eyes and bony limbs. But it was the dog Peter was worried about. The hound had gotten a taste of his blood in the barn that day, and neither of them had forgotten.

"Just down this path now, Mr. Ericsson."

Peter could see the sturdy blockhouse on the brow of the hill. "Does your family have a farmstead here, Rosanne?"

"Family? No. I—I work for the land manager, the man—"

"Brant Layton?"

"Yes. But how did you know?"

"I trade with him on occasion."

"Yes," Rosanne murmured. "Of course." As they passed through the stockade gates, she watched Simon disappear hurriedly into the store with Tynan, throwing her a last look to make certain she'd returned home unharmed. It occurred to her suddenly that the store was probably where she'd seen Peter Ericsson before, and the thought put her momentarily more at ease.

"The house is this way," she said, noticing again the strange intensity of his stare as he looked around. Unexpectedly then she felt a wave of pity for him. He probably had no one to care for him.

Peter memorized the plan of the farmhouse as Rosanne led him into the kitchen, which was empty and unusually quiet except for the squash-blossom stew Deep Spring had left bubbling gently on the fire for supper. Faintly, from the spinning room behind them, they could hear Mrs. Dare's off-key singing over the humming of her wheel. It would be difficult, Peter thought, to commit a murder within the confines of such a close-knit community.

He turned suddenly. Rosanne was holding out a leather tankard of rum. "Drink this, Mr. Ericsson. For the pain."

"I might not be able to walk out of here after this and the loss of so much blood," he joked weakly.

She tied a muslin apron around her waist, watching him from the tail of her eye. She noticed that his smile seemed strained, as if at conflict with his thoughts. She felt almost as though she'd brought a wild animal into her home. She wasn't quite sure what to expect of him.

"I'll have to stitch your shoulder."

He shrugged, and without speaking further she warmed water to wash the bits of bloodied flesh from his wound. Her face grim with concentration, she stitched the widest gash together with an embroidery needle, then applied a salve of witch hazel, castoreum, and crushed tobacco leaves—the Indians' infection fighter—and finally bound his shoulder with strips of clean gauze. He never flinched, which she privately found odd, for she knew it must have hurt terribly.

She offered him more rum and left him drinking it while she ran upstairs to Brant's room for an old hunting shirt to replace Peter's tattered one. He was finishing a bowl of stew, drinking it from the rim, when she returned to the kitchen. She stood in the doorway and watched him uneasily, the long buttonless shirt hanging over her arm.

Peter set the bowl down hastily and wiped his mouth on the back of his hand. "I was hungry," he said defensively. "And it smelled so good, I couldn't resist—"

She shook her head, "You needn't apologize." She handed him the shirt, turning away to wipe off the table while he put it on. "You'll probably have a bad scar when your shoulder heals, Mr. Ericsson. The gashes weren't as deep as I'd feared, but they were ragged. I'm sorry."

"Didn't you notice my back?"

"No, I—" She stepped back, startled, as he maneuvered around a keg of beer and angled his body to display the ridge upon ridge of puckered flesh that covered his back. She lowered her cloth, her misgivings and sense of propriety swept away in a wave of horror. "My God," she whispered. "What happened to you?"

"I was captured by Hurons on their hunting grounds. Captured and tortured."

"It—it must have been dreadful," she said inadequately. She edged around the keg, now all at once wary of his half-naked nearness, and began busying herself setting out pewterware for supper. Why would he not leave?

"May I call on you again, Rosanne?"

Rosanne dropped the bowl she'd been carrying to the sink to wash. As she knelt to retrieve it from under the bench, pretending not to have heard his request, she saw Brant standing in the doorway. Her surprised gaze traveled up his booted legs and long, buckskin-clad torso to his face. His eyes blazed with unbridled rage.

"What's this man doing in my house?"

She got to her feet, clutching the bowl. Those were not the first words she'd hoped to hear from him after his absence. Of course, she thought distractedly, he probably hadn't expected to walk into the kitchen and find her with a seminaked man either.

"I asked you a question, Rosanne. Who in hell let him in here?"

"I did. A bear attacked him in the woods—partly because of me—and I brought him here to tend his wound."

Brant strode into the kitchen, his furious gaze flashing from Peter and back to her. "Are you finished with him?"

"Yes." She dropped her voice in embarrassment. "Brant, what's come over you? We're always treating traders or farmers in here for one thing or another. This man hasn't done any harm."

"Not that you know of."

He brushed past her with a black scowl and stopped directly in front of Ericsson. "Get out," he ordered coldly. "Get out, you filthy piece of—"

"Oh, really!" Rosanne whispered, aghast.

Peter merely finished pulling on the shirt, nodding in resignation. "All right. Don't quarrel with each other on my account." He picked up his lance and shot pouch and continued in a calm conversational tone, "By the way, Layton, I have some excellent pelts left you might be interested in—beaver, fox—"

"All my business is handled at the trading post," Brant interrupted him brusquely. "Not in my home. You're not welcome here. Have I made that clear?"

"*Ja.* Fine. I understand. I'll bring my pelts down in a few days, but I want a good price. Who is working the post now?"

"Whoever can spare the time at the moment," Brant said tautly.

Peter walked toward the door, pivoting slowly for a final glimpse of Rosanne, who stood watching from the corner in confusion. "*Tack,* mistress. I will see you again soon."

"You will not bother her, Ericsson," Brant called after him in a dangerously low voice. "Not her or any other woman in Hemlock Creek, for that matter. Stay in the hills with the other wolves."

"Well, I never, Brant Layton!" Rosanne exclaimed as soon as she heard Peter leave the house. "That was the rudest display I've ever witnessed."

"It wasn't exactly the kind of homecoming I was looking forward to myself," he said dryly. "Good God, Rosanne, I never dreamed you were such a poor judge of character. Could you not see what kind of man he is?"

"It didn't really matter at the time, Brant. I felt responsible that the bear hurt him. I'd been bathing at the ravine, and he was hunting. I distracted him."

His eyes narrowed. "Oh, I imagine you did. I suppose he had a nice leisurely look at you splashing around in all your naked glory."

"No, he didn't, but think what you will." She clenched her jaw and faced away from him to count out the knives. She couldn't believe the state he was working himself into over nothing. This was not simple jealousy. It was almost as if he held a past grudge against the man. In fact, Brant *had* known Peter's name, had appeared to recognize him instantly.

She turned back toward him. "You know him, don't you? You've clashed with him over something before."

"Yes."

She fingered the sharp edge of a bone-handled knife, curiosity building inside her to know what had happened between the two men that still possessed the power to enrage Brant. "Was it . . . was it over a woman?"

"In a way, yes."

"I see." She returned to the table, banging knives and spoons together in a cacophony of sound.

"I wasn't involved with the woman, Rosanne. He was mistreating her, and I helped her get away from him. That's all."

"Oh?" She shot him a cool glance over her shoulder. "I suppose you could say you did the same for me—helped me to get away from Hugh."

He sighed. "It was entirely different. Would you stop making that damned noise and listen to me?" He stepped around the table and grabbed her hands, drawing her forward so that they stood only inches apart. "I don't want a man like that near you, Rosanne. I don't trust him. Even the other traders avoid him."

"I didn't like him either," she admitted, softening at the concern in his voice. "Still, I could not have left him at the ravine after what happened to him."

"I'd have left him to feed the bear," he said savagely, but then his face relaxed, his eyes darkening with pleasure and drinking in the sight of her as though he'd been away for weeks instead of days. "Come here and let me hold you. I'm in too good a mood to quarrel."

She complied, leaning against him with a frown. "Who was this woman?" she asked hesitantly. "Have I heard of her?"

"I've given her my word that I'd never reveal her name." His voice was gentle but firm. "She's no threat to you, if that's what you're wondering."

He framed her shoulders with his hands and tugged her closer so that she swayed against him like a blade of wheat in the wind. His eyelids drooping pleasurably, he bent his head and kissed her, kissed her with leisurely, sensual languor, kissed her until the sweet agony of his own arousal forced him to tear his mouth free in a breathless groan. His mouth climbed to her earlobe, his teeth tugging gently at the silken pink skin, then skimmed to the delicate curve of her jawline. His hands drifted downward to fondle the rounded swells of her bottom, gathering her into him, against his aching shaft. He had missed her so much over the past four days that it seemed impossible he'd ever considered letting her go. But he was a different man now than he had been then, that cynical stranger who had hidden from his own feelings behind so many carefully structured plans. And it had taken this woman to throw those plans into delightful chaos.

"I finished my business early so that I could hurry back to you," he said huskily.

"Oh, Brant, I miss—"

He leaned into her, capturing her mouth midsentence. Her heart soared. Her blood sang with the incredible joy of being in his arms again. Only now could she admit to herself that she had dreaded his return as much as she'd looked forward to it. She had been so deeply afraid that he would tell her he'd had a chance to rethink their relationship, that he was sorry but she wasn't worth the trouble she was causing him after all. Reality receded as rapture beckoned. She brought her hands up to his shoulders, holding him as if he could anchor her against the waves of sweetly tumultuous sensation that were assailing her.

"Oh, heavens, Brant," she whispered unsteadily as he broke away to draw another breath, to shower her face and throat with a string of adoring little kisses. "I forgot we were in the *kitchen* . . ."

"Umm. Are we? I hadn't noticed. Oh, woman, you smell so sweet . . ."

She shivered and clasped him fiercely as his hands molded the shape of her breasts and pushed them upward, creating a lush haven for his face. "You are in a good mood," she murmured, pressing her lips to his hair.

"I'm happy to be home." He straightened slowly but

did not release her, his eyes seeking hers with intimate warmth. "My grant was approved by the governor's council. Hugh gave in. It's over."

"That easily? I can't believe it."

"And I thought I was the cynic. Aren't you happy for me?"

"Well of course I am, but what about Jacobus Sluyter's lawsuit?"

"He never filed it."

"You saw him?"

He noticed a spot of blood, Ericsson's blood, on her gown and frowned. "I saw his son."

"Oh, Brant, you didn't fight again."

"Not at all. He offered to buy me a drink, congratulated me, and suggested a possible business proposition for shipping future grain crops to the West Indies."

She frowned as she leaned back against the table. She was aware she did not understand the situation as thoroughly as he did. She knew only that she would not trust the Sluyters. But then perhaps men could brawl one day and cordially discuss business the next. Wilderness society was like that: spontaneous, unstructured, adaptable.

"Was there any word of Hugh?" She lowered her voice instinctively, even though everyone in the house now had a rough idea of why Brant had brought her to Hemlock Creek.

"None."

"Doesn't he ever visit his lands?"

"Rarely. He thinks we're all savages who run around naked and live in caves."

She cleared her throat, trying to sound casual and failing. "Did Conrad Sluyter mention anything about Martha?"

He grinned and kissed the tip of her nose. "Who?"

Just then Deep Spring entered the kitchen and walked past them to the hearth, her eyes shining darkly with amusement. "I suppose it's stupid to ask if either of you thought to stir my stew."

They smiled sheepishly in reply.

A few moments later, Mrs. Dare appeared, wrinkling

her long nose disapprovingly at the Indian girl's stew and sneaking a handful of salt into the pot for added flavor. Sally and Priscilla appeared next, discussing pimple and boil remedies, followed by Simon and Tynan. Reluctantly, Brant moved a respectable distance away from Rosanne, slumping over a stool to watch the usual confusion of supper preparations.

"It's like militia day on the common in this kitchen," he said loudly in an effort to be heard over the voices of Deep Spring and Mrs. Dare arguing about how much salt the stew required.

"If you want quiet, go sit in the blockhouse," Deep Spring said over her shoulder.

"And take that dog with you," Mrs. Dare added.

Brant glanced at Rosanne and gave her a lazy personal smile. "We'll leave them all here when we move into the new cabin. I'll build a twelve-foot stockade around us."

Rosanne's heart stopped and then lurched into an erratic tatoo. She set down the trencher of rye bread she had been about to take into the parlor. When *we* move? He had said that, hadn't he? She'd been so caught up in worrying whether their relationship would carry from one day to the next that she had failed to consider how it would change once he left Hemlock Creek. He wanted her with him, but in what capacity? As a combination servant and mistress? Wife? She had to know—soon!

Supper later that evening was a celebration. Two formal announcements were made and toasted: the council's approval of Brant's patent and Sally's engagement to Garth Hitchcock, who arrived promptly at seven to present his newly betrothed with a nosegay of wilted wildflowers. One of Deep Spring's uncles, Little Otter, also appeared, unannounced but, as always, welcome. He had brought Mrs. Dare a live porcupine to roast in the oven, but Simon managed to smuggle the little rodent past the kitchen and free it outside the stockade.

After supper Patrick brought down his long-stemmed pipe from the mantel and filled its bowl with an aromatic blend of tobacco and sumac leaves.

"No more delaying now, Brant, my boy. We'll get your cabin raised by the end of the week. Mine can wait until after the harvest. I hear Lorne MacGavin's offered to help ye with the paneling."

Brant had to force himself to listen; he was watching Rosanne as she cleared the table, picturing her hair released from its primly twisted knot and rippling over her lovely naked body, picturing her beneath him, their flesh joined as one. The little minx knew he wanted her too. Her soft blue eyes sent him wanton messages that scorched the very air between them. Her full-lipped mouth tantalized him with unspoken sensual promises. He tossed a scrap of gristle under the table to Tynan and rubbed the shaggy chest with his foot. Little by little he was winning the hound over to him. Without doubt the dog would come to live in the cabin with his mistress.

"That sounds fine, Patrick," he said absently.

Patrick lit his pipe and looked across the table at Priscilla with his eyebrows arched. "The poor fool's in another world. Someone ought to put him out of his misery."

"Someone ought to put out your miserable pipe," Mrs. Dare said. "It is spoiling the taste of my tea."

"My tobacco smells like attar of roses compared to that stuff ye're always rubbing into your elbows, Beatrice."

"That's your wife's medicine you're insulting. It probably wouldn't work if it didn't smell."

Brant turned back to the table as the usual friendly bantering continued. Mrs. Dare's rheumatism salve—was that what they were arguing over? Bear grease and bitternuthickory oil. By God, that was what he'd smelled at the ravine that day. He had almost put the incident out of his mind. His mouth lifted into a smile. He might have accused his housekeeper of spying on him, but he knew she could never have run fast enough to elude him.

"Are ye back among us now, Brant?" Patrick asked him in an amused voice as he drew on his pipe. "May I have yer attention before she comes back into the room?"

Brant flushed lightly. "Forgive me. I had something else on my mind."

"Aye. We gathered that."

Embarrassed, aware that both Priscilla and Patrick were smirking at him and enjoying his discomfort, Brant deliberately changed the subject. "Albany is still upset over the speech Deep Spring's father gave at the Indian conference. Clinton had hoped for a formal declaration of allegiance from the Iroquois."

Patrick's face clouded. "And why should the people of the Six Nations sacrifice their lives to protect the English when the colonial governors have failed to agree among themselves to raise a militia for the same purpose?"

"That's true," Brant conceded. "Who wishes to pay higher taxes to defend a handful of settlers foolhardy enough to live on the frontier? Why should the Iroquois go to war over us when our own cannot be bothered to defend ourselves?"

A spell of gloomy silence ensued. No one spoke, but everyone felt the same black fear. If the Iroquois would not defend them, the frontier settlers were doomed. Both France and England understood the strategic importance of the Mohawk Valley and its broad river, the waterway that held the key to an empire by providing the only natural access from the Atlantic Ocean to the Great Lakes region and the unexplored west. Control of the Mohawk was, politically, worth a war.

It was Deep Spring, sitting at the fireside with Little Otter, who finally broke the silence. "My uncle has a story for us," she announced. The Iroquois were hailed by the white man as eloquent orators who rivaled the ancient Romans, but they were also master storytellers who, without a written language to record their own history and folklore, took the deepest pleasure in recounting with rich embellishment the tales, passed down from generation to generation, that embodied their chronicles and beliefs. Little Otter was no exception, and his visits always drew everyone to the hearth to listen. As he began to relate his tale in a hypnotic nasal tone, Deep Spring translated the story of a grotesque serpent that had been sent one spring by Tawiskaron, the Creator of Evil, to plague her grandfather's village.

She explained: "The reptile was so wicked that it gorged on the decaying remains of corpses and poisoned every plant, tree, and river it touched. Corn seedlings withered in the ground. Salmon died before they could spawn. Birds perished in their nests. Finally, Ga-ho, the Spirit of the Wind, took pity on the starving people and blew the serpent into a cave where it was unable to escape. But even then it continued to feast on hunters and warriors as they passed by. Within another moon, only old men, squaws, and their children were left to defend their village. And then at last the serpent grew so fat that it burst open, spewing half-digested bodies everywhere.

"Alas, only one brave had survived imprisonment in the serpent's belly. But when he emerged, he possessed great *orenda*, power. He was my brother, Black Snake, and because he fed the remains of the serpent to his hungry people, the village was saved. *Na-ho,* I am done."

Deep Spring had scarcely fallen silent when her husband pulled his chair closer to the hearth and began a long-winded recitation about the adventures of St. Patrick and how he drove all the snakes from Ireland. As soon as he finished, Deep Spring beckoned to Rosanne to leave the table, where she was preparing bowls of blackberry-cornmeal pudding as dessert, and to join the others in front of the fireplace. "Tell us your story of the maiden who was helped by the Spirit of the Pumpkin."

"Spirit of the— Oh, you mean Cinderella." Rosanne smiled and spooned out the last portion of pudding, dousing it with sweet, melting cream. After she had served the bowls, she settled down on the hearth rug between Deep Spring and Little Otter and began to recount her favorite fairy tale.

Brant left the table and sat behind her on the hearthstone, positioning his knees against her shoulders. While she spoke he ate the pudding, savoring each sweet, starchy mouthful because she'd made it especially for him. And when she reached the end of the story, he leaned down to whisper in her ear, "You little witch. You *did* know that drunken rakehell in the yellow carriage on Maiden Lane." And he laughed softly at the memory of the tipsy young man calling Rosanne Cinderella on that bittersweet night last summer.

"Do you remember what else happened that night?" she whispered back with a mischievous grin.

"I could hardly forget."

Priscilla looked up, her spoon arrested in midair. "I think I'd like to hear that story next."

"And I think it's time for bed," Mrs. Dare remarked, rising from the settee. "Simon, you too. Little Otter is already half asleep under his blanket."

"Oh, Gran—"

"Upstairs, boy."

Patrick rose and stretched his thickly muscled arms. "I'm for bed too. Oh, damnation, I forgot. I've got the blasted accounts to tally again. The rents are coming due, and Hugh will send the sheriff after us if we're late. I'll warrant he would love to see us all thrown into gaol."

"I've already taken care of the rents," Brant said. "I'll finish the store accounts tomorrow night. I'm too tired to try to decipher your calculations right now."

Rosanne twisted around on the rug toward him. "I'll do the account books. I'm good at ciphering."

"You?"

"Well, why not?"

"It would help," he said slowly. "No one else has the time, but there is a great deal of work involved."

"I'll begin tonight. Where are the account books?"

Patrick dropped back into his chair. "Spring, take her into the office where the ledgers are kept." Then, as the two women disappeared through the doorway, he leveled a thoughtful glance at Brant. "Ye're worrying me, Brant."

"I can't live without her. I want to marry her."

Brant looked up defiantly, his jaw set. He felt as if a boulder had rolled off his heart. The words had been spoken. All the knotted emotions Rosanne evoked in him were slowly untangling.

"I want to marry her," he repeated in a voice of quiet wonder.

"Aye. I understood ye the first time," Patrick said, relighting his pipe. "So what are ye going to do about it?"

"Ask her at the end of the week, as soon as the cabin's raised. I won't be talked out of it, Patrick."

"I'll not try to. I was wrong about her. I admit it. But I still think you should be concerned about Hugh—" Patrick clamped his mouth shut on his pipe stem as the two women reentered the room.

"Those are last year's books ye've given her, Spring. Oh, hell." He got up again, taking Rosanne by the elbow. "Come with me. I'll find ye the right ones and explain my personal system of accounting at the same time. Ye may as well keep these to refer to." And taking her by the arm, he led her from the room.

Brant glanced up at Deep Spring and frowned. "There is something you should know," he said quietly. "Peter Ericsson—"

"I know. I heard his voice and hid in the dairy room until he left. He is possessed by evil spirits, that one."

Brant's frown deepened. "I warned him against entering the stockade again unless he was trading, and I would not allow him even that except that I know he'd try to make trouble for you merely from spite otherwise. It would be so much easier if you'd tell Patrick the truth."

She shook her head, twisting and untwisting the fringe on her deerskin tunic. "I fear for him. You know what he would do if he learned of Peter's identity, that he was the man who beat me before. My husband has a temper like Heno, God of Thunder. Your people would hang him."

"All I know with certainty is that Patrick would be hurt if he thought you were keeping secrets from him."

They fell silent at the sound of footsteps in the hall. Several moments later, Patrick reappeared in the doorway with Rosanne. "Let's go upstairs, Spring. These two can stay up with the owls if they like."

Brant got up and walked to the door to relieve Rosanne of the heavy account books. "I'll carry these upstairs for you. I know you've been working hard this week. There's no need to start on them tonight."

"I want to. Anyway, I don't feel all that tired."

"Suddenly, neither do I."

Her heart began to knock, and she dropped her gaze self-consciously as he brushed against her in the process of balancing the ledgers. "We need to talk, Rosanne. Alone."

He looked back over his shoulder as Little Otter gave a particularly raucous snore and rolled over with a grunt, pulling the bearskin up over his face so that only his scalp lock showed.

Rosanne could not restrain a giggle. "Is that possible in this house?"

He lifted a brow. "I'm beginning to wonder." He turned back to her, his eyes holding hers captive with unabashed longing. "I'll take you to the cabin the day after the housewarming, show you my land, and explain what I intend to do. We'll talk then. Alone."

"I'd like that, Brant."

They climbed the stairs slowly, reluctant to part company now that they had finally faced the question of commitment. Brant intended to ask her to marry him properly this time, to make up for that miserable morning when his offer had been a self-imposed penance for the sin of seducing her. By the end of the week he'd have taken her to his new home, revealed his private dreams to her, and tendered her his heart, his name and his protection. And, God willing, she would have accepted. They would be married before Hugh could interfere.

"I bought you a gown," he said softly outside her room. "It's in the box on the bed." He followed her into the small chamber and set the books down on a chair, retreating hastily to the door before his self-control gave way completely. Surely he could wait another week, couldn't he?

"Thank you," she whispered. "I do need one." She turned toward him and was struck by how handsome he looked standing there in the doorway with his strong features accentuated by the play of moonlight against shadow. On impulse she moved back to him, laced her arms around his deeply tanned neck, and kissed him. "I love you, Brant."

He smiled, his chest expanding with the sharp breath he drew to slow his racing heart. "I thought about you every minute I was away," he said unevenly. "And if I do not leave this room right now, Mrs. Dare will come in with her blunderbuss and order me out." He kissed her gently on her mouth, her cheeks, her chin, his hands sliding down her sides. "Don't stay up late working on those ledgers."

"Good night," she murmured, leaning against the doorjamb as he released her.

"Good night," he whispered. "I'll probably be gone before you wake up."

For long moments afterward Rosanne stood unmoving, floating in a sweet, golden fog. Finally she roused herself enough to close the door and walk to the washstand. There she splashed tepid water on her face where the imprint of Brant's kisses still burned like tiny firebrands. How on earth could she sleep now? She felt flushed and quivery from her forehead to her knees, as if she'd contracted a malingering ailment for which there was no cure.

Her gaze fell on the large box he'd left on the bed. She opened it, her eyes misting with emotion as she lifted the garment loose from its nest of protective gauze. The gown was an exquisite creation of fawn-colored watered silk, shot through with glinting golden thread. The heavy overskirt, draped back at either side by water-pearl clasps, cascaded to the floor like sunlit waves. A clinging robin's-egg blue gauze underskirt lay beneath. The scallop-shaped neckline dipped low into a bodice stiffened with whalebone and adorned with twisted gold silk buttons. The three-quarter length sleeves were slashed; white lace as fragile as foam spilled from their cuffs.

The gift was gorgeous, and yet it would mean nothing, nothing at all to her without the absolute affection of its giver. Dear heaven, what would she do if Brant did not want her to take a permanent place in his life?

She carefully folded the gown back into the box and undressed for bed. Lighting a candle, she told herself that he cared for her. He had to. She got into bed, and soon her worries were forgotten as she began to devote her attention to the account books. Most business at the trading post was transacted by barter, so she had to struggle to translate Indian payments of pelts, wampum, and ginseng into actual monetary values. Unfortunately, those values fluctuated according to Patrick's overall mood of the particular month, and neither Brant nor the blacksmith had a head for business.

Still, the store turned an undisputed profit. In fact, one of the few agreements Hugh had honored was the one by which Brant was to keep whatever he made in the store above a fixed percentage, and Brant was slowly prospering.

He had arranged to ship his goods to several wilderness outlets as far west as Oswego. He sent his furs and ginseng to England, his flour surplus to the Indies. But he never had enough cash on hand, though his bank account in London was swelling under his father's watchful eye.

She shook her head in admiration. Perhaps she hadn't given him his due after all. He'd worked hard for whatever he had gained, and one day it would pay off handsomely. He had everything in his favor—reasonably priced goods; a prime location near the well-traveled King's Highway; and the goodwill of his customers, both Indian and white—not to mention the tracts of land that he could either rent or sell.

And then her delight in his success faded abruptly as she began leafing through one of the older ledgers. Brant, she realized, transacted the bulk of his business with the renowned house of Bedwell and Mayfield. It was one of the largest mercantile companies in Europe, and the duke of Rydenham was listed as a principal investor. The despised title glared up at her from a year-old receipt that His Grace's secretary had signed in acceptance of a shipment of silver-fox pelts. Had the vain old peacock strutted around London in his furs while his daughter-in-law rotted in a pauper's grave? Another, more recent, entry caught her eye. She slammed the book shut on her goose-quill pen, her eyes dark with all the bitterness her grandfather's memory evoked.

She felt betrayed beyond belief. How could Brant have hidden this from her? Even if he'd been conducting business with the duke since before he had met her, he might have told her of it and offered to deal with a rival company in the future.

She blew out the candle and lay in the darkness, her heart thudding heavily with the painful strokes of her hatred. If Brant cared for her, he would have to end his business association with her grandfather. If he had any consideration at all for her feelings, he would understand how deeply his association with the duke hurt her.

Chapter 23

Brant and his neighbors had the cabin raised in three days. Almost half of Hemlock Creek's tenantry had refused to participate, resenting Brant for abandoning them and for not fulfilling his uncle's promises. They had never met Hugh Layton, but they viewed him much as they did King George, a faraway father figure, too removed from their lives to seem quite real.

Still, with Garth supervising, trees were felled and split into measured logs the first day; a stone foundation was laid and the root cellar put in. On the second, logs were notched, timber crudely framed, a door made, and the roof constructed. The final day's work involved chinking the logs and the chimney and refining the cabin's interior. That same night Brant had a housewarming, but nearly everyone invited was too exhausted to dance. Brant fell asleep with his head on the trestle table in the middle of the feasting. Rosanne spent the entire evening cooking over an open fire.

The following morning Brant and Rosanne forded the Mohawk on horseback and crossed the heavily traveled road to his tract, Simon riding behind on his roan as a reluctant watch. Brant and Rosanne had seen each other only briefly in passing since the afternoon of his return, and he was too exhilarated to sense that something was troubling her.

He had everything he had ever wanted.

Soon he would be independent of Hugh, free to accept complete responsibility for his life. Pride rang in his voice as he showed Rosanne the stream where the sawmill would be built, the hilltop lot where he planned to erect a permanent stone mansion. With the late Indian corn harvest finally in, he could seriously begin girdling trees for his own fields.

It was late afternoon when they rode to the cabin clearing, absorbing the beauty of the autumnal landscape around them. Summer had faded with lingering sweetness, and smoky sunshine filtered down, its soft topaz shafts piercing the forest vaulting. Already the sugar maple leaves touched the peaceful blue sky with flame, while the foliage of the beech glowed like burnt gold against the dark green pines and flamboyant scarlet sycamores.

Brant tethered the horses to a rail behind the woodshed and sent Simon off with Tynan on the pretext of gathering nuts for Mrs. Dare. He intended to be alone with Rosanne inside the cabin.

He closed the heavy wooden shutters, which had slits for firing through should the cabin be attacked. He built a small fire in the stone fireplace—large enough to shelter a cow during a storm if necessary—and led her through the house, finally taking her upstairs to a modest-sized chamber with a built-in Dutch-style alcove bed.

"Well, what do you think?" He sat down inside the wooden boxlike frame, his legs hanging over the edge. "Cozy on a December evening, wouldn't you say?"

"It's perfect," she said quietly.

"I wouldn't go that far, but it'll suit our needs until the hilltop house is finished."

She looked up suddenly and stared at him, unable to hold back the questions that sprang to her lips. "And what exactly are those needs, Brant? What am I to you? Where do I fit into your future? I have to know. I can't stand not knowing anymore."

"Come here."

"No, no. I don't want you to touch me. I—I want to talk."

"Come here, Rosanne." His voice beckoned her with its deeply tender tones. "You haven't told me whether you liked the gown."

She drifted toward him like a sleepwalker caught between a dream and wakefulness. Oh, God, she was frightened, so fearful of what he would say next.

"It—it was lovely." She stopped herself from melting into his arms. If he touched her now, she would lose her control, and it was the wrong time. She could no longer pretend that the future didn't matter. She had to face the truth, to draw it out of him. *She had to know*.

"Please, Brant," she whispered, her face painfully earnest. "Don't try to change the subject."

"The seamstress assured me it was appropriate for a wedding. Of course, I don't know how fashionable it is. All those dresses look the same to me. Did it fit?"

"Yes, it—" Her eyes opened wide as his words filtered through her fears. "What are you saying?"

He smiled tremulously and reached out to take her hand, interlacing her fingers with his. "I want you to become my wife, Rosanne. Please don't say no again. Please."

Joy washed over her like a summer sunrise. She searched his face, searched every shadowed hollow, every copper-hued plane. He was obviously in an anguish of waiting for her answer; his expression was endearingly miserable at having put his heart in her hands. "Are you sure, Brant? Is it for the right reason this time?"

"You're making this very difficult for me," he said. "But if there's one thing I'm sure of, it is that I don't want to live without you." He drew her between his legs, gazing up at her with passionate adoration in his eyes. "I'm so afraid you'll come to your senses and realize you're too good for me. You deserve a mansion and servants, and all I can offer you now is a log cabin and endless drudgery. And my devotion . . . I promise you that."

"I'd be proud to be your wife," she whispered, her throat unbearably tight. "I've never wanted anything more . . ."

He pulled her down on top of him, falling backward onto the jacket he'd laid beneath him and closing his arms firmly around her waist. "My wife and the mother of my children," he murmured. "Lorne MacGavin is making a cradle for us. I want that so much, Rosanne, a home and sons and daughters. Oh, Rosanne, I want you so much . . ."

She closed her eyes and sank down beside him, feeling his hands and mouth moving over her with feverish urgency. He hadn't told her he loved her, and the realization touched off a bittersweet ache inside her. Were the words that difficult for him to say? Was it possible he would never come to feel as deeply for her as she did for him?

It was almost dusk when they reemerged from the cabin, hanging back in the doorway for a final lingering kiss. Simon sat waiting for them outside the woodshed, his embarrassed silence hinting that he suspected what had occupied their afternoon and hadn't wanted to interrupt.

"Do us a favor, lad, and bring the horses around," Brant called out to Simon. Then he placed his arms around Rosanne's waist and held her possessively, his heart swelling with the proud knowledge that she had agreed to become his wife.

Rosanne leaned her head back and smiled at him, the warmth of her happiness radiating out from within her. Soon this simple little clearing would be her home, their home. She pictured herself running after children and chickens, planting a vegetable garden and some flowers. "I want some of those seeds imported from England that we carry in the store. And lilac bushes—I want to plant them behind the kitchen. And we'll need—"

She stopped abruptly, feeling as if someone had punched her in the stomach. Her own mention of the store had brought back—the image of a page in an account ledger. Swept along in the joy of the afternoon, she'd managed to forget the disturbing secret she had recently uncovered. But it had been festering inside her for days, and she was convinced that only by confronting Brant with it could she check its growth. Besides, it was probably a mistake. She would learn that he didn't realize he was dealing with her grandfather.

"Brant, there's something I must speak to you about."

"Wait until the ride back, sweet. I told Patrick we'd be home by sunset, and there's a ladder leaning against the side of the cabin that I should put behind the woodshed."

"There's a tankard up on the roof, too," she noted distractedly. "A silver one, at that. You should have warned the men to be more careful."

"My dear," he said teasingly, "should you not wait until after the wedding to start scolding?"

"I am not scolding. I never realized how wasteful you were until I began doing your accounts."

"I can afford one silver tankard," he said offhandedly as he started up the ladder.

"That isn't the point." She frowned, watching him climb onto the roof. "It's the accounts I need to discuss with you, Brant." When he didn't respond, preoccupied with reexamining the long, hand-riven shakes lashed by poles onto the purlin ends with rope, she moved halfway up the ladder so that she could see him. "Are you listening to me?"

"No, I'm not." He glanced back at her with a scowl of displeasure. "Climb down before you fall. Wait for me inside the cabin."

"Brant, you're doing business with the firm of Bedwell and Mayfield."

"Well, what of it? My father recommended them. He handles all my transactions abroad. I trust his judgment."

"I don't think you understand what I'm trying to tell you. Indirectly, you are dealing with my grandfather."

"Am I? Should we expect a wedding present from him then? You know, to make up for the dowry I'm not getting." He was running his hands over the shaggy-looking shakes, admiring them, she thought in annoyance, with much the same absorption that he did her when they made love. "Well, the roof's not perfect, but it should keep us dry for the winter, if not safe from flaming arrows. If we were to live here longer, I'd have used green swamp-cedar shingles. They're more resistant to decay and splitting. I'm putting a lead roof on the hilltop house."

"What for?" she asked tartly. "You already have a lead head. I don't think a cannonball could penetrate it."

He looked up abruptly, sure he hadn't heard her properly, and his eyes widened at the unmistakable blaze of anger on her face. "Rosanne?" He crawled across the roof toward her, but she turned her head to the side. "Rosanne, is it really that important? Can it not wait until I'm off the damned roof?"

She swung her head around then, her eyes flashing. "It may not matter to you, but I find it difficult to sleep at night knowing that I'm helping to swell the coffers of the man responsible for ruining my mother's life."

"And it may not matter to you, but I get little sleep myself when I'm worrying about how I'll pay my debts." He reached backward across the roof for the tankard. "Aaah— Hell and damnation!" He jerked his hand up into the air with a yelp of pain, a long splinter protruding from beneath his thumbnail. "That should make you feel better," he said through his teeth. "My thumb will probably become infected and swell up like a pig's bladder, and I won't be able to make out any receipts, for your grandfather or anyone else!"

"Oh . . . why don't you sit on your thumb, you big infant!"

He yanked out the sliver and clamped his fingers around his thumb, his voice a menacing rumble. "Impertinence is bad enough in one's servant, but I'll be damned if I'll tolerate it in a wife."

"I am not your wife yet!"

He slid down toward her, his face flushed. "Just see if that stops me from paddling your butt."

"Don't you dare!"

She retreated several steps down the ladder, groping for an effective insult to shake him out of his callous indifference. "You—you sound just like your uncle. All you care about is money!"

"And you sound like a spoiled little brat!"

"Go back to Martha then."

From the corner of his eye Brant noticed Simon sneaking back toward the woodshed to wait out the quarrel. Glaring at Rosanne, Brant leaned forward and dropped his voice to its deepest pitch. "I don't want Martha, I want you, though at the moment I honestly can't remember why."

"Oh, I can," she said wickedly. "She wouldn't have you."

"You've gone too far," he said, swinging over the poles. "You'd better make it to your mount before I—"

He stopped and looked up, warned by some instinct. Something was wrong. He sensed it.

"What is it?" Rosanne whispered, twisting her neck to look behind her.

"I—"

A musket shot exploded suddenly from the thicket across the clearing, and a lead ball whistled over Brant's head. Acting on reflex, he flattened himself against the roof. His gaze swerved to Rosanne, and he scanned her white, startled face for some reassurance that she hadn't been hit. Standing upright on the ladder with her back exposed, she presented an excellent target for whoever had fired at them. He heard a noise from the woodshed and prayed it was Simon cocking his musket and not someone sneaking up from the other side to attack.

"Get down, Rosanne," he whispered urgently. "My rifle is sitting under the ladder. Grab it and make a run for the kitchen door."

"I—I don't want to leave you alone up here, Brant," she said, her voice a strangled wisp of sound. "And I th-think my skirts are snagged on the ladder."

"Work them free!"

His insides knotted; his eyes raked the thicket, looking for movement. He decided he couldn't wait for her to descend to safety. He could not allow whoever was hiding out there time to reload. Then all at once another musket boomed, the ball ricocheting off the chimney in a spray of clay, moss, and fieldstone. There had to be at least two of them.

"I've gotten them loose," she whispered. "'Oh, dear God—Brant, be careful—"

Jumping up suddenly to attract attention to himself and away from her, he shouted: "Simon, cover Rosanne when she runs!"

But before she could descend even another rung, he perceived a faint metallic flash in the twilight mist of the thicket. His only thought to spare her life, he dove blindly from the roof, pulling Rosanne and the ladder with him in a perpendicular crash toward the ground. Above them a tomahawk soared straight for the roof, revolving in the air as it hurtled with enough force to split a man's skull. Rosanne screamed shrilly, her mind not even registering the fact that Brant had already dropped out of the blade's deadly range.

Brant landed first and managed to lunge upward to break her fall as she toppled back, pinning them both beneath the ladder. Agony twisted through his kneecap as he kicked out with his right leg to free them. Gritting his teeth against the pain, he yanked her inert figure into his arms and rolled them both toward the cabin wall.

Dimly, he heard Simon fire a shot into the thicket; then there was a soft shuffling noise but nothing else. He glanced upward, his eyes narrowing as they lit on the tomahawk embedded in the gigantic old oak he'd left standing behind the cabin for summer shade. Whoever had thrown that blade had waited until he was completely defenseless, presenting a perfect target as he argued like a damned idiot on the rooftop.

"Rosanne?"

Relief rippled through him, mingling with his steadily mounting pain, as he felt her stir and heard her dazed groan. He groped behind him for his rifle, his eyes riveted on the thicket. Nothing. Not a sound. Not a shadow. Simon's musket fire had frightened them off.

"Are you all right, Simon?"

"Yes," the boy shouted back to him through the narrow

opening he'd left between the door of the woodshed and the doorpost, his voice wavering. "Are they gone?"

"I think so."

Brant sat up cautiously, taking Rosanne's chin between his thumb and forefinger to examine her face for evidence of shock or injury. "I'm sorry I had to push you so hard. Are you hurt anywhere?"

"My shoulder is a little sore," she replied, her eyes drifting past him and upward in slow hypnotic horror to the oak. "My God, Brant . . ."

"Go into the cabin and stay there until I tell you to come out," he said harshly, spilling her to the ground. "Go!"

She scrambled to her knees and then turned to pluck at his jacket, filled with fear as she realized he intended to go after whoever had attacked them. "Let them go, Brant! Simon, come here!"

Simon bolted from the woodshed in a running crouch with the musket at the crook of his arm and Tynan at his heels. "What's the matter?" he asked anxiously. "Are you shot, Rosanne?"

"No, she's not been shot," Brant snapped. "Just get her into the cabin and keep her there, would you? Sweet Jesus, what a pair of imbeciles." He stood up holding his rifle and wheeled disgustedly, only to come to an abrupt stop after four steps because of the excruciating pain radiating from his knee.

"Brant!" Rosanne surged to her feet to steady him as he circled and swayed like a wooden top.

He motioned her away. His face was strained with pain and embarrassment as he limped to the cabin to lean against the door. "Tracks, Simon," he said impatiently. "Light a torch and at least try to make out their tracks so that we have something by which to identify them."

"You want me to go out there alone?"

"No. Take Tynan if you think you'll get lonely. Goddamn boy, don't stand there waiting for the stars to come out!"

Rosanne came up beside Brant and pressed the back of

her hand to his forehead, encountering the cold droplets of perspiration that had broken out near his hairline. "Perhaps it would be better if we waited until morning," she said. "We should have a doctor examine your leg."

He moved past her and stared into the shadows of the dusky landscape that sloped away from the clearing and then climbed into the encroaching hills. "The doctor can wait. The tracks can't. Not this time."

Chapter 24

Jonathan Crane was not an orthodox eighteenth-century physician. At thirty-six, he had abandoned his thriving practice in Sussex, England, to come to the Mohawk Valley to study Iroquois herbalism. His former colleagues in the Royal College of Physicians had laughed at his intention to add to the *London Pharmacopoeia* the heathen remedies he was sure he would discover. But they had also laughed at his uncle, Sir Geoffrey Crane, two decades earlier, when the elderly physician had joined forces with Lady Mary Wortley Montagu to fight for the Turkish method of inoculation against smallpox to be tried on Newgate prisoners. Although the controversial experiment had been a success, the College of Physicians still remained skeptical.

But Jonathan himself had stopped caring about what his peers thought of him the first time he saw proof of an Indian wound resisting gangrene that would have killed a patient in a European hospital. Deaths during childbirth were rare among Iroquois women. He wanted to know why. And he was not without his supporters abroad, rich and liberal-minded patrons of science who encouraged him by funding his studies.

"As far as I can tell the patella is not fractured," he pronounced after a lengthy examination of Brant's kneecap. "Of course in these cases it is impossible to be certain. Cold-water hemlock poultices will reduce the swelling." His golden brown hair, glinting in the candlelight, was swept back carelessly into a queue with a frayed black velvet ribbon added almost as an afterthought. "Who will be tending you, Layton?"

"I will." Rosanne moved out from behind the settee where Brant had resentfully and rudely submitted to the examination.

Crane's intelligent green eyes swept over her from head to ankles in a swift, decidedly unmedical assessment. Then, frowning, he dropped his gaze to the bag at his side. "Sit down beside me, mistress. I'll show you how to bandage him. Deep Spring knows how to make the poultices."

Brant lifted his injured leg from the footstool and against the settee. "I don't need a bandage."

"Keep your leg up, man." Crane, his lips compressed in a thin line of impatience, forced Brant's leg back toward him with an expert yank worthy of a farrier shoeing a stubborn horse. "Not too tight now, mistress," he instructed Rosanne; he had placed the gauze bandage in her hand and was now guiding both hand and gauze around Brant's knee. "Above the joint first. That's it."

"How long will it take to heal, Doctor?" she asked.

"A matter of weeks, if the bone isn't chipped and he gives the damaged ligaments a chance to rest."

"I don't know that he'll do that," she said, glancing up at Brant. "He's not the type to sit about idle. Or to follow advice."

Crane nodded. "I've noticed that. He has a head like a block of wood."

"Like lead," she corrected.

"I could bleed him if you'd like."

"Would it help, Doctor?"

"His knee? Probably not. His hard-boiled head? Perhaps."

Brant leaned down between them, not a bit amused that they were enjoying an intimate tête-à-tête at his expense. "Hear me, you posy-picking mountebank—I am not paying you an exorbitant fee to demean me."

"I understand you've land available for farming," the

physician said conversationally in a deft change of subject. "I might be interested."

"You?" Brant eased himself back with a scoffing laugh. He and Crane had known each other long enough to feel free to trade insults. "Preserve those lily-white hands for your lancet. Farming's hard work, Doctor. How would you find time to practice your quackery?"

"I think a doctor would be a wonderful asset to the community," Rosanne said enthusiastically, ignoring Brant's remarks.

Crane gave her one of his rare smiles, a smile that changed his eyes to a lambent emerald and made his otherwise craggy face quite attractive. "Thank you, mistress. Now, do you think you can manage to keep the patient off his feet until my next visit?"

"Probably not."

To Brant's great satisfaction, Crane and Rosanne were interrupted by the boisterous arrival of Patrick, Little Otter, and Garth Hitchcock. The three men had been searching the woods around the clearing for tracks.

Brant maneuvered himself into an upright position, deliberately wedging his good leg between Crane and Rosanne so that the physician was separated from her by the intimidating barrier of Brant's thigh. He had no intention of allowing Crane's interest to deepen into something more than professional. He hadn't gotten up the nerve to ask Rosanne to marry him only to let one of his friends turn her pretty head.

"Did you find anything?"

Patrick shook his head. "Simon was right. There were no tracks. The tomahawk might have come from our own store. My guess is the Sluyters had a hand in this. They've been too quiet lately, too good-natured about losing that land. And I have not had a chance to tell ye that the sheriff was here again today, threatening to confiscate our furs. Says we're trading illegally."

"According to whose laws?" Brant said angrily. "Those arbitrarily decided upon by some greedy Albany burghers? They'd not hold up in a court of law."

"Aye," Patrick agreed. "So take it to court. Spend all yer time and money fighting the Sluyters and their friends. That's what they're hoping ye'll do. While ye're going bankrupt, they'll be in a perfect position to figure out how to wrest your patent away from ye."

Brant leaned back tiredly. "It looks as if I'll have to ride back to Albany to confront Conrad Sluyter. I should have known he wouldn't change."

"I'll go with ye," Patrick offered. "Obviously, ye can't move to the cabin now until the stockade is built."

Brant gave a morose nod of agreement, his mind struggling for answers. Were they even related, the incident at the ravine with Rosanne and the attempt on his life today? Why would someone want to kill him? God, for all he knew, the attack today might well have been the work of one of his own tenant farmers, angry at him for abandoning them to Hugh's deceit.

He lifted his head, distracted by the quiet flow of conversation between Crane and Rosanne as they sat on their respective footstools. He felt an irrational surge of relief as he realized that all they were discussing was how to treat his knee.

"She took a bad fall herself, Doctor," Brant said. "She was complaining of tenderness in her shoulder. Would you mind examining her?"

Crane nodded, reassuming his professional demeanor. "Of course." He glanced around the room. "Gentlemen, do you mind?"

Brant made to rise as the room cleared, but Crane motioned him to remain seated, ordering him in an amused tone to "rest that damn knee."

Brant subsided with a faintly resentful scowl and yet felt relieved that his jealousy was unnoticed. He swallowed hard as he tried not to stare, not to mind Crane's hands on Rosanne's shoulder, pushing back the heavy silk of her hair and probing the pale flesh with his fingers. Life was so unpredictable. Just a few hours earlier he and Rosanne were squabbling, unaware they would momentarily be facing violent death and were spending what might be their last moments in foolish bickering. Now here he sat, with his leg elevated and trussed, like some gouty old patriach. Worse, he appeared to have gained a rival in Jonathan Crane. But he would see that that didn't last long.

"You do have a nasty bruise on your shoulder, mistress," he heard Crane murmur. "Have Deep Spring make you a poultice for it too, to help draw out the discoloration. Your skin is fair and marks easily . . ."

"Are you finished with my betrothed yet, Doctor?"

There was a heavy pause. If Crane hadn't understood the situation before, he did now.

"I am." Crane collected his black cloak, hat, and bag and rose agilely. "I'll be back tomorrow to check your knee. Observe it tonight for signs of heat or undue swelling." He paused before the settee, his eyes shining with wry humor. "Good night to you both. I suppose congratulations are in order on your engagement."

"Thank you, Doctor," Brant said graciously. "We might discuss that tract you mentioned later, if you're serious."

Brant watched Rosanne walk Crane to the door, watched a smile curve her mouth as she thanked him again. But when she turned back to the settee, her expression showed her thoughts had turned inward, and he noticed her eyes avoided him.

She knelt before him with a rag in her hand and began to sop up the puddles that had dripped from the cold compress and were soaking into the pine-board floor. "Leave that," Brant said. "Sit with me instead."

He stretched out his hand to brush an errant strand of gold from her cheek, and as she pressed her face into his palm, he felt her give a forlorn sigh. "It's all right, sweet. Everything is all right. We'll find out who was at the clearing today. But no more arguing on the roof over such trivial things as silver tankards."

She drew her face away slowly. "It was not trivial to me, Brant. And we weren't arguing about the tankard, or have you forgotten already?"

A frown seamed his brow and then smoothed out as the memory of their argument over her grandfather came back to him. In his estimation it did not rank high in importance among the day's other events: his offer of marriage; his near-murder; the wrenching of his knee; and learning that the sheriff had been at the store after his furs.

"Oh, that again."

He didn't understand, she thought miserably. He was unable to understand how important it was to her that he, of all people, not become tainted by association with her grandfather. In her eyes it was an unbearable betrayal.

"You are," she said without rancor, "truly more like Hugh than either of us realized."

He looked away, unwilling to let her know how deeply that barb struck. Could she indeed have guessed how often he'd compared himself to his uncle and found a shocking number of similarities?

"Release this childish grudge against your grandfather, Rosanne. My reasons for dealing with him are entirely different from Hugh's. I can't break a business contract because of a whim."

Childish grudge? Whim?

She turned away and would have left the room had she not heard voices in the hallway. He did not understand and would not even bother to try. What could she do? She was trapped neatly within the confines of her own character. She loved him too much to leave him; she lacked the dramatic flair to even threaten that she would. But she was also too honest with herself to pretend that the issue would not affect their relationship. It was bound to, though she was unable to judge to what extent. That would have required rational consideration, and the bitter intensity of the emotions the duke inspired in her ruled out any hope of that.

The door opened just then, and Mrs. Dare's voice, crackling like dry, bare cornstalks in the breeze, filled the uncomfortable silence. "Did I hear something about an engagement?" she asked innocently as she entered the room between her two granddaughters.

"Not unless you were eavesdropping at the keyhole," Brant said crossly.

Priscilla moved to the table with a tray of hot chocolate and maple-sugar cookies. "Of course she was."

Mrs. Dare stopped at the settee, bending at the waist to examine Brant's bandaged knee. "Since I hear no denial, I assume there is to be a wedding. That should put a stop to your prowling the hallways at night." She prodded at Brant's kneecap. "This bandage feels too tight to me."

"Sit down and behave yourself, Gran," Sally said with a sigh. "Who would like a cup of chocolate?"

"We should have wine," Priscilla said. "Whoever heard of celebrating a betrothal with chocolate?"

Brant stared down at Rosanne. "I don't want anything."

"And I am going to bed," Rosanne said, coming to her feet.

He struggled up from the settee and hobbled after her. "Wait, Rosanne, I'll walk up with you."

But for once she outpaced him easily, and by the time he reached the staircase, he recognized the distinct slam of her door. He shook his head in bemusement. She didn't lose her temper often, but when she did, approaching her was like tangling with a brier rose. Refusing to acknowledge the presence of the three curious females crowded into the doorway behind him, he hit his fist against the banister and slowly began the painful ascent to his own room. There was not a whit of privacy to be had in this house. He had a game leg. Someone wanted him dead. His betrothed wasn't speaking to him. Why had he been so pitifully naive as to believe that by asking her to marry him he would end all his problems?

It was two hours after sunset the following day before anyone realized Simon was missing. The stockade gates had been closed, but beyond the blockhouse many of the settlers were still straggling back to their outlying farms, having spent the afternoon away from their fields shooting hundreds of passenger pigeons that flocked to the valley in dark-winged clouds every autumn and spring.

Rosanne had been up since dawn. Autumn was a wilderness housewife's delight or nightmare, depending on her domestic inclinations. She had begun the day pickling eels, a disgusting job guaranteed to turn the strongest stomach, and hers was already queasy that morning. Next she helped Sally put up jam, while at the kitchen table, perspiring in the fragrant steam, Priscilla and her grandmother carved up pumpkins to dry for pies that would enliven the dreary winter fare of corn and salted pork.

She hadn't seen Brant at breakfast, but she'd stayed awake half the night thinking about what he'd said. Was she being unreasonable? Should she simply overlook his dealings with her grandfather? Could she betray her mother's memory so easily? If he loved me, she thought sadly, he'd find another firm to deal with. If he loved her . . . She had to remember he hadn't admitted that. She had to remember she had more or less wedged her way into his life and made a place for herself. His wife, the mother of his children, a companion with whom to share his work— she might have to be content with that.

As the supper hour approached, Patrick came in from his shop to wash in the kitchen, and Brant finally emerged from his office where he had secluded himself all day. Reviewing the duke's receipts? Rosanne felt like asking, but as she wasn't speaking to him, she had to communicate her feelings with a cold glare, the intended impact of which was greatly diminished by a smudge of raspberry jam on her cheek.

Patrick was the first to note Simon's absence. "Where's your grandson got off to, Beatrice? He was supposed to bring back some pigeon berries for Spring to take her sister."

"And feverweed for Dr. Crane," Sally added as she removed a steaming, golden-crusted apple pie from the brick oven built into the fireplace wall.

Rosanne and Priscilla shared troubled glances across the table; the horror of yesterday's attack hadn't receded from anyone's mind.

"That young lumphead," Mrs. Dare muttered, but there was a note of genuine fear in her voice.

Patrick pulled his old buckskin jacket from the oaken

peg. "Can anyone suggest where we might begin to look for him?"

"I think he mentioned something this morning, but I wasn't truly listening," Sally said, and at the exasperated look Patrick gave her, she added, "Maybe he wandered off into the woods so that he wouldn't have to watch the men bringing down the birds. You know how hunting upsets him."

Priscilla turned pale. "Maybe he got himself shot by accident. Or those men yesterday . . . maybe they found him—"

"And maybe he's on his way home right now," Brant remarked, reappearing in the doorway with his rifle. "Sally, tell Garth to collect a party to cover the hills to the west. Patrick and I will track east and then cross the river in the event he returned to the cabin. The women are to stay here."

He hoped it was obvious from the way his gaze skipped Rosanne that he meant his order especially for her. She was just angry enough at him and fond enough of Simon to try to find the boy herself. Over the summer she and Simon had formed a strong bond of friendship based on their shared reverence for all living things. Fewer and fewer rabbits had graced the table lately. Hogs marked for slaughter at the first frost had mysteriously disappeared. In fact, he would not have been surprised if Simon wasn't engaged at that very moment in some harebrained mission of mercy.

An hour passed, long and uneventful, and then Dr. Crane arrived to examine Brant's knee. Rosanne explained Brant's absence as she led him to the parlor where Mrs. Dare sat with her knitting neglected in her lap and her small face collapsed into worried creases.

"Brant isn't here, Doctor. He and Patrick have been out since before supper looking for Simon. His knee did seem much better today though. At least I heard no complaints from him."

"I must accept partial blame if anything has happened to that boy," Crane said as Rosanne helped him off with his cloak. "I had him collecting seeds for me. I've been sending them to an avid botanist friend of mine in London. He's an aristocrat with all the wealth and time in the world to indulge his fancies."

"His name doesn't happen to be the duke of Rydenham, does it, Doctor?"

"Good Lord, no. Not that I wouldn't mind his patronage. Why do you ask?"

She shook her head, distracted by the sight of Mrs. Dare approaching the window again to stare outside. It had been only that morning that Simon asked Rosanne to return to the ravine with him, but she'd been so busy, she'd told him to wait until the end of the week.

The ravine. What if he'd slipped into the pool and hit his head on the boulders? Herbs and plants thrived in that humid hollow. He might have lost track of the time.

"That's where he has gone. I know it. Something must be wrong."

Crane blinked. "Excuse me?"

"The ravine, Doctor. I'm sure he's gone there looking for feverweed for you. It flourishes on damp soil. He wanted to gather the last of the season. Priscilla, take down that hunting musket."

"What for? You don't know how to shoot."

"I can fire it."

"She couldn't hit the middle of the moon if it dropped at her feet," Mrs. Dare said, securing the shutter. "What are you thinking of, Rosanne?"

Alarm crossed Crane's face. "You're not going out there alone. Give me directions. I'll find him."

"No. Stay here, Doctor," Rosanne urged. "If the others bring Simon home and he's injured, you'll be needed. If I find him, I'll know where to look for you."

"Oh, no, mistress. I cannot allow—"

"It's only two miles from here, Doctor. You can come after me if I don't return right away."

Priscilla moved between them with the musket. "I'll go with you. Sally, run up to the blockhouse and keep the sentries amused until we slip outside. They'll try to stop us otherwise."

"But how shall I keep them amused?"

"I don't know. Try to remember how you got Garth to ask for your hand."

The nocturnal dangers of the woods, real and imagined, held little fear for Rosanne as she raced along the now-familiar path, deftly sidestepping mossy logs and roots, slapping back branches before they could slap her. She had taken to wearing moccasins of late, and she ran as Deep Spring had taught her, with her toes tucked inward to prevent bruising and her hands held loosely. She knew Priscilla lagged not too far behind from the girl's frequent breathless complaints.

Only the palest threads of the waning moon trickled down into the clearing. The mouth of the ravine yawned just ahead of them, wide and black like a whale's mouth, except where the stream cascaded over its lip. They traced Simon to the edge of the pool below by the sounds of his weak, spasmodic wretching; he was huddled between two squat boulders and going into convulsions. Foamy spittle bubbled from the corners of his mouth. In the dim moonlight they could see his pupils were contracted, and when Rosanne knelt down to help him, he gave an inarticulate cry and flung up his hands to shield his face from some hallucinatory horror.

"Simon, it's only me. Oh, you poor thing, what has happened to you?"

Priscilla gazed down at them from the ledge, her face drawn and anguished. "Oh, my dear God," she whispered. "He's got the rabies! He's been bit by a mad animal. I knew this would happen one day, him being so trusting—"

"It couldn't be rabies!" Rosanne looked up, torn between sympathy and exasperation. "It takes weeks to manifest symptoms." She touched his hand gently. His skin felt cool and clammy, and his general appearance reminded her painfully of Gwennie as she lay dying on the *Broken Heart*.

"Simon," she cried suddenly, "what have you been eating?" She scrambled around in search of his belongings, emptied his tanned skin bag, and then noticed the mushrooms scattered beneath the boulders.

"Lower the musket to me, Priscilla. I'll try to start a fire from the gunpowder to get him warm. I'll have to find dry flint."

There was a quiet splash as the musket landed in the pool, a gurgle as it sank to the grasses at the bottom. "I'm sorry, Rosanne," Priscilla wailed. "I almost fell myself. It's so dark down there. . . ."

"Never mind. But one of us will have to return to the house to fetch Dr. Crane. Priscilla, did you hear me? *Priscilla!* It's urgent! Your brother is dy—"

"W-w-wolf . . ."

The single word, so chillingly spoken, raised gooseflesh on Rosanne's arms. She glanced around frantically for Simon's musket, which he had either lost or forgotten. "Are you sure, Priscilla?" she whispered.

"L-look," the girl stammered. "Look th-there!"

Chapter 25

Rosanne hastily covered Simon's quivering shoulders with her shawl and climbed the slippery steps, her gaze shooting to the bulky grayish shadow at the edge of the clearing. Then slowly the shadow moved, its long muzzle pressed to the earth to sniff at tracks.

"That's my dog, Priscilla," she said, more relieved than her scornful tone revealed. "Really, you're as bad as I was about the racoons."

"Then what was *that?*"

Rosanne glanced to the right and listened, suddenly and unwillingly wondering whether they might have been followed by the same men who had tried to kill Brant yesterday afternoon. She could hear footsteps approaching along the path to the ravine, a branch swishing as it was pushed aside.

"Dr. Crane— Oh, I'm so glad you've come!"

Jonathan crossed the clearing, staring around in puzzlement until he discerned Rosanne and Priscilla on the ledge. "Did you find him?"

"Yes," Rosanne answered. "Oh, Doctor, I think he's eaten poison mushrooms. He's been vomiting violently, and he—he doesn't seem to know me."

"How do we get down to him, mistress? Priscilla, be a good girl and fire my musket into the air to summon help. Damnation, it's as dark as a sepulcher down here. Where are my belladonna tablets? There's no point in giving him an emetic. It appears he's already emptied his stomach. I've warned him about eating everything he picks. Mistress, will you help me hold him still while I place a tablet under his tongue?"

She crawled around a boulder to assist him, her mocassins sinking into the soggy ground. Simon thrashed and muttered incoherently about man-eating dragons while she planted her hands on his shoulders and held him fast. Above them Priscilla gripped Dr. Crane's musket and fired above her head, staggering backward from the recoil. Then she leaned over the ledge, her anxiety conveyed not in words but by an uncharacteristic silence.

"Will he live, Dr. Crane?" Rosanne asked quietly.

"I can't tell. Half the people who are poisoned thus do not survive." His voice was hollow as he looked up into her face, an oval of anguish in a gilded frame. Where had Layton found her? he wondered irrelevantly. Even if she had not been half so lovely, he would have fallen under her enchantment because of the stubborn loyalty she'd shown tonight in trying to rescue a friend.

Simon groaned softly, and Rosanne bent over him in helpless concern. Death could and did strike without warning in the wilderness—Indian attack, snakebite, a hunting accident were only some of the ever-present dangers. Life was all the more precious for its uncertainty. I must apologize to Brant for quarreling with him about my grandfather, she decided impulsively. Seeing Simon, her gentle-souled companion, like this, so near death, altered her perspective, put her in a mood for reconciliation. She and Brant had overcome other problems—they mustn't start their marriage on a note of discord.

"He—he seems quieter, Doctor," she murmured. "What shall we do next?"

"There is nothing much else we can do, my dear, except keep him warm until we get home and then wait it out. Priscilla!" he called, glancing up. "Gather some twigs for a fire. Someone should have heard that shot by now. I know there are men in the area."

He removed his cloak, fashioned of black wool and

faced with red squirrel fur, and tucked it around Simon's shuddering frame. "Come, mistress. Sit on the boulder beside me. Your skirts are dragging in the water, and I don't want another patient. You took quite a risk coming down here by yourself. I should never have let you leave the house alone." He moved suddenly closer to her, lifting his delicate fingers to her face. "My dear, that isn't blood on your face, is it?"

"I believe it's raspberry jam," a rough voice replied, filtering down to them through the hemlock foliage that hung over the pool like a dark lace curtain.

"Brant!" Rosanne slid off the boulder with a start. She was unable to see his face, but the throbbing anger in his voice could not be mistaken. Was he upset with her because she hadn't obeyed his order to stay in the house? He will surely understand when he hears about Simon, she thought. And I'll explain that it doesn't really matter whether he wishes to continue dealing with the same firm. She began scaling the natural staircase, searching for his figure in the small crowd of men hovering above in the clearing. She wanted to hold him, to lose herself in his comfort. Simon was like a brother to her, and she loved him dearly, but she was grateful beyond belief that it wasn't Brant whose death she might have to accept.

He lowered his hand and hauled her up the last few steps to stand beside him but stepped away from her the moment she had gained her footing. Behind him Patrick and two tenant farmers were fashioning a crude stretcher for Simon by lashing branches and vines together. But all Brant's attention—his anger and his fear—was focused on Rosanne. He had returned to the settlement to the shock of finding her gone. The little brat obviously hadn't learned her lesson that night in the pitfall, and it occurred to him she might have disobeyed him simply to drive home her own anger, to flaunt her lack of respect for him. Had it been an illusion of moonlight and shadow, or had she actually been sitting as close to Crane as he feared? Did she purposely intend to drive him to distraction? Whatever her objectives, he was in no frame of mind to try to decipher them. His own emotions were rushing through him like a river to a waterfall, slamming up against the realization that he loved her beyond reason, that any hope he had had for a sane and orderly existence had ended the day he'd met her. There was no help for it.

"You disobeyed me." His voice blasted through her like cold air on an aching tooth. "Do you imagine I've nothing better to do than chase after you all the time?"

His words were a defense against the emotional backlash of his own realization. The withering rage in his voice arose from his violent relief at finding her safe with Crane, when in his imagination she had lain dead or unconscious at the bottom of the ravine, perhaps the victim of the tomahawk-wielding maniac who had been haunting the area.

She raised a hand to touch his chest, but he recoiled; he seemed to turn to stone beneath her fingertips. "Brant, you don't understand—"

"Get back to the house." It was bad enough she'd disobeyed him and led him a merry chase and that both his friends and his servants knew it, but he'd be damned if he'd show them all just how easily Her Royal Highness, the Queen of Mischief, could manipulate him. Not that he doubted for a moment it was obvious. He'd been dancing attendance on her like a bloody court jester too long to hope no one else had noticed.

"Get back to the house, Rosanne."

"Don't speak to me in that tone! You don't even know what happened—"

"At this moment I don't care." He edged away from her, his features wooden. "I don't want to hear your excuses. You'll not get around me with your big blue eyes tonight. I am so furious with you at the moment I almost regret—"

He stopped, and so did Rosanne's heart. "You almost regret what?" she demanded huskily. "Say it, you damned coward. Say it!"

"Just get away from me, Rosanne. Get back to the house before I truly lose my temper."

She gazed up at him in anger and bewilderment. Perhaps he was sorry he'd asked her to marry him. Perhaps he would use this as an excuse to break their betrothal. What could he possibly be thinking? They should be comforting each other over Simon, not drawing further apart. And then, as she stared into his unyielding features, she suddenly saw, superimposed, the face of her father, looking as it had the times he had refused to comfort her after a nightmare. The same frigid distaste she had seen in his eyes then she saw now in Brant's; then, as now, it prompted her to withdraw in devastated silence. Brant would never love her.

She darted around him and turned blindly onto the path, holding back the tears that were stinging her lowered eyelids. She would leave Hemlock Creek tomorrow. She was strong and capable enough to find work somewhere. She was fed up with trying to understand Brant's feelings for her. She would rather lose him completely than lose the last shred of her self-respect.

"You realize, of course, that she may well have saved Simon's life by finding him when she did," Jonathan remarked softly as he came to stand beside Brant.

"Yes. At great bloody risk to her own." His brow creased, Brant turned to face Crane reluctantly, having watched Rosanne vanish into the grayish night. "I must follow her."

"I suppose you must."

Brant hesitated. "What are Simon's chances?"

"There is no known antidote." Crane pursed his lips. "For either of you."

It was well past midnight before Brant finished working in his office and made his way upstairs. Candlelight gleamed through the crack in the door to Simon's room where Priscilla sat watch at his bedside. There was no sound from the chamber at the end of the hallway. He paused, listening, half afraid he would hear sounds of Rosanne packing. He wouldn't blame her if she was. He had behaved unforgivably and unfairly. After a moment's deliberation, he limped to her room and, without knocking, opened the door.

She was huddled up against the headboard of her bed with her face squashed into a pillow and Tynan lying across her feet. The hound didn't so much as growl at the intrusion, and when Brant sat down on the bed, the dog merely jumped to the floor and curled up on the carpet beneath the window with a deep sigh.

"Rosanne."

"Leave me alone." She lowered the pillow to peer at him. "Is Simon worse?"

"His condition hasn't changed. Rosanne, put the pillow down so that we can talk."

"Why? I don't want to hear another cold, ugly word from you tonight. You're just like—"

"You needn't say it. I am well aware of my faults."

He pried the pillow from her grasp, then raked his fingers through her hair, parting it to expose her wet, downcast face. His thumb rubbed the underside of her lower lip and circled upward to erase an errant teardrop from her cheekbone.

"I love you, Rosanne Mallory," he whispered. "I love you even though you've turned my life upside down. I've fought it, denied it, ignored it. I love you, girl."

She lifted her eyes to his, black pools of doubt rimmed in royal blue velvet. She was desperately afraid of allowing herself to believe him. She'd ached to hear those words for so long that all she could think of were the hundred reasons they couldn't possibly be true.

"Perhaps I came into your life at the wrong time—"

"Rosanne, you found me precisely when I needed you, before I'd become . . . become like Hugh. . . ."

"We—we're so different," she murmured, but she had begun to tremble under the artful stroking of his fingers as they found the sensitive points on her face, behind her earlobe and along her jaw, her throat, the deep recess between her breasts. There wasn't a speck of resistance to him in her whole being, she thought ruefully. "You're always throwing your differences up to me."

"Different, and yet so right together," he said tenderly. "Before I met you, I was hollow inside, Rosanne. I had my ambition, but it wasn't enough to satisfy my soul."

"But Martha—"

"—had the courage to break off our betrothal before I cheated us both." His fingers formed a lever beneath her chin, lifting it so that their mouths hovered only a breath apart. "I have resigned myself to a life of misrule, little one. I am your devoted subject, your willing slave."

"But tonight you said—"

"Tonight I was acting like a fool. You gave me a scare. Tonight I—I realized how much I love you. Don't leave me, Rosanne."

She sighed, savoring the moment, her doubts drifting away. She believed him. Everything would work out from this point onward. "Unlike you, Brant, I've never been successful at hiding how I felt," she whispered. "Oh, you were right—I've never had even one suitor before. My father kept me away at school while other girls my age were meeting young men and marrying. But I knew the moment I saw you—I *knew* I wanted to be yours."

She paused, overcome with emotion, and Brant snatched the moment to send a silent message of thanks to her father, who, bastard though he was, had by his coldhearted behavior actually brought them together.

"I do love you, Brant," she continued softly. "But I never dreamed that love could be this involved, this painful."

"It was painful for me too, sweet. The birth of anything, even an emotion, usually is."

"Brant, about my grandfather—"

"I've just finished writing a letter to my father asking him to approach another firm on my behalf. I warn you, it may be months before the new arrangements take effect, and I am legally bound to fulfill my present contract."

"No. Oh, no. It isn't necessary to make any change." she said in a breathless rush of love and guilt and gratitude. "I was wrong. You've worked too hard to let anything spoil your plans. I will not allow my hatred for my grandfather to come between us."

"And I will not do business with a man whose very name upsets my wife. I want us to be married at the end of the month, Rosanne. I want us to spend the winter together in the cabin. I want you to be in my bed, at my side, as my wife."

She looked away, overwhelmed, and when she returned her gaze to his face, her eyes glittered with both tears and impish delight. "It has taken you forever to realize you love me. Shall I make you wait that long before I agree to marry you?"

"Sweet, if you were that cruel, I'd never have fallen in love with you in the first place. And you've already agreed . . ."

His lips touched hers, heating them with slow-burning tenderness as he felt the soft, joyful moan that trembled in her throat. From the distant hills behind the house the wind gathered force and gusted through the night, carrying autumn-tinted leaves and the mournful song of a wolf. The wolf's howl sounded a subtle warning, or so, fancifully, it seemed to Brant. He deepened his kiss with sweet urgency. His hands gripped her shoulders and he grasped her tightly, as if he were struggling to hold her back from some invisible force that threatened to tear them apart. Passionate and playful, gentle and giving, she belonged to him, and he would not let her go.

He ended the kiss only when they could neither think nor breathe, clinging to each other in mindless rapture, clinging to the tip of a falling star as it plummeted to earth in an explosion of amber-gold sparks. Rosanne lay beneath him in dreamy acquiescence, her mind detached from her body, which she voluptuously envisioned as a lush-petaled water lily drifting on a pool of pleasure.

Brant, still recovering from the fright she'd given him earlier, was content to lie beside her, smiling into her heavily lashed eyes and stroking her hair with gentle sensuality.

"I love your hair," he murmured languidly, his fingers threading through the golden waves. "I love your eyes, your skin, your laugh. I'm sorry I wasted so much time trying to escape my emotions instead of trusting them. Another woman would have given up on me." He laid his head back against the pillow, drawing her against his chest, his words absorbed by her tousled hair. "Still, I wouldn't trade last summer for anything."

"Nor would I," she whispered, "though I wish we could forget Hugh existed."

She felt him tense at the reminder and wished she hadn't ruined the mood by mentioning his uncle. "When I threatened to expose him early last summer," he said quietly, "I could not foresee that I'd fall in love with you. I've no idea how he will react to news of our marriage, but I'll be relieved once we're off his land." A sudden irrational fear for her clouded his contentment. "He won't forgive me this."

"What do you think he'll do?"

"I don't know. Possibly nothing except rant and threaten. But in the meantime, no more running off without my permission. Let's not forget someone tried to cleave my skull yesterday."

She shivered and huddled closer to him, his words stirring in her mind the memory of that frightening day in the MacGavins' barn. "As if I could ever forget," she whispered.

"I don't care if it's a friend or a pigeon with a broken wing you think to rescue," he went on, "I want you to stay inside the stockade. If this war worsens . . . Well, there's no point in worrying about that yet. But please promise me you will not wander past the spring."

"I promise," she said solemnly. Her eyes grew wide with apprehension, though not from his remarks about Hugh or even the war. She'd just remembered that Simon had hidden a hog in Mrs. Dare's spinning room that morning, and it was to have been her task to smuggle it to a safer location before slaughtering began. She gave a tentative little wriggle, trying to dislodge the muscular brown arms wrapped around her.

"Brant, I—I think I hear Mrs. Dare in the hallway."

"Lord forbid," he groaned. "Well, she'll just have to

shoot me where I lie. I'm lame in one leg, and the other's asleep. Where are you going? I closed the door behind me." He found himself suddenly grasping air and felt the mattress lift as she dropped her feet to the floor. "Don't get up. I enjoy holding you."

"I'm going downstairs to brew tea for Priscilla. I promised I'd relieve her soon anyway."

He got up with a resigned sigh and watched her slip out of her nightdress and into her gown. "Love, you'll need warmer clothes for the winter." He walked over to her then and proceeded to lace her up, his expression at once ardent and rueful. "I ought to be helping you out of your clothes right now, not into them. Don't forget to put your stockings on. And a shawl. It's cold as a springhouse downstairs."

"I think I left my shawl at the ravine. What—what are you doing?"

He was guiding her toward the bed, where he pushed her gently onto her bottom while he knelt at her feet to roll her stockings on. Her legs, long and curvaceous, had always driven him wild, and it was the first time he'd felt uninhibited enough to indulge in this tantalizing fantasy. Slowly he smoothed the stocking upward, his fingertips tracing her instep, her ankle, and the sensuous curve of her calf before traveling higher to her kneecap where, with smoldering eyes and a knocking heart, he tied on the silk-ribboned garter. This arousing ritual he repeated on the other leg while Rosanne sat entranced, wet heat gathering between her thighs, burning need spreading through her belly.

"My dear," he said in a nonchalant tone that belied his thunderous pulse, "you have holes in your stockings. What a delectable mess you are."

If he moved his hand another inch higher, Rosanne thought faintly, she would melt bonelessly. His touch, whether accidental or intended, always traveled through her like a jolt of electricity to discharge its current, with devastating impact, upon her senses.

"Rosanne," he said, and his tone deepened as his fingers slipped upward. "You have till the count of five to reach that door; else I guarantee neither of us will leave this room tonight."

She rose from the bed, gasping softly with pleasure as he deliberately allowed his hand to brush her *there*. At the door, where she stopped to put on her mocassins, she felt so flustered, she could not remember why she had wanted to go downstairs—until Brant reminded her.

"By the way, Rosanne, I had to move the hog out of the spinning room. He was making rather a racket, so I shut him up in the woodshed for the night." He got up, wincing at the discomfort in his knee, and opened the door, placing one hand on her derriere to herd her into the hallway. "Here. Put on my jacket when you go downstairs. I don't want you taking ill. No excuses for Crane to examine you again, d'you hear?"

Chapter 26

Hugh Layton's amber eyes glowed with the angry incandescence of his thoughts as he strode from City Hall toward the waiting carriage. If he had been a superstitious man, he might have believed that Rosanne Mallory was a witch who had entered his life only to curse it before mysteriously vanishing into the ethers. And vanish she had, he thought grimly. His agents in England hadn't found a trace of the girl, and they had discreetly but thoroughly interrogated everyone who had known her, from her former schoolmistresses to her neighbors in the London hovel where she had spent most of her life. He'd had Roxbury Neck combed for her body, and he had spent a small fortune loosening tongues along wharves from Boston to New York for a clue to her whereabouts.

Nothing.

If he didn't find her soon, he felt he might as well move to the Mohawk Valley and take up farming with his damned nephew, because his political future would be worth naught. How long could he keep postponing his wedding? How long could he continue to make excuses for the bride-to-be his acquaintances were openly skeptical even existed. Ill fortune seemed to be blowing his way from all points of the compass.

His son Daniel had had to enlist in the militia after his mistress drowned while he was rowing her across Boston

Harbor. God, it had cost Hugh a pretty penny to squash that scandal.

The governor had proven as politically unskilled and as easily manipulated as Hugh had assumed he would be. Unfortunately, it was Chief Justice James De Lancey, and not Hugh, who had manipulated his way into the envious position of Clinton's confidante and primary advisor.

Two of Hugh's ships had been lost in a freak storm at sea. A land investment had gone sour. Some upstart lawyer was threatening to sue him on behalf of the Mohawks over a fraudulent deed that had already passed the Upper House.

But by far the most ominous piece of news was the letter he had received yesterday. A letter from the duke of Rydenham himself stating his intense desire to make amends with his granddaughter and to reassure himself she was making a good match.

His Grace was coming to America. To visit Rosanne, waiting until he'd met Hugh in person to either deny or bestow his blessing upon her marriage. But Hugh would be unable to produce the old man's granddaughter, would not even be able to explain why she'd run away.

"God help me," he muttered, and as he climbed into the carriage, his face hardened with displeasure at the woman he discovered waiting inside. "You are the last person I want to see today, Olivia. I trust this is important. I'm on my way to the slave auction to examine my latest shipment."

"So Moira told me. I'm going with you."

"You came all the way to New York to procure more slaves? Aren't you afraid of another rebellion? Why, you were the one who advised me to take precautions—"

She cut him off, her eyes glittering coldly between their almost lashless lids. "I've brought you some news."

"You—" He sat forward, his voice rough with excitement. "You've found her?"

"Conrad Sluyter has. In fact, he met her several months ago and never realized who she was."

"Where?"

"In your nephew's bed, from what I gather."

The blood drained drop by drop from his face as he absorbed her statement. "Jesus God Almighty," he whispered. "I don't understand . . . I—I thought you'd already arranged—"

"The first attempt failed, but Conrad is handling everything for you—both the girl and Brant. I hope it's understood that you'll be generous in your appreciation. You'd have had none of this trouble if you'd hired Conrad to begin with."

He leaned back heavily, shock and disbelief in his eyes. "I don't want to know any of the details, Olivia. No matter what he's done, Brant is my family."

"He betrayed you, Hugh," she said intently. "He's made a fool of you. You have no choice."

No choice . . . no choice. The words echoed a dull refrain inside Hugh's head, echoed mockingly with the clattering of the coach wheels. And as he felt Olivia watching him, her dispassionate stare quelling any protests he might have made, he faced his own cowardice with cringing fatalism and then, at last, gave her a stiffly reluctant nod of assent.

Chapter 27

It had been during harvest, when every able-bodied man was either laboring or standing guard in the cornfields, that Rosanne had first begun working in the trading post. Now, with Simon slowly recuperating and still unable to manage alone, she spent more time than ever there. The store was a stuffy log structure on a stone foundation; its shelves were filled with jars, the counters were piled high with boxes, and the walls were lined with barrels. Axes, lead, seeds, beads, shirts, blades, buttons, vermilion, and powder horns were only a few of the frontier necessities for sale. Recently, after Rosanne had spent an afternoon in a rival store in Schenectady, they had started to carry velvet as well as calico and broadcloth; lace and silk ribbons along with linen. And silk stockings, but that was Brant's suggestion.

The Indians came with brooms, wooden bowls and baskets, medicinal herbs, and venison from their recent hunting expeditions to trade. The majority of the trapper-traders had paddled off in their canoes for the winter, though a few had chosen to remain in the area. King George's War had actually improved business, for many traders who had fearfully fled remote Fort Oswego were returning to more settled regions. And that meant increased trade for Brant.

Most of the customers that autumn were farmers from outlying settlements, German immigrants from nearby Stone Arabia and frontier housewives who lived in isolated cabins and were as hungry for gossip as they were for the pretty trinkets and feminine luxuries that Rosanne had begun to stock.

In fact, Brant had had the very clothes Rosanne wore that day made by a Palatine seamstress who now lived in nearby German Flatts. If not stylish, the burgundy woolen gown with its square embroidered neckline, white velvet stomacher, and quilted petticoats provided warmth on this gray November afternoon.

She looked up briefly from the shelf she was straightening as the door opened. The store had no windows, and the lantern, lit to dispel the perpetual gloom, illuminated only a small working area.

Her eyes widened in disbelief at the sight of a familiar figure. At first she was sure she was mistaken and attributed it to the poor lighting. But then Peter Ericsson swaggered up to the counter into full view, outlandishly dressed in a lace-trimmed frock coat and a billowing cream silk shirt with maroon satin knee breeches and red leather high-heeled shoes. His white-blond hair, clean and silky, dangled in a braid between his shoulder blades. He had even doffed his plumed hat as she turned fully to face him; she noticed that his hands were scrubbed clean except for the traces of tannin embedded in the grooves of his palms.

"Mr. Ericsson?" He looked, she decided, like a buccaneer who had misplaced his frigate, but she lost the urge to laugh the moment she met his gaze. No hint of humor softened the granite eyes that were studying her so intently.

"So," he said softly, "you haven't forgotten me."

His tone unsettled her. She glanced down at Simon sitting on the floor behind the counter; he wasn't much in the way of protection, and nowadays Tynan preferred following Brant to the fields, rather than staying cooped up in the store all day.

"Can I help you with something, Mr. Ericsson?"

Peter's mouth tightened as Simon rose awkwardly and edged nearer Rosanne. The boy irritated him. Of course, he hadn't expected to find Rosanne alone today in any case. His plans had changed since the day he'd met her at the ravine. His plans now including abducting her, a pleasurable prospect that also would pay well enough for him to retire forever from trapping. He'd suspected from the start that she had a secret, that she was hiding something in her past. He'd been hunted for so long himself that he'd developed an instinct for smelling out fear.

"You, boy," he said to Simon, producing a piece of paper from his pocket. "There are some pelts and deer hides outside on the porch. I need—" he pretended to scan the list "—gunpowder, flint, a blanket, some rum, and a mirror." He chuckled to himself at the inclusion of the last item, a little joke for Luther's benefit.

"Mr. Layton doesn't carry spirits," Simon muttered. "The Mohawk sachems asked him not to."

"Well then, see about the pelts, boy. It looks like rain." He shoved the paper back into his pocket as Simon moved past him. It was a passage from the Psalms, but Peter didn't know that. His education had been interrupted before he had even learned his alphabet, and he was ashamed of his illiteracy.

He slung a bundle of black-fox pelts onto the counter. "I saved these for you, Rosanne. Repayment for your fine needlework, which left only the smallest scar. They're very valuable."

"I can't accept these, Peter." She stared down at his offering in dismay, hoping Simon would return soon. She felt heart-sorry for the poor foxes who'd gotten caught in this man's traps. "You'll have to take something in trade for them," she said firmly. "Unfortunately, I've no idea what they're worth."

"We can negotiate the price." He leaned across the counter to take her hand and run it over one of the silky pelts. "Have a cloak lined for the winter."

She drew her hand back, disturbed by his touch. What was Simon doing—counting every hair on every hide? "Speaking of winter, Mr. Ericsson, shouldn't you be on your way back north soon?"

"I'm not trapping this winter. I have other plans." He

withdrew his hand, noticing her nervousness. "What about you?"

"She's to be married. And, unfortunately, not to either of us."

Rosanne looked up with an irrepressible sigh of relief as Jonathan entered the store. Grateful for the excuse to leave the counter, she hurried forward to greet the physician. "You didn't happen to step on Simon as you came in, did you, Doctor?"

"Yes, I did. His grandmother was out there dosing him with the sassafras tonic I prescribed." He approached the counter, his face lighting up. "Damn, those are splendid furs. Are they for sale?"

"No, they're not," Peter said curtly, his gaze skimming Crane with annoyance before returning to Rosanne. "Is it true what he said, mistress? That you are to be married?"

"Yes. In a week."

"And neither of us will see much of her afterward, I expect," Crane complained. "Brant's not likely to let her out of his sight until spring."

Peter settled his hat back onto his head, his expression pensive. "In that case, mistress, I *insist* you keep the furs. As a wedding gift."

"No, I couldn't."

Jonathan shook his head. "Of course you could."

"No, I—"

At that moment Simon returned and began assembling Peter's supplies. The boy's sullen face and brusque movements gave away his intense dislike of the Swedish trapper, but Peter was too absorbed in his own thoughts to notice. Obviously, he had to work this latest development, Rosanne's impending marriage, into his strategy, and he had to do it fast. He couldn't afford to wait even another day. He grabbed his supplies and left, muttering a vague farewell to Rosanne and ignoring her request to take the furs along with him.

Crane watched his departure with a rueful grin. "Well, you've broken another heart, my dear."

"Don't be silly, Jonathan. I don't even know him."

"Or want to, I'd wager. Damned peculiar clothes for a trapper." He stroked his jaw thoughtfully as if to coax the beard he was trying to grow. "Perhaps I ought to give up medicine and become a *voyageur*."

"Not you, Jonathan," she teased lightly, at ease now that Ericsson had gone. "You like your creature comforts too much to spend days on end in a leaky canoe or camping out in the snow."

"True," he murmured. "I confess I'm reaching the age when I crave hearth and home. Still, after a morning spent peeling off some miserable old farmer's bunions, well, I could use a little adventure."

"You've come to the wrong place for that then. We're as dull as can be around here. The greatest adventure I can offer is to let you help me move these barrels back where they belong."

He moved quickly forward to block her path. "Oh, no, you don't. Not until we've examined you to find out whether we've a little Layton on the way."

She blushed with pleasure. Could it be true? She would not allow herself to become overly excited until Jonathan had confirmed it. Except for occasional queasiness, her only symptom was mild fatigue, which could also be attributed to the added work she'd taken on. She would have to wait, anyway, until after the wedding to share the happy news.

Priscilla interrupted them then with a tray of hot tea sweetened with maple sugar and accompanied by a loaf of freshly baked pumpkin-cornbread. "Gran thought you might appreciate this, since you've been working in the cold all day, Rosanne," she said breathlessly, smiling up at Jonathan as he relieved her of the tray and set it on the counter.

Rosanne hid her own smile. Mrs. Dare had brought her tea less than an hour ago, but it was no secret the housekeeper hoped to spark a match between Priscilla and the physician. It appeared it might work too, if she could judge by the flicker of interest in his eye as he watched the girl pour his tea, pale tendrils of hair peeping from her mobcap to frame her broad face.

"Jonathan," Rosanne said impulsively, "you will stay for supper, won't you? 'Twill give you a chance to examine Brant's knee again, and Priscilla does make the most heavenly pie."

"With great pleasure," he replied, his eyes darting to Priscilla, then past her to the dark-haired figure who had just appeared in the doorway. "Well, here he is now. Your knee is troubling you again, I see. I thought we had that healed. Your betrothed seems to hold a peculiar fascination for limping men. I wonder what it is."

Brant leaned over the counter to kiss Rosanne on the cheek. "What's he talking about?"

She shrugged, wrinkling her nose at the pungent odor of male sweat that drifted to her from his damp linsey-woolsey shirt. "I don't know. Ask him. Phew, you've been working."

"Girdling trees is hard work, love." His gaze dropped to the pelts draped across the counter. "Odd time for these to appear. Where did they come from?"

"The trapper with a limp," Crane supplied, swallowing a mouthful of bread. "Do you know, I think it must have been caused by either his tight breeches or the high-heeled shoes. Where do you suppose he got the money to dress like that?"

"Trapper with a limp?" Brant repeated, lost.

Rosanne braced herself, fearing Brant's reaction; he was bound to magnify the incident out of proportion. "Peter Ericsson."

His face darkened. "I told him to stay away from here."

"No, you didn't. You told him to stay away from the house."

"And you."

"He came here to trade. He didn't know I was working the store."

Brant doubted that but didn't want to argue. After all, Ericsson and his kind should be gone from the valley shortly. The beaver trapping season had started a month ago. "You're too trusting," he said to cover the jealous irritation he felt at another man bringing her gifts. "I hope you didn't serve him tea, or he'll be back again and again like a damned stray dog."

Rosanne glanced around the floor. "Tynan would take offense at that. Where is my dog anyway?"

"Begging scraps from Sally the last time I saw him." He looked past the counter to the storeroom. "Simon, your grandmother was asking for your help in the smokehouse, lad."

"And I should help Sally in the kitchen," Rosanne said, coming around the counter to take Brant's arm. "Walk me back to the house. I haven't spoken with you all day. Priscilla, you don't mind staying here alone, do you?"

"No, I don't mind."

"I'll keep her company," Jonathan offered. "We'll play a game of draughts. Let's see. What shall we wager? A kiss, Priscilla, or a slice of your heavenly pie? Which do you suppose is sweeter?"

"Oh, honestly, Doctor, you are wicked."

Rosanne had gotten Brant halfway to the door before he balked, suddenly remembering why he had come to the store in the first place. "I can't go back to the house just yet, Rosanne. I need to start an inventory. I intend to leave Hugh with exactly what he began with."

"Later, Brant," she said under her breath. "I promise I'll help you *later*."

He glanced back behind them, comprehension dawning. "So you've added matchmaking to your mischief, have you?" he asked amusedly. "Well, I shouldn't complain since it seems to have turned Crane's interest away from you."

Arm in arm they strolled back to the house, discussing the furniture that Brant had ordered to be made for the cabin. Rosanne was burning to tell him she might be pregnant but wanted to wait at least another week. He was already in high spirits; he'd just received a letter from Governor Clinton informing him that he would be offered a contract to provision Fort Hunter.

But as they entered the house, Brant became aware of a

nebulous thought nagging at the back of his mind, eluding him before he could focus on it. Had he forgotten to pay a bill, send off an important shipment, file a required form? He didn't think so, but he'd review his books to make certain.

"What is it?" Rosanne asked, noting his preoccupied expression.

He shrugged off his jacket so that she could hang it on its peg. "Something Crane said in the store. It bothered me, and I don't know why or even what it was."

"You'll remember later. Try not to think about it. Would you like perry or Madeira with your cigar?"

"Madeira," he replied, giving her an exasperated frown. "Damn. I almost had it until you asked me that." He walked slowly down the hallway and into his office, his brow furrowed in thought. By the time he'd lit the oil lamp and started his cigar, Rosanne had brought him a goblet of wine, and he'd become so involved in reading the letters on his desk that everything else was forgotten.

Rosanne sat on the edge of his desk, shuffling through a stack of receipts. "I'm not sure whether I'm pleased about the governor's contract or not. I suppose it means I'll see even less of you the next few months."

He sat back in his chair to enjoy his cigar and to indulge in the pleasure he always gained from simply looking at her and realizing she was his. "It was you who set the books straight so that I could present him with a bid. But our efforts will all be repaid one day, my dear. Our children won't have to struggle as their parents must do, God willing."

Our children! Rosanne flushed delightedly, but Brant didn't notice. He stretched forward suddenly to pick up the unopened envelope she had uncovered in her shuffling. "This must have come today too," he said. "I seem to have missed it."

"Who is it from?"

"Hans van Hoorn, Martha's brother."

Rosanne looked up slowly at the subtle change in his voice. Was it caused by excitement at possible news of

Martha or sadness at the reminder that he'd lost her? The doubts and jealous misgivings that she prided herself on having vanquished weeks before reared up inside her. With hard-won composure she slid off the desk and asked, "Would you prefer to be alone while you read it?"

Instead of the hoped-for "Of course not, darling. It's nothing important," he merely scowled and waved her to silence without even glancing up from the letter.

Rosanne backed away from the desk, studying every nuance of his expression, her apprehension growing. What did it signify when he rubbed his right eyebrow like that? What could the letter hold that could coax his lips into that maddening little smile? Had Martha broken her engagement after all? Was Hans begging him to return to New York for his sister's sake? Convinced that Brant no longer desired her company, that he probably resented her very presence, she turned woodenly to leave the room.

His voice reached out to her unexpectedly. "Where are you going?" And then, before she could answer, "Hans has formally agreed to help finance the sawmill. Lord, that's welcome news, but I wish he hadn't taken so long to let me know. He'll be visiting us before winter. Jansen wishes Wouter to come too, to discuss terms for the lumber he needs for his shipyard." He paused, his rugged face inscrutable. "He and Martha were married last month, and she's planning to accompany him. Would that upset you?"

"More to the point, Brant, would it upset you?"

He seemed genuinely surprised by the question.

"Why should it? I was thinking of you, of you having to play hostess in that little cabin. They have no idea we're to be married. I could suggest they stay in Schenectady." He resumed reading the letter before she could respond. "Would you like to hear something amusing?"

"Not particularly."

"Martha fainted dead away on her wedding night." He chuckled, glancing away from the letter as if, Rosanne thought, he were reliving a fond memory. "She always did swoon whenever she was excited . . ."

"Oh, you—you bastard!" How dared he sit there in his sublime arrogance joking about his experience of arousing another woman! And how dared he expect her to find it amusing! She could picture a scene from the van Hoorns' upcoming visit: Brant and Martha huddled together on the settee laughing over old memories while she and Wouter sat in opposite corners, glaring at their respective spouses in silent misery.

Brant's gaze swung to Rosanne's face. He loved her so completely that he assumed he could jest with impunity about his past relationship with Martha. And *past* it was, he thought gratefully. He felt about as much longing for Martha as he did for her brother.

He stood up, allowing the letter to flutter to the desktop; his face was repentant. "Poor choice of words. I wasn't thinking." He crossed the space between them in two long-legged strides, lowering his hands to her waist to draw her against him.

"Brant, don't . . . don't maul me like a bear. I have to help with supper."

"To hell with supper." He leaned into her, his eyelids lowered and his jaw, typically shadowed with stubble, abrading her cheek as he tried to kiss her. "I'll starve myself until you forgive me."

"Good idea. Tynan can have your bones."

She wriggled away from him only to discover herself backed against a bookshelf, his right arm raised to block her escape. Infuriatingly she found herself struggling not to grin at his persistence. Oh, the devil take him anyway! She didn't wish to forgive him. He deserved to suffer if only for possessing the power to render her so helpless. He realized it too, she thought furiously, her anger kindling at the smug smile she detected hovering on his lips. He played her as if she were a damned harpsichord and he a maestro, plucking her senses like strings and setting off quivering vibrations throughout her shameless body.

"May I suggest a compromise?" he asked softly. "We'll make love, and afterward I'll write a letter to Wouter Jansen. How about: 'Dear Wouter, I very much look forward to your visit and, more importantly, to getting my hands on your gold. However, I must insist you leave your swooning wife at home.' " He waited, his eyes probing hers, warm with good-humor, warm with wanting her. "What do you think?"

"I think," she said crisply, "that I shall give you three seconds to release me."

"Kiss me first."

"I'd sooner kiss a toad."

He grinned ruefully. If only she knew how she captivated, fascinated, devastated him, from his senses to his soul. It seemed so absurd to him, adoring her as he did, that she could suspect he harbored anything but the mildest affection for Martha. And yet he understood her feelings. The mere notion of her having had another lover evoked violent urges inside him.

He ran his forefinger under her jaw to tilt her defiant face toward his, the callused pad of his thumb sending sparks of tingling desire spiraling down her neck, her shoulder, her rigidly held spine. "We shall be married in a few days," he murmured lazily. "Do you hope to deny me until then?"

"Perhaps longer."

"Oh, no, not you, my wanton rose. You melt like a snowflake in August whenever I touch you."

"You beast," she said. "You conceited beast."

"Not conceited, Rosanne, merely observant. For example—"

"No. No, don't . . ."

The words trailed off as he suddenly kissed her, slowly drawing her lower lip into his mouth and playfully biting the sensitive flesh. His tongue flirted with hers, flirted and foraged for nectar, and then he broke away to glide his mouth down her neck, his fingers casually flicking back her hair and curling around the gilded strands. Hot, almost hurtful, kisses played havoc in the pearly hollow of her throat where her pulse throbbed in arousal as if to deny her anger. She pressed a palm to his shoulder to repel him, ended up, instead, by swaying against him in breathless languor. Their bodies arched together, she pliant as a bowstring, he an arrow, taut and hard, fitting against her as though by design.

"You see," he whispered, triumph rich in his voice. "And that was only from my kisses. What kind of response do you suppose I'll elicit if I were to move my mouth lower still—"

"I hate to disappoint you, Brant," she said silkily. "But you may kiss me until the cows come home, and I still will not faint away. . . ." She smiled, a devilish glint in her dark eyes as she suddenly ducked under his outflung arm and darted toward the door. "I shall be in the kitchen if you need me, master," she said, and dipped him an impudent curtsy.

"I need you now, wench." He grinned slowly, acknowledging temporary defeat. "But just remember that once we're married, you won't escape me that easily."

It rained shortly after supper that night. Everyone gathered in the parlor to play faro in front of a roaring fire. Imaginary stakes were wagered, growing more outrageous as the evening progressed. Patrick bet a leprechaun's pot of gold, Jonathan the elixir of youth. Sally lost the Red Sea, and Brant won all the pearls in the Orient.

About eight o'clock, when the rainstorm was at its worst, Rosanne served Priscilla's mouth-watering apple and pumpkin pies, smothering each slice with thick, creamy custard. After the dessert dishes were cleared away for another game of cards, Brant took his coffee to the fireside where Rosanne sat embroidering a linen tablecloth for their new home. He dropped onto the settee beside her and sat quietly admiring her flawless stitchery. She put love into every task she undertook, he thought, his heart expanding with all the emotions he had finally allowed himself to feel. And whether she cared to admit it or not, she was every inch a lady, from the refined little nose to the slim, aristocratic fingers plying the needle to the fierce devotion she inspired in the wolfdog stretched out protectively at her feet. Trade her mobcap for a veil, the tablecloth for a tapestry, and she might have been a princess in a castle turret.

And, he mused silently, that probably made him serf or a similarly unflattering equivalent.

They sat in companionable silence while behind them the others played cards and got silly on Mrs. Dare's brandy. The logs in the hearth popped. Rosanne's hands became still; with a quiet sigh, she leaned back against the settee and closed her eyes.

"Love, are you asleep?" Gaining no response, Brant knelt before her and gently secured the needle in the linen so that she wouldn't prick her finger. Then, as he was about to reseat himself, he jerked his head around in reaction to the violent blast of wind that rattled the windows.

Damn and blast, he groaned inwardly as he suddenly remembered he'd left the windows unshuttered in the cabin. There hadn't been a cloud in the sky that morning. He straightened up with a grimace, thinking of the personal effects he had moved there only a few days ago. Books, a trunk of clothes, bedding, and even his wedding present for Rosanne: a leather toilette case that contained a hand-beaten silver-backed brush and mirror, an ivory comb, a vial of perfume, curling tongs, and an assortment of herbal washballs. She had hinted that she coveted the case on their last trip into Schenectady, and he'd ridden back later to buy it and then hide it in the cabin so that it would be a surprise.

He walked to the door. Everything would be ruined in the rain, and he couldn't afford replacements. He'd sunk all his cash into supplies; he wouldn't realize any returns until spring. For God's sake, hadn't the almanac predicted fair weather until the end of the month? He'd be better off listening to Mrs. Dare's rheumatism complaints for clues to the weather—

It hit him just as he reached the hallway. Rheumatism. Limps. The medicinal scent of bitternut-hickory oil. The assailant who left no tracks. He retraced his steps to the doorway, feeling like a fool for not having suspected

Ericsson sooner but at the same time relieved he'd realized the truth before it was too late.

"Deep Spring, would you come here, please?"

The Indian girl left the table—reluctantly, since she was also leaving the first decent hand she'd held all evening. "Are you going outside in this rain?" she asked disapprovingly, glancing down at the hat in his hand.

"Spring, listen to me," he said quietly, urgently. "It's Peter Ericsson who has been stalking me. I'm sure of it."

"Why?" she whispered.

"God knows. I guess he never got over the bruising I gave him years ago. Obviously the man is too dangerous to be allowed to wander around for even another day. Tomorrow morning I'll ride out to the hills to find him. Patrick must be told. I'm sorry, but there's no avoiding it. Everyone in the area will have to be warned to watch for him."

She nodded grimly. "I won't tell Patrick tonight, not when he's been drinking, or he'll surely not wait before going out to find Peter."

"First thing tomorrow?"

"Yes." She glanced back into the room, and her eyes were troubled as her gaze came to Brant. "Where are you going now?"

"To the cabin. I left the shutters open. We'll talk about this more in the morning. Go back to your game."

He had been gone for an hour when Rosanne awoke, startled by the sound of a log shifting in the fireplace. This is dreadful, she thought, dozing off in the parlor like an old woman. She laid her tablecloth aside and glanced around the room, searching for Brant among the figures at the table.

"Is Brant in his office?" she asked, stifling a yawn.

"No, lass," Patrick replied from the table. "He's just ridden over to the cabin."

"In this weather?" She sat forward in alarm. "Whatever for?"

"Damned if I know. Spring, do ye know—"

A violent pounding at the door cut him short. He got up

and strode into the hallway, Rosanne at his side. Surely a visitor this late at night, during a storm, could only bring unwelcome news, she thought. What if something had happened to Brant? Lord, was this sick fluttering inside her a premonition or merely a mark of early pregnancy?

Patrick wrenched the door open, ushering in a gust of rain-laced wind and the short, dripping figure of Garth Hitchcock.

"By Jesus," Patrick exclaimed and stood back as the foreman shook himself like a wet dog. "Don't tell me ye've come out in this deluge to see Sally again, ye lovesick lunatic. Ye've not been gone all of three hours—"

"I've been up at the blockhouse," Garth said, interrupting him. "Two Mohawk runners just brought word that one of their hunting parties sighted Abnakis north of Indian Lake. French soldiers too."

"So the old trapper was right after all," Patrick said tersely. "Well, 'tis a long way off, and we're well protected, but there's no sense in taking chances. We'll not fire off the cannon yet though. Have ye alerted the other settlers?"

"Not yet. I came here first."

"Spread the word then, but caution against panic. I suppose I'll have to ride out to old man Tyrell over the hill. Hell of a night to cross the creek."

Garth turned back to the door. "The rain's easing up. We'll have snow within a fortnight."

Patrick wheeled and strode toward the parlor, yelling into the doorway, "Crane!"

Jonathan appeared instantly. The solemnly drawn lines of his face revealed he had overheard enough of the exchange between Patrick and Garth to grasp the seriousness of the situation. "What do you want me to do?"

"Just stay here with the women, if ye don't mind." Patrick thrust his arms into his jacket and hurriedly shouldered the musket Deep Spring brought him. "I've a few woodsmen to call on, so don't worry if I'm gone awhile."

His wife trailed him to the door, clutching at his arm as he paused to rearrange his bullet pouch and powder horn.

"Be careful when you ride through the hills," she said in a sudden surge of fear for him. "There's a trapper, a man I knew long ago . . . I—I must tell you—"

"Tell me when I get back," he said impatiently, yanking his arm loose. "I'll be fine."

Rosanne rushed up behind them, her face suddenly pale. "Patrick, what about Brant? Aren't you going to send someone out to—"

"He'll be fine too," Patrick snapped, and then he was gone, the door banging loudly behind him.

Chapter 28

Rosanne turned slowly, her distressed gaze meeting Jonathan's across the hallway. "He's out there alone," she said, her voice laced with anxiety. "I'd ride out to the cabin myself if I knew the way."

"No, you wouldn't. It's completely unnecessary." He came forward and took her hand, leading her back into the parlor where Priscilla was gathering up dirty bowls and glasses in a burst of nervous energy. "Indian Lake is over a hundred miles away," he explained. "They could not possibly have moved that fast. But if it will make you feel better, after Patrick gets back I'll ride over to the cabin later to see that Brant is safe."

Her face brightened. "Oh, thank you, Jonathan. No doubt he'll have returned long before then anyway. After what happened that day, I don't like the thought of him out this late alone. Especially if there's a chance of an attack."

"If I thought we were in any real danger of a raid, I wouldn't be here myself," he said lightly. "In another week, we'll probably learn that the Indians have returned to Crown Point, and our lives will settle back into comfortable monotony."

"I hope so." She gave him a warm smile and squeezed his hand, grateful for his reassurance. "And I'd always thought doctors were good only for bleedings and administering enemas."

"Pray God I am as adept at handling a musket in an emergency as I am a lancet."

Her smile wilted. "Pray God, Doctor, that we never find out."

"I might have stayed in London, tending hypochondriac merchants and colicky countesses," he mused. "I might be sipping a damson plum cordial this very minute, perusing my journals in some elegant townhouse on the Thames with a brazier of coals at my feet."

"Ah, but you aren't, Doctor. And weren't you just this afternoon complaining that you craved a little adventure?"

He inclined his head and gazed down at her, his eyes teasing and yet oddly resigned. "I crave many things, it would seem, that I can't have."

Rosanne looked away quickly, her gaze settling on Priscilla at the table. She dared not ask him to elaborate on that remark. She had too much on her mind for flirtatious parlor banter, with which she suspected he was attempting to divert her. She realized it was totally irrational to worry about Brant falling into an ambush with the enemy so far away, but she would be unable to rest easy until he returned to the house.

Another hour crawled by. Although the rain stopped, the wind had risen again to a menacing hiss, whistling against the windows and releasing its chilly breath to race through the naked cornfields. Finally everyone except Rosanne, and of course Dr. Crane, went upstairs to bed. Not even Mrs. Dare felt the danger imminent enough to warrant losing a wink of sleep. They were as ready as they would ever be for an attack.

Jonathan, to pass the time, sat at the table playing solitaire while Rosanne alternated between pacing before the fire and embroidering lilies on her tablecloth. Then suddenly she sprang out of her chair, aware that she hadn't seen Tynan since late that afternoon. She might not have been so concerned if she hadn't learned recently that the Indians considered dog a tasty addition to the stewpot.

"My hound, Jonathan. Have you seen him?"

"What? Oh, let me think. Mrs. Dare let him out over an hour ago."

"In the rain? He'll be soaked."

"Umm. She made some remark to the effect that she'd rather he got wet than the settee."

Rosanne pulled her cloak from the peg by the door. "He's probably in the kitchen garden."

"I'll help you look." He threw down his cards, rose, and had just pushed his chair back to the table when another knock sounded at the door.

"I'll answer it." He nudged Rosanne gently from his path. "Stay here—just in case."

She giggled, following after him. "Don't be silly, Jonathan. Raiding parties don't knock, do they?"

"Properly bred ones do," he said gravely.

It was one of the sentries, a young, lanky-boned boy whose overloud voice betrayed the nervous tension he felt at having to leave his post on what he considered to be an unimportant errand. "Mrs. Miller's baby's comin', Doctor. Her husband says it's too early, and something's wrong."

Crane frowned. " 'Tis early. But where's the damned midwife?"

"Hidin' in her cellar," the boy said scornfully. "Says she ain't comin' out till it's safe."

"Well, I can't leave here now," Crane said in exasperation. "I gave my word I'd wait for Patrick."

Rosanne moved beside him. "Go ahead, Jonathan," she urged. "He'll be home any time now. I'll collect your things."

He hesitated, clearly unhappy about breaking his promise. "Are you sure?"

"Yes. You can't let that poor woman suffer just for the sake of keeping me company. Go on. It's not as if I'm by myself."

"Well, if you think—"

"Yes, I do."

Several moments later she stood in the doorway helping

him on with his cloak. "Be careful, Jonathan. And if you have a chance—"

"Yes. Yes," he said with amused impatience. "The cabin. I remember. Now, go back into the house and . . ." His voice swirled away into the wind as, with a curt wave, he turned to stride down the darkened pathway to the stable.

Rosanne waited until he disappeared from sight; then, throwing her cloak around her shoulders, she ran outside and around the house to the garden.

"Tynan?" she whispered. Her eyes searched for the shaggy gray form. "Tynan, come on, boy."

Light rain had begun falling again, and the wind swept through the bare, tidy garden in a sudden violent gust. Drawing up the hood of her cloak, Rosanne opened the gate and jogged toward the outbuildings where the dog had likely taken shelter. Then from the corner of her eye, she saw a black-haired figure clad in buckskin; it was moving toward her. She froze, her heart lurching.

"Rosanne?"

"Deep Spring. Oh, what a fright you gave me. What are you doing out here?"

"I'm watching for my husband. And you?"

"Looking for my dog."

"He's probably staying dry under the eaves of the woodshed. I'll walk with you." She rubbed her arms, shivering as the wind swished through the bordering sugar maple branches and dislodged a spattering of icy raindrops. "Ga-ho is bringing a warning on the wind tonight. Listen . . ."

Rosanne felt a tingle travel up her spine, more from foreboding than from the cold. "Do you think we'll be attacked?" she asked uneasily.

"No. Not here." Deep Spring's dark head turned suddenly in the direction of the trading post. "What was that?"

"It came from over there." Rosanne stepped toward the sound, gathering her cloak into her body. "Oh, Lord, could Tynan have gotten locked inside the store again?

Simon must have let him in when he went back tonight to fetch the lantern."

"Leave him until my husband returns," Deep Spring whispered, hanging back in the darkness.

"What? And have Brant ranting about the mess he's made? I'd— "

She and Deep Spring froze in unison, simultaneously perceiving the two crouching figures a fraction of a second before the forms sprang off the porch and lunged toward them.

Deep Spring whirled in panic, recognition and stark fear spreading across her face. "Run, Rosanne!" she gasped. "Get back into the—" A rough palm smothered the conclusion of her cry, its wild-eyed owner grunting as he dragged the struggling girl backward into the store.

Rosanne wavered, torn between attempting to save her friend or running to the blockhouse for help. She whirled, the decision made, as an involuntary scream rose in her throat. But before it was possible to alert anyone, the second man ran up behind her and brutally clapped his hand over her mouth, flinging his arm across her diaphragm with a force that winded her. She kicked and twisted every step he forced her to take, but she was no match for his wiry strength—it was insanity to fight him—and he had little trouble maneuvering her back onto the porch. She'd gotten only a glimpse of his face, but she had recognized his long blond braid. It came to her in a terrifying stab of understanding then that Peter Ericsson was the man who had assaulted her in the MacGavins' barn. Had he been stalking her, she wondered in horror, stalking her like one of the poor animals he tortured and trapped? Dear God, what did he intend to do once he forced her inside the store? He had to be insane, she realized frantically, dangerously insane to risk attacking her inside the stockade!

He shoved her deep into the store's musty interior, sent her hurtling forward, and then wheeled to bolt the door behind him. The urge to scream again, to scream and scream in the hope of summoning help, gathered inside her. But then all at once, in the darkness, relieved only by a strand of moonlight piercing a chink in the roof, she caught the flash of a knife unsheathed, and her shocked gaze fell on Deep Spring, lying unconscious on her back beneath her hulking, long-haired assailant.

Peter grabbed Rosanne and spun her around roughly, hissing into her stricken face, "If you scream again, he'll slit her throat from ear to ear."

"She isn't moving," Rosanne said brokenly, wrenching free. "How do you know he hasn't already killed her?" She darted forward, but Peter caught her arm and slammed her back against the counter with a snarled warning.

"She isn't dead yet. But if you make the slightest noise to attract attention, or if you try to escape me, I promise you she'll die instantly. Luther has a deep-seated hatred of squaws that goes back to the time when they carved up his face." He smiled with cruel enjoyment, his eyes sliding to his companion. "Isn't that right, handsome?"

Luther grunted, absorbed in the process of resheathing his knife when Deep Spring suddenly twisted out from beneath him, wresting the weapon from his hands and leaping to her feet. Luther grabbed her and missed swaying clumsily to one side. Without thinking Rosanne reached across the counter to fling a bolt of calico in his face. It unfolded in its flight and temporarily deterred him, but Peter reached the door at the same moment as the agile young Indian woman and placed himself directly in her path.

"Be careful, Deep Spring," Rosanne pleaded, her hands sweeping the counter again in a frantic search for another weapon. Then, to her horror, she felt Luther grab her from behind and haul her roughly against his enormous frame, imprisoning her in a crushing hold that almost choked her into unconsciousness. Over the hairy forearm he had drawn across her windpipe, she watched in terrified fascination as her friend attempted to defend herself at the door. Incongruously she noticed that Peter had changed back into his hunting attire and that he seemed to be enjoying himself as he had the day she'd caught him tormenting the bear.

Deep Spring had whirled on him, slashing out blindly, carelessly, her breath coming in soft animal whimpers.

"You always were quick with a knife, Deosongwa," Peter said tauntingly, circling her with a wary respect that contradicted the mockery in his voice. "Marriage to the Irishman obviously hasn't tamed the savage in you. Doesn't he beat you often enough?"

Cornered, her eyes black with the remembered cruelty she had experienced at this man's hands, Deep Spring attacked him, jabbing for his heart. He dodged, jumping back nimbly, but not before the knife had slashed across his abdomen, leaving a thin red laceration that soaked through his roughly woven shirt. He didn't look down. He seemed not to realize he'd been injured.

But he had tired of playing and, his eyes like frozen granite, he closed in swiftly to disarm her. In desperation, Deep Spring sprang at him again, and as the knife sank into his shoulder, through flesh, muscle, and into bone, she jerked her body backward and spun wildly to unbolt the door.

Shock, unexpected pain, and then fury registered on Peter's face. He caught Deep Spring by the waist and threw her against a copper-banded barrel. She landed, dazed and quivering, at Rosanne's feet. Cursing under his breath, Peter grabbed the hilt of the knife and withdrew the blade from his shoulder, pressing the heel of his hand to the wound to staunch the flow of blood.

"Let the girl go, Luther," he growled. "I need her to bind my shoulder. She has a gentle touch."

Rosanne staggered forward as the trapper released her, hatred blazing in her eyes. "I'll not help you! I hope you bleed to death. I hope—"

"Do as I say, or the squaw dies."

"Don't fight him, Rosanne," Deep Spring said faintly from the floor where she lay, still stunned from her fall. "Do whatever he asks. I beg you."

Her face gray, Rosanne reviewed her alternatives and

realized with sick fear that she could do nothing to escape without endangering her friend's life. Numb, her fingers ice cold and trembling, she obeyed Peter's instructions, all the while hoping fiercely he would faint or, better yet, die from the loss of blood. He hadn't bled that heavily, however, considering the blade had sliced a deep ugly gash that reached to his armpit. Her eyes bright with anxiety, she stepped back when she had finished and wiped her hands on her cloak.

"What—what are you going to do with us?" she whispered.

"Be quiet!" He glanced back at Deep Spring with a contemptuous sneer. "Take the heathen bitch into the storeroom, Luther, and keep her there until I've had time to reach the river." From the canvas bag at his side, he produced a strip of rawhide which he lifted to dangle menacingly before Rosanne. "I hate to mark that soft white skin, but I've a feeling you'll try to get away from me."

She lifted her eyes to the door.

"Don't try it," he said flatly. "You won't escape me."

Chapter 29

The next quarter of an hour flashed before Rosanne in a string of nightmarish images: Deep Spring's look of terror as Luther carried her into the storeroom; Peter forcing her, Rosanne, out into the cold, stinging rain; his ugly, whispered promise—"She dies if you so much as gasp until we're outside the stockade. Luther will be watching us from the post."

She prayed they would be stopped by the sentries. But the stockade gates had been opened for the arrival of a woodsman, his wife, their three crying children, and a cow who were seeking protection in the two-story blockhouse. Patrick had left orders to admit them. The guards were so preoccupied with watching the hills for Indians they took no notice of the two shadowy figures that slipped past them.

Please, God, Rosanne prayed desperately, let one of the sentries see us before it's too late. Let Patrick return . . . or Brant. *Oh, Brant, Brant, where are you?* Her gaze scoured the darkly wooded hills around them for a sign of a rider emerging from the road. No one. Only the wildly thrashing branches of the hemlocks in the wind.

She twisted around violently, still in Peter's arms, for a final look at the stockade, an angry sob breaking from her lips as the gates swung closed. Peter's sour breath rasped against her cheek as he spoke. "Keep moving. No, not toward the highway. We cross through the woods."

Would it do any good to scream? Would Luther kill Deep Spring, and Peter her, before help could reach them? she wondered wildly. She stumbled over a tangle of rain-slick roots, unable to balance herself with her hands bound. Peter caught her before she could fall, his arm tightening around her ribcage. "Be careful. I don't want you hurt."

She shook her head in confusion. "Why are you doing this to me? What do you possibly hope to gain?"

"You are very valuable to me, Rosanne," he said succinctly, prodding her back onto the trail.

She halted, pretending to stumble again as she forced herself to fight against fear and think. Use any means to delay their progress. Keep him talking. Perhaps Jonathan would take the short way through the woods. Or perhaps it would be Brant. Perhaps the two men were even together. "What do you mean, I am valuable, Peter?"

He hesitated and watched her lean against a tree, pretending to catch her breath. His instructions had been to reveal nothing to her, to deliver her unharmed. "Someone is willing to pay a great deal of money for you. That's all you need know."

She jerked away from him as he reached for her arm. What did he mean? Was he hoping to hold her for ransom? "Brant doesn't have any money," she cried. "He'll kill you when he finds us! And he will find us." She raised her head and stared over his shoulder as if she could will Brant to materialize from the trees.

Peter yanked her toward him impatiently. "He's not coming."

They hurried on beneath a tunnel of interlaced branches, Rosanne's feet barely touching the sodden, leaf-strewn ground. The trapper seemed to possess an uncanny instinct for knowing exactly where to step, in which direction to turn. Dimly she noticed that they'd left the familiar trail, and when unexpectedly they broke onto the path that led to the pool, she was unable to hold back a fearful shudder at the realization that they'd already covered two miles without encountering anyone. The rain had stopped. A restless silence hung over the ravine. The air smelled fresh and tingled with moist cold.

Peter allowed her a minute to rest, then pushed her across the clearing to the horse Luther had left tethered in the pine grove. The animal shied away from Peter as he approached and snorted with her head thrown back, until he jerked down ferociously on the bridle. Rosanne's heart sank. They would travel so much faster on horseback!

"You'll mount first," he told her. "Come here. There wasn't time to get another horse."

"Steal one, you mean," she said, her voice sharp with rancor and outrage.

He smiled coldly. "After tonight, I'll be able to afford an entire stable."

She lowered her gaze and stared at the ground, her thoughts racing erratically. She was still near enough to the settlement to reach it on her own if she could get a good start on him, catch him off guard. She braced her hands on the saddle, slightly above the shoulder of his injured arm, as he leaned against the horse to hoist her up.

"Wait," he said. "I'll loosen the rawhide around your wrists so that you can use your hands to keep your balance, but don't think you can outrun me."

She flinched as he sliced through the rawhide with his hunting knife; then, glaring at him, she shook her wrists to restimulate circulation. She would force herself to remain submissive until the right moment. "How . . . how did you get into the stockade, Peter?"

He resheathed his knife and lifted her onto the horse. "Did I ever say I left?"

He's planned out his every move, she realized now, her dread mounting. She had to escape him before they put another mile behind them! Her right hand crept cautiously across the mare's shoulder toward a dangling length of rein, freezing suddenly as Peter glanced up at her. Furtively she drew her hand back inside her cloak. And then, in the feeble moonlight that broke through the foilage, she saw the blood on the mare's shoulder, on her own fingertips, blood mingled with raindrops. Had the poor horse been hurt, or had Peter's wound begun to bleed again? He couldn't last long if it had, she thought, hope buoying her. She stole a glance down at his shoulder as he grasped the pommel to mount. He caught her look as he swung up behind her.

"What are you staring at?"

"There's blood on the horse. She won't carry us far if she's hurt. Maybe—maybe we should walk."

"The horse isn't bleeding," he said evenly. "But her owner did before Luther shot him."

"Her owner—"

"Haven't you recognized the mare?"

In her bewilderment, she hadn't. But now, as she turned her head and gazed down at the animal, fearful apprehension filled her. "Gemma," she whispered, the name catching in her throat. "Oh, God, where is he?" she cried. "What have you done to him?"

"He's dead. Luther shot him."

"No." She shook her head, disbelieving. It was a cruel trick to subdue her, to frighten her into acquiescence. "You stole his horse, that's all! He and Patrick will track you down. And if you hurt either me or Deep Spring—"

Peter spurred the horse forward, trying to close his mind to her threats, irritated that they had any power at all to disturb him. He knew he wouldn't feel this unease if he'd taken care of Layton himself. But he hadn't been able to lie in wait for Rosanne inside the stockade and follow Brant at the same time. One of them had had to remain behind, and Peter was more skilled at hiding himself than Luther. Still, Luther was only an adequate marksman, and for a moment Peter considered riding to the ford where Luther claimed Layton had fallen face down in the cold river current. But he couldn't risk being caught with the girl. He couldn't even spare the time to cover their tracks.

"He's dead by now," he thought aloud, taking reassurance from his own words. Layton would have drowned even if the two musket shots to the chest hadn't killed him instantly. At this point, Peter almost didn't care. He'd get paid for the girl—that was what really mattered.

The dispassionate conviction in his voice knifed through Rosanne's consciousness. He wasn't feigning, she thought despairingly. He's a cold-blooded murderer, and somewhere very near Brant was lying dead, the victim of this insane scheme. She wanted to find him, to fling herself down beside him, to draw him back from death. She couldn't imagine how she would live without him. There was no point to it. He had been everything to her, the source of her sweetest joys and most bitter sorrows. Scalding tears of grief spilled down her cheeks, and her heart felt as though it would burst from her chest with the anguish it contained. *Oh, my love, my love.* And then it struck her that the blood on her hand was actually Brant's, and with that horrifying realization, a darkly savage side of herself she never dreamed existed broke through her shattered emotions to take control.

She waited, holding her breath until her lungs ached, and as Peter began to guide the mare up the hillside, she swiveled around in the saddle and violently swung her elbow upward into his throat. He rocked back, clutching his neck with a choked curse. Before he could recover, she pounded her fists repeatedly against his wounded arm, pounded until her hands hurt, and then threw herself to the ground, rolling painfully beneath Gemma's belly and down the muddy incline.

She didn't wait for his reaction. She spared no time looking back. She sprang to her feet and ran, ran on the wild chance that if she stayed within the densely crowded trees and underbrush, he would be unable to follow her on horseback. Wet leaves cushioned her frantic moccasined footfalls. Damp, thorny branches tore rents in her billowing plum velvet cloak. Close behind her now,—oh, God, too close—she heard hoofbeats pounding and twigs splintering as Peter forced the mare through the tangled forest thickets.

Then all at once, silence.

She hesitated, swallowing a sob. Her neck muscles quivering, she glanced back into the shadows. Had she lost him? Had he fainted from the pain of her attack? Surely she would have heard him fall . . . She clutched her cloak tighter to her trembling form and spun about. She would have to break out onto the trail sooner or later to reach Hemlock Creek. She prayed against logic that she would have left Peter far behind when the time arrived.

Brant—Brant. A sudden wave of grief broke over her and brought fresh blinding tears to her eyes. She wanted to sink to her knees and sob her heart out, but something kept her running, wouldn't let her stop. Oh, God, why? What motive could Peter have had? Did it have something to do with the fact that he and Deep Spring seemed to have known each other before? Was she the woman Brant had spoken of defending years ago? At the thought of her friend being held hostage by that fiend in the trading post, renewed panic shot through her system. She had almost forgotten in her own terror and grief, Peter's threat that Deep Spring would die, but now his words flooded back to haunt her. What proof did she have that Luther hadn't already murdered the girl? And how many other victims might he claim as he attempted to sneak outside the stockade? If Patrick found him . . . Patrick. He would know what to do. He would help her find Brant . . . or his body.

She cried out without thinking as her cloak became snagged on a branch and sent her stumbling tiredly against a rough pine trunk. Her chest heaved. She closed her eyes and clung to the tree. She had to rest, had to calm her mind so that she could think of ways to outwit, if not to outrun, Peter. For she knew she couldn't run much farther.

She forced her eyes open, gazing around into the black dripping grove. The ravine. Thank God! She had approached it from the northwest hills. Hemlock Creek lay only two miles south.

Drawing a deep breath, she plunged across the clearing. She never heard a footstep on the pine-needle path. Never noticed the shadow emerging from behind the tree directly beside her. Not until she stood only an arm's length away from the tall, unsmiling figure.

She whirled. Peter caught her by the shoulder, spinning her around into an inescapable embrace. His other hand crawled up the nape of her neck, where he twined his fingers in the braided knot of her hair and tugged it until he held her immobilized. They were standing in the same spot where he had tormented the bear that summer afternoon, she realized sickly. But no one would come to her rescue.

He turned her around slowly, crushing her against his chest so that she could smell the sweat and blood and excitement emanating from him. Dear Lord, what did he plan to do with her now? Punish her for running away? Rape her and throw her into the ravine? His dark gray eyes revealed nothing of his intentions; they were, she noticed, chillingly devoid of any expression whatsoever.

"I always told Kerstin that her hair was too pretty to wear tied back," he said with quiet intensity, and the effect of those strange words was somehow more frightening than the violence she had anticipated. "I cut off her braid after she died," he continued softly. "I still carry it with me. Would you like to see it?"

Rosanne bit her underlip. "N-no. Oh, please, Peter. For the love of God—"

"Kerstin was afraid too. She didn't want to be sold to an unknown master in a foreign land. She was only a little girl. I couldn't allow her to be humiliated on an auction block, to be taken from me and violated by a stranger. Could I?"

His voice had gone deadly flat, and it was all Rosanne could do to fight back another wave of panic. He had murdered his own sister. She was terrified to voice the realization, terrified even to let it show in her eyes for fear she would meet the same fate.

"P-please, Peter. Please, let me go."

"I can't. You are my passport to the fine life, Rosanne. Because of you I needn't spend another winter living like a stinking savage. Maybe I'll even return to Sweden." He frowned thoughtfully, lifting a loosened strand of her hair to his mouth in a disturbingly sensual gesture. "What a shame I can't take you with me."

She shivered, praying he wouldn't kiss her, but then

suddenly he released her. In a detached tone he said, "I'll have to tie your hands to the pommel. I can't take the chance that you might hurt yourself."

"Is it . . . is it true that Luther killed Brant?" she whispered.

"It's true." His face hardened as if the question angered him. He shoved her forward toward the mare and lifted her onto the saddle in silence.

Rosanne no longer struggled. She noted that he grimaced as he mounted, and she wondered if he were truly as impervious to pain as he had bragged he was. She hoped not. She hoped he would suffer all the agonies of hell. It was clear to her that he would be forced to seek medical attention. If only she could convince him to see Jonathan.

"Unless you have a doctor tend you, Peter, your wound will become infected—possibly gangrenous."

"I'm touched by your concern. But I'll worry about that *after* I've taken care of you. Hold on tightly now."

Taken care of me? Rosanne repeated to herself, horror underscoring every syllable.

He kicked the mare's sides, and Rosanne lurched sideways in the saddle, the rawhide strips cutting into her wrists. Peter's arm snapped out to steady her. Despairingly, she realized that he intended to avoid the road again and travel the ancient Iroquois game trails that he seemed to know by instinct. But he was a poor horseman, and Gemma seemed to sense his incompetence, slowing frequently to test him. In response Peter cursed and kicked her furiously until finally the mare lunged forward and carried them through the darkness at a steady canter.

They traveled for two hours through the low, wooded hills. Rosanne was unable to recognize even one familiar landmark along the inky terrain. Once they burst into a meadow with a cluster of cabins scattered in the distance. Although she was dazed and exhausted from her unsuccessful attempt at escape, she felt suddenly alert, every fiber of her body stirring in the hope that someone would see and intercept them.

Of course, no one did. At that hour, the chance of meeting anyone was remote. And then, as the mare descended a damp embankment, Rosanne recognized the Mohawk River stretching below, a moonlit pewter serpent coiling through the sleeping valley. They were going to ford the river, she realized in dismay. He was heading northeast, toward uncharted wilderness, into an area not inhabited even by Indians.

"Peter, where are we going?" She wriggled about so abruptly that she nearly unseated them both. "You can't mean to go north! You fool, Peter, there are reports of French Indians in the foothills!"

He gave her a look of such cold amusement that chills of terror leaped up her spine. Surely he didn't mean to sell her into slavery to hostile Indians! Or was he planning to carry her with him into Canada? She had to stop him before they left the valley. The farther away they got from civilization, the less chance there was that anyone would find her. In desperation she twisted herself around to face him. Frustrated by her immobilized hands, she butted him with her head, purposely aiming again for his injured arm, in an attempt to unhorse him.

For a moment it appeared she'd succeeded. He slid halfway out of the saddle, cursing her as he dropped the reins to raise his arms protectively. Then in one lithe move, he regained his seat and the reins and lashed his arm around her waist with such whipcord strength that it became difficult for her to breathe, let alone attempt another attack.

"You little bitch!" He dealt her a brutal blow across the side of the head, his furious voice penetrating the painful ringing between her ears. "Try that again, and you just might end up floating in the river like your lover! And don't bother to invent another absurd tale about Indians to frighten me. It won't work."

"It was not an invention," she said defiantly. "It's true! I hope the Indians capture you and roast you—"

She broke off and cringed as he lifted his arm warningly. What was the use in fighting him? He would only hit her again. And it was as futile to try to reason with him as it had been to attack him. She raised her face and stared ahead, feeling hopelessness settle on her like a heavy weight. All she could do was wait until he weakened and pray that by then it would not be too late.

Chapter 30

They stopped briefly on the north bank of the river, to rest the horse. Peter helped Rosanne dismount and stood in watchful silence as she collapsed beneath an oak tree. He had become brooding and withdrawn, she realized uneasily. His eyes held a haunted glint that did not seem human, and his face had taken on a sickly pallor. She was sure his arm was causing him great pain. She had only to bide her time.

He crouched down beside her and took several deep swigs from a canteen of rum and then thrust it at her, shrugging when she refused to drink from it. He had made an impulsive decision to cross the Mohawk and proceed along the less populated northeastern shore until they were nearer their destination of Albany. He knew they could go little farther that night. Neither the girl nor the horse were capable of it. And—damn!—that savage little squaw had done a vicious job on his arm. It would be all right though, once he cleaned and bandaged it. He'd had deeper wounds.

His head snapped around suddenly. "We're being followed," he hissed. He grabbed his musket and flung Rosanne a look that indicated that he blamed her.

She jumped to her feet. "Good! I'll make as much noise as I— "

He shot up behind her and covered her mouth with his hand. "It's an Indian," he whispered. "Perhaps you weren't lying after all. Now be quiet and get back on the horse. I'd hate to see that pretty scalp stretched out over a birch hoop."

She fell silent, her mind reeling. What choice did she have, caught between an amoral murderer and a French-Indian raiding party? But he hadn't hurt her yet. . . . For some reason he seemed intent on keeping her alive throughout this hellish journey. But at its end . . . She thrust the thought away, numbly allowing herself to be lifted back onto the mare.

He pushed the horse at a relentless pace through the narrow hill passages until they reached a remote hamlet northeast of Saratoga, close to the banks of the Hudson River. Unfortified, with its farms tended mostly by freed bondslaves, retired trappers, and former convicts, the community sprawled out beneath them in stump-scarred fields and dilapidated cabins. On its outskirts sat a forlorn wooden blockhouse, unmanned, its door banging in the wind. Behind it was the inn and trading post where Peter had spent more drunken nights than he could remember.

He hammered at the door and called for the proprietress by name, all the while clutching Rosanne tightly to his side as if they were lovers who could bear not a moment's separation. Candlelight flared behind the oiled paper that served as a windowpane. A gruff male voice shouted down an obscenity from the inn's second story. The latch lifted and the heavy door opened to reveal a wide-hipped woman in her fifties brandishing a musket, her unrefined features lit by a tallow stub in a chipped saucer that sat on the crudely carved shelf behind her.

"What in hell d'you mean by banging at my door this time of night?" she demanded. "Goddamn drunken bastards. Between you and them Mohocks— By Jesus, is that you, Ericsson?"

Peter tossed her two gold coins and shoved his way inside as she scrambled to retrieve them. "I've need of a room. Hot water, towels, food. And your silence."

The woman pulled herself erect, her eyes wandering to Rosanne with bold curiosity. "You've come up in the world, ain't you, Peter? Where'd you find her?"

Rosanne wrenched away from him, lifting her bound hands into the taper's glow for the woman to see. "For the love of God, help me, mistress. He's killed a man tonight, and—"

"You'll have to take the garret, Peter." The woman stared past Rosanne as though she didn't exist. "Mind you don't break anything."

"We'll be gone before you awake, Bessie. By dawn, probably."

The woman snorted. "You ain't got long then. But I don't suppose you came here to sleep." Taking the tallow candle stub from the shelf, she turned hurriedly toward the kitchen to heat the water he'd requested.

Rosanne turned as if to follow her, then went rigid with a gasp as Peter withdrew his knife and laid it across the madly beating pulse in her throat. "I have said you were valuable to me. But make no mistake. I value nothing above my own life. No one will help you here anyway. Will you behave?"

She nodded, her eyes dark with fear and hatred and the blood in her veins as cold as the steel pressed to her flesh. He dragged the knife, blade flat, down her throat to the rise of her breasts, then brought it back to his hip, spinning the hilt deftly between his fingers before sliding the weapon back into its worn leather sheath.

He released her with a little shove, and she backed away from him to sag against the unpaneled log wall, closing her eyes and giving way to the darkest despair she had ever known. *I will lose my mind before this night ends,* she thought. *What will happen next?*

"Get upstairs."

Her eyes snapped open as Peter grabbed her arm and hauled her up the small flight of stairs and into the dark, airless loft. He pushed her toward the corner that held a flimsy bedstead with a musty-smelling straw mattress, stripping off his gear as he went. Bewildered, she lost her balance and tumbled down onto the unwashed homespun coverlet.

He leaned down to bind one of her hands to the bedpost. "Go to sleep," he said brusquely.

Impossible. She lay back cautiously, pretending to close her eyes, but actually observing his movements through her lowered lashes. The woman he had called Bessie arrived, bringing him a pitcher of left-over wash water, dirty towels, and a tray of stale cornbread and cheese. Rosanne watched him try to bathe and bandage his arm; she heard him grunt as he stripped off his shirt and the wound reopened. She determined that if he asked her to stitch him, she would refuse. If he tried to rape her, she would fight him.

To her chagrin, she fell into a restless sleep. When she woke, it was to discover Peter leaning over the bed, untying the rawhide strip that bound her hand to the bedpost. Grayish light filtered through the window. It was almost dawn.

"Wake up. We're leaving here."

"I—I hurt all over. Won't you let me rest a few hours more?"

"The hamlet will be attacked within the hour. There are Abnaki war canoes hidden in the woods near the river."

She sat up hurriedly. "How do you know that?"

"I found them when I went looking for whoever was following us."

"Did you discover who it was?"

"I didn't have time. Now get up from that bed, dammit. This hovel will burn like a pack of cards when the Indians torch it."

She moistened her lips, shrinking away from him as she slid off the edge of the mildewed mattress. "Have you warned the others?"

"I've barely time to get us out of here and none to spare worrying about a fat old whore and her drunken patrons. We must ride away unseen." He threw her cloak around her shoulders; then, on impulse, he tore a strip of muslin from one of the sheets with the clear intention of securing it around her mouth as a gag. "A precaution—in case you decide to scream out a warning."

"No," she whispered hoarsely. "I won't—"

She tried to duck below reach of his hands, but within half a minute the gag was straining her jaw muscles painfully and filling her mouth with its musty taste. He hasn't slept at all, she thought dully. His lean cheeks looked flushed with unnatural color, and his eyes were feverishly bright.

She stumbled down the staircase, stepping on her cloak and tearing its silken frog fastening loose at the throat. The button popped off and clattered down the stairs.

Outside, in the grayish predawn gloom, the heavy velvet cloak slipped from her shoulders as they rode away from the hamlet. They did not return to retrieve it. The first spinetingling war whoops were already echoing in their ears before they reached the nearby hills.

Chapter 31

Four days? A week? How long had it been now since Peter had abducted her from Hemlock Creek? It had rained that night, she remembered, staring listlessly around the moldering hillside cavern where she and the trapper had taken refuge. And it had begun to rain again shortly after daybreak the morning of the raid.

The raid. She drew her knees up to her face to muffle a moan in the folds of her tattered woolen overskirt. Sweet Lord, how much longer could she survive this torment, her body wracked with cold and hunger, her heart numb with grief? And her mind—would it ever recover from the scene of senseless carnage she had witnessed?

The raid, she thought again, shuddering. Peter had rushed them to safety with perhaps five minutes to spare. Behind a screen of white pines on a hill, they had watched the war party swarm down on the settlement. French soldiers, *Canadian coureurs de bois*, those ruthless and independent wood runners—trappers—and painted Abnaki Indians awakening the slumbering hamlet with their ululating war whoops. Barns, filled to the rafters with their combustible harvest, were ignited into bonfires. Stinging charcoal-colored smoke had billowed above the pathetic sight of families fleeing in their nightclothes toward the safety of the river, only to encounter another party lying in wait. Rosanne had seen a young brave recover her cloak and wear it while he scalped a farmer running to rescue his children. Had anyone escaped slaughter or captivity?

Then, traveling on horseback, in a hysterical frenzy, Peter had taken her away from the smoldering ruins as fast as the exhausted mare could carry them, first through oozing swampland, then into the tangled wilderness of the southern foothills of the Adirondacks, stopping finally to take shelter (days ago?) in this cave. The raid had unleashed horrific memories of his own captivity years before, of suffering that had left even deeper scars on his psyche than were inflicted on his body. Dangerously unbalanced to begin with, slowly dying from gangrene, he was descending into an irrational delirium. His lucid moments had become frighteningly less frequent.

He had difficulty remembering who Rosanne was and why he had to take her to Albany. He swung back and forth in his mind between recollections of his childhood and those of his earliest years in America. One moment he was mumbling about the frost giants and the ugly black elves who lurked in the depths of the cave; the next he was gazing outside with his musket leveled at a hallucinatory enemy, convinced that he had seen an Indian. And each time he sprang up from the mat of branches and pine needles that served as his bed, muttering incoherently, Rosanne would huddle deeper beneath the matted bearskin he had given her, wondering whether it was merely another delusion of his deranged mind or indeed a straggler from the war party.

Several times she had actually seen members of the war party marching their prisoners past the mouth of this very cavern. Fear had kept her at Peter's side, a fear far stronger than the rawhide thongs he had used to bind her hands.

The previous night, while he thrashed and moaned in the throes of a feverish sleep, she had finally stolen his knife and freed her hands. She might have escaped him easily then, but it was fear again—the fear of not finding her way through the savage wilderness—that forced her to remain inside the cave. She hated Peter with a fierce intensity that grew every moment she spent contemplating his crimes. Yet she believed she needed him to survive;

the life growing inside her, if indeed Brant's seed had taken root, had to be protected at all costs.

Suddenly her thoughts were scattered by the sound of Peter's voice:

"*Vad är det,* Kerstin? What is wrong?" he asked, turning on his pallet of evergreen boughs to gaze at her. "I'll find the way home before dark. I won't let the elves hurt you."

She was shocked at the rasping weakness of that voice. Clutching the knife beneath the bearskin, her skirts dragging along the dank cave floor, she edged toward him. His eyes followed her from hollowed sockets; beneath a sparse sprinkling of blond beard, his cheeks were sunken, creating skeletal shadows. The stench of putrefying flesh pervaded the cave.

"Peter," she said urgently, "I must light a fire. Else we shall freeze to death. And we need food." She touched his chest, half hoping, half afraid he'd stopped breathing. "Peter? Peter, please. We're lost, and it's going to snow."

"We are not lost, Kerstin," he whispered with an indulgent smile. "Follow the path from the woodcutter's hut to the millstream."

He opened his eyes briefly, frowning in confusion, and raised his hand to touch her unbound hair. Rosanne drew back in alarm and retreated to her corner of the cave; although she knew he was too weak to hurt her now, she could not forget what he'd done to Brant and to his sister, the innocent young girl he had murdered out of a dark, warped love. She had been sleeping badly at night, keeping constant guard lest she become his next victim.

"I won't let our *mor* sell you, Kerstin. I won't let her sell you to that man in Albany."

Tears of frustration slipped down Rosanne's face; she dashed them away angrily, impatient with her own weakness. "Damn you, I'm not Kerstin!" Then, swinging her head back around to stare at him, she demanded, "What man, Peter? *Who?*"

He had slipped into a coma.

That evening, just outside the cave entrance, she collected a stack of evergreen twigs and some hardwood chips to serve as kindling. Then she lit a fire, striking a piece of flint repeatedly against Peter's knife, until the kindling caught. Without enjoyment, she ate the last of the deer Peter had killed, washing it down with bitter spruce tea. Shivering, feeding the flames by meager handfuls, she dropped into a light sleep only to be awakened in the middle of the night by the appearance of two wolves at the entrance of the cave.

"Peter!" When he didn't answer, she grabbed the musket and fired it at the long, shaggy wolves, missing both but frightening them off into the misty forest.

"Peter," she cried, her voice strident with panic. "I don't know how to reload your musket, and there are wolves . . ."

He was dead.

She crawled closer to his side and stared down at his ghastly countenance with lightheaded detachment. Scarcely pausing, she swiftly tugged off the powder horn he had refused to part with, then his moccasins, which she would lace on over her own for added insulation. Her stomach churning with hatred, revulsion, and hunger, she covered him with his own woolen stroud and dragged his canvas hunting bag toward her. His tomahawk would weigh her down, but she might need it. It was senseless to carry along the musket, but the gunpowder would serve to start a campfire, if nothing else.

An hour, two hours passed. Sleep was impossible; she was terrified the wolves would return to claim the corpse. She stumbled outside, her head spinning from the claustrophobic fumes, and gazed up through the spreading blue-green arches of spruce and fir, searching for the North Star in the frosty sky.

Where was she? How would she find her way back to civilization? There were no trails to follow. The mare had run away two or three nights before, or rather Rosanne had chased her off, afraid that Peter would slaughter her for food. Faintly Rosanne hoped the horse would somehow return to Hemlock Creek, or that someone might become suspicious of a riderless mount and search the area.

But would it be a hostile Indian, or a French scout? Her mind refused to contemplate the frightening possibilities, concentrating instead on the monumental task of survival. She would not cry, and she would not panic. She would master her fears because there was no other choice left to her.

At dawn she breakfasted on groundnuts, or tubers, and crushed acorns. Armed only with a tomahawk and a hunting knife, wearing Peter's jacket and moose-skin mittens, which were strung around her neck by a cord to prevent their loss and consequent frostbite, she struck out in what she could only pray was the right direction. She had located the morning star just before sunrise and had charted a rough southwesterly course in her mind as the sky lightened.

It was useless to try to retrace the haphazard route she and Peter had taken. He had forced the mare to ride mostly through streambeds and across rocky river banks to avoid leaving tracks. If he hadn't been careful covering his trail from Hemlock Creek to the hamlet, he had been fanatical about it after the morning of the raid.

She wandered through the still sylvan aisles, feeling like a peasant skulking between rows of displeased conifer monarchs. She climbed over cold mossy boulders, grasping clumps of lichen for support. She treaded an endless carpet of frost crystals and pine needles that crunched beneath her feet. She wriggled through tunnels formed by fallen trees that housed families of carnivorous short-tailed shrews. She slid down a hillside and nearly impaled herself on the white, pointed rocks hidden in the tangles of a witch-hazel thicket.

By noon she had decided to follow a stream and struggled over a series of tumbling hillocks into a dank hollow where, to her dismay, the channel vanished underground and she sank in black boggy mud up to her knees.

By late afternoon she was weaving dizzily, barely able to plant one sodden moccasin in front of another. Worried that she might have traveled in a circle, she mounted a heavily wooded knoll that overlooked a valley and studied the terrain. To the north, mantled in smoky blue haze, were the Adirondacks, the name derived from the Indian Ha-De-Ron-Dah, a derogatory term meaning "bark eaters" which the Iroquois used to refer to their Algonquin enemies. The uppermost foliage of the hemlocks generally grew toward the rising sun, or east, and it appeared that she had been headed west as she'd intended. But her spirits flagged as she sighted a little mist-shrouded lake gleaming blue against the tall dark pines which ringed its shoreline. That lake had been her landmark from the cave. In an entire day of traveling she had covered only about two miles. She would be dead in a week at this pace.

Just before dusk, she frightened a fox from its kill, a scrawny rabbit that was more bones than flesh. After cleaning the animal at a nearby brook, she took shelter in a hemlock grove and fashioned a spit from a green branch stretched across two vertical crotched sticks. Since she had not yet eaten, she did not have enough strength to cut down any hardwood that would hold a fire, so she peeled off strips of hemlock bark and laid them crosswise over a kindling mound of dried conifer twigs.

Crouching beneath the bearskin, her stomach contracting hungrily, she could hardly wait for the meat to cook through before she began to devour it. "Poor little rabbit," she whispered in mournful apology as she licked her singed fingers. "I'm sorry you had to die."

That night the temperature dropped drastically, and a penetrating wind howled down from the northwest. She built a lopsided lean-to from hemlock boughs on a shaky frame of cedar poles. She tried to recall what she'd learned from watching both Brant and Peter in the woods, and then unexpectedly a torrent of tears overcame her, slipping warmly down her cheeks as she was waterproofing her roof with handfuls of moss.

It should keep us dry for the winter, if not safe from flaming arrows. . . .

It had been Peter and Luther who'd attempted to kill Brant that afternoon outside the cabin. Why? Had Peter been seeking revenge for something that had happened between him and Brant years ago? Had a murderous fury been sparked inside him the day Brant had ordered him out of the house? There was more to it, she knew—a thread that pulled everything together. And it concerned the man in Albany, the man Peter had mentioned in his delirium.

Conrad Sluyter.

Who else could it have been?

But what would he have wanted with her? She cringed inwardly as she remembered the feral lust in his eyes. She belonged to his rival. She was to have been a trophy of his revenge.

She dropped to the ground, weeping grievously and rocking back and forth in comfortless desolation until she had exhausted herself. Was this the day she and Brant were to have been married? Would this be the night they were to have spent together in the cabin? What should have been the sweetest hours she had ever known stretched before her as the beginning of the lonely path her life had suddenly become. She had known pain before but never like this, never this wrenching anguish that felt as though her very soul was being ripped apart. It would never heal, she thought. Until the day she herself died she would be incomplete.

She sat up slowly, aware of a sudden wave of dizziness washing over her. Was Jonathan correct in his diagnosis that she was pregnant? She felt so wretched, so faint and weary because of the ordeal she had undergone, it was difficult to tell. But her breasts were swollen and tender, and she had missed almost two monthly courses now. A baby. Brant's child. How happy he would have been to know a son or daughter would be born on his land. How delighted she would have been to tell him of it.

She gazed into the flames, her thoughts flitting erratically from what she would eat for breakfast to what she would name the baby to how she would take her own revenge on Conrad Sluyter. And take revenge on him she would. If she survived.

If she survived.

It was not her fears or lack of food or even Indians or animals that posed the greatest threat to her now, she reflected. It was the cold. Experienced woodsmen had perished in this wilderness. What chance did she have? Laying a few more strips of bark over the fire, she resettled herself beneath the bearskin and decided she was too tired to hunt for dry wood after all. As a result, she shivered convulsively throughout the night as her body struggled to produce heat. In the morning she felt as though she hadn't slept at all.

She followed the same disheartening pattern for the next three days, at times eating only bark she'd torn off birch trees and twice bringing down a partridge with a heavy stone.

On the evening of the third day, she built a fire and collapsed at the base of a boulder that faced a shallow stream. She had reached the limits of her physical endurance. The bruises and blisters on her feet had made walking intolerable. She could barely chew the tubers she had uprooted for the numbing lassitude creeping over her.

She had no idea where she was and she didn't care. She wanted only to sleep. And when, early the next morning, she felt a moccasined toe prodding her in the ribs and rolling her over like a stone, she thought at first that the impassive-faced Indian standing before her with his tomahawk uplifted was a figure from a dream.

Then panic broke inside her as he muttered an order in his own tongue and leaned down to yank the bearskin covering from her. Instinctively she drew her knees toward her belly and closed her fingers around the hilt of the hunting knife wedged beneath her hip. She had no intention of dying without a fight, but to her horror she found she hadn't the strength even to lift her arm, let alone defend herself. Blackness closed in around her, enveloping her in its velvety swirl.

"Please don't hurt me," she heard herself whisper faintly. "Don't hurt my baby . . ."

Chapter 32

High winds whipped through the branches above Brant's head, lashing at the leaves that clung to them stubbornly and would not be shed until spring arrived. Oblivious to his surroundings, he frowned in concentration and tried to decipher the charcoal symbols the war party had painted on the inner bark of the aged beech tree. Rain had smudged the roughly drawn figures so that he could barely read them.

Dear God, it's been two weeks, he raged silently. He had lost two weeks. He stiffened, conscious of an uncomfortable constriction in his upper chest where Crane had removed the lead balls that had struck Brant as he was fording the Mohawk. He'd suffered a tremendous loss of blood during the operation, but the balls had missed his heart. They had been deflected by the shot pouch that hung from his left shoulder and contained his own supply of cast-lead bullets. Crane's surgical skill had saved his life, although Brant would have drowned first if Little Otter and his brother White Eagle hadn't found him floating in the river on their return from a council meeting at Mount Johnson to the Lower Mohawk Castle. Apparently, he had managed to entangle himself in a tussock of rushes to avoid being caught in the current. But he didn't remember that. It was not until he regained consciousness two days later in White Eagle's *ganosote*, or bark house, where Crane had been forced to perform the surgery, that Brant learned exactly what had happened. But by then, feverish and weakened from loss of blood, he was forced to endure a frustrating recuperation before he could set out on Ericsson's trail.

Rosanne had vanished sometime during the last evening he'd seen her. Patrick had searched for hours that same night before he finally found his own wife, badly beaten, slumped unconscious over the body of the man whose throat she'd slit in self-defense.

Young and eager to avenge the assault on his niece, for the Iroquois highly esteemed their women and would tolerate no violence toward them, White Eagle had wasted no time following Ericsson's tracks to the hamlet where the trapper had briefly taken refuge. He planned to rescue the pale-haired woman first and then lift Ericsson's scalp. But the brave's attention had been diverted by the Abnaki war canoes he had stumbled upon at the Hudson River's edge. Reluctantly, White Eagle had swiftly returned to his village to alert his own people against a possible attack. The dilapidated tavern where Rosanne had last been seen burned to the ground, its occupants either dead or taken into captivity before Brant could find his way there—a fortnight after the raid.

Crane had undertaken the grim task of questioning the one surviving family concerning the bodies that were found among the charred ruins and had been buried quickly to prevent disease.

"The remains of three women were found beneath the rubble," he told Brant several hours later, white-faced and shaken. "It's believed that one was the proprietress, the other her daugher, and the third a woman traveling with her husband."

"Then she was taken prisoner by the Abnakis," Brant said quietly. "There's a chance she's still alive."

Crane withheld comment, unwilling to express his own doubts. The old farmer he'd interviewed had hidden himself and his family in a hemlock thicket above the Hudson. Not one of them recalled seeing a young woman of

Rosanne's description among the captives forced into the canoes.

"What are you going to do?"

"Find her," Brant said without hesitation.

"I'll go with you."

"You should stay here. You'll be needed in the valley."

But in the end Crane had accompanied Brant on what the physician privately thought was a futile journey, canoeing upstream whenever possible, portaging over trackless terrain when the waters became unnavigable. Confident they were not being followed, the raiding party had left a blatant trail along the land carries that even the heavy rains had not erased—blood from the scalps taken, spattered over stones; spoils that had become too cumbersome to continue carrying and were discarded along the way; and, frequently, the bodies of captives who had collapsed and died during the journey.

And, arrogantly, as if to flaunt their victory, the war party had painted records of their exploits on trees that stood out prominently along the carrying places. Now Brant stared intently, forcing himself to concentrate on interpreting the crude portrait instead of submitting to the raw feelings clamoring for release inside him.

"What the hell's this one say?" Crane asked again, as he came alongside Brant, pink splotches of cold glowing in his cheeks.

Brant answered without turning his head, his tone heavy with discouragement. "The same as before. Their tribal animal. The number of scalps taken and warriors lost." He faltered, his words fading to a hoarse whisper. "One child and two of the four women prisoners are dead. One woman, represented by this figure being carried on the litter, fell ill and died, probably of injuries received during the raid. The other was thrown out of a canoe and drowned for trying to escape just before they disembarked."

Crane looked away sharply to hide the despair and disillusionment he feared must show on his own face. "The river's just over that bluff. Perhaps we'll find their bodies and know with certainty that she wasn't among them."

"After a fortnight?" Brant said bitterly. "Scavengers will already have done their work, and as far as the woman who drowned—well, she'll be long swept away by now."

"I'll look around beyond the hill. We have little time if we mean to cover any distance before nightfall."

Brant nodded but did not remove his gaze from the paintings, his hazel eyes reflecting an emotional spectrum that ranged from insensate rage to desperate hope. It occurred to him that the tracks had been almost too easy to follow, as if the raiders had deliberately laid a false trail, or had been so confident of escape that they hadn't bothered to conceal their movements. In any event, the war party, traveling in the fast birchbark canoes of the Algonquins, would probably have taken the upper Hudson River to the land carry that led to Richelieu River by now.

Would Rosanne be thrown into an impenetrable prison in New France? Would she be tortured and made into a slave or would a kind-hearted Abnaki woman adopt her into her family to replace a child who had recently died? His only consoling thought was that the eastern woodland Indians didn't rape their female captives. But as for the Canadian bush-fighters . . .

Images of the torment she might have undergone, of the cruelty she might have suffered at Ericsson's hands, tore through his mind. He felt physically ill at the thought of anyone hurting her. His brave golden love. She would protest the mistreatment of her fellow prisoners at the risk of her own life. Please, God, he prayed desperately. Let her do whatever is necessary to survive. Let me find her. She's sweet and innocent and gentle. She has done nothing to deserve this . . .

He blinked and then closed his eyes, the wind chilling his drawn cheeks. He'd promised to protect her and he had failed. He should never have left the house that night, knowing Ericsson was in the area and bent on revenge. Oh, God, why had he taken her from his uncle? No matter how Hugh might have mistreated her, she would not have suffered the unspeakable horrors to which the Indians sometimes subjected their captives. His dreams could crumble into dust now for all he cared. In fact, he hadn't even returned to Hemlock Creek since the night Luther shot him. Everyone there except the members of his own household believed he'd died of a musket wound and was buried in an Iroquois village. Spreading that rumor had been Patrick's suggestion. The Irishman still asserted that Conrad Sluyter had played a part in the affair. If Patrick was correct, it would only be a matter of time before the Dutch merchant made another move—a legal move to claim Brant's land. But Brant didn't plan to wait that long. After he found Rosanne, or what had become of her, he intended to find Sluyter and kill him.

Crane gave a sudden excited shout. "I've found something! It looks—"

Had the wind snatched away Crane's concluding words? Brant wondered. Or had Jonathan found something so grim he couldn't bring himself to finish the sentence?

Brant roused himself and jogged in the direction of Crane's voice, his heart hammering, hoping and at the same time dreading what the other man had discovered. "Is it—" He averted his face, bile surging to his throat at the unexpectedly gruesome sight of a ravaged female corpse, or what the wolves had left of it, strewn across the forest floor. It soon became clear, however, that the poor woman had had brown hair.

They buried the remains in solemn silence, each grateful beyond words that it wasn't Rosanne who lay beneath the rock-covered mound with only a bark cross to mark the crude grave.

"It's damned cold," Crane said after awhile, stating the obvious from an unconscious need to end the funereal silence and the bleak thoughts it engendered. "Perhaps we'd better make camp for the night among the hills, sheltered from the wind."

Brant got up slowly, brushing leaf mold from his breeches, his face cast into uncompromising lines. "Stay if you like. I intend to follow the river for as long as it's possible."

"For God's sake, man—"

"I never asked you to accompany me, Crane," Brant said in terse tones that betrayed the effort he was exerting to keep his emotions in check. "You may take the canoe back. I'll build a raft."

"All I meant was that we should stop for the night and perhaps devise a more rational course of action. I'll not leave you alone in the middle of the bloody wilderness, and I don't fancy finding my own way back alone."

"Why did you come along at all?"

"I told you. I felt responsible for leaving Rosanne after Patrick asked me to stay. Don't imagine there's more in it than that. I do know a lost cause when I see one."

"I'm sure Patrick doesn't blame you," Brant said curtly. "Nor do I. If it's only your conscience that's bothering you, you should have stayed in the valley."

Crane shook his head. "Not conscience, Brant," he corrected. "Friendship. Is that all right?"

Their eyes met, Crane's sad and sincere, Brant's shadowed with pain and faintly apologetic for his brusqueness. Then, glancing up at the darkening sky, he pivoted and strode toward the steep, rocky bank of the Sacandaga River, which Brant guessed the raiding party had followed to the Hudson.

Crane stared after him with concern. He refused to share with Brant his strong suspicion that Rosanne was pregnant. It would be cruel to reveal that Brant had lost not only the woman he loved but also their unborn child. He had already pushed himself to the brink of physical and mental collapse as it was. God knew how much longer he could sustain this pace. His body hadn't had a decent chance to heal from the surgery. He'd need help if, by some miracle, they reached the Abnaki camp where Rosanne was being held, though Jonathan no longer pretended to himself there was any hope they'd find her alive.

He sighed and started off at a trot toward the river. When he returned to the valley, if he didn't get himself killed before that, he decided he would start a small farm while continuing his pharmaceutical research. Priscilla would make a suitable wife—she had all her teeth, didn't cheat at cards, and made a damn good meal. His craving for adventure had been satisfied and had left a decidedly bitter aftertaste.

Brant was crouched on a jutting outcrop of rock above the swirling river when Crane came up beside him. He glanced back at the older man, his lean face looking strained and lost. God, he felt lost. "I don't know what to do, Jonathan. I'm so afraid—" He swallowed, unable to complete the thought, as if by not voicing what he feared, the fear might not be realized.

"Everything is working against us," he went on. "It's goddamn freezing up at Indian Lake by now. The war party could be in Montreal already. We've lost too much time. It's hopeless. Hopeless . . ."

He waited for Crane to contradict him, to give him even a single word of encouragement, and as the silence lengthened he leaped up in frustration, his hands curling into fists. "For Christ's sake, suggest something! *Anything*. I know I'm not thinking clearly. What would you do in my place?" He lowered his voice, but it cracked as he said in desperation, "What should I do?"

Crane shook his head slowly. "I'm not sure. I might consider returning to New York to petition the governor to help you arrange a ransom through Montreal. It would not be the first time it's been done. Of course, it would take money—"

"I'll sell my land. I'll sell every cursed acre to my uncle if I must. I don't want it now anyway." He turned to face the river, his mind seizing on Crane's suggestion and weighing it carefully. "By God," he said softly, "that's probably what I should have done all along, or at least have had Patrick working on for me." He bent at the waist to sweep up his gear and rifle, hope energizing him for the first time in days. "Have you ever run the rapids, Crane?"

"No. Why do you—" In a flash of comprehension, Crane gazed down at the black, foam-laced water rushing below them, dashing over protruding rocks in a wild race to the rapids where it plunged, surrounded by madly swirling spume, into a misty basin.

"Brant, I—"

"It's the fastest way, Crane. Portaging will cost more time than I can afford. You can still take the canoe back. I can still build a raft. I've shot the rapids before for pleasure."

"In these waters?"

"No." Brant hesitated. "I won't lie to you. There are dangers."

"Oh . . . The devil take it! I'll go with you."

They secured their belongings to the thwarts of the elmbark canoe, keeping the bow and stern light to avoid its unbalancing in rough waters, and portaged along the high bank until they reached a relatively peaceful stretch of river. Crane had always wondered what it felt like to drown. He imagined it would be a kinder death than the Indian tortures he half anticipated. Brant embarked first, settling into the stern on his knees and firing instructions as he handed Crane his paddle, explaining how to turn the blade at the end of each stroke.

Brant, riding in the stern, a position that required complete concentration, propelled the canoe into the swiftest central current. Aware that shallow waters might pose the greatest hazard, that he could not afford a single slip of the paddle or a miscalculation, he skimmed the sharp, jagged rocks that lined the riverbed. Soon they slipped around a stepped shelving ledge, gliding a distance until suddenly they were swept into the foaming main current and carried around the racing waters. Huge boulders, moss speckled and treacherous, and overhanging hemlock branches whirled past their vision, grayish-green blurs overlaid with pinpoints of icy spume thrown up from the churning waves.

Crane anticipated the dangers. But he was not prepared for the reckless exhilaration that seized him the first time the lightweight vessel veered around a curve, lingered fleetingly in flat water, and then shot out into the air and took the perpendicular drop in a shower of numbing froth, to land bobbing in the strangely still cauldron below.

Another rapid, and then a third, steeper and beckoning

in the distance, its loud, lyrical song rising into the forest as it thundered in their ears. He had quickly learned to watch for the mirror-clear surfaces that suddenly turned into restless white water and signaled the approaching drop.

Crane was actually enjoying himself now. He rotated his hips at just the right times to maintain the craft's balance. He sensed how Brant would backstroke to avoid obstacles. He attempted to emulate Layton's posture. Holding his spine erect he leaned into his paddle, now letting it brush the water, now plying the blade with all his might as the canoe darted through a rocky aperture, rounded a bend, and flung them out into space before the pleasurably breathless descent into the calm waters below.

"Easy enough once you learn the rhythm of the currents and the eddies," Brant shouted without looking up as he maneuvered around a massive blasted pine that lay partially submerged beneath the torrent tumbling over it in the water's rush to reach the nearing plunge.

"Easy with you in the stern," Crane yelled back. He had to admire the skill his friend displayed. It wasn't easy to find safe passageways between the boulders, to keep a straight course when the river twisted while simultaneously gauging the presence and size of hidden rocks by the water activity above them.

"To be truthful, Layton," he called out with cheerfully unabashed cowardice, "I haven't the courage to try this alo—" Crane's voice froze. He half rose, heedless of the hemlock branches jutting out directly above his head from the embankment, heedless of Brant's repeated warnings that the slightest unplanned shift in weight might capsize the craft.

"Rosanne— My God . . ."

The name streaked through Brant's awareness, shattering his concentration. *Rosanne?* He angled his head upward, hope overriding the message of caution that flashed through his brain, angled his head for only a fraction of a second. And in that crucial interval his gaze swung with Crane's across the water to the achingly familiar plum velvet cloak snagged on a piece of driftwood in a rock-hemmed cove. His thoughts raced off in a thousand different directions. And before he was aware of it and could shout a warning, a low-hanging evergreen bough had neatly whacked Crane across the chest and pitched him into the roiling water.

The bow of the canoe plunged into a trough; the boat was trapped in an eddy. A wave wrenched the paddle from Brant's hands as he backstroked frantically in his effort to maintain control. The stern swiveled wildly, pivoting the canoe toward the sheer-banked shore; then all at once the vessel capsized and he was hurled into the frigid current. He resurfaced gasping, the cold a paralyzing shock to his system. A splintering crash sounded behind him as the canoe smashed broadside against the rocks. He allowed the violently heaving waters to sweep him against an upthrusting boulder. The impact winded him and stabbed his chest with deep, nauseating pain. The paddle floated past him. Then a dark, bobbing head appeared, covered with arabesques of foam. He saw Crane's dazed face as the current carried the doctor toward the boulder to which Brant clung.

"Crane!" Brant stretched out his arm, hooked one leg around the squarish rock, and caught hold of the other man's coat, fighting the current for possession of its semiconscious owner. His own strength was almost spent, not from struggling against the rapids but from the cold. By the time he dragged his sputtering friend around another rock to quiet water and hauled them both onto the north shore, he could barely stand, as shivering convulsions overcame him.

"Brant? Can you hear me?"

"Y-y-yes." He dropped to his knees, seized with severe muscle cramps. His glassy eyes gazed up at Crane with dwindling recognition. "Rosanne—Wh-where—"

"It was her cloak, man. Only her cloak. Look, we've got to get you—get us both—warm. You'll die if we don't strip your clothes off and get you warm. Do you understand? God, man, can you hear me?"

Brant tried to answer. The words refused to form on his tongue. He had curled himself into a ball, contorting his torso in an unconscious effort to raise his dangerously plummeting body temperature. He was unaware of Jonathan lifting him and carrying him across a desolate meadow into the depths of a pine swamp, where an abandoned trapper's hut offered some refuge from the wind.

Inside the hut, wet and chilled to the teeth himself, Crane worked frantically to undress Brant and thaw him out in front of a fire he hastily kindled—using a flint he discovered on the floor—and fed with whatever he could lay his hands on, including a couple of stools. Brant might not have succumbed to the cold had his body fully recovered from his recent surgery, but in his weakened condition he had been acutely vulnerable. It was crucial that Brant not warm up too quickly. As heat began to return to Brant's body, pinkish and naked beneath the old trapper's duffel Crane had found on the floor and had wrapped him in, Crane rushed back to the river with an old kettle for fresh water. He would have to feed Brant boiled lichen broth for want of a better beverage. Brant needed heated fluids, but no alcohol. In any case, their rum canteens were floating somewhere along the river; the current had carried them away along with most of their supplies.

"Stay awake, Layton!" he shouted repeatedly over his shoulder.

The words dimly filtered through Brant's stupor. He was only vaguely cognizant of his surroundings. He struggled to remember where he was and what he'd been doing in the river, but coherent thought evaded him. He began to shiver. Who was shouting at him? Where in hell were his clothes?

That night he deyeloped a fever that lasted almost a week. On the afternoon of the fifth day, he woke to find himself alone in the hut. A watery soup simmered in the kettle over a cheerful fire. Faint, disoriented, but dressed in his own stiffly dried clothes, he stumbled around the room and then halted at the low pine bench built into the puncheon wall. Spread across it were the few supplies Crane had managed to fish out of the river from the splintered canoe.

And her cloak.

Brant touched it; he fingered each rent, his heart filling with unspeakable dread. Sweat beaded his pale brow. He lurched backward, crashing over a pile of logs as he made his way to the door.

"Crane!"

He wrenched open the door and stared outside, recoiling at the unexpected bite of dry, cold air on his flushed face. The temperature had dipped below freezing, and it had snowed since the canoe accident. Ice had begun to edge the river. Opalescent hoarfrost adorned the pines that dominated the swamp.

"Crane!" he yelled again. "Where the—"

"I'll wager you'll welcome a stew of these for a change."

Crane appeared suddenly from behind the hut, swinging two recently snared rabbits. "How do you feel?"

"Did you find her?" Brant asked in a low, stricken voice.

Crane glanced away, his breath fogging the air as he panted from the exertion of jogging through the snow.

"No."

"Anything?"

"Only the cloak."

An emotion-laden silence fell between them, disrupted only when an irreverent chickadee popped out of a decaying pine stump and burst into a warbling song. Brant stared dully past the snow-mantled trees that surrounded them, his gaze lighting on an owl perched on a lofty limb. The bird gazed back at him steadily, but its interest soon returned to the mouse it had sighted scurrying across the swamp. Dusk was falling, banners of lilac and gold melting into the horizon, lengthening shadows creeping across the white forest floor.

Don't let it be true, God. Make it not real.

Crane gathered courage and confronted him, his own tone distraught. "I've been out searching every morning and afternoon. I think it's time you faced—"

Brant swung away violently. "I don't give a goddamn what you think."

Then, snatching a broken branch from the ground, he hurled it at the owl, hurled it with all his pain and rage and sorrow just as the bird took silent gliding flight and swooped down upon the unwary rodent. The branch glanced off the predator's powerful wing, breaking the bird's descent so that the mouse escaped into a thicket. The owl flew back to its perch, aloofly offended. Briefly meeting Crane's worried look, Brant turned and disappeared into the long, silent shadows of the pine swamp.

It was late when he returned, his footsteps heavy as they plowed pathways through the snow. Starlight, filtering down frostily through the pines, cast his haggard features into relief. He entered the hut without a word and nodded mute thanks for the bowl of stew Crane ladled out from the kettle. Jonathan had no need to ask whether his search had been successful. There would be no more talk of ransom between them.

"How do you feel?"

"Empty."

"What will you do now?"

Brant sat down at the bench, his eyes vacant. "I don't know. I haven't thought that far ahead. I kept hoping . . . I prayed—"

His voice broke. He brought a hand to his forehead as his facial muscles convulsed and his shoulders hunched forward, shaking with the dry sobs that tore through him. She was dead. He could no longer continue to deny it. How could he return to the Mohawk Valley? She would not be there to share his success if the settlement flourished, to offer comfort if it failed. He could not live alone in the cabin, haunted by memories of the gilded afternoon they had spent there together. Oh, God! He remembered with agonizing clarity the joy on her lovely face when he'd asked her to marry him, her infectious enthusiasm as she'd talked about the lilacs she would plant and the children they would have . . . They had been cheated of so much.

He drew a deep, shuddering sigh as if to fill the hollowness inside him. Why? he wondered tormentedly. Lord, where was the sense in it all? How could he live without her? He couldn't imagine it, couldn't imagine the black, miserable future that faced him. He thought of how cynical and arrogant he had been when he first met her, so full of his righteous ambitions that he hadn't allowed room inside him for love to grow. She had saved him, his gentle little imp; she had awakened his emotions and opened his eyes to the emptiness of his existence. And now he was empty again, so cold and empty. There would never be another love in his life.

"Pray God she didn't suffer," he whispered raggedly. "Oh, Christ, Crane. I don't understand . . ."

Acutely sensitive to his friend's need to mourn, Jonathan quietly left the table and crouched by the fire to finish the snowshoes he was making for the return journey. He made no attempt to spout comfortless platitudes about time healing grief. In Brant's case, he feared it would not hold true.

Chapter 33

It was the sound of Brant's name being called that brought Rosanne fully back to consciousness. She moaned softly and pressed her face into the pillow, her mind spiraling through murky layers of memory, fright, and exhaustion. Awareness returned gradually, first with a flood of bright candlelight and then with an unfamiliar girl's voice calling out urgently to a dark-haired figure sitting in the corner.

"Mr. Layton!" the maidservant cried. "Mr. Layton, sir, she's awakening."

Rosanne heard a chair scraping against the bare floor and two voices conferring softly, then the sound of the door closing as the girl left the chamber. She tried to rise, but waves of dizziness pounded through her, forcing her backward against the rough, lye-scented sheets.

"Brant? Oh, Lord, Brant is that you?"

"Do not upset yourself now, my dear. You've been through quite an ordeal. Why, for a time there I feared I'd lost you. But everything is all right now, isn't it? You've learned your lesson, and I'm quite willing to forgive and forget. . . ."

"Hugh! I—I thought for a moment—" She closed her eyes, his reproachful face imprinted on her mind as confusion and bitter disappointment surged through her. Mr. Layton. Of course. It hadn't been a nightmare. Unless Ericsson had lied, unless Brant's death had been another fabrication of his demented mind. She forced her eyelids open again and clutched at the braided cuff of Hugh's velvet traveling jacket, desperation edging her voice. "It isn't true about Brant, is it, Hugh? That man lied to me, didn't he? He said his friend had shot Brant, that he'd—"

"It is true, my dear. Sadly true. This is a barbaric land, not at all the place for a refined little soul like you. I'd never have sent my nephew here had I dreamed this would happen. It is tragic . . ."

His voiced drifted off. He gazed at the candle flickering on the bedside table and patted Rosanne's hand in an absentminded attempt to comfort her. Surprisingly, he had no need to force the sentiments of sorrow and remorse that lent a convincing ring to his words. After all, Brant might have been like a second son to him—why, he might easily have usurped Daniel in his affections. If Brant had shared his political aspirations, they might have carved an empire out of this wilderness together. In truth, having his own nephew murdered lay heavily on his conscience, a conscience Hugh had been astonished to learn was still active after the years he had spent submerging it. But faced with the same circumstances tomorrow, he was not sure he would act differently. Yet he wished it hadn't come to this.

His grief, Rosanne decided as she watched him, appeared genuine. Suddenly, in retrospect, in view of the terrifying ordeal she had survived, he did not seem as menacing to her as he had been in memory—the memory of that night in Boston. Time had diminished her fear of him. All at once she saw him as nothing worse than a dishonest man with a foul temper who, despite his serious shortcomings, was mourning the loss of his nephew, for whom he had obviously cared despite their differences. She doubted seriously whether he'd actually had anyting to do with Franklin Newhouse's murder. Brant had never proved it, and wasn't it more likely that the vile Sluyter family were involved? Still, she disliked Hugh personally. She could only feel relieved that she had escaped marrying him. But she felt a whit closer to him today simply because he had harbored a fondness for Brant beneath his show of threats and orders and because he looked as dispirited as she felt. Tears splashed down her face, warm and silent. Brant's parents would have to be notified, and she would have to tell them they would soon have a grandchild.

"Where am I?" she whispered restlessly.

"In Reverend Barclay's cottage at Fort Hunter. An Indian scout leading a patrol found you in the forest and brought you here. Do you not remember?"

She frowned, the memory flitting through her mind as if she had dreamed and not lived it all. Fort Hunter. Dearest God, no. She and Brant were to have been married by Reverend Barclay here in Queen Anne's Chapel.

"Do you—do you know where Brant was buried?" she asked slowly; the question was so agonizing she was barely able to articulate it.

He turned his head; his gaze was level and guileless, his response carefully rehearsed. "From what I understand, he was laid to rest in an Indian village near Hemlock Creek. I suppose it was meant to be some sort of heathen honor to him. It was too painful for me to go there to claim his remains. I—I simply could not bring myself to do it."

Her frown deepened. "How did you know where to find me, Hugh?"

"Reverend Barclay is an old acquaintance of mine. You were incoherent when they brought you here, but in your delirium you mentioned my surname and thought I should be contacted. The poor man was understandably confused. You see, he remembered that he was supposed to marry you to Brant. Fortunately, I had just arrived in Albany—"

"Albany," she interrupted sharply. "I thought you disliked wilderness towns. What were you doing that far from home?"

"Renegotiating a contract. In fact, I was at supper with the Sluyter family when I heard the news about Brant. We were all shocked, naturally. Conrad and my nephew had their differences, but it was a healthy rivalry—"

"No!" Her eyes flashed up at him, twin flames of blue

drowning in tears. "Conrad Sluyter was responsible for Brant's death, Hugh. He has to be punished! I heard him threaten to kill Brant."

"That's nonsense, my dear," he said patiently. "It's another of Brant's irrational notions. I shall never understand where he got some of his wild ideas—"

"I tell you, they despised each other!" She pressed her fingers to her right temple where she felt a sudden blinding pain. Why would he not believe her? "The trapper who abducted me mentioned a man in Albany before he died, Hugh. It's the only explanation that makes sense."

"The trapper who abducted you was a runaway servant wanted for the murders of a sixty-five-year-old Philadelphian shopkeeper and his wife. Their children have been searching for years to have him brought to justice. It's also suspected that he murdered his own little sister—smothered her—on the ship that brought them from Sweden. He used to act as a go-between for the Sluyters and the Indians who trapped farther north. Jacobus Sluyter only recently found out about his past. The man was insane. Dangerously insane. How could you believe his word?"

The hammering behind her right eye intensified with excruciating force. His revelation had resurrected all the unutterable horror of those endless days and nights inside the cave with Peter.

"From what I gather, his cohort almost killed that squaw O'Rourke married," Hugh continued insensitively. "The girl got the better of him though. Slit his damned throat."

"Deep Spring is still alive?" she asked, brightening. "Oh, thank God for that at least."

Hugh glanced away, silently expressing his own unbounded gratitude that Ericsson and his companion were both dead and unable to implicate him. He'd saved himself not only a great deal of money but also untold anxiety in the future. There should be no reason for the presentiment of disaster that kept nagging at him.

His face softening, he reached for the small glass of aromatic amber liquid that sat on the table beside the bed. "Drink this, Rosanne."

She stared down at the drink suspiciously. "What is it?"

"Just an herbal tonic intended to calm your nerves. I can see that I've upset you, and I should have known better. Actually, there's no need to ever discuss any of this again. We'll try to put it behind us." His tone deepened. "And about that night in Olivia's house—well, I'm still sick about it, and I want you to understand I'd never do that kind of . . . well, it was wrong, and I'm aware of it. But if I can forgive you for running off with my own nephew . . ."

His voice droned on, the words humming inside her head. What was he talking about? Surely he didn't imagine they could start off again together and plan to marry as if nothing had changed since the day she arrived in America. Even if she could forget the sordid violence he'd shown himself capable of last summer, she could never become his wife, could never disconnect herself from her love for Brant and for the child of their love growing inside her. She had no wish to discuss the future, not with Hugh or with anyone. It was too unbearably painful to contemplate. Perhaps Hugh meant to be kind, or perhaps he still erroneously believed she could help elevate his social station. Either way, it didn't matter.

"Hugh, please, my head is aching." A lethargic haze was stealing over her, mantling her tormented thoughts and emotions. She was incapable of thinking clearly; it was difficult to even follow his conversation.

He halted his monologue, realizing that the medicine was taking its sedative effect. She had been in a pathetic state the day after the Mohawk scout had brought her into Fort Hunter. Raving, her hair tangled and wild, her body thin and bruised beneath the startling combination of Ericsson's filthy clothing and her own gown, she hardly resembled the aloof young beauty he remembered.

And yet as his shocked revulsion began to subside on seeing Rosanne respond to warmth and nourishment, he realized that, if anything, the experiences she had undergone only heightened her desirability. There was an awakened sensuality about her that had not existed last summer. There was a depth to her now, a strength that had been found and tested. Had her spirit been subdued? For both their sakes, Hugh hoped so—hoped fervently that her apparent docility would last until after their wedding. Only the week before her grandfather had sailed into Boston, where he had business contacts, and was scheduled to arrive in New York in late January. Hugh had until then to convince Rosanne she needed him to take care of her. He did not anticipate encountering her resistance, and he was unsure whether he himself was capable of bullying her again. If she had changed over the past months, so had he.

"I've overtired you." He leaned forward to kiss her cheek. "We'll talk tomorrow. If you feel well enough, we might even be able to leave here then. This is far from the safest fort I've ever seen."

His lips lingered beneath her shadowed cheekbone, scraping her skin with unpleasantly alien sensations. She averted her face, weakly raising her hand to push him away. "Don't, Hugh. *Don't* . . ."

A deep, warning growl sounded from the huge dog lying on the floor on the opposite side of the bed. His eyes veiled with unwilling respect, Hugh pulled away from Rosanne and settled back on the stool.

"Tynan?" she whispered, unbelieving, as first the unrulybrowed foreface and then the scruffy, muscular body worked its way up beside her. "Oh, Tynan," she cried, gathering the dog up in a tearful embrace. "Where in heaven did you come from? Oh, your coat is filthy, full of foxtails, and you weigh next to nothing!"

Hugh watched her, his mouth flattening with resignation. "That hound appeared out of nowhere the night you were brought inside the fort. I thought he was dangerous, but the physician who attended you advised me to let him stay. Poor fellow could barely examine you for the dog trying to attack him."

She glanced over Tynan's head, hope lighting her gaze. "Jonathan Crane? The doctor—was it Dr. Crane?"

"Who?"

"No one. Never mind." She sank back down against the pillows, her eyelids heavy. Apparently he knew nothing of the baby. She would have to tell him later. Not now. She had no desire to share that with him now. "It will be painful to go home, Hugh," she whispered. "There are so many memories."

"Memories fade, Rosanne. You'll have a lovely room with a balcony overlooking the river. Moira will nurse you back—"

"You don't understand. I—I have to go back to Hemlock Creek. I intend to live with Simon and Priscilla . . . and Mrs. Dare . . ." She meant to tell him that if she accepted his help, it would be on her own terms and only until she was completely well and capable of supporting her child. But then suddenly her voice eased into a wistful sigh as drugged sleep overcame her, and her fingers, twisted together at the back of Tynan's neck as she embraced him, fell limp.

"You'll live with me as my wife," he told her quietly. "Neither of us has much choice anymore."

He rose from the stool and composed his features as he heard a discreet tapping at the door behind him.

"Reverend Barclay," he murmured, opening the door to admit the Anglican missioner. "I was just about to leave."

"Is the young lady feeling any better, Mr. Layton?"

"Much better, Reverend. However, she's quite concerned about her reputation." Hugh frowned and scratched his eyebrow, assuming a confidential tone. "You and I are both tolerant and forgiving men, Reverend, but I'm sure you are aware that there are members of society who would spread malicious gossip—well, who would thrive on this girl's misfortune if news of her unhappy experience were to be circulated."

The clergyman nodded. "I understand completely, Mr. Layton, and you have my assurance of total discretion. Not a word of what has befallen her will leave this fort. Such a shame though, well-bred young women are a rarity here. I'd looked forward to performing her wedding ceremony."

There was a silence. In reality, the minister had more important matters on his mind than the councilor's personal problems. The reverend's own Mohawk congregation had become increasingly agitated of late, disturbed by dangerously false rumors that the citizens of Albany were plotting to slaughter their Iroquois allies. Some believed that the rumors had been instigated by a certain wily Mohawk sachem, who hoped to embarrass the British and demonstrate that the Mohawks were not to be taken for granted. Still others accredited the troublemaking to a French spy. In either event, Reverend Barclay had no time to bother with runaway young girls.

Both men moved toward the door. Hugh paused briefly, glancing back pensively at Rosanne and then at Reverand Barclay. "I never doubted your discretion, Reverend, and, of course, I'll make my appreciation known by a substantial donation to your chapel." He smiled. "You know, I can't help thinking that a recommendation to the rectorship of Trinity Church in New York would also be in order. You belong back among civilized souls."

Chapter 34

Rosanne stared at the late January moon through the frost-coated windowpane. The Indians called it Diagona, the lost moon, the second moon to rise after the winter solstice. Its appearance sparked the beginning of the Iroquois New Year Festival, a seven-day religious event marked by the confession of sins and the sacrificial burning of a white dog that would be sent as a messenger to the Master of Life to express gratitude for the blessings he had shown mankind. In the villages there would be dancing and feasting, and people would play the peach-stone game. The interpretation of dreams during this time assumed the greatest importance, for the Iroquois believed that dreams foretold the future and were divinely inspired. No doubt Little Otter, Deep Spring, Simon, and all the others were sharing visions this very night by the fireside.

She moved away from the window with a bereft sigh and returned to the mahogany four-poster bed to contemplate the dream that had awakened her, wishing it belonged to her future, but knowing it could not be so. She had dreamed she was in the kitchen of the cabin, dyeing muslin curtains yellow in a kettle of goldenrod. Suddenly Brant had appeared in the doorway, and she'd run forward to greet him. He'd taken her in his arms and kissed her, and then he had bent over the cradle in the corner to pick up the baby, the child he would never know.

Numbly she raised her fingers to touch her mouth,

which trembled with the bittersweet memory of that phantom kiss. Tears traced silvery furrows down her face. She lifted her eyes again to the window. The moon, cold and lonely in the dark midwinter sky, and the frozen landscape, bleak beneath its wan glow—both eloquently reflected the desolation of her emotions. Would her grief never ease?

From downstairs in the mansion voices rose in bitter discord. Hugh and Olivia again; the tension between them was so palpable it penetrated even into rooms they didn't occupy and sent the servants scurrying to their quarters to escape every evening as soon as supper ended. What did they find to keep quarreling about? Sometimes it was Moira and Leander, Hugh's valet, whom Olivia had banished to the Boston townhouse during Hugh's absence. Sometimes they squabbled about the way Olivia had mistreated Daniel while he was at home. Sometimes they disagreed over business. And frequently, Rosanne suspected, they quarreled about her.

She could not remain in this house. However, practicality dictated she wait to leave at least until spring arrived, when travel became easier. She would write to Patrick soon—a task she'd been so far too distraught to undertake; she would ask his assistance in hiring a guide. Perhaps Hugh would even help her. Unlike his attitude during her first stay with him, she didn't feel he intended to hold her here against her will.

In the past few weeks, she'd noticed a haunted look about him, an edginess that caused him to lower his eyes whenever their gazes met. In fact, he had changed so much she could hardly believe he was the same man she'd met last summer. From the moment he discovered she was carrying his nephew's child, his attitude toward her had altered. He no longer tried to force his attentions on her, though he mentioned marriage daily as the only solution to her predicament. It was the least he could do, he insisted, and while she knew he still hoped to gain her grandfather's patronage, she doubted that political power was now his sole motivation for offering her marriage. But what other reason was there? Desire? No, not that, for oddly he took great pains to avoid even touching her. Pity? Compassion? To her bemusement, he behaved as if he felt guilty about what had happened. Was it because he, too, suspected that Conrad Sluyter was responsible for Brant's death and he, Hugh, hadn't had the courage to investigate the possibility for fear the Sluyter family would in turn implicate him in past crimes? After the baby was born, she vowed, she would enlist Patrick's help in uncovering the truth and seeing Conrad brought to justice. But the child came first.

She glanced at the face of the mother-of-pearl inlaid clock on the dressing table. She had slept through supper again, and the servants had neglected to call her. She rose, not bothering to inspect her reflection in the mirror or even to comb her hair. She dreaded going downstairs, but she was hungry, and she knew from experience that no one would answer if she used the bellpull. She was virtually alone in this house, alone with Hugh and Olivia and their sinister secrets.

Hugh sat alone at the dining table, his features flushed with the Madeira he had been drinking since late afternoon, his eyes on the couple standing at the sideboard. Olivia and Conrad, whispering, inventing more lies to ensnare him, plotting new intrigues to draw him deeper into their deadly schemes. Not that anything could release him now. How he loathed them, and how he had come to loathe himself for allowing his ruthless ambition to smother every decent sentiment he had ever possesed. He had no choice now but to play along with them or invite a vile scandal that would destroy him socially and politically, that would destroy his life. His life. God. what a deformity it had become.

He could not sleep at night because of the relentless and unexpected guilt that plagued him, the guilt he felt over the murder of his nephew and the countless lives he had so casually ruined. Daily it grew inside him like a malignancy—the guilt and horror over his own actions. Why had he ever been so weak as to sanction Olivia's hideous plan? Brant would never have exposed him—he felt that strongly now.

And would it have been so difficult to discontinue his illegal practices? He knew himself to be an intelligent, resourceful man. He might have found a way to attain the success he craved without staining his soul with murder. Oh, sweet Jesus, he thought, covering his face with his shaking hands. He had paid for the violent murder of his own flesh and blood. Was it any wonder that refined society shunned him?

It was the girl who had resurrected his conscience. Remorse stabbed him every time he looked at her and realized she was carrying a child whose father he had virtually murdered. Incorruptible in her innocence, she symbolized all the purity he had sought to defile, all the trust he had twisted to his own advantage. He would not force her to stay. . . . He almost wished she'd run away again. But he would insist he be allowed to provide for her and his grandniece or nephew. And when the duke arrived in New York? How would he explain the situation? Would he be surprised if the old man didn't simply take his granddaughter from this house and threaten to have Hugh publicly disgraced?

Careless laughter floated toward him. Glancing up, he saw Olivia and Conrad clinging together in a lover's embrace, sharing a glass of wine as if in celebration. He got up slowly, rage breaking loose inside him. This was more than he could tolerate.

"Stop that—do you hear me? You are still married to my son, Olivia. I won't have that girl walking into this room to witness your adulterous display."

Olivia swiveled around, leaning against Conrad in blatant defiance, her mouth curved in a derisive smile. "You old hypocrite," she said softly. "How dare you condemn me. Have you forgotten that you were lusting after that girl's mother on the very day your wife died? Have you forgotten that it was your disgusting encounter with a waterfront whore that chased her away to begin with?"

Hugh darted around the table, upsetting the wine decanter by his abrupt movement. "No, I haven't forgotten," he said darkly. "Every one of my past sins is returning to haunt me. I can forget none of them."

Olivia smirked. "Can you believe him, Conrad, developing a conscience at his age? But I must admit he's right. It wouldn't do to upset the golden princess. In fact, darling, you should make yourself scarce until Hugh has brought her around completely."

"Do you think he can manage?" Conrad asked amusedly. "He doesn't look at all capable of it."

Hugh stepped forward, his hands knotting into fists. "Get out of my house, you conniving little bastard. Get out, both of you."

"Conrad is not going anywhere until your business negotiations with him are finished, Hugh," Olivia said in a taunting voice.

Hugh narrowed his eyes. "What negotiations? I agreed he would replace Brant as my land manager. I assume he kept the money meant to entice Ericsson. Considering how that maniac almost botched everything, I think your Dutch dandy has quite a nerve even showing his face here."

"Nevertheless, the price has gone up, Hugh." Olivia pulled free of Conrad and leaned back against the sideboard, her eyes glistening in the light shed by the crystal candelabrum. "I've seen this coming for some time now," she said tonelessly. "The final weakening. I cannot afford to depend on you any longer."

"What the devil are you talking about?"

"Conrad has changed his mind," she went on. "He thinks he might enjoy the political life himself. I'm sure you could find him a comfortable position. Something with prestige."

Hugh laughed in disbelief. "The hell I will."

"I don't think you understood me, Hugh. Surely you wouldn't want Conrad to make an appearance before the council. Picture your humiliation. So many nasty secrets unveiled."

In a peculiar way, Hugh felt relieved, relieved that the confrontation he had avoided for so long had finally arrived. It would be over soon, he thought. Everything. And he deserved whatever came to him.

"I don't think *you* understand, Olivia. I'm washing my hands of you. If not for your venomous influence, Daniel might still be in this house and Brant would be alive."

"And you'd be nothing," she retorted coldly. "You were crass and ambitious when I met you, Hugh. I never forced you to do anything against your will."

"I do not deny it. But it's finished now, Olivia. I don't care what you or this lump of trash threaten."

"I don't think he believes you, Olivia." Conrad shifted forward, his features hardening unpleasantly. "Perhaps he'd change his attitude if you showed him the very detailed and incriminating letter you've written to the duke of Rydenham. Better yet, why don't we call the lovely young lady down and have her read it to us over sherry? What an evening's entertainment that would make."

Instinctively Hugh stepped back toward the door, his eyes wary. "The girl is distraught enough as it is and four months with child, Sluyter. God knows what the shock would do to her. I won't have another death on my hands. But you are right about one thing: I don't believe your threats. Ruin me, and Olivia is ruined. Now leave this house, or I warn you, you'll regret it. I'm done with the pair of you."

Olivia vented a long sigh. "For a man who's cheated every person he's ever dealt with, you're disgustingly naive. You couldn't ruin me. I've stolen enough money from you and your idiot son over the years to enable me to escape to the Continent and live out the rest of my life in splendor. Of course, I could easily double my riches if Conrad and I took the girl with us and held her for ransom."

"Take the money and leave the colonies," Hugh said, his voice hoarse with contempt. "It's worth it to be rid of you. But I swear it—if I ever see you again, I'll have you brought to trial for your crimes."

"*Our* crimes, Hugh," she said simply. "However, I'm afraid you'll have to pay for them alone." She turned to raise her hand in a gesture that even Hugh, in his intoxicated rage, could tell signaled his death sentence. "Conrad . . ."

Hugh wheeled and rushed to the door, flinging it open with a startling oath to find Rosanne standing before him, her face so pain-stricken and colorless, he knew she had overheard every incriminating word.

"Get out of here!" he ordered her under his breath. "Run around the side of the house and rouse the servants!"

His words hardly transpierced her shocked daze. Horrified to her soul at the inhuman ugliness of what he and Olivia and Conrad had done, she could only stare at him and force a broken utterance from her throat.

"It was you," she gasped. "My God, it was you. To think I have even begun to pity you . . . Oh, God, how could you?"

"It's too late to tell you I'm sorry, Rosanne. Too late for Brant and for me, but you still have a chance." A blurred streak of movement at the sideboard drew his attention. He turned toward it unthinkingly, reaching one arm behind him to shove Rosanne out into the hallway. "You're in danger! Get out of here! Go! Don't you under—"

The sentence erupted in an animalistic scream of pain as Sluyter's bone-handled dagger flew across the room and embedded itself in Hugh's chest with lethal impact. Hugh circled back toward Rosanne, his mouth hanging slack, and then plunged into the hall, scarlet rivulets of blood running down his shirt and dribbling between the imported black and white marble tiles where he fell.

Rosanne backed away from his outflung body, her steps slow and clumsy, her eyes lifting with dread to the two figures advancing on her. "No. No . . ." She whispered the word over and over as if to deny the terrible scene she had witnessed, as if by denying it she would save herself from suffering a similar destiny. Her mind was frozen in shock, incapable of absorbing, of understanding the awful truths she had learned tonight. She scarcely realized what she was doing, that her feet were moving, seemingly of their own violation.

"Not another step."

Olivia took the long-barreled pistol Conrad had removed from his waistband and leveled it at Rosanne with a humorless but strangely approving smile. "I give you credit, my dear. You've certainly forced me to change my plans. Still, I think you might prove a greater asset to me than I envisioned even in the beginning. Your grandfather will pay dearly if he hopes for a reunion."

"Your scheme is as warped as your mind, Olivia." Rosanne raised her voice and spoke slowly in a desperate play for time, praying a servant would return to remove the supper dishes. She could not reach the bellpull without walking past Conrad, and she doubted she could depend on anyone responding to it anyway. Her only hope was to run for the front door and risk a bullet in the back.

"My grandfather has never cared about me," she went on, her sluggish mind slowly rousing and her muscles tensing as adrenaline surged through her in preparation for flight. "He'll laugh if you try to extort any money from him for my release."

Olivia edged closer to the door, while behind her Conrad moved around the room drawing the curtains and extinguishing candles. "You're wrong. The old man is expected here any day, my lady. He's deeply concerned about your welfare. He indicated in his letter that he hoped to mend the disharmony in your family with his visit. And when he discovers you've a brat on the way—"

The faint clopping of hoofbeats on the cobblestones outside distracted her, reminding her that Hugh frequently received late-night visitors. "Conrad, take her down to the cellar with the body until I've gathered my belongings. Hugh kept some documents in his desk that may prove valuable to us in future."

She moved past Rosanne, transferring the pistol back to Conrad. "Ready the carriage when you're done, and if the girl tries to escape, shoot her. Are all the doors locked?"

"Oh, yes." He smiled. "Hugh was fanatical about that. He was afraid someone from his past might try to kill him."

Rosanne shrank back into the shadows as Conrad began to advance on her. "The servants will hear us," she said; the threat sounded ineffective even to her ears, and she saw him smile at it. "They—they'll wonder what you are doing in the cellar this late at night."

"Fetching another bottle of wine, of course."

His smile broadened, revealing the gap between his front teeth where Brant had hit him last summer. "Anyway, the servants have been dismissed for the evening. There'll be no one in the cellar except you and the councilor. And rats." His gaze rose to the staircase; he spoke softly with suggestive undertones, as he watched to make sure Olivia had vanished into one of the upper chambers.

"Do rats frighten you, my lady? Would you like me to spend a few minutes down there with you until you're comfortable? I've had an urge for you since that morning in Albany. What a pity your lover is no longer alive to watch me take my revenge. I'd have enjoyed it so much more. Still, I'm sure you won't disappoint me." He raised his pistol meaningfully. "Will you?"

Rosanne retreated deeper into the hallway until she was trapped beside a long-case clock standing in a tapestried alcove. The mention of Brant, the prospect of this repulsive man forcing himself on her in a rat-infested cellar beside a corpse, sent her into a paroxysm of outraged panic. From that moment, self-protective instinct, primitive and unpredictable, seized control of her mind. She had no idea of how she would defend herself against him. She only knew she would not allow him to touch her. She would not allow him to harm Brant's unborn child!

"Hurry up, my lady," he said, motioning her forward with his pistol, completely oblivious to the maelstrom of emotions rising inside her, dark emotions unrevealed by her expressionless face. "We have little enough time for our pleasure. I've no intention of letting Olivia find us. She has an unholy temper."

"Don't do this," she said hoarsely. "Let me go."

He pressed closer to her. "You can beg me later. I'd like that, I think, to have you begging on your knees . . ."

Rosanne's heart pounded in triple time with the monotonous ticking of the clock, each fleeting second lessening her chance of escape. Her eyes fastened on his leering face, she slipped her hand behind the tall cherrywood clock case and hooked her ankle around its claw-and-ball foot. If he managed to get her down into the cellar, he would violate her and perhaps provoke Olivia into a murderous fury. There was only one hope left to her, a wild and feeble hope, and she prayed God would grant her the cunning and physical strength to carry it through.

"Move, my lady," Conrad said, his voice silkily menacing. "We've wasted—"

She pushed against the clock with every ounce of her might, with all the force of her fear. For one terrifying instant, she felt nothing except searing agony shooting down her arm and up her leg as the clock resisted her efforts to dislodge it. Then, all at once, she felt it start to fall, and she barely had enough time to withdraw her ankle before the heavy, swaying weight brought her down with it.

Conrad's head snapped up, disbelief flashing across his face. "Bitch!" he roared, flinging one hand up to protect his head, the other out to grab her hair.

She darted out from the alcove as he reached for her, ignoring the pinpoints of pain that ripped through her scalp where he'd caught a thick swatch of hair and forced her to tug herself free. She could vaguely hear pounding from down the hallway, a deep male voice demanding entrance. She could hear Conrad screaming as the clock crashed down upon him, crushing his thigh and pelvis and pinning him to the floor. She could hear the weights, pendulum, and musical chimes jangling together inharmoniously against the tiles, those splendid imported tiles that Brant had once described to her.

Oh Brant! Help us. Help us!

Dazedly, over her shoulder, she glimpsed Conrad trying to struggle free of the wreckage, groaning as he crawled across the floor to find the pistol. It appeared he was unable to stand, and when he glanced up toward her, his features were twisted convulsively with pain and rage.

"You won't leave this house alive," he promised with a snarl. "I'll blow your head off your shoulders before you reach that door."

A darkly glinting object, lying midway between her and Conrad, drew Rosanne's eyes to the floor. The pistol. But at that same second, Conrad's gaze also lit upon it. He lunged forward on one knee. There was no time for Rosanne to reach the weapon. Instead, she kicked it, kicked it so hard it skittered down into the darkness beyond the sweeping staircase and clattered against the wall. Enraged, Conrad grabbed the hood of the clock and hurled it at her. It struck her shoulder. Numbing pain radiated down to her fingertips.

She whirled and ran, crying for help until her vocal chords felt raw. God, oh God, the distance to the door stretched before her endlessly. Had she imagined that voice on the portico outside moments ago? The heel of her slipper caught on the fringe of the long Persian carpet. Frantically working it free, she flew headlong into the wall.

Scarcely had she regained her balance than frantic pounding at the door resounded again through the hallway. And then suddenly it stopped. Had someone, a servant or a neighbor, heard her screams? Or was it one of Olivia's henchmen stationed outside? She squeezed herself into the corner, petrified and wracked with uncertainty. Should she try to escape through a window or find a hiding place in the house? She knew she could not just sand there cowering in the dark.

And it was so dark.

Only a pallid haze of moonlight penetrated the fan-shaped window above the door to illuminate the center of the hallway. Perhaps Conrad's bullet would miss its mark if she risked crossing the entrance lobby. She didn't hear him now, she realized confusedly. Was he waiting for her to move so that he could spring out at her? Had he found the pistol? Was he hurt so badly that he couldn't walk? Olivia must have heard the commotion.

Olivia.

Cold tingles stole down her spine as she sensed the other woman's malevolent presence. Afraid to breathe, afraid that the smallest movement would reveal her hiding place, she slowly turned her head and gazed up the staircase, her heart leaping as she recognized the auburn-haired figure slowly descending.

"I see you there, Rosanne," she said quietly. "I have one of Hugh's dueling pistols in my hand. I have no desire to use it, but I will if you force me. Conrad, the other pistol is beneath the portrait to your left."

"The witch fractured my hip," he muttered weakly. "I—I can't stand properly. I was only trying—"

"I know perfectly well what you were trying to do."

"It wasn't my fault, Olivia. She—"

His whining defense died abruptly as running footfalls sounded on the five semicircular stone steps outside. Then suddenly the scrolled panels of the front door splintered open, the center stile crashing across the threshold beneath a powerful barrage of hatchet blows.

"What in God's name is that?" Conrad whispered.

Rosanne groped behind her for the priceless Mandarin vase in the wall niche and swung it above her head. A man's voice shouted her name, its velvet resonance snapping her out of her terrified trance. She stared, a soft disbelieving cry springing from her lips. She was losing her sanity. She had to be. It sounded so much like Brant, But it couldn't be . . .

"Brant! Oh, Brant!"

He kicked through the debris, moonlight silhouetting his tall frame and glinting off the hatchet at his side. Rosanne flew across the lobby, the vase slipping unnoticed from her hands to shatter on the floor as she hurled herself against his chest, her relief so intense that for a moment blackness engulfed her. But she fought it with all her will. He wasn't dead! A sweet delirium of ecstasy swept over her. She touched his face, his mouth, his throat, weeping joyously, unable to speak, wanting nothing except to hold him.

Brant caught her with one arm, crushing her to him in a

fiercely protective embrace, relief spreading across his face. She was alive and safe. He wasn't too late.

"Thank God," he whispered roughly. "Oh, thank God—"

"They're both armed!" She pulled back frantically, awareness of their vulnerable position superceding the myriad emotions swamping her. "Olivia's somewhere on the staircase, and Conrad— "

He reacted before she could finish, flinging her to the floor behind him and dropping to one knee to fire his rifle at the figure he perceived crouching in the shadows of the hallway. Sluyter had managed to discharge his weapon, but in his panic at the appearance of the man he believed to be dead, he'd wasted too much time to aim accurately. The pistol ball soared harmlessly through the doorway and out into the mist. Rosanne looked away instinctively, hearing his short gurgling cry as he took Brant's shot in the neck, hearing the thud of his pistol as it slipped from his suddenly lifeless fingers. When finally she raised her face, it was to see Brant laying down his rifle and running toward the great staircase.

She surged to her feet and started after him, renewed fear rushing through her. Didn't he realize that Olivia was more dangerous than even Hugh and Conrad combined? Why didn't he leave her for the authorities to deal with?

"Brant, don't! Oh, please, please . . ."

He was so absorbed in catching Olivia that it took several seconds for Rosanne's cries to penetrate his mind. Was she hurt? He glanced back, reassuring himself that no harm had come to her, his courageous angel. If he hadn't arrived in time . . . The thought of what he might have found enraged him, spurred him on. He would not stop—he could not allow Olivia to escape. She had disappeared into Hugh's private apartments, and he remembered that there was a back staircase in the powder closet that led to the kitchen. He took the stairs in giant steps, but as he approached the landing, he looked down and inadvertently noticed the body sprawled out across the dining-room doorway, the body of his uncle. The sight unleashed such a floodgate of conflicting feelings inside him that he halted involuntarily and could not go on.

Soft hysterical laughter impinged on his thoughts. He looked up swiftly to the top of the staircase and his gaze narrowed on the woman standing directly above him, her straight red hair hanging loose to her waist, her green eyes mirroring the madness that had destroyed so many lives. Daniel had once told him that Olivia's ancestors had been burned at the stake for witchcraft. He believed that now.

"Give me the pistol, Olivia."

"You know me better than that, Brant."

"Conrad's dead. It's finished."

"Conrad," she said with a sneer. "I'd have wanted to be rid of him sooner or later anyway."

Brant crept up another step. "The pistol, Olivia."

"Your bastard uncle has locked his closet door and hidden the key so that I could not reach the staircase," she said, hatred flaring in her eyes as she stared past Brant to the body beneath them. "I'll have to kill you. I should have done it myself in the first place."

"But you've never killed anyone yourself, have you?" he asked softly. "You've always been far removed from your victims. Let me warn you, it isn't pleasant."

"If you kill him, you won't get past me, Olivia," Rosanne said from the bottom of the staircase. Praying the other woman was unable to discern in the dark how badly her hands were trembling, she held up the dagger she had drawn from Hugh's chest. She had thrust the horror of retrieving the weapon to the back of her mind. Warm congealed blood dripped onto her skirts, its metallic smell bringing bile to her gorge. She and Brant would remain together now no matter what their fate.

Olivia smiled and aimed the pistol between Brant's eyes. "I'll take that chance. I'd say, at four months pregnant, you were at the disadvantage, m'lady."

Fear for Rosanne's life restrained Brant's immediate reaction of joy at the revelation. Inclining his head only a fraction of an inch, his eyes still riveted to Olivia's right hand, he spoke to Rosanne in deep-timbered tones of desperation. "If what she says is true, my love, I beg you to turn and run out of this house to save our child. And even if it is only another of her lies, there's still a chance for you to escape. I won't let her shoot you."

"Please, Olivia," Rosanne whispered. "Please don't hurt him, and we—we'll let you leave. Tell her, Brant. Tell her we won't try to go after her." She raised her face to his, her eyes pleading. Despairingly she realized that he hadn't even heard her. He was watching Olivia so intently that she might not have existed at the moment.

She positioned herself at the bottom step, the dagger poised, her heart beating wildly. Olivia had retreated backward on the landing several steps, but her hand hadn't wavered. From behind her bedchamber door, Rosanne could hear Tynan whining and scratching to be let out.

"You've never killed anyone with your own hands, Olivia," Brant repeated quietly. "The horror of it will follow you forever. I don't believe you're capable of it."

She moved back another step, and then suddenly, while Brant was readying himself to spring forward and disarm her, she turned unexpectedly and bolted across the rest of the landing and down the darkened hallway, back into Hugh's bedchamber.

Rosanne flung the bloodied dagger behind her in revulsion. "Brant, hurry! Let's go before—"

There was a pistol shot, a creaking shudder, and then a distant sliding scream that died abruptly into chilling silence.

Rosanne couldn't tear her eyes from the door, though something inside her knew that Olivia would never reemerge. "Do—do you think she's killed herself?" she whispered.

"I don't know. Wait outside."

"Oh, God, Brant. Don't go in there."

"Get help, Rosanne."

She watched him move cautiously into his uncle's room; then she forced herself to back away from the staircase. She broke into a run, slowing down only once to pick up his rifle. Midway to the door she heard him call her from the landing.

"It's all right."

She whirled and rushed back toward him, sagging against the newel post at the bottom of the staircase as waves of relief swept over her. "Did she . . ."

"She shot the lock off the closet door."

"She escaped?"

"No. Hugh had been threatening to tear those stairs out since the alleged slave uprising two years ago. He was afraid he'd be murdered in his sleep. It seems he neglected to tell Olivia he'd had the stairwell removed." He looked down over his shoulder, his voice low. "She broke her neck."

An eternity passed before either of them could shake off the shock of what had happened and move into the next moment.

And then, suddenly, Brant felt as though he were awakening from a prolonged nightmare. He could feel icy sweat trickling down his armpits and spine. He could feel his hammering heart slow to a normal pace. Breaking away from the banister, he ran down the staircase toward Rosanne.

With a broken cry of relief, she laid the rifle down and scrambled up the stairs to meet him. At one point she lost her footing and backslid several steps. But then suddenly he reached down and lifted her into his arms, dropping back onto the staircase to sit and cradle her in his lap. She clung to him, shivering violently and weeping against his chest. He rocked her gently with his eyes closed and his face buried in her hair until she gave a final shuddering sob.

Slowly, his fingers trembling, his face ravaged with emotion, he tilted her head back and lowered his mouth to hers, tasting her lips, her tears, the fragile sigh she expelled. In the dark silver shadows of the moon Diagona, he kissed her with tender passion until every trace of the tension that had gripped them drained away, and there was only the poignant sweetness of their reunion, the promise of their future. For only now, in the aftermath of the grim scene they had played out, did they dare to savor the achingly intense joy of discovering each other alive.

"Don't let me go," Rosanne murmured blissfully. "I swear, Brant, should you let me go, I shall disintegrate. 'Tis only your arms around me this moment that are holding me together . . ."

"I'll never allow you out of my sight again," he promised huskily.

He touched her face adoringly, brushing back the soft strands of hair that clung to her pale cheeks. How precious she was to him. How careful he would be in future to cherish her. His gaze drifted from her face to her shoulder, his eyes darkening with distress at the large bruise blossoming purple against the whiteness of her skin.

"I hurt you when I pushed you away," he said raggedly. "I was so frightened for you. No one would answer the door, and I ran around to the back of the house. And then I heard you scream, and I went wild—" He shook his head, unable to continue.

"It was Conrad," she whispered, her voice trembling as she unwillingly relived the terror of fighting for her life. "Oh, Brant, Brant, where have you been?" she cried softly. "I needed you! Why did it take you so long to find me? Ericsson swore you were dead. I didn't want to believe him. It was so awful, Brant, so a—awful . . ."

Cold fury swept through him at the senseless anguish she had suffered, that he had suffered when he believed he'd lost her forever. Would he ever understand why? Would their hearts heal unscarred?

"Hush now, sweet," he soothed. "All that's past. There'll be time for explanations later. I'll take you home. I'll keep you safe and at my side—" He pulled back with a sudden smile, his eyes moving over her in roguish delight. "Is it true, my love? Is it true we're to have a little one?"

"It's true." She laid her hand on his cheek, smiling as he angled his face to kiss her palm. "Oh, Brant." She sighed contentedly. "You need a shave—as usual."

"And you're being impertinent—as always."

He fell silent then, overwhelmed anew with relief, thanking God again for leading him here in time, for the unexpected blessing of their babe. He had feared he would arrive to find her gone, or worse. Almost three months had elapsed since he'd seen her last, the darkest interval he had ever known. The maidservant employed by Reverend Barclay at Fort Hunter had not begun to gossip about the mysterious golden-haired woman found in the wilderness until a month after Rosanne had left the valley with Hugh. And it had taken White Eagle nearly two weeks on snowshoes to bring the news to Brant in the isolated trapper's cabin where he had remained alone to grieve, and another three days for Brant to travel in a snowstorm to Albany where he had learned that Conrad Sluyter was visiting Hugh in New York. And then, finally, he had known.

He lifted his head and let his eyes travel across the hallway to his uncle's body. Unconsciously he tightened his hold on Rosanne; he felt possessive and protective, fearful of releasing her.

Why Hugh? How could you have placed so little value on all our lives? Despite everything, I thought you cared for me. I loved you once, loved you even more than my father once, but now I hope you burn in hell for eternity . . .

Rosanne raised her head, her heart troubled as she followed Brant's gaze to Hugh and felt the pain coursing through him. "He died trying to protect me, trying to make me leave the house. He had changed—"

"No."

He shook his head in vehement denial, too disillusioned to believe any good of Hugh. Rosanne was only attempting to ease his pain, the brutal pain of realizing that his uncle had coldly plotted to have him murdered. And had almost succeeded.

"But it is true, Brant," she said gently. "He was sorry in the end. I honestly believe he loved you."

"Then he loved power more," he said with heartsick bitterness. "And he deserved his violent death."

She didn't tell him of the other dramatic changes that she had recently perceived in his uncle, knowing that one day, when he was ready, he would resolve his love and hatred for Hugh by himself, within himself. But not yet.

His feelings were too raw, too entangled. And there would be time.

"Brant," she whispered. "Should we not notify someone about—about . . ."

He nodded, his face careworn and reluctant. "I suppose we must. But that means I'll have to let you go, and I don't want to do that."

"But if someone passes by, the watch perhaps, they'll see the battered door and stop to investigate." She wriggled out of his lap and stood beside him with her hand on his shoulder. "Wouldn't it be easier to explain before anyone might draw the wrong conclusions?"

He looked up at her and smiled ruefully. "I almost wish I could call on one of Hugh's high-placed friends to get us through the legal ramifications that are likely to follow."

She turned her head sharply. "Brant, what was that?"

"A carriage pulling into the drive, by the sound of it," he replied, coming swiftly to his feet. "Stay in the north drawing room until I summon you. I won't have you subjected to an interrogation tonight, after what you've been through."

"I need to stay with you, Brant. Please."

The suppressed panic in her plea was more than he could refuse.

"All right. Oh, my God, Rosanne, don't look around—"

A torch flared in the front doorway, bright orange light casting into prominence the grim tableau that before had lain hidden in shadow. Rosanne blanched and plunged her white, stricken face into her hands as if to blot out the horrible evidence. She felt Brant's arm curl around her shoulders, and she turned to burrow into his strong embrace, her soul cringing and seeking comfort in his.

Vaguely she heard footsteps approaching behind them, accompanied by a babble of shocked voices. But there was one voice that stood out above the rest, gruff but cultured, reverberating with such unquestioned authority that even she turned around to answer it.

"My God, my God. What's happened in this house? The place looks like a battlefield. Send a man back to Fort

George to alert the governor. Are you positive we've the right address, Walker?"

"Yes, Your Grace," the valet called Walker replied. Then, hesitantly and respectfully, "Would it not be wiser to send your body servants throughout the house before you venture any farther, Your Grace?"

The white-haired nobleman, frail boned and yet erect of carriage in a silver-fox-lined cloak, proceeded slowly down the hallway as if he had not heard his attendant. Dear God, had he arrived too late? It has been his intention, ever since investigating Hugh Layton's tainted background, to come to America to prevent his estranged granddaughter from marrying the man. Would he find her in this carnage? Would it be too late for him to make peace with the girl? His eyes, vivid sapphire in a commanding face, moved searchingly ahead of him and then halted at the young couple standing at the bottom of the staircase.

"Rosanne?" he called out in a hopeful whisper. "Child, is that you?"

Startled that the elderly stranger appeared to recognize her, Brant glanced down at Rosanne for her reaction. The disbelieving hatred he glimpsed etched across her face both baffled and concerned him. Without quite understanding why, knowing only that something was threatening to hurt her again and he would not allow it, he drew her back against his chest with his arms locked securely around her waist. Then all at once it struck him. *Your Grace.* The duke of Rydenham.

Rosanne also knew the stranger's identity, though she could remember seeing him in the flesh only once, very long ago. Her mind unwillingly traveled back to that day as she leaned gratefully against Brant, her heart palpitating violently against her breastbone. It had been a gray, misty afternoon, and she and Claire had been sent outside to play in the alley. The duke had passed by slowly in his coach-and-six, the magnificent long-tailed Flemish horses and satin-liveried footmen so splendid against the squalor of the street that Rosanne had involuntarily started after them for a closer inspection, aching for a glimpse into that fairy-tale world. Claire had caught her hand and wrenched her back, explaining that the man inside the coach was none other than their despised grandfather, a man of such evil deeds that he merited a place in their young imaginations somewhere between Blackbeard and Oliver Cromwell. And as the two girls stood there in their faded gowns, alternately gawking and pulling faces at him, the duke had tossed a handful of gold coins at their feet. Claire, older and more practical, had scrambled to retrieve the money, while Rosanne had remained frozen in fear and resentment, watching him as he rode away.

She remembered that day vividly. And so did he.

The duke transferred his scrutiny to Brant, his gaze taking in the taller man's protective hold on the girl, the concern so clearly etched on the rugged, sun-bronzed face. This was not Councilor Layton, he thought in relieved surprise. But there was blood on his granddaughter's gown, and a painful bruise on her shoulder. His throat tightened. Someone had hurt her.

"Release my granddaughter, sir. I've come to remove her from this house, and not a minute too soon, it would seem."

"Brant, no! Don't let him take me," Rosanne pleaded, turning to press herself against his chest. "Make him leave! Tell him he has no authority here."

If you bother me again, Rosanne, I'll send you to live with your grandfather. He has a dungeon in his castle, a dungeon that he keeps just to lock up naughty little girls in . . .

No, Papa, I'll be good. I'll be good.

"Brant?"

Brant met the nobleman's gaze, oddly moved to pity by the desolation in the striking blue eyes that reminded him so much of Rosanne's in the emotional vulnerability they revealed.

"I'll take care of her, Your Grace."

"By all appearances, you haven't been successful at it so far," Rydenham said heavily. "You realize, don't you, that I could have you put away in gaol forever on the strength of my word alone?"

"I don't doubt it," Brant said, unruffled.

The duke's expression eased. "I want only to speak with her. Can you not convince her to come with me?"

Brant felt Rosanne's resistance to the question as he held her. The duke intended her no harm, he was certain, but there were too many painful memories between them that would take time to dissolve, that he would not encourage her to relive against her will.

"She isn't ready to speak with you, Your Grace. However, if you've any messages for her, I'll accept them myself under more appropriate circumstances. As you've already noted, you arrived at a most inauspicious time."

The duke nodded in resignation. "I cannot comprehend what has happened here, but 'tis clear the child is too distraught to hear what I have to say tonight. And as for you, young Galahad, you've some explaining to do yourself. I'll warrant you'll not refuse my help when it comes to facing the authorities."

"I'll manage alone," Brant said tersely. "I've nothing to hide."

The duke gave him a droll smile. "I wasn't thinking of you. It's my granddaughter's name I'm concerned with. How this affair will affect her. Ah, that's different, isn't it? Well, we agree on one thing. That will do for now."

Chapter 35

Brant caught Rosanne's eyes across the oval mahogany dining table and raised his silver goblet of champagne to her in a silent toast. They were residing temporarily in the Queen Street house he had rented for the duration of their stay in the city. In fact, they had been married almost a week before in this same residence. Ironically, one of Hugh's lofty ambitions had been realized when both the duke and Governor Clinton attended the ceremony that linked a Layton with the illustrious house of Rydenham.

Had he done the right thing in convincing Rosanne to open their home to the duke? Brant wondered. For now it would appear so. The first time Rosanne had sat down face to face with her grandfather, however, he doubted the decision. It had been an emotional encounter—even now she hadn't fully forgiven the elderly nobleman. But the hurt of a lifetime would not be erased in a single month. And it had been difficult for Rosanne to accept the duke's claim that her mother had lied to her and Claire about their grandfather, had time after time refused his assistance when he offered her money for the girls. Lisette had clung to her hatred until her death.

"Of course," the duke had explained, "I made the offers on the condition that she must not spend even a pound to entertain her admirers or to give to my drunken scoundrel son to game away. I couldn't bear to see you girls living in that hovel and playing in filth. I begged repeatedly to have you brought to live with me, but your mother would not hear of it. She put pride above her children's good."

"You destroyed her future as an actress," Rosanne reminded him bitterly. "You destroyed her relationship with my father."

"Yes, to my eternal shame, I ruined her reputation in the theater out of petty revenge, and I tried to make amends to her afterward, as I've just explained. But I will not accept the blame for the deteriorization of that marriage. And as for your father, well, he was a rogue then and is a worse one now. He approached me only when he was destitute and needed a loan to pay off his debts. I'll have you know he'd have rotted in prison years ago without me to bail him out. I suspect he never told you that, did he? Or that I paid for Claire to come to America and you to attend school?"

"Then why did you reconcile with him?" she asked skeptically. "You gave him money. You know he'll squander it."

"He is my son, and I am an old man, a lonely man. I have no other family. Do you have any idea what that feels like, Rosanne?"

Oh, yes, she did, for all she had ever truly wanted in her life was a loving home of her own. And now, with Brant, and their child on the way, she was making that wish a reality. Could she deny this foolish old man forgiveness?

She had invited the duke back into her home, to stay, two days after that conversation, and Brant had forced himself to remain impartial, had vowed he would support her in whatever course she decided.

My poor angel, he thought tenderly, drawing his thoughts back to the present. How uncomfortable she looked in the new gown her grandfather had given her, a shrimp pink silk damask creation draped over oblong panniers that made her appear as though she had a privet hedge growing at either hip. Just wearing the thing, she'd confided in him earlier, exhausted her, for there were lead weights sewn into the bodice sleeves, which terminated in winged cuffs wide enough for the heavy cream lace trimming of her chemise to peek through. And her hair . . . He hid a smile in the rim of his goblet as he surveyed the elaborate style. What had the French hairdresser who traveled with the duke called it? A Dutch coiffure?—the gilded strands tortured into cluster upon cluster of ringlets, ornamented with pearl hairpins and a diamond riband worn across her forehead as a finishing touch.

His gaze drifted longingly to the clock.

Soon he would remove her pins and riband and spread her hair loose over the pillows in silken disarray. He would kiss away her lip salve. He would peel off the layers of fashion that concealed her voluptuous form and make love to her long into the night.

He put down the goblet with a deep sigh.

The truth was that the garments and coiffure suited her to perfection, enhancing her noble-blooded beauty. Radiant with the glow of pregnancy, she had never seemed more enchanting to him nor, at the same time, more touchingly vulnerable. He knew that the strain of the past few months had worn her emotionally and that she ached to return home as desperately as he did. But it had taken longer than he'd anticipated to smooth out the legal ramifications that had arisen from that single, unforgettable night, and there had been the matter of hearing Hugh's will; the bulk of his inheritance was left to Daniel, with Brant receiving an unsettled tract of land in Cherry Valley. Yes, he had been grateful for the duke's intervention after all. He was not ashamed to admit it, not when it saved Rosanne untold anxiety.

"Martha Jansen called for tea this afternoon while you were out," she remarked offhandedly as a servant arrived with coffee.

He looked up innocently. "Who?"

"We had a nice talk, actually," she continued. "Wouter and Hans have asked to travel back to the valley with us. They're eager to start acquiring lumber. I told them I knew of a fairly reliable guide."

"Fairly reliable?"

"I invited Martha to come too, of course, but on the condition that—"

"—she wouldn't faint dead away whenever I walked into the room?"

The duke glanced up from his wing chair by the fire where he sat perusing the *New York Gazette*, Tynan sleeping at his feet.

"Did I miss something in this conversation?"

"A private joke, Grandfather, between Brant and myself," Rosanne said archly and took a sip of her coffee.

"Hmmm. Well, I won't insist you two share it." The duke leaned forward to scratch Tynan behind the ear. The hound had suffered the indignity of being bathed, clipped, and perfumed, but he absolutely refused to wear the tiny blue satin bows that the French *friseur* had attempted to attach to his shaggy fur.

"Damned Frenchman's trying to make a poodle out of you, isn't he, boy? Does the same thing to me, with his curling tongs and silly false curls."

"Your Grace."

Walker appeared in the doorway with his customary bow and sourly composed features. "It is almost nine o'clock, Your Grace. You are to attend the charity opera with Chief Justice De Lancey."

The duke stood up, directing a hopeful look at Rosanne and Brant. "I don't suppose I might talk either of you into accompanying me? I need someone to poke me in the ribs in case I begin to doze. It's frightfully embarrassing, snoring during an aria."

"Another night, Your Grace," Brant said politely. "I fear I'd sleep through the thing myself."

Rosanne delicately muffled a yawn behind her palm. "Me too."

"Yes, well, I'll see you at breakfast, then." His head downbent in resignation, the duke walked to the door and then slowly paused, glancing back into the room. "You'll think about what I said, both of you, about coming back to England for a visit so that I can show off my great-grandchild?"

Rosanne looked down into her cup. "Grandfather, we really can't promise anything, not with plans for the sawmill—"

"A visit in the future is entirely probable," Brant interrupted gently, and was rewarded by a grateful smile from his wife. "Patrick and I had thought to make the journey in any case to recruit some tenant farmers. I'll have to spend some time with my parents, naturally, and introduce them to Rosanne."

The duke nodded, his gaze moving wistfully to his granddaughter. "We'll discuss it in the morning. After we've visited Claire again. Good night."

"Good night, Your Grace."

"Enjoy your evening, Grandfather."

They waited until his footsteps faded away and the coach had rattled off down the street. Then Brant got up and walked toward Rosanne, a slow, lazy smile curving his lips.

"I want you upstairs in my bed, madam," he said huskily. "Now."

She made to rise and found herself suddenly, fiercely, entrapped in his arms, his mouth branding hers with a kiss of honeyed fire. His hands tangled in her hair, tugging loose pins, twining the cascading tresses around his wrist.

"Brant," she whispered laughingly, "Monsieur Lucien would *weep* if he could see what you've done to his hours of work— " She gave a soft, surprised gasp as all at once he swept her into his arms and carried her to the door, along the hallway, and toward the staircase, right past the marble-faced Walker who dutifully stepped aside to let them by without blinking an eye.

"Good night, sir, madam."

"Good night, Walker," Brant replied from the staircase, and gave Rosanne a wolfish grin.

She giggled naughtily and buried her face in his shirtfront. "You've scandalized the poor man, Brant. I shan't ever be able to look at him after tonight."

"That, madam, is his loss, not yours."

Inside their room he tumbled her down gently onto the

bed, his breath catching with pleasure as he felt her hand at his waistband, working loose the ebony buttons. In a matter of moments their clothes lay in a tangled heap on the floor. His eyes glittering darkly, Brant reached back and drew the curtains to enclose them in a private world of soft love sounds and impassioned whispers, of hard bronze muscle upon silken ivory skin, flesh joined to flesh, soul to soul.

They kissed in a delirium of desire, love and longing building between them, so deliciously intense that Brant soon tore his mouth away, moaning into her hair. "My wife, my love, my life . . . I missed you so, little one. If I hadn't found you again—"

"But you did," she whispered, fervent joy filling her heart. "We found each other."

She ran her hands down his chest, brushing her fingertips over the dark, curling hairs, down his muscular flanks and then the sleek contours of his hips. He shivered and squeezed his eyes shut, the muscles of his belly tightening with pleasurable anticipation as her hands drifted lower.

"Oh, Rosanne," he whispered. "I love it when you touch me."

"I love to touch you," she whispered back. "I love you, Brant."

His mouth and hands moved over her in worshipful exploration. His palms lifted the heavy weight of her breasts. "Your body is more beautiful than ever," he breathed adoringly. "So lush . . . so full . . ."

Their lips met again and again, their bodies pressed together, intertwined and damp and sweetly fragrant. They did not hurry but lingered over each caress in prolonged sensual appreciation. At last he rolled her beneath him and eased inside her, slipping his hands under her hips to fit her to him, each thrust rocking them together, carrying them closer and closer to that realm of rapture. Release came in a tumult of distant thunder and an explosion of white-hot ecstasy, their muted cries absorbed against each other.

Sometime near sunrise, Rosanne stirred and found Brant

awake and holding her in his arms, watching her with a smile of loving wonder. "What are you thinking?" she whispered.

"How much I love you. How eager I am to meet our child."

"I—I want to go home, Brant."

"Soon, sweetheart, soon."

They smiled at each other in contented silence, and as exhaustion crept over them, they carried into sleep the image of the night shadows falling behind them into the dawning splendor of another day.

The Blazing Romances
of New York Times Bestselling Author

JOHANNA LINDSEY

WHEN LOVE AWAITS 89739-3/$3.95 US/$5.50 Can
The terrible demands of past hatreds and misunderstandings would tear Leonie and Rolfe apart again and again—until they learned the truth that only love can bring!

LOVE ONLY ONCE 89953-1/$3.95 US/$5.50 Can
Fate and scandal had thrown them together. But it would take more than that to make them admit their need for each other.

TENDER IS THE STORM 89693-1/$3.95 US/$5.50 Can
They didn't mean to fall in love...but when a man's passion explodes into violence, only a woman's desire can turn it to love.

BRAVE THE WILD WIND 89284-7/$3.95 US/$5.50 Can
In the untamed Wyoming Territory, a fiery young beauty is swept into passionate conflict with a handsome, arrogant Westerner who has vowed never to love.

Also by Johanna Lindsey:

A GENTLE FEUDING	87155-6/$3.95 US/$5.50 Can
HEART OF THUNDER	85118-0/$3.95 US/$4.75 Can
SO SPEAKS THE HEART	81471-4/$3.95 US/$4.75 Can
GLORIOUS ANGEL	84947-X/$3.95 US/$4.95 Can
PARADISE WILD	77651-0/$3.95 US/$5.50 Can
FIRES OF WINTER	75747-8/$3.95 US/$4.95 Can
A PIRATE'S LOVE	40048-0/$3.95 US/$4.95 Can
CAPTIVE BRIDE	01697-4/$3.95 US/$4.95 Can

AVON ROMANCES

Buy these books at your local bookstore or use this coupon for ordering:

Avon Books, Dept BP, Box 767, Rte 2, Dresden, TN 38225
Please send me the book(s) I have checked above. I am enclosing $_____
(please add $1.00 to cover postage and handling for each book ordered to a maximum of three dollars). *Send check or money order*—no cash or C.O.D.'s please. Prices and numbers are subject to change without notice. Please allow six to eight weeks for delivery.

Name _____

Address _____

City _____ State/Zip _____

Lindsey 12-86

Authors of exceptional promise

Historical novels of superior quality!

ON THE WINDS OF LOVE Lori Leigh
75072-4/$3.95 US/$4.95 Can

STORM OF PASSION Virginia Brown
89933-7/$3.95 US/$4.95 Can

FIREGLOW Linda Ladd
89640-0/$3.95 US/$4.95 Can

WILD LAND, WILD LOVE Mallory Burgess
75167-4/$3.95 US/$5.50 Can

PRIDE'S PASSION Linda P. Sandifer
75171-2/$3.95 US/$5.50 Can

RECKLESS YEARNING Victoria Pade
89880-2/$3.95 US/$5.50 Can

AVON Paperbacks

Buy these books at your local bookstore or use this coupon for ordering:

Avon Books, Dept BP, Box 767, Rte 2, Dresden, TN 38225
Please send me the book(s) I have checked above. I am enclosing $_____
(please add $1.00 to cover postage and handling for each book ordered to a maximum of three dollars). Send check or money order—no cash or C.O.D.'s please. Prices and numbers are subject to change without notice. Please allow six to eight weeks for delivery.

Name _____
Address _____
City _____ State/Zip _____

Avon Rom/E 2/87